This Is Not Civilization

This Is Not
Civilization

ROBERT
ROSENBERG

Houghton Mifflin Company

BOSTON · NEW YORK

2004

For information about permission to reproduce selections from this book, write to Permissions, Houghton Mifflin Company, 215 Park Avenue South, New York, New York 10003.

Visit our Web site: www.houghtonmifflinbooks.com.

Library of Congress Cataloging-in-Publication Data is available.

ISBN-13: 978-0-618-38601-7
ISBN-10: 0-618-38601-7

Printed in the United States of America

Book design by Robert Overholtzer

MP 10 9 8 7 6 5 4 3 2 1

All of the characters in this book are fictitious, and any resemblance to actual persons, living or dead, is entirely coincidental.

for Michelle

Gurbette geçen ömür ömür değildir.

Time spent in a foreign land
is not a part of one's life.

—Turkish proverb

I

1

T HE IDEA OF using porn films to encourage the dairy cows to breed was a poor one. Anarbek Tashtanaliev, the manager of the cheese factory, had been inspired by a Moscow news broadcast. From Russia the television signal crossed the Kazakh steppes, was beamed to Bishkek, the Kyrgyz capital, and then relayed up and over the Tien Shan range and into desolate pockets of the new nation. If the Central Asian weather was favorable, the forgotten village of Kyzyl Adyr–Kirovka received the world news. As a result, one Wednesday Anarbek discovered that the Chinese had successfully used taped videos of fornicating bears to coax pandas to breed. The possibility of increased productivity based on a regimen of bovine erotica seemed promising. And the scheme had the single merit of all brilliant ideas: it was obvious.

Anarbek purchased dated Soviet video equipment across the Kazakh border in the Djambul bazaar. He kept factory workers on a twenty-four-hour watch to record, on tape, the next time the bulls went at it. But the workers had no luck that fall. In the spring he sent his employees up the shepherd hill next to the reservoir with an order to film copulating sheep. Thirty days later they had recorded over four and a half hours of tape. The following summer they projected this film each night, in color, onto the factory walls, for the enjoyment of the cows.

The animals were indifferent to the lusty films, and the scheme cost the failing cheese factory a month's wages. By the end of the winter only eleven Ala Tau cows and two bony Aleatinsky bulls remained. Production had ceased.

Anarbek managed the only collective in the mountain village. During the lean years of glasnost and perestroika, and the optimistic but still lean years of independence, Anarbek had watched his veterinarian pack up for Russia, the feed shipments dwindle, the wormwood climb the concrete walls, the electricity fail, the plate coolers rust, the cows die, and his workers use their lunch hour to hawk carrots and cabbage in the village bazaar. The cheese factory no longer produced cheese. Yet every week in the factory's old sauna, raising a glass of vodka, wearing only a towel wrapped around his bulging stomach, Anarbek told his friends, "We're still making a profit."

He was well aware it was false money. Amid the collapse of Communism, in the extended bureaucratic mess of privatization, the new government continued to support the state-owned collective. A sudden change in the village name had caused the oversight. With a burst of post-independence pride, an official had decreed Soviet *Kirovka* henceforth be called by its Kyrgyz name, *Kyzyl Adyr*. Now nobody knew what to call it (Kyzyl Adyr? Kirovka? Kyzyl Adyr–Kirovka? Kirovka–Kyzyl Adyr?). The capital could not keep up with such details. The village appeared by different names on scattered government lists, and the factory had yet to be privatized. The machinery had stopped, but the Communist salaries kept coming.

Kyzyl Adyr–Kirovka was a cosmopolitan village isolated in the mountains of northwestern Kyrgyzstan. Anarbek's neighbors were mostly fair-skinned Kyrgyz, but also included Russians desperate to repatriate, and Kurds, and Uzbeks, and the Koreans whose grandparents Stalin had exiled to Central Asia. Everyone benefited from the government oversight. For Anarbek was generous; he knew the money was neither rightfully his nor the factory's, so he kept on his original thirteen workers, whose families depended on their continuing salaries. The employees showed up at the factory each morning, sat, chatted, and drank endless cups of chai.

Everyone in the village understood that the cows were barren and dying and that the cheese factory produced no cheese. But what good would come of reporting it? Money that did not find its way out of Bishkek would sink into the pockets of the minister of finance, an official rumored to drive a Mercedes-Benz at excessive speed through the streets of the capital, weaving between potholes, honking at donkey carts, trying to run over the poor. A Mercedes-Benz! While the people of Kyzyl Adyr–Kirovka suffered! For the village, money mistakenly sent from the capital was money they deserved. Anarbek, after all, was a modern, educated Soviet man—he had studied management one summer in Moscow—and the village had confidence he could still turn things around.

On a Wednesday evening, in the heat of the factory sauna, he defended his fertility scheme to six of his neighbors and coworkers. The men nodded in complicit agreement. Only Dushen, the assistant manager of the cheese factory and a man too practical for his own good, broke the spell with a question grounded in reality: "Maybe the quality of projection was bad?"

The men clicked their tongues and shook their wet heads; two of them leaned over and spit onto the hot stones. The spit sizzled into thin wisps of steam. Anarbek sighed. Independence should have been a time of optimism, yet it seemed that brave ideas for improvement were consistently ruined by such complications.

Radish, the head doctor of the village hospital, opened the sauna door, and a stiff gust of air, fresh as a cool river, flowed into the room. Entering, the doctor banged the door behind him, turned his bare jellylike chest around, and announced, "News, my friends! News! The minister of education, from Talas, came by this morning."

"That son of a bitch," said Bulut, the town's appointed mayor, its *akim*.

"Screw the whole lot of them," said Dushen.

"Send them back to Moscow," Anarbek said. "Who needs them!"

He and his friends continued abusing government officials until Radish yelled over them. "Listen. A word! A word! He has offered the village an American."

"An American?" the men exclaimed in chorus, and burst into laughter.

"An organization called Korpus Mira." The glint in the doctor's eyes quieted Anarbek. "The government of Kyrgyzstan has ordered thirty Americans. They'll distribute them across the country. To hospitals. Schools. Factories like yours."

"What do they want from us?" Anarbek asked.

"How much do we have to pay them?" Dushen demanded.

"This is the thing," Radish explained. "They don't want any money. It's a humanitarian organization."

The words *humanitarian organization,* pronounced in Radish's halting Russian, sounded like fancy foreign machinery. Nobody in the village had ever used words like those before.

"American spies!" yelled the town *akim.*

"Thieves," said Dushen. "They'll take us over."

The men shook their heads in doubt, but Anarbek was intrigued. He mused on the inconceivable idea of America—of William Clinton and his friend Al Gore, of the war in the Persian Gulf, of Steven Seagal breaking necks, of the busty Madonna who sang "Like a Virgin"—this America, their new provider. He stepped down to the rack of hot coals, grabbed a cup of water, and, using the tips of his fingers, splashed the rocks over and over until they hissed. A wave of steam swirled into a choking cloud and raised the temperature in the cramped room. The men stepped down to the lower wooden benches. Bent over, covered in sweat, they rubbed their legs and shoulders, and two of them moaned pleasurably, "Ahy, ahy, ahy," at the heat.

In the center of the floor Anarbek crouched on his haunches next to Radish. "Did you accept this American?"

"*I* cannot accept," the doctor explained, snapping his undershorts. "We, our village—all of us must demonstrate our willingness to receive this gift."

"Maybe," joked Dushen, "she will be a beautiful long-legged blonde." He too squatted on the tar-stained floorboards and hawked a gob of mucus between the wooden beams. "Like Sharon Stone."

"There's a thought," said the *akim.* "Or maybe it will be some wealthy man who will marry one of our daughters and take her to America."

"*Owa!*" the men agreed, and some of them repeated, "America."

Radish said, "They want you to find a place to house the American. When she gets here, she will work at the factory, teaching us English. Think! The economic journals. Communication with businessmen. From any country. From around the world. New machinery you can order. New products." He was waving his arms and turning from man to man. "This World Health Organization sends the hospital a new piece for the x-ray, and we cannot even attach it. The instructions on those damn things come in English!"

Anarbek leaned forward into the steam and belched. "I will find a house for the American."

The head doctor smiled at his offer and nodded twice. "But that's not all," he added. "We must appoint one of us in town to be the Kyrgyz host family. They will—in a way—adopt her."

One by one the men lifted their chins, and the eyes of each, in turn, settled on Anarbek. This was his factory, this was his sauna, they were his guests; they were yielding to his decision. He stood up.

"I will be the father of the American," he said, and patted his wet, hairy chest. The ripples of fat absorbed the blow in a slapping sound, a note of confidence.

"An American," someone mumbled. The men leaned back, and for the first time any of them could remember, there was silence in the sauna, deep and pure. For two minutes nobody moved. Stomachs rose and fell in the thinning steam.

Dushen spoke up. "Who could have imagined?"

"The world is changing," Anarbek said, thinking of his dying cows, of faulty video equipment, and of fornicating pandas in China.

The next evening, in the shaded courtyard of his home—flanked by two long buildings, the tea bed, the stone wall, and the high steel fence—Anarbek fanned the flames of his grill, waiting for Lola. The coals had reached the perfect temperature for the *shashlyk*: the ashes gleamed red when he waved the sheet of cardboard at them.

"Lola!" he shouted. "Lola, they're ready!"

He could not get used to her delays. In twenty-one years of marriage, Baiooz, his first wife, had mastered the art of anticipating his every need. She had always been a step ahead of him. How many times had he asked her to do something, and she had told him, with her feline smile, that it had already been done? Anarbek fanned the coals again, this time more violently, then stopped and swallowed. He still could not believe Baiooz was dead.

"Lola!"

It was true what his friends said: no good can come from a beautiful woman. He dropped the cardboard, lifted his heavy frame from a low squat, and stomped toward the kitchen door. Just as he opened his mouth, Lola appeared in the doorway, carrying the silver tray of marinated mutton cubes, speared on metal skewers and covered in slivers of onions.

"Where were you?"

"I was slicing more tomatoes," Lola said. "I thought they were not enough for you. I know how much you eat."

He looked at her face, her fresh soft lips: twenty-two years old, less than half his age. An Indian scarf he had bought her covered her dark hair. In the mornings she tied her hair up into a ball and covered it, like this, but at night she brushed it out in long straight strokes. She was tall, as tall as he was, and her lithe body seemed capable of great athleticism. She always smelled of exotic fruit— her shampoo, her soap, perhaps. He hardly knew her.

"The grill's ready. The coals are red. We have to cook now, before we lose the heat."

She answered him with her haughty silence but brought the tray of skewers over to the tea bed. Their floppy-eared mutt, Sharyk, rose from his guard position next to the gate and scuttled toward the meat. Lola bent and smacked him on the behind. "*Git!*" The dog sprawled out, his head between his paws.

"Make sure he doesn't eat these," she warned.

Even in warning her voice was soft, so much softer than Baiooz's had been. But he missed his first wife's flutter of activity—her noise, her endless haranguing, her stubbornness. Lola listened to everything he said, did everything he demanded. What kind of wife was that?

He placed the first six skewers on the grill, one by one, reminding himself how well Lola took care of Baktigul, his younger daughter. That was the important thing. And he was lucky to have a wife so soon. He leaned over the grill and closed his eyes in the smoke, shaking his head. As hard as he tried, six months into the marriage he could not reconcile this life with the last.

Lola was his older daughter's best friend. She and Nazira had grown up together. Anarbek could remember the two girls at Nazira's eight-year name-day celebration. The family had picnicked on kielbasa and melons near the Kirovka River, cooling the fruit in the glacial water. He remembered one May Day festival when he had bought them both ice cream and had paid the village photographer to take their picture in the square by the statue of Lenin. They still had that photo: the two girls in flowery cotton dresses, ice cream running down their arms, Lenin's hand extended above them saluting the mountains. Anarbek remembered a later summer, when he had worked at the Kara Boora region's Young Pioneer Camp, in the foothills halfway to Talas. He had taught the girls how to ride horses. Nazira had climbed on readily, but Lola, at that time so short, so timid, could not get onto her horse. He had helped her, lifting her from behind, and she felt no heavier than a housecat.

He opened his eyes and turned the *shashlyk*.

When Baiooz had died last year, just after independence, the village mourned with him. But how long could a man with an eight-year-old daughter manage alone without a wife? By October a feverish search began for someone to replace her. With the news of her mother's death Nazira returned from university in Naryn and took over the management of the house, displaying a maturity and expertise beyond her twenty years. She looked after Baktigul and did much to console Anarbek, but he had remained unsettled. He felt an urgency to give his daughter her own life. She must marry soon enough; she could not take care of them forever.

Six months after Baiooz's death, Nazira herself had proposed the solution: Anarbek should marry her oldest friend. Lola was twenty-one and had never left Kyzyl Adyr–Kirovka; she was waiting to become a wife and mother. In an emotional plea, Nazira convinced Lola. They were almost related anyway, and what could be better than marrying the wealthiest man in the village? When Nazira informed Anarbek that Lola was willing, he was shocked. He could hardly tolerate his own daughter playing his matchmaker. He refused and, two weeks later, refused again more forcefully. By November, though, his loneliness, combined with Lola's youthful beauty and Nazira's stubborn insistence, changed his mind.

"Why don't you steal her?" Nazira had asked playfully.

He had considered. Once their nomadic ancestors—the ancient Kyrgyz horsemen—had rampaged villages and stolen women. If the bride spent a night in a captor's yurt, she belonged to him and could not return to her home. After the fall of Communism and with the rise of Kyrgyz nationalism, the tradition of wife stealing was resurfacing.

"But those are old traditions," he had finally told his daughter. "We're a modern nation now. We did away with those ideas seventy years ago."

"It's not a silly tradition," argued Nazira. "It's our heritage. Many people are doing it. Also, Ata, it's romantic."

So Anarbek had followed his daughter's advice. One wintry afternoon he spotted Lola walking back from the bazaar, carrying two kilograms of potatoes in a plastic sack. He pulled up to her in his tan Lada and cut the loud engine. She wore a long brown skirt that hugged her slim waist and a striped polyester blouse that showed off her broad shoulders. Without a word he grabbed her elbow and pulled her into the back seat of the car. She struggled. It occurred to him to let her go, but he reminded himself she was *supposed* to fight, that this was a sign of her honor. Before he slammed the door, he heard her gasp. His heart sank. But when he climbed into the front seat, he was uplifted by her muffled giggles, by the way she folded her arms across her chest and stared with calm resignation out the window. He promised himself he would treat her well. He brought her back along the dirt road, half a kilometer, to the house, avoiding the potholes hidden in the mud, driving as slowly as possible, as if the young woman were a delicate tea set he might break with a bump. At home he led her to the bedroom, where Nazira had prepared a meal of *manti,* a bottle of champagne, and the silk *platok.*

Lola wore the scarf and spent the night. From then on she belonged to Anarbek: his captured virgin bride, his prize, his consolation. He offered her family a two-thousand-dollar *kalym*—his ten-year savings—more than enough to uphold his reputation in the village.

Anarbek had nearly burned the last round of skewered *shashlyk.* His dog sniffed at his side and cried two plaintive notes. The smell of the grilling meat swirled around the courtyard, over the fence, and up above the village, where it mixed with the evening scent of burning dung and alpine poppies. Anarbek lifted the skewers, examined both sides, and held them close to his face, savoring the smell and color of the mutton. He realized Lola had not brought the bottle of vinegar and pepper, and he roared for her once again. Before she appeared, he turned, and there, on the tea bed, next to the plate of onions, the vinegar was already waiting for him. He laughed at himself.

"What do you need?" Lola asked from the doorway.

"Come, it's time to eat. Get Baktigul."

"Shouldn't we wait for Nazira?"

"The *shashlyk*'s ready. Get Baktigul."

He tossed two burnt cubes of meat to the dog, who gulped them down in a single swallow and wagged his tail. Lola fetched his daughter from the street. Baktigul appeared with her ponytails swinging, a young friend in tow. The four of them sat cross-legged on the platform, tore off pieces of Lola's fresh flatbread, and alternated bites with chunks of mutton, onions, and grilled tomatoes. Here, Anarbek assured himself, was the picture of a contented household. The man feeds his family, the wife prepares delicious bread, the daughter comes to eat with her little friend, honoring the house with a guest. Elusive happiness lay in such simplicity. Life would take care of him; it would take care of them all. He watched his young daughter tear with her teeth through a strand of sinew, and he lifted his chest with pride.

But before they had finished dinner, the two girls at the table cried out and gave startled jumps. Nazira, his older daughter, burst through the gate and slammed it shut behind her. The metal clanged. Nazira's chest was heaving, and her hair, usually straight and shining, was a tangled, dusty mess. On her face—the face of his first wife—dirt stains shadowed the bright red flush of exertion. Her skirt was torn. She stumbled two steps into the courtyard, the dog bounded to meet her, but then she collapsed to a crouch, her head bent. Anarbek dropped his skewer of meat, but Lola was already up and off the bed, running to her old friend.

"Nazira," she whispered. "Come in. Come, sit. Nazira, dear."

Lola kissed her forehead, but Nazira's shoulders arched in spasms as she wept. In two steps Anarbek was standing over her and lifting her by the shoulder. With Lola's help he walked her to the tea bed. Baktigul gasped again. "Don't cry, Nazira," she said.

Anarbek handed each of the young girls another skewer of meat and ordered them to play in the street.

"What's wrong with Nazira?" Baktigul demanded.

"Quiet now," he said. "Leave us for a little. I'll come and find you in a few minutes."

He started to tell Lola to bring some chai, but she had already returned with it, and was pouring. "Drink, Nazira," he said. "Be still, *kizim*. You're okay, aren't you?"

Lola rubbed Nazira's neck, and they sat in silence for a few moments while Nazira composed herself. Her sobs abated, then rose and fell again. She pulled her hair behind her ears. Lola wet a cloth under the samovar and wiped the dirt from Nazira's cheeks.

"I was returning for lunch this morning, after classes," Nazira began, and then broke into tears again. She taught English at the Lenin School. She was a steadfast teacher; it hardly bothered her that the students immediately forgot what she taught them, or that they were the sons and daughters of shepherds and would never have use for a foreign language. Nazira was famous around the village for her lovely voice, and her English classes eagerly followed her in daily song: "May There Always Be Sunshine" or "I Can Clap My Hands, Thank You!"

She collected her breath. "I was walking just past the flour store. A car pulled up. There were three men inside. Big men. I have never seen them before, Ata. They ran out of the vehicle and grabbed my arms. There was nobody around to help. They got me into their car."

She fought back another round of tears and nearly gagged. Anarbek waited for her to compose herself. When he could no longer wait, he tried to soothe her with a soft question, but instead his words rushed out in uncontrollable anger. "Where! Where did they take you?"

Over her sobs Nazira explained that they had driven all the way to Talas. In a concrete *microregion,* in a dark, cold apartment, they forced her into a bedroom. There the mother of one of the men brought her bread and strawberry jam, which she refused to eat, and tea, which she refused to drink. The woman even opened a bottle of vodka, poured two glasses, and raised a toast.

"To my beautiful new daughter. My son could not have found a wife more worthy." The mother had then reached over and tried to wrap a beige *platok* around her head.

Nazira fought her off, ripped the scarf from the lady's hands, crumpled it, and tossed it into the corner of the room. In a soft voice the mother tried to assuage her fears. "It's an honor, my daughter. You were so pretty; you were the one he chose." She showed her cracked photographs of the family that would be hers: her new brothers and sisters, an aging wrinkled grandmother, her mustached father.

"They all had the eyes of a wolf, every one of them," Nazira explained. "The entire family held one single expression: a sneer."

She told the woman she would never be her son's bride, no matter what tradition dictated. After that she refused to speak. The mother grew angrier, drank the vodka alone. For a half-hour she raged at Nazira's silence and rained abuses on her.

"Finally she lifted herself from the floor. I wouldn't look her in the eyes. I was staring at the bottom of her dress. She called me the worst kind of donkey. 'Aren't you ashamed?' she said. 'Aren't you a real Kyrgyz woman?' She slapped me here, across the face. When she left, I thought I was free. But it was only starting."

The dark room filled with women: relatives, friends, neighbors, and young girls all brought in to console her. They urged her not to revolt too much. "Don't deny your destiny," one old woman said. "You should accept it. You should try to find joy in it." Another said, "It happened to me too. You may not love him now, but you will learn to love him." One of the sisters urged her, "You are here already. You have crossed the threshold of this house. If you leave, you will never find another husband. Don't shame yourself."

Nazira asked only one question: "*Atam kaida?*" Where is my father? She knew they had to bring him to negotiate.

"Write him your letter. We will bring him here to name your price."

And she understood: writing the customary letter would be an admission of complicity. She was trapped. She tried to steady herself, but the tears rose. As the ladies stood to leave, the mother leaned toward her and in a voice as harsh as the breaking of glass, quoted the old saying, "A woman who comes crying into her future husband's house will lead a happy life."

The room had emptied. Nazira took in a long breath, but then the man entered. He was the largest of the three who had pulled her into the car, and he was dressed in the formal clothes he had worn for the abduction: a gray wool sweater, pressed gray slacks. He had combed his brown hair so it reached across his forehead in waves and had doused himself in barbershop witch hazel. The smell choked Nazira each time he leaned close, and in that sealed space it made it hard for her to breathe. The man sat directly across from her on a purple and red *tushuk* and poured two overflowing glasses of vodka.

He told her how he had seen her three weeks before, when she had brought a class into Talas for the middle-school English Olympiad. He spoke with a husky voice, full of confidence and menace, even more frightening when he lowered it to a whisper. He said, "You were walking across the street from School Four, and I had every intention of stealing you then. I would have, but I did not know what to do about your students. Instead I stopped one of your boys from the fourth form. I asked him your name, where you were from. The boy told me all about you, and he asked if I loved you. He must have seen it in my eyes. Even a fourth-form boy! I told your student, 'You see that mountain? The tallest one? I think she is more beautiful than that mountain.'"

He rambled on like this for an hour, professing his love.

"Nonsense," Nazira explained. "He was talking complete nonsense."

"Okay now," Lola whispered.

"Go on," Anarbek demanded.

He said his name was Traktorbek, and that he had been named after his grandfather, who had been named after the tractor (a machine of wonder the Russians had brought to Kyrgyzstan in 1948). He told her how he had given up school to sell meat in the bazaar. He told her how many men he had beaten up in the past year. He told her how much cognac he could drink in one sitting, how women who came to buy his mutton fell in love with him and he gave them discounts. He had not planned to marry so young, he said. He had wanted to make his fortune first, then find an apartment in the capital—he had been there once—where he had dreams of opening a gas station. But he had seen Nazira, and his plans had changed.

All the time he spoke, he was drinking. Nazira hardly listened. She asked herself how she was going to escape, and if it were possible, and if she did, what people would say about her.

Traktorbek then squatted beside her and pulled over two thick mats. Before she knew what was happening, he grabbed her face with his callused palms. He was kissing her, pushing her down.

Anarbek listened now with pain. He looked up through the rustling leaves of the courtyard at the darkening sky and then back down. He fingered a piece of meat, lifted it to his mouth, then threw it onto his plate. His wife looked away. Neither could face Nazira.

"I kicked him so hard between his legs that he shouted," she said. "I've never heard a man yell so loud." She laughed at the memory, but the laugh brought on a fresh round of tears. "Then he hurt me," she murmured. Her head sank. "After, I pushed my way out of the room, through the mother and the father. All the other people were there, as if it were some kind of holiday *mayram*. There was music, and they were clapping and dancing in the sitting room. They were calling my name and saying the worst kinds of things. But I grabbed a pair of shoes at the door, and I've never run so fast. I asked my legs to carry me like the wind. I was barefoot, and I ran out of the *microregion* and into the park by the Ferris wheel, across from the cinema. I hid behind the memorial statue and put on the shoes. They weren't mine. They were the mother's high heels! Too small for me. I stumbled to Prospect Chui—but look at me!—I must have looked sick. No cars would stop. I was afraid to stay on the main road. I went off to the stadium and hiked five kilometers along the river, through the Talas forest, all the way to the *otovakzal*. A truck was parked between the buses, and the driver was heading past the village. I begged him to take me home."

Anarbek sucked in a deep breath, astonished at her courage. "You were stolen. You were stolen and you ran away." He was trying to assess the extent of the damage—what, in these times, her escape actually meant. He unfolded his legs and refolded them. In his chest a rough pride swelled at his daughter's hardheadedness, but then a sharp dread pierced his stomach.

Lola had misunderstood him. "How can you say such a thing?" she burst out. "Look at her. Think of what she has been through."

"Soon the village will know," he said. "The bad tongue will begin. This man, he was not the kind you could have married?" Both women stared at him with open mouths. He was trying to think practically. If Baiooz had been here, she would have known what to say, what to do for their daughter. Now he imagined the excuses he would have to give in the sauna, the rumors that would consume the town, the impossibility of Nazira's finding a husband.

He knew by custom that he was not supposed to accept his stolen daughter back into his home—it was his duty not to. She had crossed the threshold, and now she was spoiled. Still, they lived in a modern world; these traditions hardly mattered anymore.

He stared at the table. He could eat nothing else. For minutes they sat in silence and swirled their cups of chai. Above the courtyard the branches of the plum tree swayed. Shouts flew over the high fence, sounds of the children playing on the street.

A sudden pounding on the metal gate—too rough to be Baktigul—startled them. Nazira half stood, then glanced at him, panic in her eyes.

Anarbek raised himself off the tea bed. He strode to the gate and behind him heard Lola say they should go inside. The metal hinges creaked with a high-pitched screech, like the call of a buzzard. Framed in the light blue gateway was the very picture of shattered youth. The young man had thin piercing eyes, and his wavy hair was disheveled. But he was wide-backed and powerful, with a wrestler's build so thick, his shoulders stretched the sleeves of his striped gray sweater. He did not bother with the customary formalities: no *salamatsizbih,* no *asalaam aleikum,* no *ishter kondai.*

"Where is she?" he demanded, and staggered forward.

Anarbek's ingrained sense of hospitality told him a visitor must be invited into the home, seated comfortably, offered bread and tea, and fed a meal before he was questioned. Now, for the first time in his life, he stopped a stranger at the door. He stretched a tremulous arm to block the entrance.

"You are not welcome in this home," he said. The impropriety disturbed him. He was certain no good would come of breaking tradition. Yet Nazira must not see the man again.

"I know she has come here," Traktorbek said. "The children told me." He pointed down the dirt lane where his Lada was parked. Next to it Baktigul and her friends were gathered in a circle, chattering around a boy on a fallen bicycle.

"Nazira is here. This is her home. What would you like?"

"I would see her, *agai.*"

"It seems you have already seen her. She would not see you."

Traktorbek searched past him into the courtyard. Anarbek shifted to his left, and from pale desperation the youth's face turned to red anger. The muscles in his neck flexed, and he stared up into Anarbek's eyes, only then comprehending his entrance was blocked. For a long moment they stood face to face.

"It is your obligation to return her to me. Your duty, and your family's duty. You know the ways."

"These are old ways, Traktorbek."

The young man started at the sound of his own name. He collected himself with new energy and glared, his eyes calculating. Nazira had been right: the face—the eyes—held the menacing sneer of a wolf. "Do you know anything about honor?" he demanded. "Do you think of your family's name? Do you think of your *factory's* name?" His choppy voice grew louder, and Anarbek could smell the vodka on it. "I will see her. I have made my decision. She will come back with me. She has spoken with my mother. Arrangements have been made."

"Arrangements will be forgotten." Anarbek fought to keep his voice calm. Like this young man he too was prone to passion. He knew how quickly, how often, he lost control of himself. But passion would not quiet passion. He was guarding his home from an invading presence, but the invasion felt larger and more pervasive than this simple lovesick youth standing before him.

"I do not have to tell you again," Anarbek said. "You must leave her alone now. She will not be your wife. She's made it clear. She will not have it."

"*She!* She is a woman!"

"I will not have it either. I have other plans for Nazira." The word *America* flashed like lightning across Anarbek's mind. He had no idea where it came from. Quickly he refocused.

Traktorbek's body had stiffened. "You are obligated, yet you won't give me back your daughter." He clenched and shook his fists. He reminded Anarbek of the costs of this decision, of the shame he was bringing on himself, and ended with a volley of grave threats, vowing revenge.

To his own surprise Anarbek remained calm. "Leave now," he said, stepping back from the gate and pulling the door. The young man clutched the swinging metal with his fingertips and cried out, "If you shut this gate on me, you can't know what it means to be in love!"

The outpouring drew an unexpected feeling from Anarbek. He nearly liked the boy for it. He respected the fervor of youth, its steely nerve, its determined siege before a closing gate. How men suffer in the name of women! Yet this Traktorbek was too young, too brash. He refused to face reality, and Anarbek could not approve of the animal violence he exuded. He would never have done for a husband; Anarbek could see that now.

"Son," he said, "you don't know what it means to be a father."

He pulled the gate harder, and the final image of rejected youth was transfigured into complete despair. Traktorbek's fingers slipped from the door. The gate clicked, and in a single massive blow the full force of the young man's body crashed outside, rattling the metal. Anarbek stood still. He waited for the slow shuffling of feet, the quieting of the children, and the angry growl of the car engine.

In the kitchen Lola and Nazira were seated on low stools. His wife was kneading dough for tomorrow's *leposhka* on the flat wooden table. As he entered, both women straightened up and watched him, unblinking. From the sink, rinsing his hands, he glanced back at his daughter. Conjuring the image of his dead wife, he prayed inwardly, "Baiooz, tell me I have done what is right."

He turned and reached for a towel. Their faces were set, awaiting his decision.

"You'll come with us tomorrow," he said into the sink, drying his hands. "Two days from now the Korpus Mira inspects the house I've found for the American. We must beat out the rugs and hang the curtains."

2

JEFF HARTIG had unlocked the reservation's Chief Alchesay Teen Center on Thursday afternoon and found the place destroyed. The computer monitors were bashed in. *Fuck You Bitch* had been written eleven times on the chalkboard of the meeting room. Someone had taken a knife to the pool table and had bent in the feet of the Ping-Pong tables. The library books, most of their pages torn out, lay strewn across the floor. The stereo, the VCR, the speakers, and the boom boxes had all been stolen. In Jeff's office someone had defecated on his desk, burned his piles of grant applications and business correspondence in a fire on the floor, and put it out with what smelled like urine.

The message was clear, and Jeff did not want to think about who had sent it. Later, he would remember this moment and wish he'd had the strength to persevere in the face of the insult. But he was only twenty-three years old, this was his first failure, and he did not yet have the heart to think about putting the place back together.

He locked up the teen center, walked the half-mile past the Lutheran mission over to the tribal offices, explained to Councilman Dale what had happened, and offered his resignation.

Larson Dale leaned back deep into his chair, looked straight at him, and said, "We'll get an Indian to do the job. That's what should have happened in the first place."

Everything Jeff owned lay spread out in the dusty shade of the old cottonwood, at the center of the town of Red Cliff. His pots and pans, his Tupperware, his coffeemaker, his rowing machine, his microwave, his thirteen-inch television, his plaid comforter, his desk chair, his *Oxford English Dictionary*, his acoustic guitar. He was moving on, and he didn't want this stuff anymore. He wanted lightness, mobility, and flight. One year he'd been on the Red Mountain Reservation, and the village was no better for his having come. But he refused to blame himself. The world was large, and other places needed him if this one didn't.

He heard footsteps approaching on the bridge over the creek, and his assistant at the teen center, Adam Dale, all legs and arms, appeared around the gnarled trunk of the cottonwood. His thick, dark hair curled down to his black Metallica T-shirt. He was carrying a Walkman and wearing headphones, from which tiny murmurs of heavy metal escaped. He squatted next to Jeff, removed the headphones, and tossed the Walkman onto the blanket. Jeff looked away. A hummingbird darted between the white blossoms and spikes of a yucca to his right.

"You just leaving then?" Adam asked.

Jeff stared at the ground. "Yeah. Packing it in."

"Just gonna give in so easy?"

"What do you want me to do? Hang around to fix things up? Have this happen all over again?"

"I'm saying you come here to help. We blink, you're gone."

Last summer the center had struggled for its first six weeks of operation. Hardly anyone had used it. In September, in coordination with an after-school work-for-credit program, Jeff had hired Adam. The kid had been the only student at the high school trailer with the attendance record to qualify. Adam had bestowed a palpable legitimacy on the center, and soon his friends and basketball teammates were showing up. Packs of teenage girls appeared. Younger brothers and sisters started tagging along. The Chief Alchesay Teen Center, once deserted, suddenly bustled seven days a week.

"You said you were here for the long haul," Adam murmured.

"Come on. I'm not wanted here."

"You only think that 'cause of what my dad said to you. About taking an Indian's job?"

"I'm not holding any grudges."

On a lark, Jeff had applied for the manager's position straight out of college and was surprised when he was hired. He had put himself through school at Arizona State, working as a residence counselor in a troubled-boys home in Phoenix. By his senior year he was practically running the place. The Chief Alchesay Teen Center, then, had seemed like a manageable new challenge. Before graduation last May he'd come up to the reservation, four hours from Phoenix, for the interview. The center, he learned, had been organized through the donations of all twelve churches in town and grants from both Indian Health Services and the Department of Housing and Urban Development. Its advisory board—three priests, a female IHS official, and Adam's father, Councilman Dale—had been impressed by his experience in working with troubled teens. During the interview they complimented his knowledge of Apache history (he had always read heavily on the Southwest). Later he was told everyone on the board had chosen him over four other candidates—everyone except Adam's father, who had refused to accept the hiring of a white man for the position.

The center occupied the abandoned movie theater next to the post office in the Commercial Center, the town's single burnt-out strip mall. The main room had been converted into a small auditorium, and adjoining that was a library, an arts and crafts room, and a game room. As manager Jeff had run a program of after-school activities, including Friday night films on the wide-screen television. Teens could sign out boom boxes. The dance floor on the stage had a large stereo and two enormous speakers hanging high on the wall, so the kids could come in and "jam out." Through donations from two pharmaceutical companies in Phoenix, Jeff had built a computer center and by Christmas stocked it with fourteen Macs and three color printers. The meeting hall he repaneled, and in the winter, officials from IHS used the center for counseling programs on teen pregnancy and diabetes. He'd had plans to buy a drum set and organize a local rock band.

The job came with a small, rent-subsidized house up by the Day School, where he retired late at night, the sounds of blaring metal music and screaming teenagers echoing in his head. He read in the torn-up armchair he'd owned since college and slept on a mattress on the floor. He had never gotten around to furnishing his place; his salary had been paltry, and though officially the teen center required fewer hours than the boys' home in Phoenix, he volunteered most weekends in order to keep it open.

Adam was saying, "You think it's hopeless, then. You think we're hopeless, isn't it."

"How do you want me to answer that, Adam? I don't think

you're hopeless. Get yourself to college. Find someplace better than this town, someplace with a future."

"I'm talking about the tribe."

Jeff didn't answer. Adam had given more than his share of time to the center too. He'd helped Jeff keep some semblance of control when fights broke out, when neighborhood kids would show up high on weed or glue, when strangers from other towns tried to get in. Without his help, Jeff knew he never would have survived the job for more than a couple of months.

Now a truck had pulled off the road, facing them, and an entire family—the Peaches—sprang out. The five children were all named after Chris, the father. There were Kristen and Kristina and Krissy and Krista, and the only boy, Chris Junior. Jeff could never keep the names straight.

One of the children—Krissy, perhaps?—hustled straight to Jeff's thrift-store rowing machine and started kicking the handles back and forth. Mrs. Peaches was piling up dishes and Tupperware in her arms. Two of the younger girls adjusted the size of his baseball caps, then tried them on. Chris Senior lifted a double-bladed camping ax off the blanket and ran his finger along the dull edges. "How much?" he asked.

Jeff said he could have it for a buck.

"The Tupperware?" Mrs. Peaches yelled over the shouts of the children.

"You can have all the plates and silverware. Three dollars."

"Dad! Dad!" screamed whichever Kris was on the rowing machine.

Mr. Peaches pointed over to her. "How much for that thing?"

"I'm trying to get rid of it. You just take it."

Chris Senior stood over the rowing machine, his hands on his hips; then he adjusted his large black sunglasses. Slowly he pushed his daughter off the seat, sat down, and started rowing, alternating arms.

Adam walked over to help him. "Do them both at the same time, like this. Build your back muscles up something big, isn't it?"

"You're never gonna use it," Mrs. Peaches was mumbling. "It's gonna sit and take up space."

In his denim shirt and Stetson hat, the large man was getting into a rhythm, pumping his arms furiously. "I'll use it," he said. "Just like this, I'll use it."

The girls circled around their father. "Let me! Let me!" Mr. Peaches wiped the sweat off his forehead.

Adam yelled, "Help your husband get rid of that gut, eh, Mrs. Peaches?" She raised her eyebrows and went back to examining Jeff's silverware.

In a few minutes they left, the cookware and the dishes and the rowing machine piled into the back of the truck, as were the children, each wearing a different-color ASU cap. Jeff had charged them ten bucks for everything.

Adam watched them drive away. He was silent for a few minutes, sitting on the edge of Jeff's blanket, staring out at the empty road. Adam had thin arms, a chest that showed mostly ribs when he played in pickup basketball games, but his shoulders were well defined and his fingers especially long. He slid over into the shade. "Don't want to get any darker," he'd once told Jeff. Jeff, for his part, didn't mind picking up a little sun, though he'd have to be careful—the pale skin on his legs was already burning. He was wearing worn running sneakers without socks, and he noticed his ankles were filthy, covered in the red dust that blanketed the town.

"The teen center," he said. "I want to know, Adam, why'd they fuck it up? Maybe you understand something I don't?" When he had first arrived last summer, he'd been convinced the center was what this place needed. People in Red Cliff had spent a lot of money on it, years of hard work. "I don't get it. It was a gift to the community."

"Maybe someone here didn't want your gifts."

"You think that's true?"

Adam was silent. No, Jeff thought, the kids had liked it, and they had come. They played pool, Ping-Pong, foosball. Video games on the computers. They checked out magazines from the library: *Sports Illustrated, Field and Stream, Seventeen.* They weren't home arguing with their parents, or out in the woods all tanked up, or brawling, or getting each other pregnant.

He heard the sound of a truck racing across the bridge, and suddenly a purple Toyota, freshly washed, squealed its brakes and skidded onto the gravel. Jeff spit, staring out at the red sandstone bluffs in the distance. The truck door slammed, and he heard Levi, Adam's cousin, greeting them. The voice was guttural and bearlike. Jeff said nothing in return.

"Hartig!" Levi was calling. "Hey, Hartig, you selling this shit?"

He was pointing at the blanket with the television and the stack of CDs.

Jeff nodded, clenching his lips.

"How much this TV?"

He considered not answering, then changed his mind. "Sixty dollars," he shouted.

"Sixty dollars!" Levi yelled. "You being stingy with me?"

"Cost me a hundred," Jeff said under his breath. After months of grief and confrontations, he wasn't going to give in to this kid. Levi was stocky and had swollen, permanently bloodshot eyes. He was famous in Red Cliff for his tremendous appetite. At a teen center barbecue Jeff had seen him eat eleven hamburgers with a double helping of onions and hot sauce. He also possessed artistic gifts: last fall he had painted an eagle and a roadrunner mural on the wall outside Jeff's office. That mural, too, had been defaced the day before.

"I'll give you twenty."

"Sixty."

"You keep it then. I got enough for a while, keep me busy." Levi laughed, patting his cousin on the back. "You going over there?" he asked Adam quietly, referring to the Sunrise Dance for Adam's sister, Verdena. "You need a ride?"

"I'll be over in a little bit. Nothing going on till six."

Levi said something to Adam in Apache, pointing to Jeff's truck. In English he said, "It's a piece of shit."

Adam shook his head. When Levi left, he sat back down in the shade by Jeff. "I thought you was just getting rid of this stuff?"

"That's right."

"Sixty dollars for that TV?"

"What'd Levi want?"

"Wanted to know if you agreed to sell me your truck."

"I told you I would."

"You haven't said a price."

"Two thousand."

Adam's eyes opened in surprise, but he held back the smile.

Jeff said, "I'm only doing this for you. For all your help. And I need a ride down to Phoenix on Sunday."

"I gotta ask my dad."

"You'll let me know."

Adam lowered his voice. "You shouldn't have been so strict all the time."

"Strict?"

"You shouldn't have kicked people out so fast."

"Who'd I kick out?" If the kids had been drunk, or high, or dealing, they couldn't come in. It was a teen center, and he was the manager. There were rules. He was just trying to keep it safe. "We never kicked anyone out," he said. "We asked them to leave for the night. They were always invited back."

"Except Levi."

"Oh, come on." Jeff tossed a white rock at the trunk of the cottonwood. He missed.

"You should have let him back in."

"You're saying that because he's your friend."

"My cousin."

"So he can break the rules, because he's your cousin?"

"I'm just saying, you shouldn't have kicked him out so many times."

"I liked Levi. I wanted him to hang out. I used to ask him to come by the center in the afternoons, I'd tutor him for the math GED. He ever come? He's a fuckup, your cousin. I'm sorry I've got to say that. You know it, though."

Adam didn't answer. For three years, Jeff knew, Adam had been trying to get his cousin to come back to school with him. The town's biggest problem was its lack of a real high school. Kids attended elementary at the Bureau of Indian Affairs' Day School on the hill or at the Lutheran school behind the red church. Most stopped there. Children who wanted to complete their education at a real high school had to endure a sixty-mile bus ride, each way, through the mountains to Blackriver. Red Cliff had no tax base to fund a school of its own, and though the councilman had campaigned for funds from the state congressmen and the BIA, the town was too small—it was too easy to ignore.

A few years ago Adam's father had appointed himself head of the school board and called for a series of emergency meetings. He railed at the passivity of the other board members. He explored far-fetched possibilities and came up with a plan. The Day School made extra money: all its students qualified for federal lunch programs and special ed funds. Where did that money go—toward unread textbooks, canned lunch spinach, Halloween decorations? If a little of this money was skimmed, ever so gently, off the top, they would have enough to start a high school and eventually make it grow. So the school board redirected Title IX funds into a private account in the Cottonwood Gymnasium's name and laid a concrete foundation at the edge of the Day School playground. A double trailer was towed to the site; the board recruited two retired Mormon teachers from town. And Red Cliff High opened that fall—the class of 1993, four students, including Adam.

"You'll see. This is just a start," the councilman had promised. "We'll do it our way, we'll do it ourselves." He talked all the time about building a reservation casino to bring in real money. That would fund a *real* high school. He swore to Adam that one day their school would have everything other American children had: a gymnasium with bleachers, a library with computers, a morning bell. They'd even have Apache cheerleaders. "Why not?" he'd ask.

Four years later they still had none of that. Adam had suffered through these years in his father's trailer against his will—he had wanted to play basketball for Blackriver High—but he hadn't stopped trying to convince his friends to attend school with him.

Now Jeff asked, "Did Levi have something to do with the teen center? If you know, you've got to tell me."

Adam started unlacing his high-tops, then relacing them. Jeff lifted his eyes to the blank blue sky. In the distance a falcon was circling in slow motion over the canyons and arroyos. Jeff said, "The police report says no one broke in. Someone got hold of a key."

"They don't know that," Adam said. "Someone could've just busted the door open."

Jeff stared at him. "No evidence of forced entry. Someone had a copy of a *key*, Adam. It wasn't *my* key."

They were quiet for a moment. Jeff stood and moved the guitar to make it more visible from the road. He considered for a moment keeping it. His father had taught him his first chords back in eighth grade. Jeff had always played passably by ear and had even begun to write his own songs—slow, wistful folk and blues, mostly. But he'd never learned to read music, and he knew he had no real talent. He walked back over to Adam, who was concentrating on his sneakers. Jeff stood over him. "When I hired you, I gave you a break. You wanted things to change here. I trusted your judgment."

Adam kicked at the dirt. "You still coming to the Sunrise tomorrow morning?"

"Doesn't matter anymore."

"You gotta come. You want to see the real Apache? This is it."

"Is this an apology?"

"I'm just saying—" His voice softened. "My sister asked if you'd come."

"Your dad'll be there."

"There'll be so many people, he won't even see you."

"I don't know." Jeff shook his head, stepped away from Adam, and glanced down at the long curve in the road. He had been looking forward to the Sunrise Dance—the Ceremony of Changing Woman—for months. Adam's younger sister had just turned thirteen, and for four days the extended family camped in the woods in branch wickiups, sharing feasts with the entire town. Tomorrow, at dawn, Verdena would become Changing Woman incarnate, the first Person, the only survivor of the great flood, mother of the Ndee. For a day she would share the blessings and bounty of her womanhood with all who came to witness the ceremony. The community would re-create itself, as it had for centuries. But now, instead of the connection Jeff had hoped to feel, the tiny step closer to understanding these people, he would watch from a distance, as a visitor who had descended on the tribe and just as quickly abandoned them, as little more than a tourist.

"I'm asking you to come," Adam said. He stood, brushed off his basketball shorts, clipped his headphones back on, and walked without another word back over the bridge, then out of sight.

Jeff sat very still, trying not to think, not to blame. He had never imagined his motivation, his determined goodwill, could be sapped so easily. He was ineffectual. And where would he go now? He had no desire to see his father up in Idaho and even less to return to Phoenix. He could return to work at the boys' home—for a few months, at least; he could handle that until something better came up.

By midafternoon three more trucks had stopped at the cottonwood. Sam Goseyun bought the television for twelve dollars. In an hour everything had been sold except for a Frisbee and Jeff's garlic press.

The next morning, in the predawn darkness, afraid of letting Adam down, Jeff followed his directions to the pasture. He drove his pickup along first gravel, then dirt roads, turning at the Indian Ruins and then at the abandoned Medicine Ranch, passing the wandering cows, the dense groves of ponderosa pine, weaving his truck up and down the muddy slopes. At the side of the road the occasional cornfield swayed in the first light. Each field was owned by a different family, and in the spring a few elders still moved out here and lived in brush-covered huts, planting their corn, tending their peach orchards.

He parked on the edge of the road and hiked up toward the pasture, avoiding the prickly pear, now laden with purple fruit, and the sharp spines of the jumping cholla. He walked slowly, aware of his feet sinking a half-inch into the soft, rusted earth. The fire cherry trees with their blackish fruit clusters. The hairy silver leaves of the white oak. He would miss this isolation—the nearest shopping center was an hour away. He would miss the sharp greens and grays of this chaparral, the vegetation like that of some other planet. He spotted the tracks of deer, then an orange butterfly, and followed the branch of the spring-fed creek until it brought him back out of the woods, to the pasture.

The clearing was a wet field surrounded by scrub oak and juniper. He saw that two camps had been established, one by Verdena's parents and the other by her godparents, who funded the four-day festival. Already in the gray dawn at least fifty dust-covered trucks and cars were parked at scattered angles along the edge of the woods, all the way over the small rise of the hill at the far end of the field.

Adam's aunt, Marie Anne, waved to Jeff and led him over to the family's camp. She was a heavy white-haired woman, the clerk in the town's only trading post. In the shade of the ramada, built of interwoven branches, she seated Jeff on the improvised bench of a fallen log and offered him coffee and a powdered doughnut. The family—Councilman Dale; Adam's mother, Lorena; and Adam's uncle Sparky—were sitting in silence. Jeff gave each of them a self-conscious nod and ate his doughnut, looking at the ground. When he had finished, Marie Anne brought him a second doughnut and touched him softly on the back of his neck—a show, Jeff thought, of silent pity.

They had problems, he knew. Adam had often come to work upset, with tales of his father's household rage, of the helplessness of his half-deaf mother, of Marie Anne's getting back together with Uncle Sparky, only to leave him again. But here, awaiting Verdena's rite of passage, they seemed more cohesive than the family Jeff had known. He found himself fighting back jealousy. He had grown up an only child in Tucson; his family moved to Phoenix when he was fourteen—but neither place seemed like home. His mother had died of stomach cancer during his freshman year of college, and his father, a real-estate lawyer now living in Idaho, had remarried only two months after the funeral. Furious, Jeff hadn't attended the wedding and still refused to meet his new stepmother. His father had recently tracked down his phone number on the reservation, and every few weeks left a short, tired message pleading for Jeff to return his call.

Adam joined them in the ramada. His black eyes were reddened, his thick hair disheveled, and he looked as if he had not slept in days. He didn't greet Jeff but squeezed down on the log next to him, so their shoulders touched. He told his father Jeff had offered to sell him his truck. Councilman Dale raised his leathery face just slightly.

"What year's it?" he asked, not looking at Jeff.

"Eighty-seven," Jeff said.

He blew on his coffee. "How many miles it got?"

"Under seventy thousand."

"How'd it get so rusty? Didn't you take care of it or nothing?"

Jeff said, "Two thousand dollars is nothing for that truck. It's only six years old. It's worth twice that." His own dad had given him the vehicle as a high school graduation present, and he'd never cared what happened to it. He'd never washed it, rarely changed the oil. Now he just wanted to get rid of it.

Larson was leaning on his knees, but he sat up slightly. Adam looked at his father, met his glance, and looked back down at the ground.

Their faces were distinctly similar: the roundness of the bones, the flat nose, the light brown skin, the slightly Asian eyes. Larson Dale's features were fuller, though, in every sense, his flesh hanging, his neck thick. Adam was leaner, with sharply molded features.

Councilman Dale asked his son, "You got the money for that?"

Adam nodded, but clicked his tongue.

"How much you got?"

"I got fifteen hundred."

"He's going to need some wheels for college," Jeff said.

"I know what he needs."

"It'll give him a good few years, Larson."

Councilman Dale pursed his lips and sipped his coffee. "Toyota?" he said. "Why didn't you buy American?"

Jeff thought he was joking, but he was the only one who smiled. He looked over to Adam for some support, but the teenager's face was solemn and downcast. Larson Dale had a stranglehold of power on the town. From the start Jeff was intimidated by him and had tried to win him over. Now he couldn't care what the councilman thought. None of the Apaches ever complained, but Jeff had heard rumors from the Lutheran pastor that Councilman Dale had fathered children off the rez, that he was spotted in Phoenix bars, that he took vacations on tribal money, that he was driving the town into bankruptcy.

This was high living for a man who had worked as a machinist at the Red Cliff Apache Sawmill until seven years ago, when he'd been elected councilman. According to Adam, the dive into politics had not been Larson's idea. Adam's father had possessed not the slightest inclination toward civic duty. But Uncle Sparky (Levi's father, not with Marie Anne) got him elected.

Sparky used to work at the sawmill as well but left to pursue a different calling. Once a month he drove down to Phoenix and picked up cartons of heroin, marijuana, and cocaine and with a fearless lack of precaution smuggled the narcotics up to the reservation. After two years of dealing, he had developed a connection down in Hermosillo. Each week at a set time, a small Mexican plane glided low over the village, circled the forest-fire runway out by Lonely Mountain, and dumped round bundles into the clumps of cholla and agave. When the plane disappeared over the horizon, Sparky retrieved the drugs, distributed them, and in this way earned more money than anyone in Red Cliff. Jeff had seen the man running business off the porch of his HUD home, sitting deep in a green mildewed lounge chair. His dark hands were constantly pulling at his camouflage pants; his greased rat-tail clung to his neck. Appearance was not important—the business needed little marketing, and his influence expanded. Eventually, according to Adam, the tribal police, under pressure from the tribal government, started giving Sparky a hard time. They warned him they might have to arrest him or something. For protection Sparky decided to get a new councilman elected. His brother-in-law would do.

Over that summer Adam and Levi had spray-painted big corkboard campaign signs and erected them at the Turnoff, the corner of Highway 60 and the paved road to town:

DALE FOR COUNSILMAN
VOTE DALE
DONT SCREW UP VOTE DALE

In the sawmill, the trading post, the gymnasium, Larson's friends urged him on. An article appeared in the *Apache Scout,* announcing Dale was running: it praised him as a hard worker, it claimed he was the great-grandson of Chief Alchesay himself. The article was soon followed by hourly KNNG rez-radio advertisements, reminding listeners that Larson Dale held the Red Mountain tribe's record for antlers. Supporters gave away frybread at the gas station. They spread rumors that if elected, Dale would reopen the burnt-out liquor store on Route 260 and build up the Red Dust Rodeo grounds. No one took any polls, but before the September 18 election that year everyone had known who would win—it was just a matter of counting families.

Now the sky was growing lighter. As if on cue, the women stood and began preparations. Larson and Sparky strode over to talk to the medicine man, and one by one more trucks rumbled into the clearing. The women grew busy, rushing in and out of the branch shades. Across the field Adam's sister emerged from her wickiup, dressed in a buckskin outfit, with eagle feathers tied to her shoulders and an abalone shell tied to a lock of hair that hung over her forehead. Bells and beads dangled from the buckskin, ringing softly with each step. Her godmother—a woman in glasses, with loose gray-streaked hair—laid out a deerskin, facing east, over a pile of eight blankets. The medicine man's two helpers brought out another abalone shell full of yellow pollen, then a burden basket filled with coins and candy. Around the skins, one by one the women laid boxes of fruit and candy, ears of corn, and soda pop.

Jeff and Adam joined the crowd, which circled around Verdena at a respectful distance. The women were dressed in colorful camp dresses, the men in cowboy hats and jeans, their flannel shirts tucked in over their guts. With staunch concentration Verdena and her older cousin, her partner, took their places on the deerskin, facing east. The singers lifted their drums to their chests in anticipation.

Over the grass ridge the sun appeared, at first no more than a dot, then with each moment an expanding curve of light. The first rays struck the shell pendant on Verdena's forehead, and the drums started quietly, slowly rising in volume, beginning the six hours of dancing, the "full of great happiness" songs.

Up and down now, Verdena and her older cousin stepped in place, a quiet march, sometimes turning or stepping slightly forward, then slightly back. Jeff could discern no pattern. The dance was subtle, meant to conserve Verdena's energy for the long day ahead, but at the same time it was sensual, and it mesmerized him. Verdena was light on her feet (supported, the Apaches said, by the eagle feathers on her shoulders), and her legs never stopped moving. In her right hand she carried an oak cane, hung with long colored ribbons and oriole feathers. The cane guaranteed her a long life, and as an elder she would one day use it to help her walk. Bells at the end of the top curve jingled as she danced, echoing the bells on her buckskin dress. Song after song she stepped and planted the cane on the earth. Her godmother rushed to her now and then, to wipe off her neck and to offer her water.

Jeff and Adam sat down on the open bed of a nearby pickup. The dancing, Adam said, extended over the four straight days—this was only the third. It was a feat of endurance, and Adam had helped train his sister. For the past few months he had jogged with her every other morning, two miles, so that now she wouldn't tire.

The crowd around them watched, respectfully quiet, and Jeff grew less self-conscious. After nearly two hours of dances the godmother took Verdena's cane, twisted it into the dirt, and directed her to kneel on the deerskin. Verdena raised her arms heavenward, the way Changing Woman had when the sun's rays first entered her body on the mountaintop, the very first morning of the world. The singing of the medicine man softened; the godmother guided Verdena to sway side to side and then to lie facedown. Circling her four times, she massaged the young girl with her hands and feet, to ensure a strong, agile body into adulthood. At last Verdena was drawn up and stood before the people in confidence, refreshed. The pains of the previous days of dancing were healed, her energy renewed for the two days to come.

Finally the medicine man dusted Verdena with yellow pollen and emptied an embroidered burden basket of candy, coins, and corn kernels over her head. Everything around her—the sweets, the food, the corn—was now sanctified; and the children jostled one another to get the holy bubblegum and soda pop from the boxes. Before them Verdena stood transformed, in a single body both young woman and White Painted Woman. The crowd gathered closer, and she offered blessings to the long line of celebrants. With her fingers dipped in pollen she touched toddlers' heads and lifted babies up to face the four directions. The elders held out their aching joints to her. In this incarnation, the teenager had the power to heal and strengthen the tribe.

Verdena rested in her wickiup for the afternoon, and Jeff drove home to finish packing and cleaning up his house. Everything he owned fit into three large duffle bags and a single backpack. But that evening he returned to the ceremony in the woods. Above the night was dark, bands of white clouds streaked the sky, and the occasional satellite popped in and out of the ribbons of gray. Ghostly forms filled the darkness around the trucks: flirting teenagers, shouting children, adults who had walked the two miles from town. The mood remained solemn—scattered conversations in whispers, now and then a single shriek of laughter. Occasionally drums beat in the distance. The crickets were loud in the woods, and Jeff heard a rustling there that sounded like animals afoot, but was probably just children running along dark paths, through piles of dead leaves. The ripeness of the air mixed with the mud of the ground, the settled coolness of the forest, and the smoke of the bonfire in the center of the pasture.

He approached the edge of the firelight, where Verdena was standing with three other girls, all dressed in buckskin. After a moment Jeff heard behind him the jingling of bells and the terrified shrieks of young children.

Five crown dancers, the Gaan, emerged single file from the forest, shirtless, wearing black executioner-style hoods, their three-foot white crowns jutting at angles from their heads, the bells of their knee-high moccasins clinking to the drumbeat, their prodigious stomachs and backs painted gray with black dots and geometric patterns, and the belts around their waists holding a spray of spruce branches. In each hand the dancers grasped painted wooden wands.

It was easy to understand why the children were afraid of these spirits. They had once been called "devil dancers" by American settlers who had witnessed this ceremony—Jeff had seen that label printed on a post card in town. But they were benevolent, and they had come to offer their special protective powers to Verdena and the celebrants.

In one line the Gaan raced up and down the clearing in a vigorous, twirling dance, swinging and ducking their great white crowns. Behind them their leader, the clown, his torso painted white with red dots, carried a wedge of wood on a length of cord. He twirled this in wide circles around his wrist, in imitation of the whistling of the mountain winds. For minutes the Gaan moved in circles, thrusting their wands into the ground. Then Verdena and the other young women joined the dance. It was elaborate—far more difficult than the simple stepping of the morning ceremony—and involved wide arching movements and sinuous turns. A few men tossed more wood into the bonfire, and the ashes swirled up over the crowd, over the spiraling dancers.

Jeff was breathless. Here it was, authenticity, the culture for a moment preserved. Yet Adam complained that sometimes these Sunrise Dances were nothing more than a large outdoor beer party. Many young Apache girls were already deciding not to go through with it. Jeff couldn't help but think that the Apache men drove Nissans to round up their herds, logged the forest with chain saws and dynamite, and shopped for Christmas gifts at Kmart.

He told himself he would not descend into guilt. This was not his culture to save, and these people had made that clear enough. It was a tiny village, missing from most maps. A place nobody had ever heard of. What difference did it make if he could have helped improve things here?

As the Gaan were winding down their fourth and final dance, Jeff began to shiver. He was suddenly unnerved by the crown dancers, by the unnatural motion of their bodies, their rolls of fat jiggling up and down, the thrust of their hoods forward and back, like hunted animals in the final throes of life. By the light of the fire they did not look human.

Among the Gaan the girls were dancing with renewed energy. The children had quieted down, and their young faces, dimly lit in an orange glow, showed an infinite capacity for belief. Suddenly the drums stopped and the dance ended. In single file, chests heaving, the spirits made their way into the forest again.

Jeff was negotiating the darkness to find his truck when he felt a hand on his shoulder, pulling him back.

"Hartig," the voice said.

He turned and saw two dim figures. One he couldn't recognize, but the other, a compact, powerful young man, he knew. It was Levi, swaying on his feet.

"Adam told me you're taking off tomorrow."

"Yeah, I've gotta go."

"When you leaving?"

"Your cousin's driving me down to Phoenix in the afternoon. After the painting ceremony."

"Maybe I'll come."

Jeff stiffened. "If you want, Levi."

"I'm just kidding."

"Whatever you want to do, you do."

"You leaving 'cause of what happened to the center, isn't it?"

"Yeah."

"It sucks that you're leaving."

"It does suck."

"I'm sorry that all happened to you."

"It didn't happen to me, Levi. I wasn't the one it happened to." Jeff paused a second. "You know who did it?"

"I don't know nothing."

"You sure?"

"Man, don't ask me again."

"I'll see you then." He squeezed past the teenagers, toward his truck.

"You probably won't. See me, I mean."

Jeff turned back. The young men were laughing at something. He said, "All right, we'll say goodbye now." He reached to shake Levi's hand, but the gesture wasn't reciprocated. Jeff's hand hung there, and slowly he lowered it. He got into the truck, slammed the door, and as the engine roared, he was sure he heard Levi shout, "You bitch!"

Jeff drove through dense night along the unmarked logging paths, back to the main road. Halfway home he realized that he was driving with both hands, digging his fingers into the rubber grip of the steering wheel. He dodged a lame dog and five minutes later was turning onto the school grounds, onto Teacher's Row, the white man's housing.

The next day, on the ride to Phoenix, Jeff told Adam, "You can take her for a thousand. We'll straighten out the title and papers. And make sure you get insurance."

"What you gonna do now?"

"I'll crash with some college friends for a few weeks, till I figure it out." Last year, he explained, before he took the job in Red Cliff, he'd applied to the Peace Corps. He was going to see if he couldn't reactivate the application and get placed overseas.

"Another country?"

"Yeah, another country."

"You could just go like that?"

"Well, you go where they send you."

"You'll let me know where you are?"

"Why's that?"

"So I could pay you back. For the truck and all."

"Don't worry about it."

They passed through the mining town of Globe and stopped at the final light on Route 60. A gospel song was playing on the radio, and Adam lowered the volume.

"Hartig," he said. "I let him borrow the key."

"I know you did."

"He said he was just gonna go in and jam to some music. Him and some of our friends."

"Well, that's not what they did."

"It's fucked up. I trusted him."

Jeff shook his head, and his tongue felt heavy. He almost wished Adam hadn't admitted it. The light turned. He pulled the truck forward and raced it past seventy onto the open highway.

Adam stared out the side window and asked, "You'll still write me?"

"What difference does it make?"

"You write me. I want to show you."

"Show me what?"

Adam didn't answer him.

"Show me what, Adam?"

"We could still be friends."

Jeff fought back the smile. He turned the gospel music back up and Adam threw in a Megadeth cassette. They rode without a word past the last stores of Globe and over the pass to Phoenix. Two hours later, outside his old college roommate's house in Tempe, Jeff handed over the keys for the Toyota.

"Take care of this thing," he said to Adam, kicking the truck's front tire. "It's an heirloom."

"Yeah."

They shook hands but did not say goodbye. There was no Apache word for it.

3

ANARBEK AND NAZIRA had been waiting for the American to arrive since seven o'clock that morning. Anarbek insisted they remain in the house; he wanted to make sure they did not miss their guest, and he needed Nazira to help translate for him. She had busied herself with the final touches, ironing all the curtains for a second time, sweeping out of the cupboards any crumbs that had escaped her many cleanings, folding towels, scouring the bathtub, and counting silverware to make sure there were eight full sets of knives, forks, spoons, and teacups. By mid-evening both she and her father had fallen asleep in the living room. They were awakened by the crashing of a bus over the dirt humps of Karl Marx Street. Anarbek rushed to the door and Nazira hurried to the bathroom to brush her hair. She arrived in the living room just as her father was pulling Dushen and the American into the house.

She had never seen anyone like him. He looked . . . healthy. He had a fleshy face, curly auburn hair that was beginning to creep below his ears, broad shoulders, a thin waist, and a perfectly white, perfectly straight set of teeth. In greeting, his voice was high pitched and uncertain, his Kyrgyz accent comical, but his blue eyes, though tired and reddened by the long trip from the capital, glowed with kindness. He acknowledged her only with a cursory nod—this alone brought the blood rushing to her cheeks. Her father immediately led him over to the Brezhnev-era refrigerator groaning in a corner of the living room, tugged it open, and gestured with a flourish inside. The rusted racks were filled with seventeen blue cans labeled Judah Maccabee.

"These must have cost a fortune," the foreigner said.

"Americans always have a refrigerator full of beer," Anarbek announced. "I saw it in the films."

The Peace Corps had placed Jeff in the Kyrgyz village to teach English to rural factory workers. The recent independence of Central Asia after the collapse of the Soviet Union had created a new frontier, and a wave of humanitarian, business, and religious groups had already flooded in. Jeff's assignment was straightforward: under the English for Specific Purposes program, he would offer basic language classes. After his failure on the reservation, he had grown staunchly motivated. He wanted to be useful in a practical way, in a place that needed him, and he was determined to forget Arizona.

He had spent the summer in Bishkek, completing the three-month Peace Corps orientation program. Each morning he had dropped off letters to his friends in America at the main *pochta*, then walked to school through an unkempt park with dried-up fountains, ready to face a day of language study and teacher training. The capital was a pleasant Soviet city with wildflowers and marijuana growing amid the sidewalk weeds. Sheep grazed downtown. On a walk one dark evening, staring up at the enormous moon, Jeff fell into an open manhole. He caught himself at the elbows, his feet dangling in the blackness below. He had lost a Birkenstock but was grateful he had not broken his back. When he pulled himself out and staggered to the *microregion* of his host family (the former manager of a state-run radio program and his frenetic wife), they informed him that manhole covers had become prized substitutes for barbell plates, so he should watch where he was going.

In language classes he struggled along with the other volunteers. They ridiculed each other's efforts to master the accumulation of Kyrgyz suffixes. One of his friends could perfectly imitate the grammatical rule their teacher kept referring to as "wowel harmony." Midsummer they went to Lake Issy-Kul in the northeast mountains for a three-week teaching camp. By day the volunteers planned their lessons, taught in a practice school, and observed one another's classes. By night they flirted and drank. Jeff hung back, more interested in absorbing the scenery than in reliving college life. In order to ward off mosquitoes he ate four cloves of garlic a day and didn't shower. Thrilled by the sense of remoteness, by the distance from America, he spent a good deal of time walking alone. In the fragrant summer evenings, after his daily teaching evaluation, he would wander over to the pier and dip his feet into Issy-Kul (Hot Lake), stare out at the shadows of the Tien Shan (Mountains of Heaven), and count the shooting stars.

On his return to Bishkek for the final month of training, his host family showed him off to friends and relatives around the capital. For centuries their nomadic ancestors had never turned hungry travelers away from their mountain yurts. Now, despite their poverty, the Kyrgyz welcomed strangers like him into their Soviet-era apartments with traditional zeal. Homemade jams, pickles, round loaves of nan, walnuts, melons, raisins, honey cakes, fried dough, yogurt, and sour cream were spread before him. When he had eaten his fill, he was told that dinner had not yet begun. Soups, dumplings, and a mound of pilaf were on their way. He finished and thanked the hostess for the fine meal. She assured him the main course would be ready shortly. *Shashlyk* and *beshbarmak* (the national dish of greasy noodles and boiled mutton swimming in a broth of onions, eaten with the hands) were served. Vodka and cognac were poured. Singing and dancing were inevitable. And though the average family earned twenty-five dollars a month, to Jeff's dismay his hosts sometimes killed their only sheep in his honor. He would be asked to carve its boiled head.

As a final exam, the Peace Corps sent trainees on the dreaded Village Visit—an independent weekend excursion meant to test resilience and language ability. Jeff found himself in a Russian dacha two hours west of the city. Over three long days the hosts seemed puzzled by his mispronunciation of the simplest Russian words. The family gave up trying to hold a conversation and instead forced large amounts of vodka on him, fed him mounds of potato *pieroshkis,* dressed him for comfort in the father's floral pajamas, and holed him up in a private villa guarded by six dogs, a sow, her piglets, and a coop of noisy chickens. In the middle of the second evening, bursting, he blundered outside in the dark in search of the toilet. The barking dogs pursued him. They woke the hens and swine. Reeling from the stink of the outhouse, he found every light on the street turned on, neighbors rushing around in slippers, lighting candles, trying to discover what on earth had aroused such a tumult in their once peaceful town.

In this way he passed his Village Visit test, and the following week at the Hotel Dostuk the ambassador swore him in. After the ceremony Jeff met his site representative: a man named Dushen, the assistant manager of Kyzyl Adyr–Kirovka's cheese collective. Together, they left the capital on a rusted minibus for the journey into the mountains. To get to the Talas Valley, they had to ride west, out of the country, across the lower steppes of Kazakhstan, then wind through a steep mountain pass and enter back into Kyrgyzstan. With independence the borders had changed, but the roads had not.

Twelve hours and six champagne bottles later, the bus deposited them in front of a dark house blanketed by night. Jeff felt a bulge in his throat. He was alone. He could sense the mountains around him, cutting him off from everything familiar. Along an uneven stone path, ducking under the branches of what appeared to be apple trees, Dushen helped drag his bags up to the concrete porch of a townhouse. The lights flickered on from a first-floor room, and a huge man with a pockmarked face, tousled gray hair, and eyes still half-asleep greeted them in the doorway. Dushen introduced Anarbek Tashtanaliev, Jeff's village host-father. As they shook hands the man's daughter, pale with scattered dark freckles, appeared behind him. She offered Jeff a gentle, closed-lipped smile while his host-father pulled him over to a refrigerator full of Israeli beer.

In Kyzyl Adyr–Kirovka Jeff received what felt like a hero's welcome. Over his first few days his neighbors on Karl Marx Street introduced themselves in a continuous wave. Expectations were high; they seemed to believe he could change their lives. The attention was jarring—in Red Cliff he'd always been kept at arm's length by the community. But here the villagers offered gifts of warm bread, eggplant and cabbage from their family plots, strawberry and cherry compote, boiled mutton, and plastic bags filled with cold triangles of fried dough. They explained just to what length Anarbek had gone to refurbish the old brick townhouse. The previous year the occupants had repatriated to southern Russia. The house had served a six-person family for three decades, so the village deemed it large enough for one American. Anarbek had arranged for its purchase with the village *akim*. For an entire month he had shown up each day with his wife and two daughters to renovate the home and bring it up to Peace Corps standards. He had installed a Western toilet (the bathroom did not have running water; Anarbek would work on that, they said) and a series of electric radiators (the street's electricity seemed sporadic; he would work on that). His daughters had hung printed curtains made from bedroom sheets, pounded out the carpets, and scrubbed the several years' accumulation of Central Asian dust off the floors. From the *akim*, Anarbek requisitioned a heavy steel gate for the front door, a strict requirement stipulated by the Peace Corps, but in the neighbors' opinion an unnecessary precaution. For the previous quarter of a century, Kyzyl Adyr–Kirovka had known no crime.

Anarbek had even installed a telephone. It was a red, hollow, plastic device with a single thread of exposed wire that looped out of the top step on the second floor, perfectly situated to trip Jeff and send him flying down the stairs. On his third evening in the village, finished unpacking, he checked the telephone to see if he could reach America. There was no dial tone. When he picked up the receiver, he could hear the strumming of a *kumooz* and the high-pitched wailing of a Kyrgyz folk song. The telephone picked up radio signals.

Anarbek came by three times a day to see how Jeff was settling in. The round man arrived sweating, his shirt stained in large damp patches beneath his arms. He carried the smell of wet leather into the home. He fingered Jeff's hiking boots, he fingered his books, his Bic pens, his serrated knife. How had he slept? he asked. What had he eaten for breakfast? Whom had he talked to? Where had he been wandering at eight that morning? (One of the village children had spotted Jeff taking out garbage. Word had spread.) What would he do this evening? Would he come over for dinner?

Jeff accepted dinner each night for the first week. He dined in a sitting room alone with Anarbek, served by his quick-stepping wife, Lola, a slim, fair-skinned woman of his own age. She appeared carrying a new mutton dish each night: mutton dumplings called *manti*, a mutton and turnip stew called *lagman*, the mutton kebabs called *shashlyk*—and what Anarbek claimed was a special delicacy, known as "refrigerator jelly": a wobbling glob of congealed fat from the previous day's mutton.

By the end of the first week Jeff decided he would have to learn how to refuse his host-father's invitations. That Saturday he fumbled an excuse in grammatically poor Russian. Anarbek's face colored, his eyes dropped, and, head hanging, he left the house, checking the metal gate behind him. Five minutes later a knock on the door sounded. Jeff's neighbor, Oomar, wanted to know if he would join them for dinner.

In this way two weeks passed. Jeff settled in and began to plan his English lessons. He checked the village *pochta* every day for his mail. At last, at the end of the second week, he received his first letter, a one-page note from Adam, telling him he'd enrolled at Northern Arizona University. A university grant, combined with his BIA scholarship and tribal land settlement, had amounted to a full ride. Jeff doubted Adam would make it through first semester, but then rebuked himself for his bitterness.

That same afternoon Anarbek drove Jeff to the cheese factory to show him his classroom. At the entrance gate squatted what looked like a tollbooth, with a chipped barrier arm painted in black and white stripes, which a watchman raised by pulling a frayed string. They drove into the complex and parked in a gravel lot. In front of them lay a discolored concrete building—long and low, like a bunker—whose entire left half appeared to be sinking into the earth. Anarbek explained that the foundation had shifted ten years ago in a small earthquake. He laughed, explaining how he had been working that very afternoon in his office, and his desk had slid backward and pinned him against the wall. But nobody had been hurt, only surprised. This sunken building connected to a high warehouse structure with missing windows. Across the lot stood a similar building, backed by a white silo that leaned at an angle, like the Tower of Pisa. Anarbek indicated the cow stables, then pointed to a large square shed in the far corner of the lot and with a smile told Jeff it was the factory sauna. A light shone from the sauna windows, and steam drifted from a pipe on the roof—the only signs of life in the complex.

The bunker's unlit hallways were strangely quiet, and on most doors hung freshly painted signs with the word *OPASNIE!*—DANGER! Anarbek hurried Jeff past these, straight to the door of his classroom; but when he triumphantly turned the loose knob to usher Jeff in, he found that the door was locked. This apparently was a surprise. Anarbek cursed, fumbled in his pocket for the keys, and finding none, promptly bashed the door with a thunderous front-thrust kick. It swung open; the knob fell and rattled on the ground. Jeff stepped in and saw that his classroom was a converted closet, with six tables, and milking stools for seats. A warped brown chalkboard had been hung on the back wall, and in front of it, on a flimsy desk, sat a box of Soviet chalk. When he picked up a piece, half of it disintegrated in his fingers. The chalkboard, he found, was ancient and frictionless—he tried to write his name, and the chalk barely left a trace.

His classes would begin on Monday. He glanced back at Anarbek, who was cleaning his ear with his pinky. Jeff smiled. Through the room's lone, thin window, he could see two snowy mountain peaks reflecting the high Central Asian sun.

"*Prekrasna*," he said, his voice resounding in the empty halls of the silent factory. Perfect.

Peace Corps trainers had warned Jeff about a debilitating state of mind, common to many volunteers, called the fishbowl effect. With his hooded hemp Baja shirt and his leather sneakers, in his every movement, Jeff stood out in full relief. People stared. When he bought his eggs in the bazaar, all eyes fell on him. The faces of babushkas jostling at the counter in the *pochta* locked on him a unified, threatening glare. Old men hobbling along Karl Marx Street halted before his gate and watched him gathering fallen apples. On the porch, after dinner, he would look up from an old copy of *Newsweek* to see an array of children's eyes poking through the slats in his fence, their hands resting above the posts. He knew no privacy.

On a bright Saturday morning in mid-September, a Soviet army jeep swerved in front of the house, and Anarbek stumbled out. Without explanation he dragged Jeff across the yard and pushed him toward the vehicle. "Just tell me where we are going," Jeff pleaded, but his host-father waved vaguely at the highest peaks in the distance.

Two fat Kyrgyz men in camouflage suits sat up front, but Jeff was shoved into the back, where he found the director of the Lenin School, his wife, their two children, Anarbek's daughter Baktigul, a case of vodka, two watermelons, fishing gear, three hunting rifles, and a bucket of sunflower seeds.

Following the course of a swirling river, they bounced through high, dry country along a primitive dirt path into the mountains. The road climbed to a cliff overlooking the water. Anarbek took the treacherous curves at a furious pace and kept turning around to ask questions.

How much money does your father make?

Do Americans believe in God?

How many floors are there in the Empire State Building?

When will you marry a Kyrgyz woman?

Jeff coughed a loud nervous laugh, pressed his head to the window, and stared out over the precipice, certain they would plummet over it at any moment. The rough-edged peaks rose high above. Little air circulated inside the crowded jeep. Anarbek leered left and right, swerving the vehicle with each turn of his head. Jeff wondered what his own father would do when he learned of the impending jeep wreck. And why did everyone else seem so calm?

After nearly an hour the Kyrgyz thrashed the transmission from fourth gear to first, jerking them all to a halt. The men hurried from the vehicle, loading their rifles, and shot off a thunderous volley at what appeared to be an empty side of the mountain. Jeff cringed, watching Anarbek dash up the slope across the steady line of fire, then dive behind a boulder.

He reappeared without bullet wounds, swinging four dead pheasants by the feet. The crowd in the jeep applauded the bloody birds, and his host-father laid them as a gift on Jeff's lap. He forced a smile. Blood dripped out of a pheasant's mouth onto his sneaker.

They drove higher; the slopes of the mountains swam upward in steep vertiginous angles and jutting overhangs of rock. Occasionally the landscape leveled into a valley or a long brown field of rustling grass. They stopped three times to slaughter more large fowl. After one assault their hosts encouraged Jeff to practice shooting. He missed rocks and closely placed bottles. "*Amerikanyets!*" someone laughed from the back of the jeep.

Anarbek informed Jeff that he was not keeping the rifle steady. "The secret of hunting," he said, "is keeping the hands still." He provided an immediate solution: vodka toasts.

To friendship.

To peace.

To a full table.

To guests.

Two hours beyond any trace of civilization the jeep bumped over a haphazard wooden bridge and swerved before a mud-brick farmhouse surrounded by horses. A ceremonial nomadic yurt had been set up behind the house, and beyond it a wide field stretched in both directions, cut in half by the tumbling river. The noon sun leaning over the highest ridge cast the mountains half in shadow. Groups of strangers, apparently Anarbek's relatives, rushed out of the yurt, greeted them with a round of *salamatsizbih,* and swept them into their fly-infested home.

The nomads crouched around a stained cloth spread on the floor, their chins upturned, eyes wide, examining him. They wore traditional Kyrgyz dress: *kalpaks* (tall white-felt national headgear, which Jeff could only associate with a dunce cap), high black boots, the men in weathered sports jackets, the women in head-scarves and dresses that looked like floral tablecloths. Years of tending sheep in the alpine sun had burned their faces terra-cotta red.

It seemed that everyone had gathered to celebrate the first birth-day of Anarbek's nephew, a gurgling round-faced toddler with flushed cheeks. From a stained bowl Jeff drank *kumyss*—fermented mare's milk—and managed to keep it down with shots of chai. The hostess never filled a teacup completely, worried it would be cold before one finished it. Instead there commenced the endless ritual of sipping, slurping, then passing of the cups around the circle back to the samovar. A tablecloth covered the center of the floor, and breads, apples, grapes, raisins, apricots, sauces, candies, jams, nuts, and teacups were spread upon it. The indoor picnic was arranged with a delightful scattered precision, and Jeff reminded himself how little these families had, how generous they were being with their food.

Lola set before him a large mound of pilaf and a full cup of chai. To Jeff's left knelt an old man, bent over, facing the southwest corner of the room, reciting loud Arabic prayers. Clothed in a long black overcoat, a worn suit jacket, black stockings, and a silver skullcap, he bobbed his bearded face back and forth at the floor. Anarbek told him the man, his first wife's father, was approaching a hundred years of age. For half an hour the praying figure did not acknowledge the company. Finally, with a slide of his hands over his face—"*Omen!*"—he finished the ritual, raised his eyes to the center of the room, greeted Jeff with a toothless smile, and joined him at the mound of pilaf.

They ate with their hands, and Jeff tried not to drop any food in his lap. He watched the old man's withered fingers clenching the moist rice. One hundred years old. What had this man seen? A rise and a fall of an empire. Two world wars. Stalin's purges, the concentration camps, the gulag? Perhaps he knew nothing of these things. Perhaps he had led only a sheltered village life, ignorant of the trials of the larger world. He looked wise, but could he even read?

"*Abdan tattoo*," Jeff said. Very delicious. He broke the silence of intense feasting and lost a handful of rice on his socks.

"*Azamat!*" Good boy! The old man licked the oil from his wrinkled palm and patted Jeff on the arm.

"*Elma*," he said, holding up an apple.

"*Bilem*," Jeff told the old man. I know.

"*Elma!*" he demanded.

"*Elma.*"

He lifted walnuts, hard candy, a spoonful of sugar, various breads, the dusty raisins. He said the name, Jeff repeated it; he said it a second time with greater force, Jeff repeated it louder. Finally the man reviewed the items, asking one by one, "*Bool ne?*" Everyone nodded vigorously when Jeff gave the correct answer.

The meat on the pilaf was unusually lean and tasty, not like the greasy mutton he had come to expect. When at last he was invited outside to rest his stomach, he discovered why. Anarbek pulled him into a shed behind the house, where a group of young men squatted in the shadows around a three-foot pile of charred meat. "*At!*" they pronounced proudly, gesturing like game-show hostesses. Horse.

They cut him more and handed him a raw onion as a side dish. He nibbled politely. Anarbek explained that eating horse was rare in the autumn—it was usually saved for the end of winter, when meat ran low. "Horse meat has many calories," he said. "It will make you strong." He pointed to Jeff's groin, curled his finger, and straightened it rigidly up into the air. Jeff shifted away from him.

When Jeff could stomach no more, he was led outside and seated before another spread of food, laid out on a cloth in the sharp grass. Again the vodka flowed. If he refused to drink, his hosts clicked their tongues in disappointment, lifted the glass, and forced it into his hands. To refuse again would be an insult. "*Davai!*" the men shouted, glasses raised, vodka spilling. Come on!

Anarbek paced around the circle of family and friends, answering questions about his American. Jeff nibbled triangles of *borsok,* which, like frybread, he dipped in honey, shocking his hosts. This apparently was not done. He inhaled a long heavy breath, the pressure in his stomach unrelenting. His mind swam through a blurred vision of Central Asia, the mountain pasture, the singsong language, the generosity of these strangers, their laughter, their smiles, their friendly whacks on his back. More vodka was poured. He drained his glass and it was filled; he drained it and it was filled again.

When he could put no more into his body and did not know if he would be able to stand, the athletic events began. Male participation, Anarbek warned, was mandatory. First came the races. The men sprinted across the cow field, and even a crippled uncle, leaning on a walking stick, hobbled along. Slowed by a stomach full of horse organs, Jeff found himself in less than top form. He finished the race fourth, ahead of the crippled uncle, and vomited into a ditch next to a cow.

A ceremonial birthday race came next. To begin, the parents tied a ribbon around the nephew's bowed legs, and he wobbled in front of the crowd. Then, from across the field the other children raced to him. Anarbek's daughter Baktigul won the event, and the adults awarded her a pair of scissors. She snipped the child's ribbon between his legs, a symbolic cutting: the boy, now a year old, was ready to enter the race of life. The toddler took a few uncertain steps and everyone cheered.

"*Azamat!*" Good boy!

After this came feats of strength: pushup contests, a tug of war, and most exciting of all, the wrestling on horseback. Two men lined up their horses side by side, facing opposite directions, and with embroidered leather whips they urged the animals into a slow spin. Gathering momentum, whipping the stomping horses still faster, each rider grabbed the other's shoulder, then tried to dismount the opponent by tearing at his shirt, hair, and flailing limbs. The relatives shouted while in a display of wild acrobatics the riders sweated and the horses grew dizzy, tossing their heads until one man fell.

As Jeff watched, applauding, Anarbek's older daughter, Nazira, sat beside him. She slanted her feet below her skirt, offered him a piece of fresh bread, then gestured to the horse wrestling and proclaimed in hesitant English, "It is an excellent sport for watching.

But more exciting, to my mind, to play." She turned to him and asked, "Would you like to attempt?"

Jeff simply laughed. "How do you speak such wonderful English?"

Nazira had long, straight black hair. She giggled and her mouth opened slightly, like the budding of a rose. He caught a glimpse of two gold molars before she covered her mouth quickly with her hand. "I studied in university," she said. "And now I am the teacher."

The next match had begun and they watched it together. Anarbek sneaked up behind them; his shadow spread across the food. He leaned down and spoke in Jeff's ear. "I see, Jeff, you are talking to my daughter." With his dirty fingers he lined up three glasses and filled each from an open vodka bottle.

Nazira told him, "You must not drink if you do not want. But it is our way."

Jeff smiled. "I thought you were Muslim. This drinking is not, well—very religious."

Nazira laughed again. "We are very bad Muslims, Jeff Hartig. Very bad. But you must remember—the Russians brought this." She tapped the empty bottle with her fingernail.

It was time for the traditional wrestling. The competitors tied pieces of cloth around their waists to use as a grip. Jeff mentioned he had wrestled in high school; after much arguing he consented to take on a young cousin of Anarbek's. Nazira helped tie a belt around his waist. When he turned, though, he saw two men had locked arms over piles of fresh horse manure. The men flipped each other, the dung flew, the crowd cheered. It seemed the Kyrgyz drew little distinction between shit and dirt. Jeff untied his belt and sat down.

A few minutes later the relatives called for the women to wrestle. "They are joking, aren't they?" he asked Anarbek.

But to everyone's laughter, the modest, soft-spoken Kyrgyz women paired up, grabbed each other around the neck, yanked each other's scarves, and in elaborate knotted holds pummeled each other into the filth. The men wagered vodka shots on wives and sisters and groaned when they lost a bet.

In the final match, in a show of enormous strength, with a grunt and a twist, Nazira herself flipped a great-aunt onto the pungent ground. She raised her arms in victory, her stained skirt whipping in the breeze. In Jeff's life, the event was memorable for more than its hilarity. Even covered in horseshit this woman was stunning. She was slight and strong, with gentle Asian eyes, dark freckles, and a grace and modesty in her playfulness. Jeff lay back on his elbows in the grass, staring at her.

Nazira watched the sun begin to set beyond the mountains. A row of haystacks gleamed orange across the field. Groups of her intrepid aunts stirred meat in woks over fires and rolled flour and water into long noodles. Large Russian samovars boiled chai for the guests. One of her uncles had set up a unique contraption: gasoline dripped out of a plugged vodka bottle, ran down a long ramp, and fueled a fire under a metal vat, boiling water for the dishes.

She crouched with Jeff near the fire and watched a circle of men playing *durag*. The card players waited for their opponents to throw their hands, grumbled, and smoked cigarettes rolled from homegrown tobacco and last year's newspapers. She observed with fascination how patiently Jeff answered their questions, but she was embarrassed when one of the players asked if he would marry a Kyrgyz woman, and why it was taking him so long.

At dinner she guided him into the fly-infested farmhouse with fourteen other men and sat down to administer the samovar. Jeff was given the most important seat, farthest from the door. A young nephew, circling the room with a kettle and basin, poured steaming water on each person's hands, then the women carried in the plates of *beshbarmak*. As the guest of honor Jeff was given a sheep's head to carve. Nazira hid her smile when he could not negotiate slicing through a nostril with any degree of grace. She asked one of her cousins, a powerful man to Jeff's left, to help him. He directed Jeff to the eyes of the sheep. The foreigner grabbed one with his slippery fingers and tried to dislodge it, but the thin red veins kept it well attached, stretching like bands of rubber with each pull. At last her cousin helped Jeff, jabbing the knife between his fingers until the eye was free.

Tradition dictated that Jeff give the eyeball to someone he wished to see again soon, but it was too much to hope he might offer it to her. He passed it instead to her grandfather, who had spent the evening in prayer in the corner of the room. Her cousin dislodged the second eye and with a bow of the head offered it to Jeff himself to swallow.

The American held the eyeball in his palm for an unusually long time, his Adam's apple lurching up and down his throat. Slowly he placed the eyeball into his mouth, seeming to curl his tongue around it. On his first swallow his throat failed him. Nazira leaned forward. He tried again and again and finally squeezed it down, then chased it with a nearby apricot.

"*Azamat!*" she cried out, and everyone around her drew a collective breath.

She joined her father and the family in the packed vehicle for the twilight ride home. As the jeep jostled them through the mountains, she sat crunched between Jeff's hip and the three squirming children. The men's conversation centered on him.

How do you like our Kyrgyzstan?

How much does this knife cost in America?

And bread?

And a house?

Do you have apples in America?

What do you think of our privatization?

Perhaps you will stay longer than two years?

His Kyrgyz answers were growing mildly comprehensible, and he was relying less on Russian, which pleased Nazira. Through much evasive language, the American was able to explain something called carjacking and something else called money laundering. He informed them that in New York City an apartment the size of two of those jeeps cost one thousand dollars to rent.

"A year?" Anarbek asked.

"A month!"

In the front seat, the eyes of the men opened in wonder.

When there was at last a lull in the conversation, Nazira's father bellowed, "Sing!"

Anarbek possessed a powerful voice and a deep Kyrgyz love of song. Inspired by the alpine air and the bottles of vodka, he and the school director pretended to woo Jeff with a resounding love serenade. In turn Nazira sang a solo ballad in her soft soprano voice. It was the first song her mother had ever taught her, about the beauty of the mountains—how the snow leaves in the summer and one might think it gone forever, but every winter it returns. Shy, she did not look at the American, but her voice quavered when she felt her shoulder press into his.

Finally it was Jeff's turn. He claimed he had never performed for an audience before, but Anarbek would not accept such a flimsy excuse. In the end he appeased them with a song called "Ninety-nine Bottles of Beer on the Wall." Everyone in the swerving jeep picked up on the words, and Nazira would never forget the American's strong voice leading the chorus, the swaying men in the front seat, her scarved aunts and the children piled in back, in heavy Central Asian accents, all counting bottles of beer on the wall. It was the first time since escaping Traktorbek that she could see the possibility of a new and better life before her.

Jeff awoke each day sick from the previous night's food, but he appreciated the luxury of his own indoor toilet (which he flushed with a bucket of water). First thing in the morning he stared out at the mountains; the snow crept lower across them each day. Now in the November dawn frost appeared on the ground. Horses grazed on the remains of his garden, and crows called from the apple trees that blocked his view of the kindergarten across the street.

Each weekend Jeff left the village and took the three-hour bus ride to Talas to shop at the larger bazaar there. In good weather he hiked into the mountains or camped next to the glacial Talas River. On a routine visit the Peace Corps country director complimented him, saying he had proved himself a tough-minded volunteer dedicated to his job, able to suffer the most difficult privations with grace and resilience. The director appreciated how he had persevered in his village work at the Kyzyl Adyr–Kirovka cheese collective.

Jeff understood that this typical overblown Peace Corps flattery meant only that he didn't complain about the failing water supply or the lack of heat in his home. The Peace Corps office knew absolutely nothing about his factory students, their constant need to review material, their expectation of attaining instant knowledge (without, apparently, any studying), their mumbled incoherencies, their reluctant classroom participation, their intense doubt and refusal to accept the fundamentals of English grammar. For weeks at a time Jeff struggled to help the factory electrician, engineer, accountant, and dairy maids memorize the conjugation of the verb *to be*.

In the evenings he graded homework and responded to his students' weekly journals. On Friday afternoons he organized a volleyball club. After months of persistent wrangling with the state bureaucracy, he managed to open the English Resource Center in a room adjoining the *pochta,* where twice a week he taught classes to adults from neighboring villages and on Sunday afternoons offered karate workshops to eager crowds of village children.

To help Anarbek, Jeff translated the cheese factory's machinery inventories and production reports and edited applications for capital grants and agricultural exchange programs. The figures all sounded pretty good, and only in November did it occur to him that he had never seen any cheese. There was none for sale in the bazaar, none in the village's near-empty store. Anarbek answered Jeff's inquiries evasively: the factory was adjusting to changes in the market. They were reassessing production capabilities. Business was fully expected to pick up next year. There was no need to draw attention to the problem.

"If the cows are unproductive, perhaps you should consider a change in product," Jeff suggested. "Report your troubles to the government. See if you can get some money together for a joint venture. You can make leather boots or wool scarves. You can build on what you have."

"This is a dairy factory, Jeff. I've been running it for over thirty years. It's what I was trained to do. We don't make scarves here."

Jeff pointed to an inventory he had translated. "But you're reporting to Bishkek eight hundred kilograms of cheese for each eight-hour shift. That's not true."

Anarbek chastised him. "This is Kyrgyzstan you're talking about, my friend. Much you don't see is true."

Sometimes, in the evenings, Jeff fooled himself into believing that his townhouse home would grant him respite from the fishbowl effect. But the village kept track of his every move. No sooner had he returned from a long day of teaching at the factory than the knocking would begin. At the door the neighbor's children offered him *kumyss.* An old mother knocked, dragged her daughter into his home, and asked him to teach the girl English, there and then, in one try. Sometimes the pounding on the door was Anarbek, armed with shanks of mutton and bottles of vodka. Or it was Nazira, offering him fresh bread. She alone declined his obligatory invitation to come inside.

He came to live in a state of dread and started pretending he wasn't home. The village was not fooled.

One rainy December afternoon the door shook for a full thirty minutes. Jeff was resolute; he would not answer it. Through his window he heard an unfamiliar voice speaking to the neighbors' children.

"Is the foreigner home?"

One of the kids answered, "The *eenostranyets* got home one hour ago. The *eenostranyets* was carrying a bag of carrots and a jar of milk. The *eenostranyets* was wearing that bright green rain jacket that looks so funny. He has not shaved in weeks. He gave me two lollipops yesterday. Just keep knocking. The *eenostranyets* usually answers."

Jeff opened the front door and gate and found, standing on his porch, an elderly Russian man. The veins on his red nose protruded in blue lines; thin gray hair was slathered across his forehead. His stained army overcoat was soaked, and a torn leather rucksack was slung across his shoulder. "*Zdrastvooitye,* Jeff Hartig!"

"*Zdras.* Come in."

As the stranger entered, Jeff noticed the dark clouds on the tips of the mountains begin to break. The rain had stopped, and a chorus of drops from the eaves of his house pattered to the earth. Once inside the man removed his boots and extended a quivering hand. "Yuri Samonov! It's a pleasure to meet you. A pleasure."

"It's a pleasure," Jeff repeated in Russian. "I apologize about the door. In the rain—and I was sleeping—"

"*Nyechevo!* I understand, Jeff Hartig." There was a sparkle of intelligence in his eyes, an ironic expression on his weathered face. Jeff invited him upstairs to dry off while he prepared the chai and warmed yesterday's bread. When Jeff returned to the living room, the man was thumbing through a stack of old *National Geographic*s that Jeff's aunt had recently shipped.

The Russian's hands shook as he held one out and opened it. "This is the greatest magazine in the world," he said. "My favorite." He turned a page. "My favorite." He slammed his palm on the pink plastic tablecloth, startling Jeff.

"You can take a copy or two, if you like."

Yuri was quiet for a moment, mouthing the words of one of the captions under a close-up photo of a bat with its wings spread. He finished and looked up with bright eyes. "I wrote for this magazine," he said.

Jeff assumed the man was drunk, but he insisted that he had written two articles, in 1972 and 1977. Over tea Yuri explained how he had worked as a geologist and mountaineer in Bishkek for most of his life. He had climbed the three tallest peaks in the Tien Shan, some of the highest on the planet. But after independence he could no longer make a living as a geologist. With his Kyrgyz wife and teenage son he had moved to the village. Here they could feed themselves from a private crop grown on land owned by his wife's family and raise money by selling vodka and cognac at a table in the bazaar. He had been watching Jeff these past three months. As an intellectual he felt it was his duty to come and introduce himself.

He glanced again at the *National Geographic*. "They translated my Russian poorly. I will bring you copies of my articles. But you must let me borrow this one. This is the greatest magazine in the world. I have not seen it in years. Decades."

"You can have that one. Take two. Really."

"Two! Two! I couldn't. Two?"

"Please."

Jeff's aunt had sent twelve copies, dating from the mid-1980s. Yuri Samonov was silent as he selected two of the golden issues carefully, as if choosing his fate. When he had made his decision, he said, "Thank you, friend. Thank you."

The light was fading. Jeff stood to turn on a lamp, but Yuri told him to wait a moment and pulled him by the shoulder toward the window. The silhouette of the mountains rose over the kindergarten across the street, breaking through a gray line of clouds. To the southwest the shrinking edge of day shone pale yellow with an outline of pink as it fell through the crags of the peaks.

"You have landed in the middle of nowhere, haven't you?" Yuri whispered conspiratorially.

"I know it."

"Moscow is halfway across the continent. Here, your America exists only in our imagination. This is not civilization. They drink horse milk. This is not civilization." Yuri turned to Jeff. The blue veins across his nose stood out more prominently than before. "Are you lonely here?" he asked.

"No, not yet." In four busy months Jeff had not much considered loneliness, or what, if anything, he missed about America. But the question gave him pause. "Sometimes," he said.

"Have you saved Kyzyl Adyr–Kirovka's famous cheese factory yet?"

"The factory's in trouble. I'm trying to get Anarbek to face the truth."

He chuckled. "You Americans love truth, no? You have come here to serve us, but see what you are up against? Nobody can help this place."

"It's your new country, and you've already given up on it?"

"It's not my country," Yuri said, indicating the mountains. "We built this place up, every centimeter of every road, every phone line, and now they are kicking us out."

"Well, we will see. Perhaps I can help."

"You will help! Ha! You're far from home, Jeff Hartig. When you write a letter and tell your friends where you are, they cannot understand. They do not know where Kyrgyzstan is located, and if they do, they do not know where our Talas Valley lies. History has forgotten us. Your letters might be from outer space. Here." The Russian picked up a letter Jeff had begun writing to Adam the night before. He rubbed it between thumb and forefinger, as if to smudge the ink. "Feel this."

Jeff reached for the rough tan paper, the only kind available in the region. It seemed unremarkable.

"It's paper," Yuri whispered.

"Yes. Paper. *Shto?*"

"Look out the window. You are in the middle of nowhere. Do you see the mountains here, to the south, and the smaller range to the north, that parallels it? And you have seen the winding Talas River, which our road follows." Yuri stretched his arms and crossed them at the wrists. "Past the source of the river these ranges intersect. It makes crossing the mountains difficult in summer, impossible other seasons. There is only one way out of our valley. That is there." He raised one finger and pointed west.

Jeff said, "I know this. We travel through Kazakhstan to get to the capital."

"You don't know! Here is the important thing. In the year 751"—Yuri lifted a pen and scribbled the number on the corner of Jeff's letter. He went on to describe how the Chinese Tang dynasty had conquered all of Central Asia and then kept moving steadily west. Here, along the Talas River, they had come across an army of Arabs, Turks, and Tibetans and were driven deep into the valley. "You see through this window, there is no escape. In its history, it was the greatest loss for the Tang Chinese." The Russian clapped his hands. "It stopped them cold! And with the victory of Arabs and Turks, Islam came to dominate the region."

Jeff tried to grasp the point. "So in the history of religion, this valley is an important place. Is that what you are telling me?"

"*Nyet!* Not only the history of religions. Not only the history of Central Asia. The history of the *world*."

"You're exaggerating now, Yuri."

"Listen. With the Chinese defeat, the Arabs took prisoners. These prisoners knew important Chinese secrets."

"Silk. Of course."

"Yes, silk making was one. The Arabs brought this knowledge back with them to Middle Eastern cities, across Africa and into Europe. It made them rich. But a second art was more important still." Yuri lifted the letter again and ran his fingernails along the edge, back and forth, producing a sound like the gasp of a throat.

"*Boomaga*," he whispered. "When they were brought to the Arab cities, the Chinese prisoners revealed the art of *paper*. With the Arabs, papermaking spread to Europe, then, as you know, around the world. Without paper, how would your technology, your philosophy, your money, your literature exist? A person could argue your civilization owes much to these mountains, to this very place, in the middle of nowhere."

"*Boomaga?*" Jeff repeated, taking back his letter.

"*Boomaga!*" Yuri stretched each of his arms through the sleeves of his musty overcoat and took up his copies of *National Geographic*. "Paper! This very place. Thank you for the tea, Jeff Hartig, and your company. You are very generous. I will return these to you."

In a letter that took eight weeks to reach him, Jeff had learned that Adam had begun school at NAU and that in September he had slept with his first white woman. She was a free spirit from New Orleans who hunted him down in the dormitories, followed him into the library, kept popping up behind him in the bookstore, and finally appeared one night at his dorm room. Adam wrote that, riding him backward, "She called out louder than any of the Apache girls I ever slept with. Do they all do that?" And then he was let down: the next time he saw her, she pretended not to know him.

What was Adam doing, writing him this stuff? Did he want some help? Advice? Jeff decided coarseness was his best response.

"You bastard," he wrote in reply. "I wish I could reciprocate with details of my own sordid lifestyle. Unfortunately, I'm living a monastic existence at the moment. Neither my Russian or Kyrgyz is strong enough to impress a woman with my usual wit and charm. I sound like a four-year-old when I speak."

Jeff had imagined he might stop hearing from Adam once he got caught up in college life, but over the next months he found that, among old roommates and ex-girlfriends who sent scattered letters and the aunts and uncles who scribbled proud notes and birthday cards, it was Adam who wrote with unmatched regularity. This surprised Jeff because of the Apache's staunch guardedness. In their letters back and forth neither mentioned the teen center, or even Jeff's time in Red Cliff. More than anything Adam seemed to want Jeff's approval; but the letters disturbed Jeff, too, each a nagging reminder of his failure on the reservation, and they had the effect of temporarily disorienting him.

Adam detailed in short, single-page notes the classes he had enrolled in, his midterm grades, and that he'd made the NAU basketball team. Jeff responded with something akin to the pride of an older brother. His own letters were filled with exaggerated details of his hard work, making his teaching schedule sound more demanding than it really was.

"I'm both optimistic and frustrated with the lessons," he wrote. "Before I came, I had visions of introducing Shakespeare to the shepherds of Kyrgyzstan, but my students are just getting confident with the alphabet. I've been reviewing for this verb-tense exam I'll give at the end of the week, and the factory workers have forgotten 99 percent of what I've taught them. They don't study. How can I blame them? Getting food for the winter is more a priority than mastering the present progressive."

As the correspondence continued, Jeff found he was revealing more than he wanted to of himself—his uncertainties about what he might accomplish in Kyrgyzstan, memories of his own troubled relationship with his father. He wrote how the man had cheated on his mother throughout the years that she was sick, and how his mother had known but put up with it. Jeff had never understood the reasons. Lately he had come to believe she endured the marriage only for his sake, to keep the family together; and Jeff confessed to Adam he often felt that half the choices he made in life reflected a desire to prove himself a better man than his father.

Eventually Jeff came to depend on these monthly letters simply to vent. He had grown tired of communicating only in basic Russian and Kyrgyz, conversations that mostly rode on the surface of things. Yet he never knew how to sign off to Adam. *Sincerely* was too formal, *Love* too bizarre, *Take care* too blank, *Your friend* ridiculous. Adam, for his part, didn't even sign his letters; they ended, usually, with a simple question, such as *What kind of gun did that guy shoot the pheasants with?* or *You think I should take Intro to World Lit pass/fail?* The lack of a signature gave the note an informal immediacy, as if he and Adam were chatting on the porch of the Red Cliff Trading Post, not sending letters that took months to cross the oceans.

Anarbek grew visibly worried about Jeff's first winter in the village. As temperatures plummeted and snow mounted, the town's electricity went out more frequently. This was followed by the failure of the pumps and the loss of running water. When water was not restored, Jeff was invited to thaw out and cleanse himself with the village elders in their Wednesday evening sauna at the factory.

In the makeshift bar adjoining the sauna, the wooden walls were smattered with the calendars of smooth-skinned Chinese and Kyrgyz models, calendars Anarbek had collected over the years on his various trips to the capital. On Jeff's first visit, the manager ordered Dushen to fill a kettle with water for tea. Anarbek's friends arrived and greeted them with handshakes. Bakyt, the Lenin School director, carried in boiled legs of mutton wrapped in newspaper and a jar of pickles. The *akim* entered with a hunk of butter and three greasy tails of homemade kielbasa. Radish, the doctor, came straight from the region's hospital, swaggering through the door with a bottle of vodka in each hand, his towel folded under his arm.

From the bar another door led to the changing room, where two showers (the only showers in Kyzyl Adyr–Kirovka, Anarbek bragged) worked at high pressure when the water was running. In this room the men undressed and then entered the sauna, some naked, some in grimy underpants. Jeff stripped hesitantly to his plaid boxers, and Anarbek reminded him to take off his watch so the metal would not burn his arm. Inside the sauna, as the room grew hotter, the men stared at the sweat dripping off Jeff's head down into the curly beard that now grew from his face. Anarbek pointed to his bony chest and visible ribs and announced, "That is not healthy!" When it was obvious Jeff could no longer stand the temperature and was about to pass out, they directed him to squat on the ground where it was cooler. Around him the other men sweated and moaned, and slapped each other's backs in elaborate massages. Finally the heat became too much even for them, and Anarbek gave the nod. Dushen swung open the door, and they ran, one by one, out of the steam, grabbed their towels in the changing room, and sprang to a room adjoining the bar, where a large in-ground tub had been filled with freezing green water. The men hopped in and shrieked, "Oh! Oh! *Sohhhk!*" Cold!

They tried to push Jeff into the tub, but he resisted. "In America," he called over their moaning, "we think you could die of shock doing this."

"What do Americans know?" the head doctor retorted, splashing him. "It makes your body stronger. You'll handle the winter better. Now get in!"

On emerging from the ice water the wrinkled men dried themselves and returned to the bar. Anarbek started the rounds of vodka toasts, offering Jeff spoonfuls of butter and slices of kielbasa as chasers.

To guests.

To health.

To a full table.

The chai was poured and slurped. The men, shifting on their seats, unleashed a pestilential torrent of gas.

"Time again!" Anarbek announced. The ritual continued: burning sauna, freezing tub, shots of vodka.

At the end of the evening Anarbek slumped next to Jeff on a cushioned bench in the bar, beneath a wall calendar of a grinning Kyrgyz model. He took an exaggerated breath, sighed, and asked, "So, is there progress?"

Jeff was holding a full glass of vodka and shivering. "Progress?"

"With my factory workers? How is their English?"

Around the bar the village elders focused on him, intent on his answer. Jeff hesitated, his mouth hanging open. "So much progress," he finally said. "The students are eager, and I think they are learning quickly. Soon they will be able to write advertisements. They'll sell your cheese to any nation in the world."

The *akim* turned to Dushen. "You've been taking his classes. What can *you* say?"

Dushen cleared his voice. "Whad—is—yaw—nem?" He pointed

to a red towel and said, "Red." He pointed to the mutton and said, "Ship." He pointed to Jeff and said, "My teycher!"

The elders murmured in approval. Anarbek stuck out his chest and gave Jeff a swift, hard pound on the back.

Jeff hated his own duplicity. There was no progress. In a country whose guiding principles seemed based on the art of deception, he was as guilty as the next of saying one thing when the opposite was true.

"You know," the *akim* said, nodding at Jeff, "Anarbek's daughter teaches English too."

"Yes, I have met her."

"She is a beauty," one of the workers murmured, and Anarbek squinted at him until he lowered his head. "Too beautiful for me!"

"She is not married yet," Dushen said.

"What about you, Jeff Hartig? Will you stay with us here? Will you marry a Kyrgyz woman?"

Jeff glanced at a calendar model through the corner of his eye. A bit of her white neck was just visible beneath the high collar of her blouse. It occurred to him that Nazira was more striking than this woman, and he wondered what it would be like to live with her, to be a Kyrgyz man, to remain here. What would it be like to stay in this village for fifty years, to live the rest of his days surrounded by the highest mountains in the world, to measure time by the rise and fall of the snow on the peaks, to have her cook bread for him, to raise children with her, to forget the dreary realities of car-insurance rates and commuter traffic? For long moments he entertained the fantasy of settling in the village and giving up the more complicated world.

Jeff smiled and answered the question with one of his stock Russian phrases. *"Posmotrim."* We will see.

Anarbek patted Jeff's knee and laughed heartily. "*I* will see. Don't you worry, my friend. *I* will see." His hand clenched Jeff's bare kneecap, now covered in goose bumps. "Our guest is freezing!" He grabbed a towel from a far seat and draped it over Jeff's shoulders.

Radish stood and brought over his *kalpak*. "Put this on. Do you know what is so special about the *kalpak*?"

"Tell me."

"In the winter, it traps the heat and keeps your head warm. In the summer, the air inside stays cold and keeps your head cool. It is the only hat in the world with this kind of *microclimate*."

Jeff sat back on the cushioned bench, the tall *kalpak* on his head. He adjusted the towel, wrapped like a cape over his shoulders. He sipped his chai, belched, then slurped the last drops. He had never felt more Kyrgyz.

The organization that was overseeing privatization, USAID, had just opened its first satellite office in Talas. Jeff was on his way to pick up his monthly salary at the bank when he passed it for the first time. The office had taken over the abandoned hall of sports, next to the boarded-up cinema. There was a carnival atmosphere around the building; a crowd of hundreds had gathered on the street, vendors were selling potato *pieroshki,* and volunteers were handing out *limonad*—an undrinkable carbonated imitation of soda. Ten wide stone steps, shaded by an immense concrete over-hang, ascended to the entrance, where two hefty speakers were blasting a Kyrgyz rap song—"Amerikan Girl"—out over the square. A banner proclaiming MENCHEEKTESHTEEROO, the recently invented Kyrgyz word for *privatization,* was draped above the doorways, and out of every window hung posters proclaiming PRIVATIZATSIA in Cyrillic block letters.

Anarbek had been railing against privatization that very morning, saying it would certainly mean the end for the village. A system of auctions was to be held in the coming months, and coupons would be distributed to all state workers, based on salary and years of service. The public could use the coupons to purchase shares in private enterprises or could sell them as stock on the newly opened exchange in Bishkek. Nobody believed any of this would work. Jeff had asked Anarbek what he expected to do if the factory oversight was discovered, if they lost the wages. Anarbek told him they always had their fields to farm. Potatoes and beans: that's what they would resort to.

Around the square, volunteers were distributing plastic buttons and T-shirts decorated with the emblem of the new nation's flag—a rising red sun—and the word MENCHEEKTESHTEEROO. Handful by handful they threw the gifts into the crowd. The children who caught the shirts put them on and immediately drew jeers. The shirts came in only one size—extra large—and reached their ankles.

As Jeff watched, a young official stepped onto the street and handed him a button. The man wore a thin gray suit that made him look absolutely official, from the tips of his shining brown loafers to his combed fox-hair *shapka,* and he possessed in common with other government officials the stoutness of a mule, a grating voice, and the brusque manners of a high school football coach. Jeff introduced himself, and the man was especially impressed to hear he worked in the tiny village of Kyzyl Adyr–Kirovka. "I am certainly honored to meet you," he said, "someone who has worked so hard to help improve our country." He gripped Jeff's shoulder. "My name is Bolot Ismailov. You will join us for lunch and sit beside me."

Jeff twisted free of Bolot's firm grip, apologizing and explaining he had to hurry to the bank, before it closed, in order to get his salary. The official seemed only mildly insulted. Jeff stuffed the button in his pocket, reminded himself to hide it from Anarbek, and continued on. He sloshed his way through the mud in the park, past the memorial statues and the Ferris wheel, up to the bank—a one-story stucco building with corroded metal gates attached to the front door. Each month he had collected his living allowance here. The Peace Corps claimed to pay volunteers roughly the average salary of the local population, but Jeff was uncomfortably aware that he made ten times what the villagers earned each month. Inside, after a thirty-minute wait for service at the wooden counter, he filled out forms in triplicate, presented his passport and work visa, and received a receipt for his full salary, stamped four times in blue. This he carried to the single window in an adjoining room, where customers jostled in a rugby scrum for position, then barked at the overwrought cashier.

Earlier in the year Jeff had been timid, and it had taken most of the afternoon to receive his cash. He had also been embarrassed when the pensioners around him watched the cashier's fingers double-check his enormous salary. But by now he had become a veteran customer. He elbowed his way past an elderly woman and two young men and received his money with hardly any wait at all. As the teller counted the stack of bills to herself, one man to Jeff's right—a thick-necked youth in a gray sweater—counted each bill out loud. When Jeff pocketed his money, the man turned and announced the American's salary to the crowded room.

Outside it was growing dark. In the park Jeff noticed the man from the bank, accompanied by two tall friends, following him. At the memorial statue he prepared to smile, nod, and let them pass. But they beckoned him, and he knew he was in trouble as they approached more quickly. He could tell from their swollen eyes they had been drinking. All three wore MENCHEEKTESHTEEROO buttons.

"American?" one asked in English, a puff of breath swirling from his mouth.

"Gooddayhowareyousir?" another said.

The third, the one who had counted aloud in the bank, rubbed his red fingers together and said, "Excuse me money."

His heart racing, Jeff hesitated, turned, and started off in a sprint. He had not made it five yards before he slipped in the mud and they were on him. They tackled him to the ground, kicked him in the knee and the groin, then raked his face against the stone walk. They turned him over so the memorial statue loomed above: the colonial Russian on horseback, waving his sword. The thick-necked man leaned over his face and pounded him with a fist, once against each eye. He pulled Jeff's long hair, jerking his head back, while his friends tugged off his ski jacket, groping for the stack of bills in the inside pocket. They emptied his pants pockets as well; one of them shouted, "Traktorbek, *speshi!*" and their footsteps faded off into the park.

Jeff stood uneasily, drew on his torn jacket, then stumbled to the road. They had stolen his identification card and wallet, and he didn't even have enough for the bus back to the village. He staggered through the park.

The young privatization official, standing alone outside the former hall of sports, spotted Jeff and gasped. "What has happened, Meester Hartig?"

"They took my money. Can you help me? Can you find me a police officer?" He touched a welt rising on his forehead and checked the blood caked on his fingers.

The official clicked his tongue. "I am not sure that is a good idea—it may have *been* the police. Here, my friend, come inside the bathroom, let us clean you off." Bolot Ismailov led him to the old locker room, but the water was not running. He swiped at Jeff's bloody face with a dirty rag, chafing the skin under his eyes. Jeff winced and told him he was making it worse. He said he simply wanted to get home and asked if Bolot could lend him the fare. The privatization officer insisted on driving him instead.

Along the road through the valley Bolot's Lada seemed to nail each and every pothole. Jeff's head pounded. Bolot inserted a cassette into the ancient stereo and a fuzzy version of Michael Jackson's *Thriller* blared from a single speaker. Jeff passed out for the second half of the ride and came to only as they turned in at the village *otovakzal*. They sped by the sign for the cheese collective, and suddenly Bolot slowed the vehicle, turned down the music, and said, "I didn't know there was a collective here."

Jeff panicked, but bit his lip.

"That's a cheese factory back there?" Bolot asked, craning his neck.

"No, there's no collective. I teach at the Lenin School."

"I saw the sign."

"Well, there certainly is no cheese factory here. I . . . I should know. I have to travel to Kazakhstan to buy cheese if I want it."

"Perhaps I'm wrong," Bolot said and shrugged.

"Yes, I'm sure you were mistaken."

"It's happened before."

Jeff directed him to Karl Marx Street, and when the Lada swerved to a halt in front of his fence, he thanked Bolot profusely for the ride and asked how he could repay him.

"It was no trouble," Bolot said. He looked straight ahead, the slightest smile on his lips.

Nazira heard Baktigul scream, "Jeff *agai!*" and saw the foreigner stumble into the gate of their lighted courtyard. She and Lola quickly ran to him, grasped his arms, and escorted him inside the house to the couch.

Jeff was out of breath. "I need to talk to your father. Please get him."

"Yes, yes, Jeff," she said. "But first let us take care of you." She ordered Baktigul to find their father and Lola to bring him water to clean the blood off his face. Nazira rubbed a spoonful of her homemade yogurt under his eyes, explaining it would act as a balm.

"Jeff, I am very embarrassed this has happened to you," she said as she finished. She screwed the lid back onto the jar, then wiped a drop of excess yogurt off his upper beard. "You come to help, and do you see how our people repay you?"

As she and Lola adjusted some pillows behind his neck, she heard her father bang into the house. He appeared with a cold bottle of Chinese beer, which he ordered Nazira to hold against the swelling of one of Jeff's cheekbones.

"Who?" her father thundered. "Who did this to you?"

"There were three of them, but I didn't get a good look."

Nazira pressed the beer bottle into his face, and Jeff winced. She had never seen him vulnerable and beaten down like this. Month by month he had been growing steadily more impressive in her estimation. To have given up the comforts of America! To have volunteered to help in the struggles of their new nation! He had brought with him the knowledge of the West—New York, California, Washington—places where real history happened. He had brought the outside world in and opened their eyes. For this fact alone he seemed more durable, more vital, than anyone she knew. An American's life, she thought, was of more consequence than their own small village lives.

Jeff was shifting out of her grasp. "I'm fine. Just forget it," he said. "Forget it ever happened."

"That is best," Nazira whispered in English. "That is what I always do."

Jeff turned to her father and spoke in Russian: "Anarbek, I have something to say."

"What is it? What has happened?"

"The factory. I think they might know."

II

4

THREE DAYS BEFORE Adam left for university, everyone was home except his father, and they had no idea where he'd gone. His mom had on her purple camp dress with wide white trim and long open sleeves. She was beading jewelry on the opposite end of the couch from her sister, her swollen fingers racing with the precision of a spider's legs. Aunt Marie Anne sat straight up, intent on a word search in the *Apache Scout*.

A basketball game blared from the television. Sitting next to Adam on the floor, Verdena crushed an empty beer can with her heel, then straightened it, then crushed it again. "Where's Dad?" she called. The noise bothered Adam—he couldn't hear the game —but it did not bother his mother. The winter he'd been born, Lorena had grown feverish in the cold, had battled a month-long pneumonia, and since then was slowly losing her hearing. Half-deaf, she relied on Marie Anne to keep her up to date with the world.

They watched the basketball game until their father came stomping through the back door. Marie Anne didn't bother looking up from her word search.

Lorena said, "You been gone two days."

"Home now," Larson said, his back to her.

"Why don't you just leave altogether?"

"I should," he muttered. "Should."

"You didn't even leave us any—"

Larson faced her. "I'm home now! Just come back! Why don't you let a person take his jacket off?"

"Don't take it off. Get out."

"Starting this again, Lorena."

"You even smell like her. Go on, just get outta here. Go on back with her."

"Say this in front of your own children?" He pointed at Adam and Verdena. Their father had the thickest arms Adam had ever seen.

"You don't think they know? Wonder where they think you are?"

Adam left the house before it got worse. In the backyard he walked slowly past the swing set. The seesaw, slide, rings, and monkey bars all lay completely destroyed. His dad had bought the set for Verdena when she was eight, down at the Sears in Phoenix, and they had hauled it to the reservation in the pickup, the parts rattling in a box for four long hours. A month later, sleeping with their parents, Verdena had wet the bed, and their father got angry. In the middle of the night Larson went out and smashed the jungle gym. He tore off the pipes and beat the seesaw against the fence, bent it in two and toppled the whole thing, took a hatchet to the plastic seats, and then cursed at the stars until all the dogs of Red Cliff were wailing. Adam watched from the door with his mom, her arm draped around his shoulders. "It's good," she had whispered. "Let him do that."

Outside now, Adam began to shoot baskets in the yard. He followed his old pattern: start from the laundry line and step farther back with each shot, until he was past the ruined swing set and had to heave the ball with a running start over the Joshua trees. He heard his dad get into the pickup, slam the door, and in a whirl of dust and exhaust pull off the property.

Before the dust had cleared, the truck reversed and squealed back up the dirt driveway. His father called in Apache, "Hey, we're hunting in the morning. Tell your mom to make us food."

"It's not season yet," Adam said.

"I'll worry about that."

Adam went in through the back kitchen door and found his mother trembling by the counter, covering her right eye. Aunt Marie Anne sat at the table shaking her head, and continued her word search.

Adam said, "He wants to hunt tomorrow."

His mom nodded. He helped her find the ingredients, fry up the tortillas, and boil the eggs. She was going to make sandwiches but he told her, "Dad says not to bring meat with us hunting. Elk could smell the meat."

She smiled and ran her hand over her lean face; her eyes grew moist. For the next two hours she and Marie Anne made the frybread. The kitchen warmed with steam. Adam helped them spread the beans, and together they wrapped the Apache burritos in foil. His aunt rubbed his mother's hair and kissed her on the forehead, then looked down at Adam and said, "You'll have lots of food."

Before dawn he heard his dad come in through the dark, clomping around the house in his boots. He didn't get up until he felt the warm hands shoving him.

"Hey, you got some whitetail to shoot."

Adam rose and stretched his palms toward the woodstove next to his mattress. The fire had gone out, but the house was not too cold; he would let his mom light it.

Verdena got up too and joined them in the kitchen where their father was packing the food into the cooler. She watched for a minute as they got ready, but she was curled asleep, a pile of warmth, on Adam's mattress by the time they left. Adam made sure the screen door didn't slam and went out into the dim morning.

Uncle Sparky was waiting in the cab of the pickup. "Mr. University!" he shouted. They loaded the icebox and the packs of bullets and the 30-30 and the other rifles.

"Got Adam with us today," Uncle Sparky said. "Always bring something home when he comes, isn't it?"

"Kid's good luck," Larson said. "Get him an elk before he takes off on us."

"We don't miss nothing when Adam's here." Sparky squeezed the rim of Adam's cap and turned it around backward as he always did, so Adam had to fix it.

His dad and uncle slammed the doors almost in unison, and he climbed into the bed of the pickup and sat facing the rear. His father drove west through the gray light, and beyond Indian Ruins the road became dirt; then at Iron Mine they crossed Canyon Creek and turned up a logging road toward Foot Canyon. Adam kept lookout from the bed of the truck. All the roads looked the same, but he could have negotiated the forest as well as his dad did.

An hour into the drive, near Medicine Ranch, he saw two brown streaks of elk and pounded his elbow twice on the rear window. The truck skidded, and Uncle Sparky and Larson were out and looking in their sights. Two blasts. The elk loped in a panicked curve around the road, making for a grove of cottonwood. The men, all blocky legs and heavy hips, chased to cut them off, but at the bend the animals had already vanished up the hill into the dense trees.

They lowered their guns. At the truck his father laughed. "You missed, Spark. You just scared 'em away." His pockmarked face exploded in a rare smile, and he punched Sparky's shoulder.

Sparky said, "I never miss when Adam's with us, isn't it?"

"You're full of shit," Adam said.

"Well," Sparky looked both ways and winked. "Don't tell no one about that."

Another ten miles down the cratered road they pulled off in a clearing beneath the ponderosas, took their rifles, and split up. Adam felt the drizzle and the wet wind on his face. He followed his father's heavy legs against the wind and knew they were heading the right way. On one hill they sat by the trunk of a low scrub oak and listened for a long time. They hiked back down and Adam watched his father's boots. When he was little, he used to try to match him stride for stride. Now his legs were already longer than his dad's.

After a few minutes Larson stopped and knelt next to him. He balanced on his haunches, his right fingers touching the ground. The air was still; the beaded grass and mud smelled both sweet and acrid.

"The secret of hunting," Larson whispered, "is a prayer you'll never come home empty handed."

Again they set off and had nearly reached the truck when Adam heard a branch break. He clicked his tongue and pointed with his lips across the clearing, to where a cow elk and her calf were standing, rigid and alert.

Adam hesitated to lift his gun, but in one swift, gentle movement his father raised his rifle to his shoulder, aimed, pulled, and shot. The calf dropped. Its mother bolted out of sight with two great leaps. Adam stood still. The echo of the blast died off in his head, the rustling sounds of the fleeing elk grew fainter. He stared at the fallen calf.

Larson looked at Adam. "The meat's more tender," he explained. They approached the dead animal and his father held back a step. "You know what to do."

With his left hand Adam grabbed the calf's warm head and with his other hand the right front leg. His father helped him pull it around, clockwise, so the head faced where the sun comes up. In the truck they found a sharp knife, and by then Uncle Sparky had joined them. First they sliced the stomach and took out its steaming guts and kidneys. They cut parts of the upper legs and hips and the back and the neck. They wasted no meat; that would bring bad luck. They raised the heavy skin and shook it over the meat and prayed four times that they would always be lucky hunting. Adam had to carry the soft head as they hauled the skin back to the truck bed. He packed the dripping red meat into the cooler and wiped his hands in the grass.

They breakfasted in silence. Adam and his uncle leaned against the cold side of the truck, peeling hard-boiled eggs and flicking shells off their fingers into the mud.

That afternoon they fished Canyon Creek, and near dusk they hiked in the rain single file over the hills, looking for whitetail. Manzanita crunched beneath their boots. Above, a single crow dipped and curved in the dark sky. The pale green hills lay empty — the day had yielded all it was going to yield, and his father decided it was time to head home.

Their old Nissan had only two-wheel drive, so running up the muddy trails was difficult, and they sometimes slid going down. At the bottom of one hill the truck reached a flooded wash where the monsoon water crashed over polished white stones. Larson didn't hesitate; he raced the engine, threw it into first, and crossed half the churning river before the water exploded against the door and came leaking into the cab.

There was no choice but to climb out. They splashed into the freezing current, carrying guns and ammo high over the water. In a defeated line, the rain sliding down their necks, they retreated a mile back to Indian Ruins and found an abandoned trailer. They left the guns there to dry and returned to the truck to get the food and blankets and to cover the hide. By then the rain was letting up.

Back in the trailer Uncle Sparky scratched his crooked nose. "Nobody knows where we're at."

"Game warden'll be around by morning," Larson said. "He'll see the truck."

"The fucker's gonna fine us."

"I'll take care of it." His father turned to Adam and said in Apache, "Always tell someone where you're going, or else you get lost like us."

Late that evening the plastic tile of the trailer floor grew frigid, and the men spread two damp wool blankets to share among them. They stretched out, hands beneath their heads, and gazed up as the ceiling darkened. Uncle Sparky teased Adam about how many bottles of Miller he could drink and how many girlfriends he had. "You know Apache love?" he kept asking. "A hickey and a black eye. You ever do it? You will soon enough." Adam remained silent while the two adults laughed at him. He felt the blood running to his face, and he heard his dad's laugh, so loud the floor of the trailer shook. Sparky gave up on Adam and said to his father, "Lorena's gonna be worried 'bout you boys."

"She'll worry about him," Larson said.

Sparky sucked in a long breath. "Not a bad thing, having a woman worrying 'bout ya."

Adam said, "Mom don't worry about Dad 'cause he's never home anyway."

The blow came out of the darkness, the shot of his father's hard hand, once across the lower forehead, then again across the bridge of his nose. His head smashed into the metal base of the wall. The scuffling of shadows. His uncle pulled his father off him. "Leave it, Larson. Kid's right. Leave it!"

"Kid doesn't know. Needs to—"

"Leave it."

With the pain the room around Adam collapsed into white blank space. He kept his eyes clenched shut and lay immobile, refusing to check the size of the pounding welt on his forehead or to wipe the warm wetness spreading in back of his head. He disappeared into the wilderness of pain, amazed by the expanse of it all, by what it was possible for one body to take.

Some time later the pain wore down. His eyes were sticky when he opened them, and he reemerged from the distance to hear his uncle and father discussing someone. Did they think he was asleep? They talked about her as if he didn't know. A white teacher from off the rez. Not his mother.

It would be easy, he thought. He would wait for both of them to sleep. He would rise and take the long serrated deer knife from the cooler. He'd slice open his father's stomach first, then pull out the steaming guts and kidneys. After, his mother would be better off. She wouldn't worry; she wouldn't have to fight anymore. He thought he could do it. Everyone thought Adam was quiet, harmless, but he knew he had it in him.

Then he questioned it, and told himself he was too young to kill anyone. He hadn't even started college yet.

In Flagstaff, after a week of tryouts, Adam managed to walk on to the NAU basketball team. He never expected to start; the recruits were too strong. The Lumberjacks had won their division each of the past three years and had played on national television in the March tournament. It was a thrill just to make the team.

Adam had learned basketball from his father. Like most Red Cliff families, the Dales had set up a makeshift plywood goal on their camp, and Larson had shown him how to shoot—first underhand, standing straight beneath the rim, then a two-hand push shot, banking it off the shaky backboard, and at last a set shot, which Adam practiced with his cousin Levi defending him.

Larson sometimes joined the boys in the backyard for a game of horse. They tried to outdo one another's unlikely shots. They played with different words, such as *frybread* and *Geronimo,* and even Apache words like *llkaad dijege,* which meant candy and had no real spelling and made the game funnier. They played a version of twenty-one—one person took foul shots while the others rebounded and put the ball back into play. By age twelve Levi was already a strong young point guard. Despite his weight he had naturally quick hands and rarely missed from the baseline. Adam surpassed him, though: he could do just about anything with the basketball, and he was faster than anyone in town, much faster than his limping father.

Still, Larson was tallest, and he showed the boys little mercy rebounding.

"You gotta block me out!" he once yelled at Adam. "You can't let me get into your area! This space"—he bent over and with his heel dragged a line in the dust where the key would have been—

"this area, this, this, this, and this, belongs to *you*. Why are you letting me get in there?"

On the next shot Adam tried it. He held his father out and grabbed the rebound, and for a second he felt victorious. But with the strength of years of hauling wood, Larson yanked the ball out of his hands and laid it into the basket for his own points. "You just gave me that!"

Adam squinted and stepped away.

"You better protect that ball once you got it. Watch me." His father tossed the ball against the rusty rim and went up and took the rebound. He came down and covered it in his powerful chest, twisting right and left, his elbows pointed to throw the boys off him.

"More elbows!" shouted his father. "You've got to throw those things around. They're your weapons. Your shotguns. Keep other people away. You give a guy a good shot—pow!—early in the game, they won't be trying to get the ball off you anymore, isn't it?"

From that time on Adam went up for rebounds and always came down throwing first his right then his left elbow—even when no one was threatening him. By the time he was in college his game had grown so intense, he felt that the rebound—the spinning globe in the air—was his, and nobody could take it from him. His elbows, his weapons, guaranteed it.

NAU practices were held in the immense white dome on the southern end of campus, sometimes twice a day, mornings and evenings. Substituting did not bother him. He enjoyed the competition of scrimmages, scoring on the starters, occasionally stealing the ball. The other players came from Arizona, California, and even as far away as Michigan and New York. For preseason games he traveled through nearby states on the team bus. As they bumped along, his teammates played cards and traded rap CDs for their Walkmans. In the long hours of travel Adam gazed out the bus windows at the unfamiliar names of towns, the wide-open spaces and empty roads. Not only was there a world beyond the reservation, there was a world beyond Arizona—there were other lives to be lived.

This he would contemplate while training on weekends in October, getting in shape by jogging three times a week to the top of Mount Humphreys. He drove to the trail in Jeff's truck and circled ten thousand feet upward through the flaming aspens to the parking lot. From there he paced himself up the shaded trail. The trees ended, the final quarter-mile of boulders could not be run, and he scaled the rocks until he reached the twelve-thousand-foot peak. Standing alone, in cargo shorts and a long T-shirt, surrounded by photographers and day hikers in Gore-Tex jackets and fleece hats, he looked out past the town below, in the direction of the Red Mountains. The reservation was too far away to see. To the north lay the Grand Canyon, on clear days the crack just visible from the peak. Pink streaks of the Painted Desert ran along the dry eastern horizon, across the Navajo reservation.

His mother had once told him that from a mountain like this the Apache crown dancers descended to cure the evil ways of their tribe. As children, at the Sunrise Dances he and Verdena used to scream when the crown dancers got close, and his mom laughed at the two of them. From the highest point in Arizona, breathing hard, he could see the world below as the mountain spirits might have seen it: in miniature, no more than a scrap of wreckage against the surge of land and sky. He would squat for twenty minutes on the cool ground, catch his breath, and begin his descent.

He wrote Jeff once a month from school. Life was easier, he told him, off the rez. He forgot the dangers, the infighting between families, the need to be cool. His head was clearer; the constant pressure and disappointments slowly seeped from his mind. In a single-paragraph letter, in late October, he wrote that he had managed to pass all his midterms.

Uninvited, Councilman Dale appeared on the campus one bright fall afternoon as Adam was walking to his logic and rhetoric class with two of his teammates. His father smacked him on the back of his head and insisted on shaking hands with his two friends. Larson claimed he was in town on some vague tribal business. He walked along with them to class and plied Adam with embarrassing questions about college, then delivered private news from Red Cliff: news of the family, what kind of crossbow he was shopping for, who had gotten whom pregnant. At the classroom door Adam paused while his friends went in and found seats.

"What are you doing here?"

"Passing through, I told you."

"Could have called. Told me you were coming."

Larson glanced into the classroom. "Thought I'd surprise you.

See how things are going, schoolboy." He laid a heavy hand on Adam's shoulder.

Adam tensed up. "Semester's just normal. Nothing happening yet."

His dad dropped his arm and stood with his legs apart. Adam turned to enter the classroom without saying goodbye, but Larson limped in beside him. The seats were arranged in a horseshoe around three long tables. His father squeezed down in the chair next to him, and Adam felt the weight of twenty students' eyes. At last the young professor hustled in. She was just about to begin lecturing when she paused and asked Larson who he was.

"Adam Dale's dad. You just go on teaching, Miss. Pretend I'm not here."

"I see." The professor looked at Adam, her lips pressed. "I see."

For the duration of class his father read over his shoulder, first the textbook, then the copy of a student's paper the professor was critiquing. Adam sat erect, paralyzed with fear that his father would raise his hand. Larson's shoulder pressed against him; his warm exhalations smelled of last night's beer, his unwashed jeans stank, and the rise and fall of his heavy chest made it impossible for Adam to think straight. Once, during a particularly oblique explanation by the professor, in a voice entirely too loud, Larson hissed, "Bullshit." Half the heads in the room turned to face them.

When the lecture ended, Adam was first out of the classroom, and he didn't say goodbye to his father. The following weekend he spoke to Marie Anne on the phone, but apparently neither she nor his mother had any idea Larson had visited. Adam decided not to tell them.

His father appeared a second time in January. On a blustery winter night, snow whirling around the streetlights outside the dorm, Adam pulled the blinds to go to sleep. A pounding on his door woke him some time later, the sound echoing off the concrete walls of his room. He jumped from bed. In the hallway his father balanced himself against the doorframe, his drenched windbreaker covered in melting white flakes. Thin wet curls of gray hair shone in the fluorescent light, and drops of water clung to his ears and nose. Adam pulled him into the room and Larson lurched forward; the mud on his shoes left brown streaks on the tile floor. The dormitory lay in complete silence, punctuated only by the distant flush of a toilet from a higher floor.

"What the hell you doing?" Adam whispered.

"Come up to see ya."

"Jesus Christ."

"Thing is," his father said, "you're Apache." He fingered the CD collection on a shelf, twirled and lifted Adam's Lumberjack backpack, kicked down the whiffleball bat leaning against the closet, and stood transfixed by the poster of Pamela Anderson, her white teeth shining like a beacon in the dim room.

Adam guided his father to the bed, sat him down, peeled off the freezing jacket, and struggled with the knotted, icy boot laces. He undressed him, pushing the large unsteady body back on the bed, unzipping the pants, and tugging the soaked jeans off each powerful leg. Larson's skin was rough and goosebumped, and a thick purple scar from a sawmill accident lined the bottom of his knee.

"You doing it like this—this all the time?"

"Fuck off, Dad."

Adam directed his father's wide limbs into dry sweats and an NAU T-shirt. He waited for him to pass out on the bed, snoring, and he slept that night on the floor, bile in his throat, recalling the trailer on that hunting trip six months ago, the first time he had imagined this man dead.

The dorm was quiet in the morning when he shook his father awake. They had a silent breakfast of western omelets at the Village Inn Diner. He could tell his father was preoccupied, and after Larson polished off his eggs, he spoke. "BIA's changed its goddamn mind," he said. He explained how that fall they had reversed policy on building the high school in Red Cliff. The elementary school had reached four hundred children, and taking notice, the Bureau of Indian Affairs ordered the town to build its own high school to accommodate the numbers. "Not like I haven't been trying myself five years now!" his father said. He had protested and pressed his boss, the tribal chairman in Blackriver, not to rush into any outside plans. "If they'll wait until the casino's built, we'll fund the largest damn high school of any rez town in this country."

But already the BIA had taken matters into its own hands. In Blackriver the tribal chairman researched Dome Technology, the fastest and cheapest way to put up a building; then the tribe purchased a plan from an Idaho construction company. The fifteen-ton fabric lining was flown in from France, then shaped in Houston; fiberglass filling and rebar were ordered from Albuquerque, and a Mormon-owned construction company from Holbrook was contracted. By late autumn at the building site the earth had been flattened and the foundation poured, but then funds stalled, bickering over contracts wasted time, and progress slowed. "I didn't think they'd ever get the goddamn thing started," his dad said. But now the bulldozers were moving again, and they'd raised a ten-foot concrete stem wall. This spring, when the weather warmed, workers would truck in the fabric from storage, attach it to the stem wall, and seal off the doors and windows. By summer they would inflate the bubble with a giant blower, supplanting with air his father's vision of a high school.

Larson was agitated, shaking his head and cursing under his breath as he told the story. Adam paid for the breakfast—his father had no money on him, not even an ATM card. After the meal, still wearing Adam's sweats, Larson climbed into his Nissan and peeled out of the one-way entrance to the parking lot. Though he had said he was heading back to the reservation, Adam didn't believe him. His father was on a tear, and there was no stopping him.

After the visit Adam threw himself more fiercely into his studies and basketball practice. Like his teammates he declared a communications major. In the last meaningless regular season game, up in Salt Lake City, his coach gave him five minutes of playing time, and Adam hit a twenty-footer. They were his only two points for the season, but they were something.

Late in May Adam drove back to Red Cliff for the first time to work the summer with Marie Anne at the town's grocery store. Officially its name was the Red Cliff Trading Post, but everyone called it the Tom's Store. Tom, a Mormon from off the reservation, managed the business and took in the profits. The Apaches sometimes started their own trading posts—but they kept giving free food and clothes to their friends. New stores opened, lost money, and within a few weeks were boarded up. The Tom's Store, though, was operated by an outsider, and it had prospered. Marie Anne worked the busy counter, and on his first day of stocking, Adam enjoyed seeing her waddle up to shelves to pull off cans of Spaghetti Os, pails of Crisco, and jars of pickled pig's feet.

The town was smaller than he remembered it. Compared to Flagstaff, the reservation had so little traffic it seemed abandoned, yet within a week the place had swallowed him. Adam found himself out until all hours, drinking beers at the creek, sleeping with old girlfriends, and staying in bed later and later each morning. Disconcerted, he felt the eyes of the houses watching him, as if with a single consciousness. In Red Cliff, barely the slightest instant passed between an action and public judgment.

His first Friday after work he walked over to Uncle Sparky's house, looking for Levi. On the porch he heard a muffled shouting from behind the cardboard-covered garage door. He knocked, waited a few moments, knocked again. For another ten minutes he continued knocking. Inside the yelling grew louder, but nobody answered. Finally a threatening hush fell. The door opened a crack and a voice he recognized but couldn't place cursed:

"Get the fuck out of here, schoolboy."

That night Levi showed up at Adam's house. Since Adam had been away, his cousin had gotten heavier and blocky, double-chinned, wide-cheeked, yet he had the same blood-red eyes.

"Cuz," he said, "let's shoot."

Out back Levi wobbled and could hardly hold the basketball. They shot in silence for almost an hour. Winded, Levi took a break and staggered around the old swing set. Neither suggested they play any of their old games. Finally Adam sat on the ball, and Levi approached and stood uneasily straight, as if balancing on two legs took his full concentration.

He showed up at the Tom's Store the next afternoon. Adam was stacking cans of Spam on the uneven counters when, through the window, he saw his cousin pull into the gravel lot in a new purple Ford Ranger, with fluorescent yellow sport stripes—a sixteen-thousand-dollar truck. Levi honked three times. Tom, the owner, was reading a newspaper behind the counter and didn't say anything when Adam left. Outside he strolled over to the truck and tapped its warm metal hood. He asked Levi where he'd gotten it.

"While some of you schoolboys are off in college, others of us putting food on the table." Levi patted the dashboard with his palm, sounding two hollow thumps. Adam leaned in through the window, inhaling the stale beer odor of his cousin's breath. Levi adjusted the side mirror with his lean, muscled arm, now tattooed in black ink with some kind of Phoenix gang sign.

That evening after dinner Adam found his father on the porch, sanding down a handle for a broken ax. Adam watched him work for thirty minutes. Finally he blurted out everything he was thinking—about Levi's new truck, about how he was picking up Uncle Sparky's bad habits. Larson continued working, as if he didn't hear. He finished sanding the wood, laid the head across two bricks, and in powerful strokes close to the metal, sawed off the old handle.

"Do something," Adam begged. "You're not gonna let Levi get into all this shit?"

His father lifted the ax head to drive out the remaining wood with a chisel. "What you want me to do? It's a family thing."

"That's why you gotta do something."

"That's why I can't." Larson took up the new smooth handle and forced it tight through the ax head. "I'm supposed to have your uncle arrested?" He lifted the saw and began cutting off the extra wood on top. "You want me to put your cousin behind bars? That what you want?" He finished sawing, stood the ax straight on the cement step, and with a hammer drove a small wooden wedge deep into the slot. Finally he stopped, breathing heavily, and stared up at the sky. Adam followed his gaze. Stars were sprayed across the summer night. Larson said, "You don't go betraying blood."

With the ax lying straight across the bricks, he sawed off the extra inch of the wedge.

A deal went sour. At 1:20 on a bright Thursday afternoon, mid-August, word reached Adam at the trading post: Sparky had been shot.

His uncle had been driving in his red Corvette out to the highway with a new girlfriend, a plump San Carlos Apache woman who had witnessed the whole thing. A rival dealer from Phoenix, a Mexican, was waiting for them at the Turnoff. He strode into the middle of the intersection and pulled the car over, signaling with a shotgun. Sparky was bent over fumbling for the 9-millimeter pistol he always kept beneath the passenger seat when the Mexican blasted twice through the window. Glass shattered across the girlfriend's lap and bloodied her chest and face. She screamed one piercing note while the Mexican slid calmly into his black Mercedes, and she had not stopped screaming five minutes later when Pastor Wyckoff, heading down to Tucson, pulled over in his minivan and found Sparky dead.

Red Cliff had lost its dealer, and the town went into mourning. Adam's old friends printed black T-shirts with Tupac Shakur's

"Rebel of the Underground" rap lyrics on the front and a portrait of Sparky on the back. Half the procession at the crowded funeral wore the shirts. Sparky was buried on the hillside cemetery above the creek, inside the barbed-wire fence that kept the coyotes out. The site was surrounded by other graves marked by freshly painted white wooden crosses. Councilman Dale helped lower the casket, his face expressionless, rigid as stone, and Marie Anne bent over the grave, bracing herself with her hands on her knees. Levi was nowhere to be found.

At the Turnoff that weekend Sparky's friends erected a permanent memorial stone, decorated with pink and red plastic flowers and inscribed with his real name and the dates of his life. To get to Red Cliff, you had to pass it.

There were no fishing trips, no barbecues, no rodeos for the duration of the summer, and the only thing that raised Larson's spirits was the construction of the casino. Adam drove him up for the final weekly inspection that August, and on the ride back his father seemed pleased. The building stood ready for the slot machines, the poker tables, and the buffet lounge. It would open in late fall, just a few months away. At the Turnoff Adam swung his father's new Toyota 4×4 onto the paved road, past the memorial. Over the final ridge to Red Cliff he dodged a spotted cow, the truck handling nicely; its power steering responded to the slightest touch. Adam rounded the steep downhill curve, and it was then he saw it—the white pimple on the face of their valley, the bubble. That morning, when he and his father had driven out of Red Cliff, it had not yet been visible in the rearview mirror. Now it shone in the spotlight of the four o'clock sun.

"They're inflating the dome," Adam said.

"I see that."

As Red Cliff's councilman, his dad should have been able to stop the construction. But it had been forced on them by Washington, by the BIA, by Larson's boss, the tribal chairman—outsiders, his father called them, outsiders who could care less, outsiders like the man who killed Sparky. Adam stepped harder on the gas.

"What the town needs is *money*," Larson said, "not some instant school, built on the cheap, like someone bought it with food stamps."

Adam knew the construction plan: his father had approved it

only through pressure from the chairman. The dome would take twenty-four hours to inflate. Once it was up, they would spray an initial layer of fiberglass inside to lend structural support. Over thirty days, layers of concrete would be spiraled to the top, and in a month the instant building would stand on its own.

From ten miles off, the future school seemed to crouch on the hilltop like a UFO. Half-inflated, it already dominated the idyllic valley. Adam hit the gas pedal, the truck flew closer, and over the final five-mile stretch the dome grew higher and wider and more grotesque. Slowing as he entered town, Adam saw that people had climbed onto their rooftops for a better view; they were pointing and chattering.

"Even the neighbors don't know what we need," his father mumbled. "Cheering handouts from Washington!"

They found Lorena, Verdena, and Marie Anne watching from the porch outside the house. The high school dome loomed in the west, gleaming in the orange light. Adam drove into the dirt driveway and cut the engine. His father gathered his papers from under the passenger seat, and with the door open Adam heard Verdena questioning their aunt. "There gonna be computers in there? There'll be a cafeteria, isn't it? How many teachers they going to need?" His mom held Verdena around the waist while Marie Anne answered patiently. None of them took their eyes off the dome, not even to greet Adam and his dad.

"Our own goddamn family," Larson muttered under his breath, slamming the truck door.

Verdena was chomping a grilled cheese sandwich, and between bites she pointed with her crumb-encrusted lips and said, "Looks like a big egg, Dad, isn't it?"

Lorena said, "Supposed to hold five hundred students!"

Larson faced them with a wry smirk, squinting. "Looks like a big old birdshit to me. You gonna go to school in that thing, Verdena?"

Verdena told him she didn't mind. It was better than the trailer.

Larson laughed. "Going to school in a big ol' bird turd. That's all right with my kids. They don't care."

Adam glared. Marie Anne said, "What you telling them? You should be happy about this. It's what you wanted."

"I wanted a real school for my children!" He turned to Adam and said in Apache, "Never would have seen me in a school like that."

That night Larson told Adam to get in the truck and they'd check out the dome. They drove through the dark streets up past the Day School to the top of the hill, where his father parked by a power shovel. The high school, illuminated by a sliver of moon, seemed to hover ahead in a white phosphorescence. The generator was grating away, blowing hot air into the bubble, a roar Adam imagined could be heard for miles.

They stepped carefully around the dome to what would become the main entrance. It was sealed with boards to prevent air from escaping. His father pried loose two six-foot beams, then tore them off with his bare hands. A heavy stream of warm air rushed from the hole. The space was just wide enough to squeeze through if they sucked in their stomachs. Inside, the dome was darker than night, a sky without stars, lit only by the faint opaque glints of boarded windows in the stem wall. Adam clapped his hands, and the sound went off like thunder, reverberating off the fifty-foot ceiling and the cement floor, a storm only they could hear.

Back outside, Adam tried to reattach the boards to the entrance, but his father said not to bother. They drove down the hill. At the house Larson kept the truck running and wouldn't get out.

"Where you heading?" Adam asked.

"Just go inside."

Behind Adam the truck took off again. In the middle of the night he heard his father crash through the living room and step over his mattress, stumbling past the woodstove. Adam pretended to sleep.

That morning Larson feigned outrage when the town woke to the deflated bubble, to a school that was no longer there. Someone had shot up the inside of the dome, fifty rounds at least, the fabric decimated. As councilman, he vowed to find out who had done it—who had destroyed the future of their town. He promised to get the BIA to replace the fifteen-ton fabric from France. They never did.

Adam told no one on the rez what he knew. To blame his father would only cast suspicion on himself. But in his only letter to Jeff that summer, in two scribbled pages, he unburdened himself.

The next week it was a relief—the relief of escape—to drive Jeff's truck, loaded with his stuff, back to Flagstaff, where basketball would be starting up soon.

5

ANARBEK BENT DOWN on his hands and knees and crawled under his office desk, searching for the thumbtack he had dropped. He was attempting to hang the factory's first MANAS 1000 YEARS poster. In an effort to proclaim its identity and connect to the outside world, the new nation of Kyrgyzstan had announced that it was throwing the biggest party the earth had ever known, to take place the following summer. The government had chosen to celebrate the thousandth anniversary of the *Epic of Manas,* the story of their country's mythical hero. The Kyrgyz boasted that the *Manas Epos*—double the combined length of Homer's *Iliad* and *Odyssey*—was the world's longest poem. Traces of the ancient oral tradition remained. Illiterate men still wandered remote mountain villages and could sing the entire epic from memory in a trancelike state.

Manas was a giant who could toss boulders across the peaks of the Tien Shan and pull trees out by the roots and shoot them like arrows. Legend said he was immaculately conceived when his elderly father had begged Allah for a son. He had been born in the Talas Valley, not far from Kyzyl Adyr–Kirovka. As a child he vowed to free his people from oppression. His life played out in a series of noble campaigns epitomizing the heights of bravery, until he was at last betrayed and killed. To this day, if anyone approached the hero's secret burial place, the heavens protected it with thunder, lightning, and a torrential rainstorm that could be quelled only by reciting the epic.

With independence had come an effort to revive interest in the Manas tradition. Young schoolchildren now memorized entire chapters of the epic, and nobody was better at this than Baktigul Tashtanalieva. Nazira had coached her, and Anarbek had watched his daughter place first in the yearly oblast-wide school competition, where, dressed in elaborate felt costume, her hands flying in fierce gestures, she recited the verses perfectly to mesmerized crowds. The prize won Baktigul a part, as an extra, in next summer's outdoor dramatization of the epic. Baktigul's recitation had also won Anarbek this poster.

He was still crawling on the floor when the government official arrived unannounced, slapping the hollow door with the palm of his hand. Startled, Anarbek jumped to his feet as the man strode into the room. He was wearing a solid green tie and bore a leather briefcase with an imprint of the Kyrgyz flag—the red sun rising on a yellow background. The word *mencheekteshteeroo* had been embroidered in black on the leather. He introduced himself as Bolot Ismailov. Anarbek offered him a seat, and the stranger flopped the briefcase onto the desk and clicked it open, so the flag and its label faced Anarbek upside down.

"Will you have some tea?" Anarbek asked. Behind him the Manas poster slid off the wall.

The squat man adjusted his glasses and cocked his head slightly, as if Anarbek had implied something illicit. "Perhaps later," he said. "We need to have a conversation. Pressing business."

Anarbek was overcome with dread. Jeff had warned him, and he had been expecting the visit, but now he decided it was best to play innocent. "Of course," he said. "What have you come to talk about, brother?"

"I've driven from Bishkek today. I'm overseeing privatization of businesses in the valley. We've been in your oblast for nearly six weeks now. Are you aware we've opened an office in Talas?"

"Perhaps I have heard."

Bolot explained that he had been sent to inspect state-owned farms and factories, in order to produce a list for this year's coming auction. It would be a cash-and-coupon auction—the government was distributing vouchers to all state workers, who could now take part in the purchase of the former collectives or any industry in the country. "We're making progress, you see. You can own your own factory now."

Anarbek spoke quietly, respectfully, examining his own fingers.

"I understand how it works. But even with the coupons, we will need credit, no? And foreign investors?"

"Certainly. A great deal of credit. With a fine, productive factory like this, I can't imagine that would be a problem."

"No. Of course not. We have an American working here."

"Ah, wonderful. I didn't know that. As I said, I've been sent to inspect the state-owned farms and factories—in order to create the list of enterprises for the privatization auction."

Anarbek hesitated. "Yes. Would you like me to show you around?"

"Certainly, but first . . ." Bolot leaned back in his chair, stretched his legs, and with some effort crossed his right foot onto his knee. His brown leather shoe was rubbed to an impressive shine. He thought for a moment, his hand pulling at his rough-shaven chin, then he suddenly spoke in Kyrgyz. "Tell me! How are things in the village?"

Anarbek tried to answer calmly. "As you know, sir, it has been very difficult these few years." It pained him to have to show deference to this short, stubby man, perhaps twenty years his junior.

Bolot asked if the government salaries were still arriving on time, and Anarbek told him not always, but regularly enough. They both agreed that the state of affairs in the country was very much up in the air. The official assured Anarbek that the changes would be for the long-term good.

"It is a difficult time right now," Bolot said. "For everyone it is a difficult time. I myself would like to marry sometime soon, but it is so expensive to start a family."

"I know. I have married twice."

"A *kalym*. One thousand, sometimes two thousand dollars for a woman from Naryn. But even that won't be enough. You understand me?"

"Yes, *agai*." Anarbek shook his head and clicked his tongue in agreement.

"And one day she will want to have a house, and children," Bolot added.

"I also have a young daughter. Two, in fact."

"Is that right? Well, then you and I both must consider the costs of a wedding. Quite expensive, in the capital, for someone like me, with so many friends. So many very *close* friends, in the government."

"I see."

"Do you pay rent here?" Bolot asked. His eyes had narrowed into thin dark slits, like roasted sunflower seeds.

"For my factory?"

"For your home?"

"No, of course not. I built it myself, with my own two hands."

"How wonderful. In the capital, you know, the rents have increased. Out of control. Many buildings have private owners now."

"Yes, I've heard."

"And we cannot grow our own food, as you do here. We must buy everything—food, clothing, butter—in the bazaar. Ten som for bread! Can you believe it?"

"It's hard to believe the costs nowadays," Anarbek said. "I don't know how we live."

The stilted conversation continued. Every time Anarbek tried to mention the factory, Bolot shifted in his seat, adjusted his tie, and changed the subject, relating the many hardships of city life. Anarbek listened impatiently, waiting for the guillotine to drop. He offered nods of commiseration, but behind the desk his knee quivered. At last Bolot searched his briefcase and drew out a notebook with orange carbon papers inserted beneath each sheet. He cleared his throat, and his voice turned solid, more official.

"Well, enough personal talk," he said in Russian. "As you see, I'm compiling the lists of factories to offer for sale this year. You're familiar with our law, 'On the Basic Principles of Destatization, Privatization, and Entrepreneurship in the Republic of Kyrgyzstan'?"

"Yes, brother."

"Then you know, of course, that the State Property Fund is the institution responsible for these sales." Bolot went on to explain that, since independence, the government had closed two hundred state-owned enterprises and privatized the service industries in full, along with 50 percent of construction enterprises, 70 percent of housing, and 25 percent of all agricultural firms. The president had declared he would like to complete the privatization of agricultural firms this year.

"Will it happen?" Anarbek asked.

"Well, things sometimes progress more slowly than our leaders would like. You do not see the president coming to your village, inspecting your cheese factory, do you?"

"No."

"No. It is only I. I'm the one who drives through the mountains, far from my home. I'm the one who organizes the auctions. I'm the one going from village to village, making the official lists for Talas."

"Yes."

"I write it here, you see. On this piece of paper. With this very pencil."

"Then you'll be assessing the value of our factory?"

"Perhaps . . . but not just yet." He eyed the open door for a long moment and then returned his gaze to Anarbek. Anarbek rose, closed the door, and secured the bolt.

Bolot continued. "I can write the factory name here, like this."

Slowly Anarbek seated himself, watching. Legs still crossed, Bolot was pretending to write and simultaneously exaggerating the words, "Kyzyl . . . Adyr . . . Kirovka . . . Cheese . . . Collective." He lowered his head, winked at Anarbek, turned the pencil upside-down, and pretended to erase. "Or I can erase the name." He smiled and laughed a discomforting guffaw, slapped the pencil on the desk, spun the notebook in his lap, opened his palms, then brushed off his hands. "What factory? You understand me, Tashtanaliev? What factory?"

Anarbek tried to smile, but his lips stretched only halfway. He thought for a second, weighing his choices. The silence in the room was oppressive. Finally he took the plunge.

"How much?" he asked.

Bolot leaned forward and whispered in Kyrgyz, "A small percentage of what you earn, Anarbek. Very small indeed. No one need know. We can get you a few years yet."

Jeff did not mean to be cynical about the planned festival. One year into his Peace Corps service, he was making every effort to stay positive. Yet with the novelty of Kyrgyzstan fading and another winter ahead, he found himself sinking deeper and deeper into a morass of cynicism.

He had first learned of the extravaganza at the bazaar, where he had run into Nazira. She had pointed out a poster pasted on a kiosk, advertising next summer's Manas celebration. Jeff was skeptically bemused. Nazira tried to explain the importance of the epic. "The legend brings our people together and gives us good examples to live by. You see, Jeff, our president has announced an international celebration and invited the world." She spread her arms wide, as if to embrace the entire bazaar. "They say even President Clinton is coming! Your father and your friends from America must also attend."

Jeff laughed. "We'll see. When will it start?"

"We don't know. May or June. It will last all of next summer. My sister will be one of the stars."

"How are they getting the money for this?" he asked. "Shouldn't the government pay unemployment or pensions first?"

Nazira blushed. "It is our ancient tradition," she explained. "Nothing is more important than that. Some of the people have forgotten Manas, and that is very bad."

Jeff recognized in Nazira his own foolish idealism. Last summer he had charged into Central Asia thinking he could preach the virtues of democracy and the necessity of basic human rights. Instead he was teaching the simple past tense to unemployed milkmaids for the fourth time. He was culturally exhausted. Life as a volunteer was becoming too much for him: too much vodka, too much attention, too much goodwill, too little progress. As his second summer ended, he did his best to escape the constant feasts. More and more he made up excuses. He avoided handshakes in the bazaars. And still, fearing unreasonable requests from his Kyrgyz friends, he refused to answer the door at night.

He reached his breaking point in mid-October. The American embassy, in support of Peace Corps volunteers involved in agricultural projects, had mailed Jeff a newsletter and application detailing a promising initiative of tax credits and loans available to dairy farmers. Before classes the next morning Jeff approached Anarbek in the factory office, showed him the information, and explained that it was the perfect opportunity for the doomed collective—even if it meant notifying the government of the oversight concerning salaries. "Look, you simply sign on," Jeff said. "I promise you. It is the only way there will be a future for your factory."

"Future?" Anarbek lifted the application papers between thumb and forefinger, as if they were wet laundry. "What future is there if the salaries stop? Half our village cannot get food now. You want to starve the other half?"

"I am not trying to starve anyone. Soon the government will discover that they have been mistakenly sending you money. What will you do then? Each year you check the privatization announcements and pray your factory is not listed. And now you're paying off Ismailov. I am telling you to *let* the inevitable happen. I am telling you to get some legitimate money in here, rebuild, and work toward a joint venture. This application can ensure success. You just have to come clean, Anarbek. The state is doing this gradually. They will not let you fall into financial trouble. They are trying to find investors abroad. It is not in their interest to see you fail. Listen." Jeff took back the application and read, "'Additionally the government is concerned about the flow of dairy products out of the country. In an effort to regulate the sector, the Kyrgyz Agro organization has been established to help newly privatized corporations handle problems associated with operating in a developing market.'" Jeff waved the papers in the air. "You are perfect for this."

Anarbek was shaking his head. "Jeff, you don't understand. The finance ministers, the governors of the oblasts, are filling their own pockets. They are buying up companies for themselves, and they are the only ones with the money to do it. Regulation? There is no regulation! No stability, no laws. Would you want to chance that? In your country you can afford to take risks. You have money; you have security. If you lose one job, you find another. That is not how it works here. They'll buy us out and close us—we could never compete with them. The village will starve."

"Compete? How will you compete now? There are hardly any cows! You have almost no milk! You make no cheese!"

"Cheese! Who cares about cheese? We still have our salaries. Soon perhaps we will start over, Jeff. We will start small. Maybe we will try to produce yogurt or *kefir* to sell in Talas. Simpler operations."

"You talk about corruption. It is you, Anarbek! You are the one stealing from the government, corrupting the system. Listen to me. You need to forget about the salaries and begin thinking of the future. All problems have solutions. You just need a change of—how do you say it?" Jeff laid the application papers on Anarbek's desk, pulled out the dictionary from his backpack, and flipped furiously through the pages. "*Mentality*," he said, pointing to the Russian word.

Anarbek stared at the word and seemed to lapse into thought. With each silent second Jeff felt his hopes multiply. If he could keep the factory from sinking—if he kept the workers in business—the village might not only survive but prosper. The free market might take off, and democracy might eventually take root here. Anarbek studied him; his eyes narrowed. He glanced down at the papers, lifted them from the desk, and held them closer to his face. "No, Jeff. Thank you, but for the last time, no. It is too much risk." With a resounding tear he ripped the application in two, then into small pieces.

The signs for the festival hung everywhere by winter's end. On every store around the oblast, every frozen highway billboard, every icy school gate, and every rusting bus: MANAS 1000 YEARS. Despite the lack of visible preparations, for Nazira these signs meant the festival was a certainty. In February she read a notice in the *pochta*, declaring the Manas celebration would take place over two weeks in June. The following Saturday a new notice corrected this, claiming the celebration would be held only the final week of June, after school let out.

"It is almost March already," Jeff told her on a dinner visit to his host family's house. It was a particularly frigid evening, and he had hardly touched the borscht or the *manti* Nazira had made. "In Talas they're just breaking ground for the first hotel, near the stadium by the river. That is not much time to build a five-star Presidential Hotel."

"It is the Kyrgyz way," Nazira assured him. "Relax, relax, relax, and at the last minute, work, work, work."

Jeff had only three months left, and Nazira realized she was running out of time. Soon he would leave—forever, perhaps—and in the larger world of teeming Western cities he would forget her. Her father made things no better with his constant questioning, with his prods, his schemes. "How are things between you and Jeff?" he wanted to know. "Have you brought him bread this week? Have you invited him to dinner? Is there progress?" She had stopped answering; there was too little time to hope.

In May Jeff spent an end-of-service weekend in the capital and returned to break the news that President Clinton was unable to attend the Manas festival; he had sent his regrets.

In late June Nazira traveled to Talas to secure festival tickets for her family; the event had now been shortened to three days. In town nothing was happening, although people claimed the celebration had already begun. It seemed the *kumbooz*, the central site of the festival, lay fifteen kilometers away, in the foothills. Since no hotels had been completed, international dignitaries would now sleep in yurts at the site. Nazira had hoped to impress Jeff—she had hoped the town would be full of parades, street musicians, *shashlyk* stands, and vendors capitalizing on this historic event. Perhaps it would all start tomorrow.

She wandered to the Talas airport. Near the dirt runway the town's schools had assembled six yurts to welcome the invited presidents. Anxious people were pacing. A terrifying Russian babushka guarded a display of mannequins dressed in sequined national costumes. A group of bored schoolboys tortured a falcon chained to a post. Children in felt dresses and conical hats, waving flags of the new nation, had gathered on the road. In one yurt a school director explained that the presidents would all fly in at seven the *next* morning.

When Nazira brought this news back to their village, Jeff was incensed.

"This whole production was concocted just to welcome the dignitaries. Propaganda, that's all it is. Why didn't anybody tell those people at the airport that they were waiting one day early?"

She told him not to worry; the people were used to waiting. The *akim* of Talas had decreed that festivities should not begin until the visiting presidents arrived from the capital. To encourage promptness, the road to the *kumbooz* would be closed by seven in the morning. The performers, including Baktigul, had to arrive before then. The family would therefore have to leave the village by four in the morning, so Jeff must stay overnight at their house. And only the *chong kishi*—big people—like themselves, who had tickets, could attend.

Lola woke Jeff at three the next morning, and over breakfast he was surprised to see that Anarbek's entire family had dressed up. While Jeff wore only his ASU Rugby T-shirt and a faded pair of sweatpants, Anarbek had put on a sports jacket and a brand-new stiff white *kalpak*. Lola wore a long blue printed dress, and more elegant still were Nazira and Baktigul, in matching equestrian costumes: lacy ruffled skirts and tight burgundy vests made of felt and embroidered with antler designs. "You look beautiful," Jeff told Baktigul, who beamed and blushed. Anarbek placed a hand on his daughter's shoulder and said, "She is our Hollywood star today.

She is our Cybill Shepherd, our Yulia Roberts." Nazira poured the chai, and when breakfast was finished she fetched Jeff's boots for him. He laced them up next to the door and watched Nazira slip her slim, delicate feet into her high heels.

They drove two hours in Anarbek's sputtering Lada, but when they approached the site, officials forced them to park a few kilometers away. As a group they began the hour-and-a-half hike to the *kumbooz*. Every other family in the area was doing likewise, a procession of zombies trudging through the yellow mist of morning. Jeff asked, "What time is the festival going to start?"

Anarbek told him the road closed at seven.

"That is not what I asked," Jeff whispered to Nazira in English.

"It is Kyrgyz time," she whispered back. "You will see."

Police were everywhere, twirling their batons as if showing off, and they screamed at the lines of shuffling people for no apparent reason. Yet everyone kept hiking; fifty thousand had to be on the mountainside by seven, before the presidents arrived. Fifty thousand began the slow march to the opposite side of the grounds; they were directed to sit on a far hill to watch the celebration, which would take place in the immense hippodrome below. The organizers had cleared a path through the brush two meters wide, which wound around outhouses, yurts, puddles, and creeks. Fifty thousand had to jump stones to cross a pond, negotiate single warped planks that bridged pools of shit, and clamber up the muddy slopes. Jeff was furious, but Nazira, in high heels, did not complain. Approaching the hill at last, she turned to him and declared, "We must have walked five kilometers. Or eight!"

In the center of the grounds stood a small stadium with the exclusive seats. Only those with special colored tickets could enter. Security guards tried to let the performers in, but the teeming general crowd swelled at the gates, trying to force their way in as well. Just as Nazira kissed her sister goodbye and directed her to the performers' gate, the police twirled their batons, and a mass of people surged back in uncontrollable waves. Baktigul shrieked. A few children fell and were nearly crushed. The celebration, Jeff thought, had begun.

No time or place had been set to meet up with Baktigul after the performance—this disturbed Jeff, but he shrugged it off as a typical Kyrgyz laissez-faire attitude. With the crowd they came to rest on the far hill, a half-kilometer from where it looked like the show might take place. Once again the waiting began—an hour passed, then two. The people sitting in front of Jeff began to play cards, and their neighbors clicked their tongues in disbelief. Someone chided them: how could anyone think to bring cards to the historic Manas celebration? From his backpack Jeff pulled out Dostoyevsky's *Crime and Punishment*.

Buses rumbled down the road that separated the general crowd from the exclusive stadium and dropped off the diplomats destined for the coveted VIP seats. The buses obstructed the general audience's view of the stadium. But the Kyrgyz merely smiled and waved at the tinted windows.

At ten in the morning the crowd was still waiting in the dirt. Jeff reminded himself not to complain. He eyed Nazira—how gracefully she bided the time, with what assurance and good-natured acceptance she waited: laughing, telling jokes, taking deep breaths of the grassy air.

Finally, two hours later, the speeches introducing the thousandth anniversary of the *Epic of Manas* began. A single staticky loudspeaker broadcast the message to the general crowd on the hill. Nobody listened. Jeff could hardly make out, through the forest of *kalpaks*, over the buses, the distant dot of the speaker. One or two diplomats rattled on, and then a representative from UNESCO offered an incomprehensible dedication. For another hour the crowd sat, waving at the buses.

Every ounce of Jeff's patience had dried up. Seething, he said to his hosts, "It is good so far?"

"Very good!" Lola agreed.

At one in the afternoon, with an uproar, the main performance finally started. Over the heads of the crowd, Jeff could see the hippodrome come to life. For the next thirty minutes a humongous cast of actors from the capital, dressed in bright flowing costumes, reenacted battle scenes from the epic. Acrobats performed on horseback, dancers twirled in lines, rainbows of fire shot over the field, gongs rang out, and banners were unveiled in synchronized patterns—a show worthy of a Superbowl halftime. Jeff was awed by it, and chastened himself for being so cynical.

Over the loudspeaker he recognized the voice of a *manaschi* singing the opening notes of the epic. Nazira scooted over excitedly and whispered in his ear, "Do you know what this is?"

"I can't understand everything. Can you translate?"

"He is just beginning. I shall see." In a sweet low voice, close to his face, she did her best with the lyrics:

> "Oh, oh, oh, the ancient fairy tale,
> It is high time to begin it . . .
> For fearless Manas's sake . . .
> We will tell you energetically
> For the sake of Manas's memory . . .
> Innumerable years have passed
> Since dressed in chain armor,
> Running when seeing an enemy,
> Fast like the whirlwind,
> The man ferocious like the tiger has passed.
> Who was it, if not the hero?
> So many people have passed through the centuries!
> Since that time
> The sea got dry
> And turned into a desert.
> The mountain peaks reaching the sky
> Have vanished and turned into a swamp.
> The peoples living on earth are getting less!"

"It's wonderful. It's really wonderful," Jeff told her. Energized, he straightened his legs and settled down to enjoy the spectacle.

Anarbek had spotted Baktigul and pointed her out. She was playing a cousin or a niece of Manas—Jeff couldn't be sure—and riding double on horseback behind one of the principal actresses, who was supposed to be fleeing a wartime burning village. Baktigul held on to the actress's shoulders as the horse galloped across the field. Anarbek and Lola shouted and waved.

Jeff began to think this festival might have been worth it. Even if it wasn't a season, or two weeks, or one week, or three days, or even two full hours, still, for this tiny new country, it was *something*. The celebration of a new nation meant something. His being here, at this historic moment, meant something.

Just as the performance was reaching a climax, the electricity and music cut off. The throngs of dancers, actors, and acrobats ignored the problem and continued marching, tumbling, and reenacting battles through the silence. After nearly a minute the loudspeaker coughed back on, and a voice apologized to the diplomats, the nine foreign presidents, the international community, and the Kyrgyz people. The voice directly addressed the performers and asked them to return to their original positions.

"Excuse us," the voice said. "We have fixed the music. Please do it again. Our deep regrets. Please start over. Excuse us."

Anarbek, Lola, and some of the crowd laughed. Nazira shrugged. A few people hissed and clicked their tongues. On the loudspeaker the *manaschi* opened the epic again. The music failed twice more during the second performance, but it no longer seemed important. The show continued in spurts. Baktigul fled the burning village a total of three times. Finally the hero Manas saved the Kyrgyz nation. Fireworks shot across the hippodrome. Gunshots, gongs, and the horsemen's shouting resounded, flags from around the world were unfurled, and a magnificent hot-air balloon, made of brilliant orange taffeta, was inflated and lifted off, rising into the sky like a second sun.

"It is so beautiful," Jeff said to Anarbek, sweeping his arm across the crowd, the Talas hills, the Ala Too mountains fringed with snow. Together everyone's heads turned upward as they followed the path of the balloon.

Past the stadium the balloon floated, lost altitude, then crashed into a hill. The basket collapsed; the fabric fell, burst, and ripped into shreds.

Jeff's heart ripped with it. Around him the Kyrgyz gazed, spellbound, at the balloon's immolation. They did not appear disappointed. They simply turned away and resumed their chatter. Anarbek was inspecting his *kalpak,* and Nazira looked serene and content. No, Jeff thought, this was a disaster. As much as he wanted this new nation to develop, to flourish, with or without his help it was going nowhere. He was finished here. Let the hero Manas save the cheese factory.

The spectacle had ended. It occurred to Lola and Nazira only then, for the first time, that finding ten-year-old Baktigul in a crowd of fifty thousand was going to be a problem. Jeff separated himself from his host family and slouched around the festival grounds, looking for the girl and avoiding invitations to eat *beshbarmak.* Eventually he met up with Nazira and Lola. They had not yet found Baktigul, but now, together, they were pulled into a yurt by an enthusiastic Kyrgyz family overjoyed to meet an American. Their hosts sat them down, carried in the sheep's head, and handed the knife to Jeff. Just as he cut into the ear, they proclaimed with unwavering smiles:

"Wasn't our Manas celebration perfect?"

*   *   *

Jeff learned from Anarbek that it was a Kyrgyz tradition to throw oneself a farewell party. He could barely fathom another evening of forced vodka and excessive generosity. He had packing and cleaning to do, and he was busy organizing his belongings to leave for village friends. In an effort to travel as lightly as possible, he had carried most of what he owned up to his bedroom, where he waded through shoes, a tape player, his dubbed blues cassettes, a pocket calculator, and his Italian spices. He had always hated goodbyes and had hoped for a quiet, graceful exit. In leaving he was abandoning the factory and the village to a state of uncertainty, and he wanted to get it over with as quickly as possible.

But Anarbek forced him to relent. "I'll mention the party to a few people," Jeff said. "Just a few, though."

The following morning he cooked *leposhka* pizzas, using the flat loaves of bread from the bazaar. He boiled down a vat of spicy tomato sauce, chopped up his last precious hunk of imported cheese from the capital, then baked it all in a covered frying pan. He was impressed with the results. For his closest village friends, ten pizzas would suffice: a final taste of America.

The crowd began arriving at nine-thirty in the morning. Scarved women charged into his home, pointed to his pizzas cooling on the kitchen table, and laughed. They were followed by their husbands and children, who tracked mud inside and hauled Jeff's furniture out the front door under the apple trees. Before he could object, three enormous tables had been improvised, covered, and set Kyrgyz style—the usual nuts, fruits, candy, and jams spread over them. Jeff heard protesting sheep dragged into the back of his yard, he heard the clanking of bottles as they were set up on the tables, and he braced himself for one final day of submission to traditions beyond his control.

Village children arrived. Upstairs the kids unpacked all of his bags, then made off with journals, photos, and his ASU sweatshirts (he would not know they were missing until weeks later). By noon Nazira was outside playing the *kumooz,* Jeff's tape player was jammed into a window frame, and electric Indian film music blared out into the dusty street; babushkas gossiped under the apple trees, the neighbor's dogs jumped up on the tables and stole pieces of *borsok,* and a group of men squatted around a bottle by the raspberry bushes, tore off berries, and swallowed them after each toast. Jeff brought out the pizzas and his guests scarfed them down in a matter of seconds, then complained how lousy American food was. The boiling of the sheep commenced, followed by the cleaning of the offal in the irrigation ditch, and Jeff was pulled inside his living room, where, as a gift, some of his neighbors recorded dedications on cassette; they thanked him for his two years of help and sang mournful farewell songs at ear-piercing volume; then they dragged him outside, where warm champagne was uncorked. Loaves of fresh bread arrived from the bazaar, someone brought homemade yogurt, and his students abandoned the factory and arrived with hunks of butter. A fight broke out between Dushen and Bolot Ismailov ("Former KGB," whispered Anarbek), and it ended with both men half-drunk, half-beaten, and slumped, hugging each other, on the roots of the plum tree. Late in the afternoon a cow wandered into the yard and lapped up jam from the table while children took turns throwing sticks at it. The villagers gave Jeff presents, more presents than he had planned to give away himself: carved chess sets, a Kyrgyz lute, watercolors of the dried-up reservoir, and, most impressive, an embroidered riding whip, with his factory students warning him, "Always take it with you, wherever you go, and you will never be lost."

Songs erupted outside, the dancing began, and the party spilled beyond his fence into Karl Marx Street. Swooning now, Jeff stared across the riot of his front yard, where he had enjoyed so many peaceful evenings reading, writing letters, and contemplating the mountains. In the growing frenzy of song, dance, and drink, it occurred to him that the entire village was there to say goodbye. His temples throbbed: he felt dizzy and sad.

"Are you okay?" The voice was Nazira's, his ballast of equilibrium in the insanity of this place. She was standing beside him, and he realized she had been hovering close to him for much of the afternoon.

"I can't believe all this." He gestured to the raucous crowd.

"The Kyrgyz can make a holiday of any occasion," she said. "We do not want you to forget us."

"How can I forget this!"

By six in the evening the yard was finally abandoned, the sun setting behind the recently plowed fields. Drunk, exhausted, melancholy, Jeff wandered from room to room of his overturned home, trying to determine how he was going to clean up the mess before he left in the morning. He gave up and passed out on the shag carpet of his living room.

At midnight a gentle but persistent knocking woke him. He stumbled to the front door and found Nazira.

"My father has sent me over to check on you. I saw the lights on. I thought you might use my help."

She stepped into his house, and with the instincts of a woman trained in the art of perspicacity set to work. At first Jeff followed her from room to room, amazed by the efficiency and confidence of her every movement. But after five minutes he retreated to the bathroom sink. The water, thank God, was running. He splashed his face, rinsed his dry mouth, and realized he was utterly unable to focus.

He found Nazira sorting effortlessly through the soiled dishes piled in the kitchen. She had begun to boil water; she had emptied three wastebaskets and was now in the process of clearing off plates. Jeff stepped in to help. He dropped the first glass he touched and it shattered on the hard stone floor.

Nazira smiled. "Why don't you start cleaning upstairs?"

Jeff found his bedroom ravaged. He noticed the dusty footprints of the children. They had jumped on his pillows, unpacked his bags, torn out pages of his favorite novels, rifled through his two-year stack of letters, and smudged every single one of his photographs. It had taken him weeks to organize all of his things: what to ship, what to carry home, what to leave for the future Peace Corps volunteers, what to leave for his village friends. His work had been for nothing. Lost in the depths of cloudy judgment, he began stuffing items into any bag they would fit. When he had filled the luggage, half of his belongings remained on the floor. He realized he was getting nowhere, dumped it all out, and went downstairs again.

Nazira had finished the dishes and had swept the large chunks of mud off the living room carpet. Jeff was thoroughly impressed. Now, at two-thirty in the morning, she was trying to clear the thick brown cobwebs off a corner of the ceiling—a job he had never, in two years, gotten around to. She could not reach the highest webs with the broom handle and dragged over a wobbly chair.

"Nazira," he said, "you are a goddess for helping me, but really, it's late. This isn't very important right now."

She climbed onto the chair and with a smile answered, "These things might not be important to you, but they are important to me. Some person must live here."

Jeff secured the shaking chair. She swiped at the cobwebs with her broom, stretching higher, and her leg slipped a few inches. He caught her calf and held her steady by both legs. It took her only a moment to clear the cobwebs, but he found, gripping her soft knees, that he was desperately aroused. She hopped down, and he turned away.

"How are you doing upstairs?" she asked.

He shook his head.

"Let me see." Nazira marched him up the staircase.

"Uff! Jeff, Jeff, Jeff." She clucked at him, observing the mess. She sat down among the T-shirts and sneakers and all of his worldly possessions and began folding clothes. He watched her noble face, her determined eyes, her constellation of freckles, and he opened his mouth in astonishment as she packed a pair of his boxer shorts.

"Really, enough, Nazira. I'll take care of all this." He tried to pull a pair of jeans from her hands. With a teasing smile she refused to let go, and the next thing he knew, they were locked in an embrace, rolling over hard lumps of his stuff, bumping their heads against the floor and the bedposts. Very soon neither had anything on—their clothes and bodies and cries mixed with the great disorganization of the room. She hugged him close and shook beneath him. Her thin legs were strong around his waist, her chest soft and flat; the musky taste of her neck could not have been more foreign, or more familiar, and inside her he thought he might never want to leave.

The nine o'clock sun slanted through the open curtains and Jeff awoke, alone, to a brilliant headache. He stood and tried to retrieve fuzzy lost pieces of the day before. What he could remember did not square with what he found. His clothes were perfectly folded in the room, all of his belongings packed and zipped in bags. He walked naked past the open bedroom windows; the air was cool and scented with wildflowers of the early alpine summer. Still naked, he crept down the groaning steps and found that the living room furniture had been brought in from the yard. The dishes had been cleaned, dried, and piled in neat rows; the kitchen table had been wiped to a shine, and on it two flat loaves of *leposhka* had been left for him. He lifted one warm loaf, and as it gradually cooled in his hands he thought, What have I done?

That morning he said goodbye to his students, to Altin Eje at the post office, to the fat Russian telegraph operator, and, with a great hug, to Anarbek. At the bazaar he said goodbye to the Kurdish milkmaids. He left all of his *National Geographics* with Yuri Samonov. He bid silent farewell to the drunks sleeping under the poplar trees by the statue of Lenin. He waved to the cheeseless cheese factory and left the village of Kyzyl Adyr–Kirovka, hitching a ride with his three oversize canvas duffle bags to Djambul, where he found a bus to the capital. The real world came rushing back to him, and the farther from the village he got, the more he dreaded America, massive wealthy modern America, waiting resolutely for his return.

III

6

IT SEEMED NOTHING new had arrived in Kyzyl Adyr–Kirovka in a decade. Everything in Jeff's old townhouse—the furniture, the appliances, the wallpaper—dated back to the days of Communism. As the excitement of the initial years of independence faded, Nazira and the people of the village grew increasingly nostalgic for a time when their world had been fresh.

This bleak February evening her key did not work in her front door. She usually forced the key in and leaned against the door to slide the bolt open, the metal scraping metal. But on frozen winter days, negotiating the lock was impossible. She carried her two-year-old son around to the other side of the house and jiggled the wooden back door, up and down, up and down, until it slid open. Any thief could get into her house—but what would he steal? He was welcome to her poverty.

She plugged in the cement hot plate, put the soup on to heat, and turned on the television, praying it would work.

With each of the past three winters, the electricity had become increasingly sporadic. One year ago, in January 1996, it had gone out for a month and she had to move back to her father's home. The family had used the bread oven to heat the kitchen, and slept there, huddled on red *tushuks*. By the end of the week their dry wood had run out, they could no longer keep a fire going, and they resorted to vodka. Since then each household in the village hoarded mounds of coal in its garden for winter emergencies.

These stockpiles were guarded with ferocity. Nobody could afford to share.

The concrete hot plates—little stone tables with a network of slight depressions through which an electric coil was threaded—that heated homes had become the predominant cause of failing electricity. When one was plugged in, the hazardous coil burned like a thin trail of lava, and the house lights dimmed. In an hour a single hot plate could warm a well-sealed room, but if too many were lit at the same time the main street fuse blew. Nazira's intrepid neighbors, Oomar and Alex, then crunched through the ice past the kindergarten, past the frozen bull shaking itself in the snow, to the fuse house at the end of the street. From her frosted windows Nazira could see sparks flying out of the shed and hear Russian and Kyrgyz curses, meaning one of the men had shocked himself. Occasionally Oomar and Alex fixed the problem and the people of Karl Marx Street promised they would be less frivolous with the heating coils. But if the neighbors failed to rewire the fuse house, Nazira camped under thin covers, trying to keep her son warm. She shivered through the night, and the next morning would find her dishes filmed with ice in the kitchen sink.

The people on the street would have to send for the Russian electrician in Pekrovka village, thirty kilometers away. In past years they'd managed to pay him with a single bottle of Stolichnaya. With each ensuing winter, however, the fuses went out more frequently, and the price went up to two, then three bottles. The Russian fiddled with the wires, drank, and grumbled. Since independence he had insisted he was leaving this damned country and returning to Russia. Kyrgyzstan, he said, no longer welcomed his kind; there was nothing left for him here.

When the electricity went out, the village water pump ceased to work. People kept emergency supplies in large metal vats where they had previously stored milk. After a few days without running water Nazira's vats went dry. She trudged a kilometer down to the creek and waited in line behind the Kurdish girls bearing pots and pans, the old Uzbek women in muddy skirts. One by one they leaned over the dribbling pipe that emptied into the stream. The pipe was the only clean source of water, and it ran, even when the village pump stopped, by gravity. Nazira carried the heavy pails home one at a time, her breath rising in little clouds as she prayed for water to run again the next day.

Back in the time of the hero Manas, she imagined, a village had survived without pipes and electricity. The Kyrgyz had lived in warm felt yurts, not in concrete apartment blocks or cold brick townhouses. Water flowed from clean streams; it was not dammed up in a polluted reservoir at the edge of the village. Her people knew how to make warm coats from sheepskin; they did not journey a half day to Kazakhstan on rusting buses to purchase imitation-leather jackets.

But she always snapped out of her daydreaming. What good was nostalgia?

Their once-developed nation had become the Third World. Her outhouse was clogged; another one needed to be dug. The faucet handle fell off every time she used it and clanked in the sink. Mice attacked her store of carrots, apples, and potatoes in the cellar. When the wheel of her canning press grew loose after six turns, she tightened it with a chipped screwdriver.

Her one retreat from the disorder came now, on these rare days when she had heat, water, electricity—and the television worked. The huge Brezhnev-era machine inhabited a large part of her upstairs living room. A few of its massive color tubes were missing, so after the signal had swept all the way from Russia to Kyrgyzstan and climbed over the mountains, it played only in green. Weeks of brownout caused the circuits to fail, but sometimes, with a proper slap on the side, the television would come back to life.

This evening it blinked on, and—nursing her son—she was able to watch a rerun of the American soap opera *Santa Barbara*. Across the humming screen lay a world beyond her imagination, a place where a person's only real problem was love.

Nazira too had known love and had decided it was a danger she had no time for. She had borne her pregnancy and the consequent scorn of the village with a quiet acceptance. Even before Jeff, from the day she had escaped Traktorbek, she had settled into a ruined reputation, and she knew it could get no worse. She refused to reveal to her closest friends the father of the child growing inside of her, hinting that he was a handsome Russian she had met in Talas. If people had other suspicions, let them think what they might.

Many times in those nine months she found herself wondering when Jeff would contact her, until finally she had taken action herself. On a winter morning, late in the pregnancy, she was shambling across the icy winter road to school. As she descended the high embankment of an irrigation ditch packed with snow, she slipped and fell. She would have landed straight on her stomach, but at the last instant she managed to twist around and hit her side instead. The fall jarred her. She shuffled in pain to the Lenin School. There was no heat, few students were attending, and in the freezing classroom, with its cracked windows and warped wooden floors, she experienced a crisis of fear. Before second period she removed the gloves she usually wore while teaching and wrote a long, desperate letter to Jeff, in Idaho, America, telling him she loved him.

The weeks passed, and though the factory workers and her father received letters from Jeff, none included a response to her. Had she placed too much faith in the unreliable Kyrgyz postal system? She mailed off another letter, but still she heard nothing. He had dismissed her, and with the loss of hope she regained her former strength.

Her one solace had been that Lola was also pregnant, carrying the child of Nazira's father. Anarbek was counting on a son. Lola beamed as her stomach grew, and she bore the weight effortlessly. The women of the village said she would be a natural mother and would not let Anarbek down. The two old friends bathed each other, shared dieting advice, and discussed possible names, if it was a girl, if it was a boy. Lola joked that, without a husband, Nazira had the unique advantage of control over the child's name.

"The problem with your child," Nazira would retaliate, "is that he'll look like my father."

Anarbek, for his part, hardly seemed concerned with his daughter's state, as if he wanted to ignore the scandal. But in the eighth month, he had reminded her that Jeff's old townhouse on Karl Marx Street was still vacant. She took this as no subtle hint: after the child was born, he wanted her to move out. Such face-saving punishment hardly bothered her. The possibility of living alone with the baby suited her independence, and the house was only a short walk away.

Her father had disappeared for two straight evenings when her water finally broke. Lola sent Baktigul out searching—to the factory, to the bazaar, to his friends, but Anarbek was nowhere to be found. In a rush of panic Lola telephoned the hospital. It took three attempts to connect. She begged Radish, the head doctor, to send the ambulance quickly. "We'd love to help," he yelled back through the rough connection, "but our ambulance is out of benzene." So with the aid of an old, senile neighbor, Nazira had delivered her son in the same home where she herself had been born. As the labor progressed, the old woman kept calling her by the wrong names, but even in her senility she retained her midwife instincts.

"How wonderful!" she kept repeating. "To be having a baby in the house! It's just like old times! How wonderful!"

Nazira's screams roused the village. A group of women gathered in the street in front of the tall blue steel gate, clicked their tongues, and complained about the lack of discretion. In the end Baktigul rushed out of the house and announced that her sister had given birth to a boy and that his name would be Manas. The village women murmured, thrilled by the new scandal. When Anarbek returned late that evening, he refused to hold the baby.

The following month Lola also gave birth to a son, Oolan. The two childhood friends, who had once shared dolls and pieces of bubblegum, who had attended music lessons together, now, in their growing poverty, were united by the trials of motherhood.

Tonight the strong wind was whistling through the window cracks, and the television screen fell into static. Nazira lay Manas on a blanket and slapped the TV's side. The *Santa Barbara* signal wavered, then came back again stronger. She lifted Manas to her swollen chest, and he sucked hungrily. As Nazira could follow the episode, the character C.C., with the help of Santana, had caught Mason in bed with Gina. When Mason found out he took revenge and told C.C. that Channing was gay. This information (equally shocking to Nazira) had sent C.C. into a coma for months. The evil Gina, knowing C.C. would disinherit her if he recovered, was now scheming to pull the plug on C.C.'s life-support system—but she wanted to make it look as though Eden had done it.

Nazira feared Eden would be unjustly blamed.

In the summer of 1998, leaving Manas with Lola, Nazira traveled by bus to Bishkek to visit her cousin, Cholpon, a business student at the Technical University. Cholpon had written to tell her about a new business venture she had discovered, one she promised would supplement Nazira's low teacher's salary.

The rest stop outside of Djambul, an elevated teahouse and a row of five smoking *shashlyk* stands, marked the halfway point of the eight-hour journey. Hungry from the long bus ride, Nazira chose the least vile skewer from one man's grill. The vendor pulled the mutton off the skewers, sprinkled vinegar and raw onions on top, and served the meat to her, along with a doughy hunk of *leposhka,* on a yellowed page ripped from a hardbound copy of Tolstoy's *What Is Art?*

Her hunger turned to nausea after the second rancid piece. She tossed the rest of the meat to a group of well-fed feral dogs and soothed her stomach with a few bites of the bread. The nausea brought on a pressing need for the toilet. Behind the tea stall, a mud path led to a cement outhouse: men to the left, women to the right. She waited in line, reeling from the stink. One by one the women from her bus rushed out of the cavelike hole, gasping for air. In turn she entered the foul chamber. The floor was wet with mud, urine, and blood. Lifting her skirt to squat, she saw that a pile of shit rose out from the stuffed hole in the ground, and she noticed, on top of it, the collective squirming of maggots. She fled the toilet, crying out in disgust.

In the bus her stomach churned at the smell lingering on her clothes and the taste of the rancid meat. The bus continued on; it would take four more hours to reach the capital. Nazira rejected self-pity. She should not pity herself; she should pity her people, all the women who had used the outhouse, silently suffering the everyday hell of their lives. During the rest of the ride she tried to relax by daydreaming of *Santa Barbara,* speculating on whom Eden would marry.

The bus broke down only once, an hour outside of Bishkek, just over the Kazakh border. Passengers emptied out and watched the driver and conductor argue over how to fix a broken pipe. It was getting late.

In the capital, just before they reached the Bishkek *otovakzal,* Nazira read a brightly lit new billboard, on the right side of the road, painted in both Kyrgyz and Russian. It showed a heart in the top left corner, a globe in the bottom right corner, and the silhouette of a couple embracing beneath a telephone number.

American/European men want to marry you!
Call 53-76-7943

At the station five minutes later, Nazira was repeating the number softly to herself as the bus screeched to a halt. Around her the passengers scrambled to be the first to escape.

She stayed with Cholpon in her fourth-floor apartment one block from the history museum. Her cousin revealed the secret details of her infallible business venture: the brewing of homemade vodka. It was a simple, inexpensive recipe, involving primarily sugar and yeast, and one could easily control the strength of the alcohol or create special flavors with various fruits and peppers.

"This is what you're learning in business school these days?" Nazira asked, laughing. But she became an eager student. Money was short, her salary was often delayed, and she had too much pride to ask her father for help.

In exchange for the lessons, Nazira shared the number on the billboard she had read, and at the end of the week the cousins placed marriage ads. Cholpon dressed Nazira in her best blouse—lightweight, short-sleeved, printed blue muslin—and a pair of blue jeans, unlike anything Nazira had ever worn. In the cramped studio on Prospect Chui, next to the telegraph station, they filled out questionnaires and applications. The Russian photographer took their measurements and added them to their forms. For Nazira's shot he undid her top button—she squirmed at his touch—forced her head to a tilt, and snapped her photo twice. The picture captured her seriousness and charm; her chin was raised, and her wide eyes appeared bright and searching. The photographer explained he would publish the classified ads in an international magazine distributed to wealthy businessmen in Europe and America.

"But would someone want to marry a woman like me, with a child?" Nazira asked, beginning to doubt herself.

"A woman as radiant as you?" the photographer said. "Absolutely! See, we have women with *more* than one child advertising with us. Many Western men are looking for a family." He showed them last fall's glossy magazine, filled with color photographs. In the information boxes, a number of the women from Bishkek, Tashkent, and Alma-Ata revealed that they were divorced, and at least one on each page claimed to have a child—some had two or three. "It doesn't make a difference," the photographer said. "They see your face, they fall in love. I guarantee it."

He would send a copy of the new magazine to her village. They just had to wait to hear from someone interested in marriage. He promised responses. Nazira and Cholpon exchanged a glance and paid two hundred som each for the service: a month's wage.

Nazira returned to Kyzyl Adyr–Kirovka and began brewing vodka, which she sold secretly to her neighbors. In the months that followed she never saw the magazine, and she never received any marriage proposals. She punished herself for trying to change her fate. Nothing would ever come of it.

7

THE SPRING OF Adam's senior year the NAU bas-
ketball team won its division title and earned an automatic bid in
the NCAA tournament. The reservation was a pocket of excitement. Crowds jammed around televisions in the HUD houses,
watching on DirecTV satellite. During time-outs, applause erupted
from Red Cliff homes whenever the camera caught Adam at the
edge of the huddle. The women laughed and pointed at him. It was
comic: the short white coach shouting his fierce directions, the
dark NAU players circled around him like a fence. When Adam
patted his teammates' butts, the Apaches jeered louder still. They
made fun of his extra-long shorts, which Lorena Dale worried
would fall down on national television. She said she would have
tightened the waistband if Adam had been back recently. Larson
told her to shut up and watch the game.

Through sheer consistency Adam had advanced to the fourth
forward on the team and was occasionally awarded playing time
when games were no longer close. The Lumberjacks were a strong
regional squad, but they could not compete with giant programs
from major conferences like the Pac-10 or Big East. The tournament had awarded them a fifteenth seed in the first-round game in
Phoenix, against St. John's, the powerhouse out of New York City.
But despite their status as eleven-point underdogs, the Lumberjacks still entered the game believing they had a chance.

Adam watched the first half from the bench, occasionally clapping, then bending low between his knees when the team fell quickly into a seventeen-point deficit. But near the end of the half, they settled down and played strong defense, extending each possession with strings of consecutive passes, and managed to cut St. John's to only a ten-point lead by the buzzer.

Through the second half the Lumberjack players hustled, dove for loose balls, and fouled hard to prevent easy baskets. A team with nothing to lose, they stayed in the game through utter determination; but time was growing short, and the entire starting lineup fell into foul trouble. The clock ticked down to three minutes, they were still behind by eight, and their two best players had fouled out.

A late-game surge carried the Lumberjacks into striking distance—consecutive fast breaks, a three-pointer, and they were only two points down. But on the next possession an overzealous power forward hacked a St. John's player dribbling past him—his last foul as well. NAU's coach fell into hysterics, paced up and down the sideline, then crouched in a dramatic pose, his face in his hands.

Lacking options, he sent Adam into the game.

The Apaches watched Adam on television walking onto the court, pulling up his shorts. He wiped the bottom of his sneakers with his palms, and an unsettled silence blanketed the reservation. But for the next forty seconds he did not touch the ball. The St. John's players ran the clock to just under ten seconds, and Adam, hopping around the court as if stepping on hot coals, was finally able to foul.

"First time kid plays on TV," Larson Dale said, "only thing he does is foul."

St. John's missed both free throws, and with eight seconds left the Lumberjacks used their final time-out. The coach drew up a long pass play to their center at half-court. It called for him to dish it to the dashing guard, who would get a chance at a three-pointer for the upset.

The center was slow to the point. The inbounding forward looked up, saw it would be a mistake to toss it to him, and hurled the ball instead to a surprised Adam open in the corner. He was quickly marked. For an eternal five seconds he drove up the floor, through three defenders, once dribbling behind his back. Past half-court, just as the clock was about to expire, he pumped a fake, drew the careful St. John's guard away from him, and then heaved the basketball from his chest. Hurtling without an arc, it spiked off the backboard glass and banked in.

The packed Phoenix Arena erupted. On television the ESPN announcers screamed themselves hoarse; they replayed the shot seven consecutive times. The entire population of fifteen thousand Apache Indians on the Red Mountain Reservation leapt from secondhand couches, spilled buckets of potato chips, *kee-ahh*-ed, and rolled on the floor in hysterics.

Adam raised his fists and his teammates ran to embrace him; then they remembered there was a final second left on the clock, and they scrambled back to defend the inbound pass. The long throw overshot the St. John's player at midcourt, and the upset belonged to the Lumberjacks and the state of Arizona.

On the reservation the Apaches watched television in tears. It was their finest moment, and suddenly it got better. The ESPN announcer, Shannon Silverstein, was interviewing Adam about the shot. "Adam Dale, when your coach put you in, he never expected you would bring this kind of last-minute luck to your team." She swung the microphone to his mouth.

"Luck! I've practiced that shot my whole life." He was panting, covered in sweat, and hardly thinking about what he was saying. He had never known this kind of euphoria.

She brushed back her golden bangs. "I just mean it was a very long shot." Her mouth closed, her enormous smile faded, and her lips curled in confusion. Lumberjack players swirled behind her, and large hands shot across the television screen to touch Adam and rustle his hair.

"I knew it was going in," he said. He was much taller than the pretty white announcer, and looked down at her. "You ever shot a basketball?"

She put one finger in her ear and gasped, "I'm having trouble hearing you. Congratulations again! Adam Dale, the last-second hero of the game. Now back to you, Jim."

The reservation was in hysterics. It had been years since anyone remembered a moment of such intense Apache pride. Over slow-motion replays and pumped-up rock music, the ESPN announcers yelled, "Adam Dale, out of the Red Cliff, Arizona!"

That Saturday the Lumberjacks lost their second-round game by twenty-five points, but back on campus the student body welcomed the team with a rally. A crowd of five hundred frantic students, shaking banners, were waiting for them, and they chanted his name as he stepped off the bus.

AD-AM! DALE! AD-AM! DALE!

The glory of the NCAA tournament soon faded. Adam graduated and returned jobless to the reservation. At first he pumped gas at the Tom's Store. Then the pastor at the Lutheran church—which Adam used to attend sporadically with his mother—gave him some part-time filing work. After he had been home a month, his father secured him a position with Healthful Nations. Early that fall Healthful Nations organized a diabetes fair in the Cottonwood Gymnasium. Adam was disappointed. Despite balloons, free door prizes, Kool-Aid served in paper cups, and a basketball raffle, the fair was poorly attended, and the microphone didn't work for the announcements. Healthful Nations also ran the Feeding Center. In his pickup Adam delivered food to elders who had no transportation, but he never figured out how to ensure that the elders, and not their families, actually ate the food. Healthful Nations had him organize biannual dental examinations at the Day School, with the Mormon dentist who taught the children to brush in circles and not to forget behind their teeth.

"This Healthful Nations is an okay idea," Adam told his mother, "but I don't know if it's doing any good."

"In this town nobody cares," Lorena said. "You might be the only one."

Red Cliff had a population of twelve hundred people. That year fourteen teenagers killed themselves.

The first was his old friend Garcia Armstrong, who used to swim with him at the creek near White Springs. He sawed off a shotgun and blasted it into his chest. Indian Health Services radioed a helicopter from Navapache Hospital, and in less than forty minutes they had evacuated the young man up over the mountains, across the Sonoran Desert, down to Tucson's University Medical Center, and onto the operation table. By some miracle Garcia survived, and Red Cliff celebrated his return with a party at the Catholic church. The town swamped him with get-well presents; his mother brought his favorite food, Pizza Hut pizza. Six weeks later he shot himself again, successfully.

A plague of copycat suicides followed: dropouts, ex–rodeo stars,

rejected lovers, single mothers, two gay teenagers. The tragedies culminated in a suicide pact: four girls swallowed six bottles
of sleeping pills and left a note claiming a ghost in the eighth-
grade English classroom had ordered them to do it. The deaths
mounted. In the fall of 1998 three separate groups of teenagers
died in drunk-driving accidents. One week after the third accident,
Adam's sister, on a joyride up to the newly opened casino with two
friends, hit an elk and rolled their truck into a tree. Only Verdena
survived.

The night of the car accident, waiting for his sister to be released
from the Navapache emergency room, Adam demanded of his father, "Do something, dammit. You're our councilman. You gotta
do something."

His father acted. He ordered the police to tow the wrecked vehicle up to the Day School playground, next to the ruined dome, and
to keep it there as a warning: this is what happens if young people
drive drunk.

This solution infuriated Adam. Verdena hadn't even *been* drunk.
The very afternoon he heard about the smashed truck on the
school grounds, he hurried into his father's office.

"That's not gonna help, Councilman!"

"What are you talking about?"

"Daniel's pickup. The wrecked-up truck."

"What's going to help, Mr. University?"

"Scaring the kids is the answer? Is that what you think?"

His father stood up at his desk. "You kids! You don't make no
effort. My generation, when we were young, we didn't go out
cruising or nothing. This town was enough for us. We never spoke
to elders the way you speak to us. We respected *tradition*."

Adam sat down on a metal folding chair. "You can't just sit
around wishing times didn't change, wishing we acted like you
when you were young. You're councilman. Ain't it your job to figure out some way to stop this shit?"

His father snorted like an angered horse. "Work our asses off.
Twenty-five years. Hauling wood, chopping trees. Give you kids
everything. And what do your friends know how to do?" He
pointed at Adam. "*Your* friends. Out cruising, drinking and driving. Need to be taught lessons."

"*Enough* with the lessons. There's two kids dead! You put that
car up on the school campus, what the hell does that teach any-

one?" Adam stopped, took a breath, and swiped his face with his hands. "It depresses people, Dad. You know what you gotta do?" He looked up. His father's brow was furrowed, his forehead deeply lined. "You gotta make life *better* than death. You put that car up at school; that's death looking us in the eye, tempting us. You gotta give kids something to *do*."

"Day *you're* councilman, you make the calls," Larson bellowed. "Till that day comes, you shut your mouth and trust me."

"Trust you to do what? Open a casino for old white folk from Phoenix?" Adam swung out his arms. "How about a teen center, or a high school maybe?"

Larson pointed to the door. "Out of here, you son of a bitch! There's things you don't understand. You think you know politics? How to get money together? Winning votes? How to pass laws? Lobbying? You understand nothing. Telling your father what to do! Go on, get outta here then! Why don't you—"

But Adam had already fled the office. He slammed the door behind him so hard, the windows in the hall shook.

He drove his truck to the Lutheran mission to talk to Pastor Wyckoff. In his office the pastor listened for a long time until Adam had told him everything and had no more to say. The pastor said Adam needed to take it easy, let things roll off him a bit more. He told him his father was a decent man and wouldn't let the tribe fail.

They sat silently for a few moments. Adam twisted from side to side on a swiveling desk chair until finally he realized the noise he was making and stopped. The pastor sighed and blew his red nose into a handkerchief. In a soft voice he reassured Adam. "He's good, your father, deep down. He just can't control the rage. There's talent here in this town, you see. Talent. And your father knows it. Just nobody's telling these young people. And they're not going to hear it from outside, from someone like me. All your friends, wanting to die, they don't know what they're worth. What life's worth, for that matter. This suicide, this death wish—it's gypping them. Life's a miracle, Adam. You understand me? I pray your friends will see that. I pray every day they will see that."

Nobody was worse off than Adam's cousin Levi. Since Sparky's death he was gradually losing his mind, and Adam would spot him wandering stoned around the village or hiking into the arroyos, where he hunted cottontail and turkey with the same 9-millimeter pistol his father had died reaching for. Six months after Adam returned from university, his cousin broke into a shack and robbed a blind mother of two. Nobody pursued him. With an air of invincibility, Levi walked freely around town.

"Do something!" Adam urged his father again. "You gotta talk to him." But the councilman did nothing.

In January the Apache police were on high alert after a series of break-ins. The crimes followed the same pattern: a window busted in with a thin metal rod. Everyone knew that Levi—tripping, high on something—was robbing the houses. He grew so brazen, one Sunday he even broke into the Dales' place. Late in the morning Lorena and Marie Anne pulled up the driveway and saw the young man, a rifle across his shoulder, a sandwich in his mouth, hopping the rusted fence at the back of the camp. The kitchen was turned over, he had stolen a pocketknife and an extra set of house keys, but he had found no money.

The next night he broke into the Catholic church's trailer, the home of the female deacon. At two in the morning he forced his way into her garage, gave her dog a pound of frozen hamburger, and scared her awake. She fled in her nightgown across the playground to the Lutheran mission.

Now Councilman Dale had no choice but to allow the police to find Levi and put him away. Adam dreaded news of the arrest, but for two days his father came home complaining his nephew had disappeared. The tribal police couldn't locate him.

Levi appeared five nights after the robbery at the foot of Adam's mattress. Adam awoke to a rough shove of his leg, and opening his eyes, he saw the dim figure of his cousin, fingering the bobcat pelt on the floor. Adam did not know what to do. With quiet steps he led Levi to the kitchen and gave him some cold frybread, which his cousin folded in half and devoured in a few bites. Adam shook his head and told Levi he could crash there a few hours, but he had to get out by dawn, since the police were stopping by pretty often and giving their father updates. They climbed onto the mattress together. Levi smelled like a stale watering hole. He whispered he had been hiding up in a trailer out by Medicine Ranch, but he didn't have nothing to eat and was afraid to go to the Tom's Store because he'd be caught.

In the morning when Adam awoke, Levi was gone. At the

kitchen counter, toasting bread for breakfast, he told his mother he knew where his cousin was and asked what he should do.

"One day you're going to have to find the strength to go against your father," Lorena said. "I never had it, and look what he's done to me." She spoke quietly, as if talking to herself. Adam realized for the first time her hair was ashen. Her words were garbled from so many years of not hearing her own voice. "We raised you to be strong. Strong as possible. I wonder we raised you strong enough to do what's hard. Even if you're told not to. We raise you strong enough to make up your own mind?"

Adam said nothing.

Three days later he came home from a long afternoon—he had skipped work at Healthful Nations and shared half of a case of MGD with his old school friends. Mom and Verdena were in town, shopping. His father was out, probably up at the casino. Adam answered two loud knocks on the backdoor, and there Levi stood, dirtier than the other night—with mud streaked across his cheeks—and thinner, more nervous. His slightest movements were uneasy; still, when he greeted Adam, his maniacal laugh held a sickening note of innocence.

Adam slapped his cousin's hand in greeting. "You got the munchies again, eh, Leev?"

In the kitchen he fried some grilled cheese and bologna sandwiches for both of them. At the table Adam said, "Shit, man. You stink like hell. Family won't be back for a while. Go take a shower."

He brought Levi a bath towel. When he heard the water running, Adam strode into the kitchen and dialed the tribal police. In three minutes they had stormed the house and were arresting his cousin in the shower. They dragged him out naked. His slimy hair was matted and dripping. From across the living room his red eyes flashed at Adam. Stoic, Adam tried to stare back, but found his gaze pulled to the floor. The police held Levi tight; he did not struggle. They dragged a shirt over him and were directing his legs into his underwear when he called out to Adam: "Before my father got shot, know who took 20 percent of the drug money?"

Adam looked up and stepped back.

"Your dad," Levi said. "Twenty percent, fucker."

The police put the handcuffs on him.

"Twenty percent to the tribal councilman, isn't it?"

They led Levi out of the house. They pushed him through the doorway and he stumbled over the uneven porch. He shouted, "Hey, Adam, remember the teen center?" Suddenly he laughed — an insane squawk. The police forced him into the jeep, and Levi yelled one final time before the door slammed:

"Thanks, cousin!"

They were the last words Adam heard from him. He was locked up in Blackriver on multiple charges, then sent to maximum security in the desert down by Winkelman.

That afternoon Adam drove to the Lutheran Mission again, seeking some kind of forgiveness. The pastor made coffee in the Sunday School kitchen and served it to Adam in a mug with a big green cross on it. Adam asked if he thought calling the police on Levi had been a sin. The pastor told him, the way he saw it, he'd done nothing he needed to be forgiven for, nothing to be ashamed of. They were the words Adam needed to hear, but somehow he was not reassured.

Late that night his father accosted him in the kitchen. "My nephew would have been caught himself, but you gotta turn him in. You know what a traitor is? They teach you that at university?"

They stood silent, practically nose to nose. Now in the leathery wrinkles of his father's face, Adam saw it, spelled out: the rage. Adam understood that rage now — he knew it himself, it was his inheritance — and he could not forgive him it. He had no doubt he would kill the man if he moved even the slightest muscle toward him.

Larson must have sensed it. He turned and stomped through the house out to the backyard. Adam watched his steady course toward the wooden backboard he had built for them fourteen years ago. He watched Larson heave his shoulder against the rotten pole, cursing; he watched the pole bend against his weight and finally crack halfway up its height. He watched the makeshift basket fall, and Larson crush it, snapping pieces beneath his boots. He watched his father kick the backboard frame over to the rusting refrigerator of past days of rage, and stumble out of the yard, secure in the knowledge that the desecration of the family was complete.

Adam had his sister drive him over the pass to Highway 60. At the Turnoff Verdena swerved onto the gravel shoulder, stopped Adam's pickup, then cut the engine. "Where ya going?"

"I dunno. But I won't be back. Verdena?"

"What?"

Adam shook his head, looking straight at the intersection. "You'll get outta here—to college or something."

She hesitated, reached into her purse, felt around, and pulled out an abalone shell, the one she had worn for her Sunrise Dance. "Here."

Adam closed his fingers around the textured shell—smooth and warm. He climbed out of the truck and lifted the duffle bag from the rear of the bed. Verdena leaned through the window. "Hey!"

"Yeah."

The engine roared. Adam was fingering the sharp corner of the shell with his thumb.

"I ain't going nowhere," his sister said. "I'll be here."

"Yeah."

"I mean it."

"Yeah."

The truck circled back in the dust, picked up speed, and grew smaller in the hazy distance. Its bumper flashed as it rounded a curve and was gone.

Vowing never to return, Adam hitched a ride in a Winnebago with some senior citizens down to Phoenix, where they dropped him off at the Greyhound Bus Terminal. He wanted to keep moving, to get as far away as possible. A white banner draped above the ticket counter announced a special: SIXTY-THREE DOLLARS TO ANYWHERE. From Phoenix the bus crossed New Mexico to Amarillo: then he was on to Houston, New Orleans, up the Mississippi River to Birmingham, Memphis, all the way to Pittsburgh, then across the last stretch of the continent toward New York City.

Three days of buses, terminal toilets, and fast food had sickened him, and when he arrived at the Port Authority, he was shaken by the crowds. The people of the city came in colors he had never seen; they rushed at him from all directions. They seemed to know where they were going and wanted to get there fast. Outside the information kiosk on the second floor, he leafed through a free copy of the Village Voice and found an advertisement for a cheap hotel.

He'd bus tables, he'd mop floors; he'd give New York a try. And if it wasn't far enough, he'd go farther: other countries, other continents. Jeff was always inviting him out to Istanbul. Hell, he'd go there.

8

ON A FRIDAY AFTERNOON, wearing his striped Chinese Addiddass sweatpants, Anarbek hurried through Kyzyl Adyr–Kirovka. He pushed his lumbering frame into the *pochta,* shoved past the scarved Russian babushkas fighting to collect their late pensions, and leaned on the cracked counter.

"Beautiful!" he called in his loud, exultant voice.

He was beckoning the postwoman, Altin Eje. She had two moles on both sides of her nostrils, a swollen throat, thinning gray hair, and a mouth full of scattered gold teeth. The teeth that were not gold were missing. Altin Eje scuttled to the counter and blushed, as she always did when he teased her.

"Come away with me, Altin Eje. We can ride my horse into the mountains."

"Only to meet your seven other women there. Not me. I'm no fool."

"Oh!" Anarbek said. He turned to the crowd of old women. "Did you hear that? Did you hear what she said to me?"

The babushkas were not amused by his game. They wanted their pensions.

"Do you have anything for me, Altin Eje?"

He was hoping for the certificate of deposit. The government payments lagged, skipped months, but just when Anarbek thought that the factory oversight had at last been reported and the payments had dried up, the money always seemed to arrive again.

"Nothing from Bishkek," Altin Eje said. She sifted through a shoebox full of letters, yellowed with age, and found a crisp envelope, conspicuous in its poorly shaped Cyrillic letters, the kind sloppy first-formers scribbled before they learned to write. She handed it to him. "This is from the American, I think."

"Great. Big thanks, Altin Eje."

"Good leaving."

"Good staying."

Anarbek examined the envelope, postmarked in smudged red ink: January 12, Istanbul. Disappointed, he saved the letter for Nazira to translate. He stepped outside again into the bright village afternoon, ignoring the smell of a smoking pile of trash, and hurried opposite the park and the statue of Lenin into the bazaar, where the Kurdish milkmaids called to him. At the butcher Nurgazi's table he shook hands, scrutinizing the cuts.

"*Aaaaaasalaaam aleikum!*"

"*Aleikum asalaam.*"

"How much a kilo?"

"Twelve som," Nurgazi said. "Take it."

Anarbek clicked his tongue. "I'll kill my own for that much. How does anyone afford to eat in this village, with you selling meat at such a price?"

"I haven't sold a piece all morning," Nurgazi said.

"Give me a half-kilo of the kielbasa."

Three times a day Anarbek visited the bazaar. He bought kilos of rice and stringy mutton, plastic toys and bars of Iranian soap, and even the inedible cabbage salad from the Koreans. Everyone was grateful; often it was the only sale they made that day. Nobody considered that his small family—Lola, Baktigul, and young Oolan—had no possible use for so much stuff. His efforts had kept half the village fed. The people of Kyzyl Adyr–Kirovka depended on the funds he distributed, and for seven years he had trusted their discretion. Nobody mentioned the cheeseless cheese factory. It remained, he thought, a village secret.

At Yuri Samonov's alcohol kiosk he eyed glinting bottles of lemon vodka, an expensive pepper vodka, and three cans of German beer.

"I'm celebrating, Yuri. I really need champagne."

"No champagne today. But you should try this cognac, Anarbek *agai*. Or some vodka. Highest quality."

Noted geologist Yuri Samonov held up the bottle of homemade vodka. The Stolichnaya label he had glued on its front was peeling. There was no champagne, but Anarbek had to buy something. He was keeping the geologist alive.

He watched for a second the sad man before him—the displaced Russian mired in his swamp of suffering. A month before, Yuri had lost his only son to the copper-wire epidemic. Across the nation young kids were dying, their bodies charred. In a national shortage the value of copper wire had increased twenty-five times. People bartered with the scrap metal in the markets, then vendors melted it into ingots and sold it to wandering Chinese traders. Young men from penniless families succumbed to the temptation of lunatic acts. They scaled poplar trees, telephone poles, or rusting steel towers in an effort to snip the wire. Not only were these children plundering the antiquated electrical grid, but they were setting entire districts of cities, entire regions of the mountains, back into darkness.

The president had declared a national emergency. The declaration had not helped Yuri's teenage son. Last month on the dirt road along the reservoir, clutching a set of pliers, the boy had scaled a power pole. He had believed he was safe because his friends had stolen the wires connected at both ends of the structure. But he had lost his balance and grabbed hold of a metal bar hanging between two chipped ceramic insulators. The live current devoured his hand, raced through his insides, tore his intestines and groin, seared the inner right thigh, and then threw him, smoking, twenty feet to the ground. The boy's friends had found the body. Yuri had been drunk ever since.

Anarbek pointed to a box of Israeli bonbons.

"How much is the chocolate?"

"Thirty-five som."

"Thirty-five som! You cheat me every day, Yuri. I can't believe it. Give me one."

"Take it, brother."

"And—another one."

"Thank you, brother. Good going."

"Good staying."

In his tan Lada Anarbek tossed the letter from the American, the kielbasa, and the box of bonbons onto the passenger seat, tightened the rearview mirror, and drove an hour out of town, thirty kilometers past the village of Ak Su. He hurtled by the dreamlike mountains and mud farmhouses, the blackbirds perched on grazing horses, and he let his mind wander, anticipating the pleasures of the evening ahead, until he turned south off the main road onto a dirt track. The small holes he had been avoiding became craters. He slalomed toward the Ala Too mountains, and the track climbed and swept through dusty curves, through fields of wheat and patches of potatoes. He passed a donkey cart piled with tinder. When he honked, the driver waved back with a whip.

It was difficult to imagine a village more isolated than Kyzyl Adyr–Kirovka, but here it was: a solemn collection of mud-brick homes without a name. He pulled around the abandoned one-room village school and at the next house sounded the horn.

Darika appeared in her soiled velvet work vest, patting her face, adjusting her scarf, and blushing. Her young blush thrilled him.

"*Salamatsizbih,*" he said.

"*Salamatchilik.*"

"Come to Talas with me."

"I cannot." She approached the car. "We're canning strawberries. You didn't tell me you were coming."

"How can I tell you I'm coming? You have no telephone. What can I use? Satellites? Smoke signals?"

Darika coughed in the dust. "Women have to work, don't you realize?"

He leaned over and found one box of chocolate on the passenger floor. It had slid under the front seat, its contents had melted, and each heavy turn had crushed the box against the door.

"Here. I brought these for you."

"You can bring something more useful than chocolate next time. Like flour."

"Come to Talas with me. We'll get flour for your family."

Darika rested her hands on her hips; she looked at the ground and back up at his car. Her black felt vest hugged her figure; her ruddy cheeks thrilled him more and more as he stared at her. He had spotted her last fall in the Talas bazaar, eyeing a plastic Chinese mirror on a low plywood table. He had haggled and bought it for her for thirteen som, and he had taken her back to Talas three times since then.

"Let me tell my mother." Darika disappeared behind the gate.

Anarbek cleared his throat and spit. He flung his elbows twice behind his back and opened and closed his fingers in front of him, imitating the cosmonauts he had once seen on television. He was as strong as ever. He stuck out his chest and breathed the fresh spring air, remembering twenty-nine years ago, when he had wooed his first wife, Baiooz. He was aging, it was true, but his power of persuasion had diminished little. He would be no slave to time.

Darika returned wearing a fluffy pink jacket. In the car he readjusted the rearview mirror, which kept shifting with the potholes. As they bumped along the road to Ak Su, Darika opened the box of melted bonbons and ate them in little bird bites. Once Anarbek swerved the vehicle so hard she was thrown against him. He stopped on a hill overlooking the northern Talas Mountains, lit golden in the afternoon sun. Through a distant pass the yellow Kazakh steppe stretched to the horizon. Anarbek shut off the engine, leaned over, and kissed the young woman, first on her cheek and, when she turned her head, on her chocolate-stained lips. She did not resist. She hardly moved.

The main road into Talas was lined with poplars planted by past generations of Young Pioneers. The car jounced by the button factory, two abandoned collective farms, and the crowded orphanage at recess. In the center of town, in a park overgrown with thistles, seven boys on horseback were playing *oolak* with a lamb carcass. He pointed as they passed.

"I used to be the best in the whole Talas region."

"I heard. People from Kyzyl Adyr are known to ride well."

"I had the longest arms and I had no fear. The other men couldn't catch me. And I stole the sheep in the crowd without them knowing. There are secrets."

"What were your secrets?"

"They're secret. I still play."

"You're too old."

"Too old, nothing!" he boomed. "I still play."

"You'd break an arm. You're too old to ride fast and steal sheep."

"Careful, or I'll steal you."

"And what will your wife say then?"

The Talas bazaar was twice the size of Kyzyl Adyr–Kirovka's. Anarbek searched for champagne and finally found a Russian lady selling two bottles between piles of turnips.

"*Atkooda?*" he asked. Where'd you get this?

"It's from Moldova."

"No, where did you *find* it?"

"It was an anniversary present."

"Give me one."

They also bought a sack of flour. Two boys helped him drag it to the Lada and plop it into the trunk, sinking the car in a billow of white smoke.

In the central town square, Anarbek took the long way, around the park, to avoid the former hall of sports. They drove past the broken Ferris wheel. Though children tried to push it, the enormous machine was ancient and rusty and, with a will of its own, moved only when the wind blew in from the steppes. Recently five children had climbed into one of the swinging cars, the wind had blown, and they had been stuck at the top for three straight nights. The telephone wires above the Ferris wheel had disappeared.

His secret apartment was in Microregion 4. Everybody knew where it was, and most people suspected what he did there, though he hinted at these assignations only to his closest friends in the sauna. The stairwell smelled of urine and the lights did not work. He fumbled in the darkness of the second-floor apartment until he finally found the circuit. They plugged in the cement hot plates and Darika started the chai. He lounged on the embroidered *tushuks,* the only furniture on the bare floor, while she served him steaming cup after cup. They bit into chocolates and he opened the champagne.

To health.

To friendship.

They chased shots of champagne with bites of kielbasa. Darika protested, pretending she'd had enough.

To Talas.

To family.

She was giggling and swallowing bonbons whole.

To flour.

To us.

When the bottle of champagne was empty, Darika stuffed and swaying, Anarbek rose.

"Where are you going?"

"More champagne," he said, slipping on his plastic sandals. "I'll just run to the bazaar. I'm coming right back."

She leaned back on the red *tushuk* as he closed the door, a suspicious smile on her face.

He hustled over to the Talas telegraph, where he could call Lola and make some kind of excuse. But as he passed the police station, he saw the all-too-familiar figure approaching—shoulders hunched, elbows splayed out to his sides—and it was too late to turn away.

"Anarbek!"

He feigned surprise. "Bolot *agai!*"

They greeted each other with a handshake and the usual courtesies.

"I haven't seen you in two months," the privatization official said. The man's doughy chin had doubled—he was growing heavier each time Anarbek saw him. He had on a bent pair of glasses, and his shoes, usually scrubbed to a shine, were chalky from the dust of the street. Bolot dug into his pocket with one fist, then held out a handful of roasted sunflower seeds in offering, and Anarbek accepted them and dropped them into his own pocket, trying to calm himself.

"I've meant to—to stop by your office," Anarbek fumbled. "I have last month's payment."

"And this month's?"

Anarbek couldn't say that he had already distributed it. "Yes, yes, that too."

Bolot set him at ease with a smile and a wave of the hand. "You can forget it, Anarbek. Forget both months."

"Really?"

"Really. It's a favor from me to you." The official spit a sunflower seed on the ground and draped one short arm around Anarbek's shoulders; they walked across the street. Over the past three years Bolot had often described the many pleasures of married life—after a long search he'd found a wife, and they'd quickly had a son—but now he was complaining about the heavy responsibilities of a family. He led Anarbek to a beer stand, where on a grimy bench beneath a plane tree they sat down.

"As I said, you can keep the money from the past two months. I'm going to need more than that."

Anarbek's head shot up. "How much more?"

"Twelve thousand dollars."

"Bolot *agai,*" he pleaded, "I can't pay that."

"Now I know you've been hoarding money, Anarbek, all these years. It's no secret, your apartment here in town, your fancy sauna. The presents you've been buying certain ladies. You have your needs, but I have needs too. My wife would like to buy a house in Bishkek. We're cramped in our old apartment. Micro-region 8. Twenty minutes outside the city, on a busy road. We don't even have a garden. And she would like another child."

"But I tell you, I don't have that kind of money."

"I tend to think you do."

"Twelve thousand dollars." Anarbek looked up. "And what if I don't pay it?"

Bolot Ismailov gripped his shoulder. His nails were neatly cut and clean, but his stubby fingers smelled of the blood of butchered sheep. He pulled Anarbek closer. "It's a simple matter. You pay. Or I report the factory to the capital. You'll be shut down in a month."

"You couldn't do that. Our village depends on the cheese factory, Bolot."

"Cheese factory! What cheese? What factory? Your village depends on me. And my generosity has limits, like any man's." Bolot let go of him. "You think you're the only one? I'm being squeezed too. I've risked my own job for what I've done for you, Tashtana-liev. Twelve thousand dollars. In dollars!" he warned with a hiss of his vinegar breath. "Not this worthless *som* crap. And the bills better be new. Nothing before 1991." He stood.

"When do you need it?"

Bolot bit down on his bottom lip, made a fuss of adjusting his collar, and straightened his tie. "I need it now, Anarbek."

"I won't pay this!"

He stretched out his arms and shrugged. "Either way, you'll pay." With that he walked off toward the telegraph station.

Anarbek got up, brushed off his pants, and spun twice around, his heart galloping. It frightened him that this man, not even from his village, knew so much about him. Where would he get this kind of money? No, he decided, it was impossible! Bolot was lying. He would not report the leaking funds; he needed his graft. But then, what if he did?

Shaken, Anarbek forgot about the telephone call to Lola. He staggered over to the Talas bazaar, found the turnip woman, and bought the last bottle of champagne.

In the apartment Darika was already asleep. Anarbek peeled off her clothes, first her velvet vest and then her thin floral blouse. He unhitched her skirt and tore it in the process, tossing it against the cement wall; then he yanked off her bra. She hardly needed a bra: it had been a flattering present from him, bought in the Talas bazaar the last time they had met. The bulbs of her young breasts perked up in the frigid air.

"It's c-cold," she said sleepily, crossing her arms.

And he was over her, his stomach flailing urgently, his chest hair awash in sweat. His mind strobed in flashes: dying cows, his wives, Bolot, and this life that would not offer the slightest respite. He barely felt Darika beneath him. The village girl clawed at his back and breathed in desperate spurts. Her flushed eyes spun at the touch of his hands. Then suddenly it was no good; he felt—nothing. This had never happened to him before.

"Don't you love me?" she asked.

"Yes, yes. One day—I'll take you—to America," he managed. And he collapsed, rolling off her. They lay awhile in silence on their backs, his hands propped behind his head, and soon he found himself drifting in and out of an uneasy sleep.

Anarbek dreamed he was flying in an airplane, a luxurious multifloored vehicle like the one he had seen in *Air Force One,* starring Harrison Ford, on the Moscow channel last week. Unlike the film, the villains of his dream were not nuclear terrorists from Kazakhstan, but Bolot and that young Traktorbek and a gang of Talas *hooligani*. In the dream Bolot once again demanded twelve thousand dollars. Anarbek refused. The men threatened his wife and children; and they also threatened his mistress Darika. He still refused. He was armed with his hunting rifle, the one he used for shooting pheasants. His enemies were unarmed, but they had seen many Jackie Chan and Steven Seagal films—they had lethal limbs.

Action music played in the background of the dream while he hid behind piles of suitcases and picked off young thugs as they spun kicking in his direction. The emergency door opened, and in a flash and a roll he somersaulted down the aisle and slammed the butt of his rifle into Traktorbek's gut, spinning him out of the aircraft at ten thousand meters.

Nobody was flying the plane! They had killed both pilots! Anarbek jumped behind the computer control panel, pushing buttons, steering, searching the rearview mirror that kept coming loose.

"Damn thing," he yelled, tightening it.

Action music grew louder. He spotted Bolot making a final dash and picked him off with his rifle. With the other hand he steered the plane amid flashes of lightning. The Kyrgyz-speaking air-traffic controller directed him through the storm. He glided the airplane over the Golden Gate Bridge and landed safely in San Francisco. Bill Clinton and Monica Lewinsky had been hiding on board. Anarbek had saved their lives and was now a world hero. Before he awoke, the American people slaughtered many sheep in his honor.

"Twelve thousand dollars. Twelve thousand dollars," he mumbled as he drove Darika back the next morning. The vehicle, laden with the sack of flour, could make it uphill only in second gear.

On his return to Kyzyl Adyr–Kirovka he found Nazira at his house, eating lunch on the tea bed with his wife and two of the neighbors. In the breezy shade of the courtyard, his grandson, Manas, and his own son, Oolan, chased Baktigul around the walnut tree. At the sight of him Lola left the platform and vanished into the kitchen. The neighbors glared. Nazira frowned, her gentle face darkening a deep red that covered her freckles. She followed him inside to the sitting room. "Did you have a good night, Ata?"

He hesitated. "Of course."

"Where were you this time?"

He wanted to say, "The sauna." But just as it had once been impossible to lie to her mother, he found it increasingly difficult to lie to Nazira. She had inherited Baiooz's power of detection. Directed at her searching eyes, a lie fell flat.

He stared at her, not knowing what to say. She was a wonder, as lovely as the moon. He had seen her last week at the May Day parade playing the *kumooz*, the tips of her fingers working at breathtaking speed. She could play the instrument upside-down and even behind her back. She slaughtered sheep. She could beat many of the village men at racing a horse. She danced in the annual harvest festival with grace and improvisation that enraptured the crowds. And despite her endless talents, like him she too was ruined.

He sank deep into the sofa, his mind racing, until his daughter said, "Lola is not stupid, Ata."

"I never thought she was."

"This is not a good way to treat a marriage. A marriage I set up."

"You do not understand," Anarbek pleaded.

"What would Ama think?"

"This is not a daughter's place to say."

"You seemed to love Lola, and I went out of my way for you. There were difficulties."

"Has Lola done badly for herself? She has everything she needs and wants."

"Except a loyal husband."

"Nazira."

"It is one thing to marry a man twice your age. But you would expect such a man to respect you."

"I take good care of her."

Nazira clicked her tongue. "She's not your daughter. She's your wife. She needs more than to be taken care of."

"It's not the same." He stood and walked to the wooden cabinet, where he kept a collection of pirated beta cassettes—Schwarzenegger, Bruce Lee, Jean-Claude Van Damme. He ran his gnarled fingers along the titles.

"What's not the same?" she asked.

He faced his daughter but tripped over his words. "She doesn't seem—I don't feel—"

"Did you treat Ama like this?"

This was too much. He lurched forward with an angry stomp and stood tall before her. But Nazira stayed on the offensive and quickly added, "*Oui-at bay sin bah!*"—You should be ashamed. She turned her back and hurried to the doorway, where she stood facing away, thinking. This ability to punish with her back, he realized, was an instinct entirely her own.

He remembered the letter from the American—the first they had received in two years. That would change the subject. That would please his daughter. He left the house and went back to the car, where he fished around on the floor for the envelope and found it encrusted in golden dust.

When he showed Nazira the letter and told her it was from Jeff, she flushed and tore it open. He listened as she read the strange English aloud, then translated it sentence by sentence for him into Kyrgyz. The letter was unusual: it mentioned Nazira twice and specifically asked if they were able to get by, if they needed some money. Midway through, her voice grew soft and she looked up at the cracked plaster ceiling, searching for the right words.

Anarbek was filled with great hope. Why had he not thought of him? Of course! Their old friend! The American! *All problems have solutions.*

9

IN A HOT, POORLY LIT office on the European side of Istanbul, Jeff struggled to get off the telephone. "Thanks," he said. "Yeah, thanks. Thank you for your help. I know you went out of your way. Thanks again."

He placed the phone down with a sweaty hand, cutting the connection to Damascus. The hollow receiver weighed almost nothing. Insubstantial, he thought. In America telephones weighed something.

"Are you all right?" Andrew asked from behind Jeff. "Bad news, I suspect?"

"Suicide." Jeff fingered his goatee and stared at his desktop. "This Palestinian I interviewed. Alwan Said. Killed himself. I was the one who told him he didn't have a case."

"Did he have a case, Jeff?"

He lifted his head and turned to his boss, the dark mustached Kuwaiti. There was authority in his British inflections — high pitched, intelligent, yet callous. The voice told all: too many years of processing refugees. You see great suffering and people become faceless. Jeff had promised himself he'd never stay around long enough to let it happen to him.

He said, "Canada might have taken him."

Andrew nodded. "Canada's doors open wider sometimes."

"He was former PLO."

"Frightful mistake."

"It would have come out eventually, right? State Department check."

"Who can say with that?" Andrew tapped the corner of Jeff's computer monitor. "Slight chance it wouldn't have mattered. Quite honestly—"

"You should have seen this guy, Andrew. He was burly. His nose was broken in a hundred places. He comes right out and tells me he's a boxer, and that once, as a teenager, he served with the PLO. Wants to know if either will hurt his claim." His boss was listening, shifting on his feet. Jeff shrugged and managed a smile. "I laughed. What could I do but laugh? He had no case. I told him there was no way our State Department would clear him. My last day in Damascus, he comes back and tells me to forget it. He wasn't former PLO. He took it back. Wants to know if he could erase it from the record."

Jeff raised his eyes. Above his desk the fluorescent ceiling lights were blurry with dead insects. He lifted a pen and twisted the cap. He had told Alwan Said it was impossible—he couldn't erase his past. But if the man had simply lied from the start, they would have gone ahead with the case. They would have interviewed him for refugee status, written up the application, and sent the poor guy to Utah or North Dakota, somewhere safe and quiet in America. The United States: that exclusive club, for which he now moderated the invitations.

Andrew was feigning patience, nodding slightly. "I've been doing this twenty years, Jeff, and worse things have happened. You were simply doing your job." There was exhaustion in his tone.

Jeff opened a random application folder. "The job is placing refugees. We didn't help him."

Andrew laid a hand on his shoulder, then walked off in stiff long strides, and that was supposed to be the end of it. Jeff returned to the piles of papers cascading across his desk. Nearly three years on this job, and he had been behind from the very start. He should have been more organized; he needed efficiency, detachment. But these stacks of profiles would have intimidated anyone. Lives hung in the balance—a person's future, a family's safety—while they waited in hostile lands for him to get to the bottom of this pile.

He straightened the papers, signed a completed application, dated it January 11, and closed the folder. Inside his drawer he fumbled for a lemon cough drop. As much as he loved this old city on the sea, Istanbul had the dirtiest air he had ever breathed. His throat was permanently sore, and in the evenings, when he blew his nose, the tissue turned a sooty black. He slipped the lozenge onto his tongue, tossed the wrapper back into the drawer, and swallowed in pain.

Since he had left Kyrgyzstan, life had led Jeff in unexpected directions. With the Peace Corps readjustment allowance, he had traveled alone for the summer through Southeast Asia, from Tashkent to Bangkok to Hong Kong to Jakarta and back to Bangkok. In what seemed an endless flight, he had finally crossed over Asia to Turkey. The variety of foods served by the stewardess was disquieting. In that plane he had seen for the first time a woman with pierced eyebrows breastfeeding her baby. It hit him: things had changed; he was returning to a world two years older than the one he had left.

He put off the inevitable last leg of his flight to the States. In Istanbul he taught English for six months, living first in a hostel and then sharing an apartment with an Australian graduate student. Jeff was losing touch with his former life: he had not written to his college friends in over a year, had never answered a letter from a high school girlfriend, and for months put off sending his new address to Adam. He spoke to his father in Idaho once on the telephone, a stilted five-minute conversation in which Jeff assured him that he was in good health and asked him to forward his mail. Hearing his father's voice after two years had shaken him. The person on the telephone, mentioning a wife Jeff had never met, was not the same man he once knew. He didn't miss him, not in the least.

That first year in Istanbul he received sporadic letters from Kyrgyzstan. The mail took up to three months, if ever, to reach him from the village by way of America. (His father forwarded mail faithfully; he could be relied on for that, if nothing else.) At first he received no replies to the letters he had written to Anarbek and the factory workers, only desperate notes in Russian and broken English, asking why he never wrote back, demanding he not forget them. In the margins the adults penciled little birds carrying packages or shadowed hearts with arrows—a sweet habit they retained from grade school. With his Russian dictionary Jeff pored over the letters, puzzled by the rough Cyrillic handwriting, but savoring the taste of a distant land he thought lost to him.

In April that year he received two letters from the Tashtanalievs. One, a single page from Anarbek, written on the notebook paper that also doubled as toilet paper in the village outhouses, told of failing electricity, a devastating drought, and the first-ever Kyzyl Adyr–Kirovka election for an *akim,* which had ended in violence. The factory salaries had skipped a month, making it impossible for Anarbek to keep up with payments.

The second letter, from Nazira, was still more disturbing. Written in a careful, loping English script, it consisted almost entirely of Kyrgyz pleasantries (*How is your work? How is your family? How is your health? Here our health is fine.*), but in a single line toward the bottom of the last page, Nazira wrote in capital letters that she loved him. He read both letters twice, full of deep shame; and unsure what to do, he told himself he would deal with the letters later and buried them under a pile of old correspondence.

He had come upon the advertisement for the job with the Development of Human Resource Organization in the *Turkish Daily News.* Based in Istanbul, the position required experience in counseling, teaching, and living overseas. The DHRO staff interviewed him in their drab office, a converted bakery in the old embassy district on the European side, and hired him on the spot. Over the two-month refugee-repatriation training, his boss, a former UNHCR worker, would count on his fingers and intone: "Your job is to do two simple things. Verify the facts. Verify the claim."

Verifying the facts meant reams of personal forms for each refugee: name, date of birth, place of birth, nation of origin, spouse's name, children's ages, medical history. It all seemed simple enough—the kind of information a schoolchild should know. But sometimes verifying the facts took days. The refugees did not know their dates of birth. Jeff was trained to list all Somalis as born on February 10, all Iraqis as born on April 4, and all Sudanese as born on August 15. The refugees could not spell their names in English, and Jeff did not know Arabic. They claimed they had been born in countries—Kurdistan, Palestine, and Chechnya—that did not exist, and they refused to allow another nation's name to be written on the forms. It would take hours of patient needling and translating for Jeff to explain that, unless they complied with the rules, their applications for American resettlement would be void.

When he had verified the facts, it was time to verify the claim. Through the translator he asked two simple questions:

"Why did you leave where you came from?"

"Why can't you stay where you ran to?"

With a stone face Jeff would listen to tales of rape, torture, persecution, and flight. In his very first case he processed a Lebanese man who had paid smugglers to ship him to Italy. The smugglers kept him locked in their boat's cargo hole for seven days, then finally pulled him out and told him he had arrived. The man left the boat, spent a happy afternoon admiring bikini-clad tourists on the black stone beach, and then discovered he was in Cyprus, not Italy, trapped on an island in the Mediterranean without a penny, a document, or a single friend. The tale at first seemed far-fetched; but as the weeks progressed, Jeff came to understand it was typical.

He wrote everything on the applications, whether the person had lied or not. If the story seemed impossible to believe—strange diseases, unprovoked cruelties, wild coincidences—still he documented it. One person's truths were as impossible to believe as another's lies. He did not judge; he was simply their advocate. He interviewed Baha'ists who could not worship in Iran, a Sudanese woman whose toes had been cut off, and Kurds rejected at every border, unwanted anywhere. Jeff wrote it all down. In this, the daily struggle for resettlement, he had never worked harder. He was helping change lives, making his small difference.

He saw now that he had floated through his twenties, adrift on waves of good intentions, from country to country, but this job, more than his others, had anchored him. It had provided an apartment, the opportunity for monthly travel, a modest living, and a sense of being useful. It was no small satisfaction to think he had remained in one place for four years, but those years were starting to feel like ages, and sometimes he felt the currents tugging again.

The lemon cough drop had not yet dissolved in his mouth before the phone rang once more. He ignored it. A sudden movement in the front office vestibule had caught his attention. Hurrying around the desks to the soundproof windows, he saw that another family had come.

Somehow they kept getting the office's address. The Development of Human Resource Organization did not advertise services, so it was a mystery how these people learned that they placed refugees. Perhaps relatives living in the States, or a family the office had once processed, tipped them off. The DHRO operated under Christian auspices—Andrew was convinced that local churches were referring them. It made no difference; they found their way.

The organization maintained a strict policy against assisting people who walked in off the streets. If they listened to a single case like this, hundreds more of the Middle East's destitute and homeless would soon flood the office.

Now, thick arms outstretched, the security guard was following policy and herding an entire family—the mother and daughters in sequined headscarves, the father in a ragged suit jacket—out the door. The woman, clutching to her chest a baby wrapped in sacking material, was trying to rein in two runny-nosed toddlers behind her. The guard was at first patient and polite; but the father forced his way back in, and Jeff sensed violence. Through the glass he heard the muffled voices—"*Olamaz!*" and "*Bir dakika!*"—as the father, dirty stubble on his weathered face, refused to leave. The man's voice rose. He wanted to state his case. The guard shoved him back, two hands to the chest.

Armenian? Kurdish? Iraqi? Jeff couldn't tell. The baby wailed as Jeff stepped into the vestibule. He could smell the putrid smoke in their clothes, the familiar sweat and sheep-stench of some distant village.

The guard was delivering his set piece in Turkish. "Call and make an appointment," he was saying. This man probably did not have enough change for a phone call, never mind enough for the bus ride back to their ghetto. "Contact the Red Crescent Society by mail," he was telling them. But Jeff wondered what the chances were that they could even write.

The father would not be denied. His wife was pulling him out the door, but he ripped his hand from her grasp, and when the security guard touched his shoulder, he flung that hand off as well. The guard's eyes narrowed. Jeff stepped between him and the family.

He smiled and told the guard, "*Ben, ben.*" Me, me.

He turned to the father: "*Dinliyorum.*" I'm listening.

Chest heaving, the man examined Jeff. His eyes rose and fell and settled on his red silk tie. He spoke. He unfolded his tale of woe: the descriptions of poverty and the great distance they had traveled, the abuses they had suffered, the injustice of it all. Jeff could understand only a few of the words, yet he knew well the rising intonation, the glistening eyes and rapid hands, and he listened and nodded. After a minute he lifted a pen and paper from the reception desk and with the guard's help wrote down the family's name.

He kept nodding as he wrote the baby's name and the children's names and the wife's name and the father's name. He gave them one of the DHRO's business cards and told them to call tomorrow, miming the word *call*.

The father, having been allowed to speak, now accepted the shoves of the guard out the door. The thick metal clanged, and a dusty silence settled in the vestibule. Jeff knew he would never see that family again, and he fought off thoughts of what would happen to them, where they would go, now that the door had shut on their backs.

He worked the next three hours through early evening and ended the day by typing a quick, long overdue letter to Adam. He described the call about the suicide, the family rejected at the door. "To get help in this world," he wrote, "it seems you need to file the necessary paperwork." He summed up his plans for the weekend: a night out at the W. B. Yeats pub with his girlfriend, Melodi; a Saturday spent reading and relaxing; a chance to catch his breath after the Damascus trip. Half joking, he suggested Adam come visit him one day, come see Istanbul; they'd smoke a hookah together. He posted the letter to the reservation and placed it in the outgoing box.

On winter evenings the endless rains fell in a heavy slant, pounding the beaux arts buildings of the ambassador's district. After work Jeff ran through the rain along Istiklal Caddesi and took refuge in the heat of the musty bar where he'd planned to meet Melodi. He bought a drink and found his friend Oren Cartwright hunched over a smooth mahogany table. Oren eyed Jeff's brown bottle of Troy and said, "You're the only one I know who can stomach that piss."

"Not all of us can afford your six-dollar Guinness." Jeff pulled out a stool and sat down.

The W. B. Yeats, the only Irish pub in Istanbul, had walls of dark wood. Its low lights and fish-'n'-chips menu, its dartboard and snooker table, its back room with a couch and VCR and a few dozen films, were supposed to make expatriates feel closer to home. His friends in the Hash House Harriers ("Drinkers with a Running Problem") arrived after their evening jogs, quenched their thirst with shots of whiskey, and inhaled cartons of cigarettes. After Thursday rehearsals, members of the Foreign Drama Club came to the pub under the pretense of practicing their lines. By midnight they were dancing on tables. The émigrés gossiped. They scowled. They did not like one another, but they could not live without one another. A few bottles of bitter Troy and they divulged all: personal tragedies, sexual proclivities, financial debacles, past addictions.

Oren raised his glass in a slow toast, sipped his Guinness, and licked the foam off his lips. Jeff found it comical to what lengths the expats went to imitate home. When, for instance, had he ever stopped at a Dunkin' Donuts in the States? But overseas he often craved a Bavarian Kreme and would travel an hour through traffic to get it. Friends like Oren went out of their way for Kentucky Fried Chicken. They bought newspapers—the *Guardian,* the *New York Times, Le Monde*—at outrageous prices two days late, in Taksim Square. And who, he wondered, among these compatriots at the Yeats, braved a Turkish dentist? Like him they went to the American Hospital, for even a simple cleaning.

On the dance floor, amid a circle of friends, Melodi was waving. Jeff smiled at her.

Oren said, "Your girlfriend's the most incredible dancer I've ever seen."

"It's the hips," Jeff said.

Oren squinted. "She's not thin. I was noticing."

"I like that. Turks call it fish meat. *Balik et.*"

Oren leaned across the table and started telling Jeff about his recent unlucky string of dates. He'd had three dates with three different women in the past week: a short athletic Turk, a long-legged Jew, and a dark Armenian with auburn hair. For the first two dates he had planned a film, but the women, as if conspiring against him, both showed up with a friend. With the Armenian he tried something different. They had arranged to meet at a fish restaurant on the shore in Beylerbey. It was Oren's choice, a romantic setting on the Asian side near the Bosphorus Bridge, where the summer palace reflected yellow off the black water. One of the teachers at the girls' *lise* had set them up, and he had been confident about his chances until his date showed up at the restaurant with her mother.

"I think we hit it off," Oren said. "The mother and I."

Jeff laughed in reflex, watching Melodi dance. He had barely been listening to the story. Oren sensed his distraction and changed the subject, lowering his voice. "She's leading you on, man."

"She's not making me do anything I don't want to do. I can break it off as easily as she can."

"You know you wouldn't do that." Shaking his head, Oren watched Melodi a few seconds more. "I'll say this once, and you're going to have to forgive me. You're too good for her. She's a flirt. Nights you're not here, I've seen it."

Jeff laughed again. "Listen who's dishing out the advice on women." He glowered at Oren. His friend taught English at a prestigious Turkish *lise*. He had effortless good looks: blond hair to his shoulders, green eyes, a runner's build. His left arm was covered in a network of tattoos that people struggled to decipher—an attention that Oren enjoyed. One tattoo showed a cartoon devil with a pitchfork; another, a snake swallowing a globe; the third, Krishna riding a chariot. Oren ran marathons and bragged he had finished the New York under 2:45. He owned a complete collection of Elvis Presley records on vinyl. He was confident and laid-back, and Jeff suspected he'd always had a crush on Melodi.

Oren said, "Consider yourself warned." The two of them admired his girlfriend, her sequined halter top pulsating under the colored lights. Oren mumbled, "Where do these Turkish women learn to dance like that?"

She was twisting her arms, palms up, over her head. Her wrists rolled left as she gyrated her hips to the right. She made eye contact with Jeff, pointed, flung her hips twice in his direction, ran her hands over her breasts, and to the beat of the pop tune pulled her finger back three times, as if casting a spell. Cher was singing *Believe*—a song it seemed nobody in the world could escape. (Jeff would rail about the Turk's love of Cher, but at home, alone, he hummed her songs to himself.) He smiled at Melodi and shook his head. She pretended to sulk and when the song ended strolled over to their cocktail table and leaned her head on his shoulder.

"Why so late?" she asked in Turkish, in her deep raspy voice. She took a quick sip of his beer.

"I got caught up."

"Ah, yes. I see. Such a hard worker he is, no, Oren?" She was teasing him: nobody worked harder than she did, as a nurse in Bakırköy. She labored through twelve-hour shifts, five days a week. Once a week she worked overnight at the hospital. These shifts annoyed Jeff. She could never get out of them, and to make it worse, she was always agreeing to cover nights for her fellow nurses, a generosity rarely reciprocated. They could go for days without seeing each other, and it hardly seemed to bother her.

She sat on his knee and draped her arm around his shoulder. Her eyebrows were damp, and Jeff could smell the lilac-scented lotion she used on her face, the tanginess of her sweat. He was just beginning to tell her about work when the music started again—another Cher song.

"I love this song!" Melodi said. She whispered in his ear, "Dance with me."

"A little later," he said.

"You, Oren! Come!" Melodi kissed Jeff, grinned, and pulled Oren to the dance floor. Jeff yelled over the music, "Bring him back in one piece."

He watched them strolling away. Oren was right: she was fleshy, not thin, with a straight, strong build and powerful legs, the kind Jeff liked, though they were thicker than his own. Her hair, died red with henna, ran down to her shoulders. What had attracted him first was her lovely, generous smile—so different from the sour looks he often received from Turkish women. He had met her the second summer after he had arrived from Kyrgyzstan. She was one of Oren's private students. Jeff ran into them at a café in Kadıköy, and Oren had urged him to sit down so Melodi could practice her English. Under the cool shade of the awning they wound up speaking for over three hours. The coffee trays came and went a half-dozen times, and Melodi read their fortunes from the muddy grounds at the bottom of the cups. Looking into Jeff's cup she had said, "You will have a long life, and deep love." She told Oren, "You have a long journey ahead of you." Two years later Oren was still bitter about that.

The pub was growing crowded. It usually filled up on weeknights by eleven. Stylish Turkish women in tight silk blouses, hints of red in their naturally dark hair, arrived in groups of four. Some had boyfriends—large, chain-smoking men who circled around them like secret-service agents. Others came to the pub on the prowl, hunting for a husband and a golden visa. They would meet a foreign man and with little shame start prying. "Where are you from? What do you do? That's a pretty good salary, no?"

Rags of smoke wafted through the dance floor lights, up to a second-story loft. All evening couples climbed the wooden stairs to this platform, leaned over the candlelit tables, and held hands. It was one of the few places in the city where young Muslims, living with their families, could be alone. At the beer-soaked table Jeff glanced from couple to couple until he spotted Melodi near the far end of the dance floor.

Tonight they would have to take the ferry to the Eminönü tram, which ran to the end of the line, and then walk twenty minutes through the usual war zone of construction to her home. The apartment, all the way out by the Atatürk Airport, was the only place she could afford. Early in the relationship Jeff had asked her to consider moving in with him, but it had been out of the question. Her conservative parents wanted her to move back down south, out of Istanbul, to their house in Konya—they thought the city was too dangerous for a single woman.

Watching her dance now, he wondered how her feelings could have changed so dramatically. Their first months together they were inseparable, obsessed with each other. They had skied at Uludağ, earned their scuba certification in Antalya, and hiked together the ruins of the Lycian trail. He could not stop thinking about her: the depths of her voice, the way she slowly brushed back her bangs—once with each hand—the skill with which she cooked traditional meals, her combination of Islamic modesty and modern style. She was a woman still in touch with what was best about her culture. She taught him Turkish; she showed him the secret corners of the city: the best places to buy *lokum,* a famous confectionary on the old cobblestone streets of Moda, the *fasıl* club where her friends listened to gypsy music. But over the two years he had become increasingly aware of the small changes. She would take all day to return his calls on her cell phone. Over dinners with her coworkers she had stopped translating for him when he lost the thread of a conversation. She wore too much makeup for his liking, too much blush on her cheeks, strange-colored eyeshadow that he had not noticed earlier. He had been completely mistaken about the modesty of Turkish women. They were obsessed with manicures, pedicures, and facials, and they were constantly having their legs waxed (from all accounts of his expatriate friends, in the salons the stylists were brutal tearing wax off the skin). Yet, despite it all, he loved her, and the more her feelings seemed to fade, the more his grew.

Jeff had never seriously entertained the notion of settling in one place, with one person. But last year, surprising himself, he had broached the subject of marriage. Melodi apologized, saying her parents would never allow her to marry a man who was not Muslim. And even if they did, with marriage would come the immediate expectation of children. She said neither of them was ready for this. Jeff argued that *he* was and that she was already twenty-seven—past the age at which most Turkish women married. She said she had no intentions yet of becoming a Turkish wife, straddled with children, laundry, and housework, on top of her career.

Now each night they spent together seemed to cement the ridiculousness of the situation. Here they were, trading off turns at each other's apartments, practically living together. All the tiresome precautions to uphold propriety! To avoid scandal! He could not telephone her at work, he could not answer the telephone in her house, and to make excuses, she called her family and friends from her cell phone whenever they were together. Last summer they had even taken a trip south to Konya, where they met her parents for the day and she had introduced him only as a friend, a visiting doctor in her hospital.

These cultural gaps cut too deeply, and Jeff sometimes wondered if it wasn't the impossibility of the situation that made him love her. He half-expected she would tell him one day that her parents had found the right eligible Turkish man for her. "You understand, Jeff, don't you?" she would say. "I was always honest with you." Until then he was simply her foreign adventure, her secret rebellion. Oren was right: one of them needed to end it. Jeff was afraid it wouldn't be him.

Under the disco lights Melodi had abandoned Oren and strutted over to a table of sweaty men from the Hash House Harriers. Oren was talking to a brunette in triangular glasses on the edge of the dance floor. As the second Cher song ended, he leaned close to this young woman, and Jeff could see her shaking her head. Soon Oren returned from the dance floor alone. In the strobe light his blond hair was a mess of tangled strings, his face dark red.

"How'd it go with her?" Jeff yelled over the music.

"She won't go out with me."

Jeff laughed.

"Said she needed to know me better. I asked her how she's going to know me better if she doesn't go out with me. Says that's for me to figure out."

"Give it up, man."

Oren searched the dance floor again. "Do I look like a man who can give up?" He took a few consolatory sips of Guinness.

Melodi rejoined them and promptly sat on Jeff's lap. He clasped her warm back loosely. She wrapped her arm around him and steadied herself not by his shoulders but by grasping the edge of his chair. Her cheeks had the chestnut flush she got when she drank too much. She was stroking her top lip, brushing at an invisible mustache she'd recently waxed.

Jeff nodded in the direction of the runners. "How are your friends?"

"They are all idiots! Do you know what they were arguing about? Whether Turkish women are servants because they don't divorce unfaithful husbands. Mike says he knows a woman whose husband goes to the general houses every week, and she will still not divorce him. I told him the Turkish woman is *faithful* to her man. I told them they did not understand the Turkish woman. Divorce is not an easy thing for our families to accept. It is a tragedy when you spend so much time building the love, and then it is ended. Don't you think it is a tragedy, Oren?"

"I'm going to get another drink."

"No! You stay with us. I am talking." Melodi lunged across the table, and Jeff directed her to the chair next to him. She regained her balance, sat up, and said, "What do you think, Oren? Do you think foreigners understand us Turks?"

Oren's face colored. "You want to know what I honestly think?" he said. "I think the Turks are the most put-upon people on earth. You think everybody is always picking on you: 'Europe doesn't want us. The Arabs hate us. America uses us.' You Turks spend your whole life complaining no one understands you. You're obsessed with the opinions of others."

"Don't listen to him, Melodi."

"No, Oren, you are right. We Turks are fools. We need others too much." She picked a single roasted chickpea from the bowl on the table and bit it in half. Chewing, she said, "We Turks. Yes, the problem is, we don't trust. Europe or Asia—we don't know which direction to look. We want both. We want everything. But that doesn't solve the problem. Can foreign men understand Turkish women? I think not. Those men at that table, they say we are all Oriental belly dancers. Everyone in America, they told me, thinks we are Oriental belly dancers. Or wearing the black sheets." She covered her eyes with her hands, peeking through her fingers.

"I never thought that," Jeff said.

"It is because I taught you differently. When I visited America on my exchange, everybody thought we were speaking Arabic. Always I was telling them we are not Arabs. One person thought Turkey bordered with India. India! Somebody asked me why Turkey wants to destroy Israel. I must teach them, we are the only Muslim friend of Israel. We are one of the most important countries in the world. How is it nobody knows us?"

Oren smiled, mocking her. "You see. 'Nobody knows Turkey. Nobody understands us! The Turks have no friends!' "

"You, Oren, do not understand because you have not loved a Turkish woman. Jeff understands us, don't you?"

"I try."

She laughed and looked back at the group of runners, who had raised another round of Troys. "Now," she said, standing, "I must go tell them what I think." She headed off through the crowd. Oren shook his head. Jeff rose and elbowed his way to the restroom.

Above the sink the pub owners had papered the walls with pages from Yeats's *Selected Poems:* "Who Goes with Fergus?" and "The Man Who Dreamed of Faeryland." Jeff wet his face and glanced in the mirror. He could feel the Istanbul grime on his skin, especially around his nose. His auburn hair was beginning to recede, his cheeks were getting looser. In college, when he had played club rugby, his neck had been taut, his shoulders broad. But now it was harder and harder to stay in shape. He had thinned out, faded, drooped. He would turn thirty in February.

He pulled twice at his goatee nervously, a habit he had to stop. He'd been experimenting with facial hair since he had left the Peace Corps. Over his first months in Istanbul he had grown a Grizzly Adams–style beard; but when the DHRO had hired him, he was warned that only imams in the mosques wore beards that long, so he had shaved, for the most part. He had kept a simple red goatee, whose ends he obsessively twisted into two tusklike tips. Tired of this, he attempted mutton chops, big thick, curly sideburns that wandered from his earlobes to his central cheeks; with the razor he could round the ends off or angle them so they pointed toward his eyes. His third year he shaved the chops entirely, replacing them with a bushy 1970s porn-star mustache. This he neglected to trim. For Melodi the mustache was a source of constant anguish—so much so that one night as he slept, she came at him with a pair of scissors and snipped off half. For nearly a month afterward, having his revenge, he sported a red soul patch, like a piece of shag carpet pasted to his chin. Melodi at last ordered him to grow back the less-repulsive goatee. She couldn't appreciate a man's need to experiment.

He found her still talking to the Hash House Harriers, her arm slung across the back of one man's chair. Just as Jeff was greeting them, she pulled him onto the dance floor for two straight Tarkan songs. Afterward, they finished another round of drinks with the runners and agreed to call it an early evening.

Jeff searched out Oren to say goodbye and spotted him in the back room, behind the pool table, at the computer the owners had set up for Internet access. They charged practically nothing—a dollar an hour—to check e-mail or to surf the Web. All day expats lounged in the old green easy chair, searched the pages of hometown newspapers, and read reviews of the latest movies, which would not arrive in Istanbul for months.

"Jeff!" Oren yelled as he entered. "Check this out. Your old home." He was flanked by Tom Delaney and two of his Swedish friends, and the four of them were surfing porn sites. Oren pointed at the computer screen, where he had typed *Russian, Women* into the flashing search engine. One of the results read "Women of Central Asia Seeking Love and Marriage."

With a click, a grid of thumbnail photos showed heavily made-up Russian, Kazakh, and Kyrgyz women, wearing their best dresses, striking extravagant poses, their heads tilted, their chests raised. The site offered eighteen pages of women. Each one contained ten profiles. Oren clicked on random faces, sometimes hitting the nose, sometimes an ear, sometimes the neck. Piece by piece the half-screen photographs appeared, accompanied by text. Jeff felt his fury rising as he read:

> Aisha #17562
> City: Bishkek
> Age: 25
> Weight: 117 lb., 53 kg
> Height: 5'7", 170 cm
> Measurement: 35-24-35, 89-62-89 cm
> Eye color: black
> Hair color: black
> Marital Status: divorced

In two lines of text below each picture, the woman described herself. Aisha liked volleyball and traveling. She was looking for a man devoted to his family. She spoke intermediate English.

Beneath this description two boxes appeared: *Add Aisha to my order* and *See more women of Central Asia.*

Tom Delaney said, "Aisha's not bad."

Jeff gritted his teeth, reading a line of blue text next to the photo: *Overall I am extremely pleased. My responses as a result of using your service were excellent. CRA is one of the best investments I have ever made. I met Aisha one month after spotting her on your site, and she is everything I could have dreamed of in a woman. You should feel very good about what you do. I wonder if you know how many people's lives you improve through your service. Keep up the good work.—Tom S., January 1999.*

Oren clicked on more women. Michael and the Swedes crowded closer to the computer. They argued over which photos to follow, which pages to skip, which woman would be a good wife, which a good lay, until Jeff—his forehead burning—cried out:

"Stop! Go back. Once more."

He thought he had seen Nazira. She was number 17463. He tore the mouse from Oren's hand and scrolled down. She was wearing a black leather miniskirt, and her printed red blouse was open to her chest.

He scrolled farther down to the bottom of the page, but there was a different name. Gulnara. From Uzbekistan. It wasn't Nazira.

"You like Gulnara, Jeff? Gonna order?"

"I thought I knew her."

"You what?"

"I thought I knew this woman," he said.

IV

10

LOST IN THE Egyptian Spice Market, Adam was jostled and spun by crowds vying for piles of turmeric, hills of saffron, and mountains of almonds. The hawkers shouted from beneath dangling confections of dates. Around him foreigners gawked at endless candies stacked high in boxes. A sign above a carton of Turkish delight read TURKISH VIAGRA. The scent of apple tea lured tourists into lighted shop fronts, where, like flies in a spider's web, they were trapped by salesmen, who blocked the exit and with eager smiles descended upon their victims.

Adam pushed through and escaped the hordes. Outside, crossing the steps of the Yeni Mosque, he scattered a flock of pigeons, then hopped the tram lines and found his way up the waterside along the Golden Horn, toward the terminal marked ÜSKÜDAR. The ferry across the straits, from Europe to Asia, took fifteen minutes. He sat outside, at the rear of the boat, and watched the sun blur behind Topkapi Palace. He had arrived this morning without hopes or expectations; he had sought distance and achieved it. Fleeing home, he had found this—the weathered mosques, the sharp minarets, the hills rising above the maze of waters: the other side of the world.

Foam splashed against the ferry's bow, and Adam thought how his mom would love it here. She delighted in the sea, the waves, things that, because they lived in Arizona, they had seen only once in his lifetime, on a family trip to Kino Bay, Mexico. He remembered swimming out through the choppy bay, digging for sand crabs with Verdena, buying shrimp with his parents off the boats docked at the fishing village. Driving home, the family had been mistaken for Mexicans and held for an hour at the border. His father had locked horns with the immigration officials: "We're Americans, dammit. Let us in!"

Over the railing the foam churned in the ferry's wake, and he tried to force the man's face from his mind, to imagine what lay ahead—what, for instance, Jeff might look like now. Adam hadn't seen him since his senior year of high school. He had called from the airport; Jeff sounded surprised when he heard that Adam had decided to visit, and then confused when Adam said he'd already arrived.

As the ferry approached the shore, he stood and flung the duffle bag over his right shoulder. Inside he had stashed his extra jeans, three pairs of cotton boxers, a second pair of high-top sneakers, Verdena's abalone shell, and two crumpled T-shirts (his Red Cliff: Apache Proud! shirt, with the tribe's great seal, and his faded Northern Arizona University 1997 Division Champions shirt). In his other hand he clenched the folded napkin on which he had jotted Jeff's directions to his apartment.

Three white stone mosques towered ahead of him on the shoreline. Humming, then growling, the ferry docked. Adam crossed the wobbling blue gangplank and, past a row of magazine kiosks, dove headlong into the winding streets. Between wooden tables hawkers sold socks and winter hats and old men splashed water over bins of squirming fish. On the napkin he had written *Fish and Sock bazaar.* He was heading in the right direction. Up the street he stumbled on a circle of fruit and vegetable carts, with tall pyramids of tangerines surrounded by rows of pomegranates and piles of a green fruit he had never seen. Behind one cart a wizened old man used a dagger to slice the tan skin of a fruit. Juice dribbled out, and he offered Adam a red seed. Adam was too shy to take it; he could not ask what it was, he didn't speak the language.

He followed Jeff's map to a taxi stand, past a stall of nuts and a busy bakery with its rich brown scent. His head was foggy from the long flight, and the fume-filled air of this city made breathing difficult; but he had sat cramped on the airplane, and it felt good to stretch his legs. Three corners over he arrived at a hill too steep for vehicles, with cobblestone steps climbing its length. At the bottom of the steps a gypsy in a purple headscarf, nursing a baby, sold yellow roses. Adam consulted his napkin. *Lots of stairs,* it read. He switched the duffle bag to his other shoulder and ascended.

On the balcony Jeff, Oren, and Melodi studied the quarter crescent crown of the mosque across the street. They had just finished their second bowls of chili and were washing them down with glasses of *raki* when Jeff heard a soft, uncertain knocking from inside.

He flipped the dead bolt twice to the right, turned the keys in the doorknob to the left, jiggled them, and pulled open the door of his apartment. Framed in the light of the doorway stood Adam, seven years older than Jeff remembered him, a green duffle bag flopped over his shoulder. His hair was a mess, and his now-crooked nose gave a heaviness to his expression. He wore baggy Wranglers and a ragged Iron Maiden T-shirt under a denim jacket.

"I still can't believe you did this," Jeff said, smiling. When Adam had phoned that morning, he hadn't said why he'd come, and Jeff assumed something had happened on the reservation.

Adam slapped his hand in greeting. His face was creviced from teenage acne, which lent a textured hardness to his stare as his eyes strained to take everything in. He entered, then lowered the half-empty duffle bag to the floor.

Jeff asked, "Mind taking your shoes off in the apartment?"

"No problem." He bent and removed his left sneaker.

"You change your name?" Jeff pointed at the duffle bag, on which the words *Larson Dale, Red Cliff, Arizona* had been written in black marker, then crossed out in a thick, slanting zigzag.

"It was my father's, is all." Adam looked back down. "Goddamn knot in this one." Jeff saw that the laces of the right sneaker, a dirty Adidas high-top, were tangled. Adam picked at the shreds of cloth with his fingertips—his nails were bitten to nothing. With the knot still in place, he managed to tug the shoe off.

Jeff offered him a drink, but he refused, so he showed him into the living room, which ran the western length of the apartment. They crossed the hardwood floors over the chain of violently colored kilims. Jeff motioned through the windows north to the straits, west across the water to Europe, the Aya Sofia, the Blue Mosque, and then south, where the adjoining building partially blocked the view of the sea.

"Some place you got." Adam stopped at the window and took a

long look at a Russian tanker gliding north along the straits. "You sure it's all right, me staying here?"

"I invited you. Let's check out your room." Jeff tried to show enthusiasm, though he was slightly put off by Adam's sudden arrival and the imposition of an unexpected guest.

He walked Adam down the hall, embarrassed by the extravagant living conditions. It was wasteful, a single guy living in this three-bedroom apartment. When he had taken the job at the DHRO, he had not been looking for anything so luxurious. But how could he have turned it down, with its view, and the price fully within the housing allowance? He showed Adam into the second bedroom. Last spring a friend had visited from Tucson, and he had set up a foldout bed for him, which had gone unused ever since.

"Look, you can stay in here. The couch pulls out. TV gets five channels. You can practice your Turkish. That duffle's all your stuff?"

"Don't want a lot of stuff when you're moving around."

"Makes sense. So, the bathroom's down the hall. Most of the time there's hot water." He stopped for a second. "You look like shit, Adam. What the hell have you been doing with yourself?"

"I was in New York."

"New York! How long were you in New York?"

"Over three months. I worked security. At the Museum of Modern Art."

"How'd you hook up with that?"

"I read it in the paper. The *Village Voice*." Adam shrugged. "I applied, and they told me they needed more Indians working there."

"Christ." Jeff laughed. "And where'd you stay?"

"I found this old hotel. Ninety-third and Broadway. Three hundred a week."

"I guess that's not bad, for New York."

"It was expensive as hell, and the place was a piece of shit. I didn't even have a TV."

"So you came here."

"Once I got the passport and had enough for the ticket."

"Adam fucken Dale," Jeff said, shaking his head.

He led him out to the enormous balcony, which wrapped around the entire top floor of the building. The evening air had grown cool and wet. Oren and Melodi were lounging in the wicker chairs, their feet resting on the concrete wall. They introduced themselves.

"So you're Indian?" Melodi asked.

"Apache."

"Shit," Oren said, "first Apache I've met in Istanbul."

"First Apache I've met anywhere!" Melodi added.

"That right?"

Oren asked about Arizona and the reservation, and Adam mumbled his answers slowly, and finally said he didn't feel much like talking about home. He stood silent, gazing out over the balcony.

Jeff was at a loss for something to say, but Melodi, with her indomitable instincts of hospitality, roused them. "We must show Adam our city. Come." They walked halfway around the balcony, and she pointed north in the distance. "It is our Bosphorus Bridge. The sixth-longest bridge in the world. We used to be able to walk across it. Only too many people were jumping off, so they have closed it for walking."

"Jumping to swim?" Adam asked.

Jeff laughed. "Swim? Christ, no, not to swim. Something like thirty people jumped off it one year."

Adam squinted hard in the distance. "You'd think they could survive that, if they hit the water right."

"One guy survived," Oren said. "His jacket spread out in the wind, like a parachute. He floated down and landed soft enough to live. A fisherman dragged him out of the water."

Adam said, "Some kind of miracle, isn't it?"

Jeff watched the Apache staring across the steady waters at the bridge to Europe. He was a strange sight, and Jeff realized now his own memories of Red Cliff—the teen center, the Sunrise Dance, his old truck—were all linked to Adam. He wasn't entirely comfortable having Adam here, crossing into this stage of his life. It made him self-conscious in a way he had not felt since Arizona.

Jeff ushered them back around the balcony and inside to the living room. "You sure you don't want a beer? Pop? We're drinking *rakı*." Jeff pounded his chest. "Lion's milk, they call it here. And we've got some chili, too, if you're hungry."

"I wouldn't recommend the chili," Oren warned.

Jeff gave him the finger. "It's the last time you'll see Oren in this apartment."

"A shower first, if you don't mind," Adam said. "Then a beer. Look, you sure about this? You tell me if there's a problem."

"No problem. There's plenty of room. Stay as long as you want. Only one thing—I'm leaving Saturday on business."

"Well, shit."

"I'm telling you, it's no problem."

"What kinda business?"

"It's an interviewing trip, for refugees. I've got to go to Yemen."

"Don't even know where that is."

"Kind of south, near the Persian Gulf, Saudi Arabia." Jeff led him back to his duffle bag at the front door. "Over there, all day long people chew this leaf called *qat*. All the men, they have *qat*-chewing parties for lunch. By noon, the entire country's sort of tripping."

The Apache smiled. "That right?" It was the first Jeff remembered seeing him smile—a subdued grin, only the slightest hint of teeth, with the edges of his lips turned down, as if this gesture, like everything else, was burdensome.

"Makes it hard to get anything done," Jeff explained. "Takes us a week. Paperwork we should be able to do in a day."

"*Qat,* isn't it?"

"I'll bring you back some, if you're still around." He pointed to the duffle bag crumpled on the floor. "Well, go ahead, make yourself comfortable."

Adam made himself so comfortable, three weeks later he was still there. It seemed an arrangement of mutual convenience, for him free rent, for Jeff someone to keep an eye on the apartment when he went abroad or stayed at Melodi's. Space was no issue; the duplex was large enough to lose each other. Money was not a problem: the apartment came with Jeff's job, a benefit the DHRO provided to make up for his meager salary.

When it was clear to Adam he would stay awhile, Jeff copied him a set of silver keys. He showed him how to unlock the three bolts to the downstairs door, an elaborate procedure.

"It would be easier," Adam said, "just to kick the fucker in."

Jeff led him on an instructional tour of the apartment's defects. "The place looks nice," he said, "all done up and everything, with these parquet floors and wood trim and all. But take a look at that. See how the molding's about to fall off. There's hardly a right angle in the place. Come in here." He led him to the kitchen. "Look under the sink at that plastic pipe. You know how many times a month that breaks off? Shoddiness! It's all a cover-up, Adam. That's how you know you're in a developing nation. Think about it. In America, you can flush toilet paper. You can't do that here. Flush a square, and plastic pipes like that'll burst."

"You complaining?" Adam asked. The apartment was more spacious than any house in Red Cliff.

"No, I love it. I love this shoddiness. America's so—easy. Everything works. You know what I'm saying?"

"Easy?"

"What I'm saying is, even on the reservation, you could flush toilet paper."

Adam said, "Growing up we had an outhouse."

Jeff promptly changed the subject.

In general he seemed glad for some noise in the huge apartment, for someone to throw ideas off of once in a while. And he respected Adam's quietude. Only once did Jeff complain, saying that being in the same room during his guest's silent spells made him edgy. But soon Adam found that when he was in a sour mood, Jeff kept his distance.

On his first Saturday, with Jeff gone, Adam met Oren and his friends at the W. B. Yeats for a beer. He kept mostly to himself, drank his Troys stoically, and simply watched what was going on. Oren checked on him now and then.

"You gonna stay in the city awhile, Adam?"

"I don't know. Why?"

"I've got a job offer, if you're interested." It was possible, Oren told him, to earn fifty dollars an hour teaching English to wealthy Turks. There was little actual teaching involved: the students simply wanted practice. Oren, in addition to his responsibilities at the girls' *lise*, had too many students and needed to unload one.

This was Burak Ekmekçi, a powerful twenty-five-year-old water-polo player on the Turkish national team. Queens College in New York had recruited him and offered an athletic scholarship. To be admitted, he had to pass the TOEFL exam with a score of 550. So far, benefiting little from Oren's rushed sessions, the athlete had failed twice. According to Oren, Burak Ekmekçi was not a person who handled defeat easily. He was getting desperate. His wealthy parents believed a future depended on graduation from an American university, and determined to break 550, Burak wanted more tutoring hours, as many as possible. His father would pay generously. Oren simply did not have the time.

"You just sit there with him and go over his mistakes on his practice tests," Oren explained. "At the end of two hours he'll hand you a hundred-dollar bill. And I told him he was getting a genuine native speaker, so expectations are high. Only one thing—he's a little intense."

"I don't know. I never taught anything."

"Think about it. But let me know by tomorrow."

The stuffy air of the pub became too much for Adam, and he left early. He preferred the long solitary walk in the wet evening air along the decrepit city streets. He liked the warmly glowing windows of apartment buildings, the shadows passing back and forth, the screams of children and rebukes of mothers. He spotted old men hurrying to neighborhood mosques after the call to prayer. It amazed him how, in the *dolmuş*—the shared minibuses—his money was passed up to the driver and back along the line of strange passengers; he would never have trusted half the people on the rez this way. And he especially liked the midnight ferry ride back to Asia, the palaces lit up on shore, the black tinfoil water reflecting the city. Rows of headlights glittered across the Bosphorus Bridge: cars full of people going somewhere.

He decided to take the work.

At Burak's urging the daily sessions began the next day. Adam met him in an open-air card house in Ortaköy, beside a gleaming white mosque on the waterfront. They sat among the old men battling over backgammon, and the slamming of plastic pieces grew so loud that Adam suggested they find a quieter place. The Turk said he liked the noise, though—it helped him concentrate. Adam watched him puzzle over practice TOEFL tests and explained the meanings of difficult words. He had the sense the two of them made a comic pair. Adam was tall and athletic, but Burak was taller still, twice as wide, with hulking biceps and a back that stretched his tailored silk dress shirt. They sat hunched for hours over a stack of paper. Burak's palms perspired as he worked. He smudged the answer sheets, and sometimes his thick fingers broke the pencil in half if he pressed too hard. He was brutish but sensitive. If Adam reminded him for the third time that the past tense of *begin* was *began,* or if he tried to correct his habit of pronouncing *v*'s as *w*'s, the big man's eyes watered. Adam attempted to be gentler in his criticism, but it wasn't much use. After a careless mistake, Burak would pound his head on the table.

"You're going to hurt yourself," Adam warned him.

"Exactly the opposite," he said. "It helps me to think."

Burak asked endless questions. The teaching was Adam's first taste of expertise, and though it seemed ridiculous to be considered a master of English, a language he had taken for granted his entire life, it was also somehow flattering. Following Oren's advice, the two spent the final half-hour reading *Newsweek* magazines and the *Turkish Daily News*.

"Our national hero," Burak said in a proud voice, referring to an article about the founder of the republic. He leaned over and murmured, "But sometimes I do not like."

Adam had never heard of the man, but his student guaranteed he had seen the somber face a hundred times: national law required that every public room in Turkey display the founder's photograph. Burak had memorized his schoolboy facts. In a practiced English speech he explained that his people called the founder "Ata," the father of the country. In the Great War he had helped win the Battle of the Aegean, but only after his life had been saved by a money clip in his breast pocket that stopped an Australian bullet. After the war the general had united their people and had driven out the occupying French, British, and American forces, as well as the enemy Greeks. He established the government without religion, then changed the alphabet from Arabic to Latin in order to better connect the new nation to the modern world.

In his water-polo captain's voice Burak intoned, "Everybody loves Atatürk!" He bent over the table and whispered, "You know this man died alcoholic. He was not a—a—" He stopped and looked the word up in the dictionary. "He was not a *saint*. 'Future future future,' he used to say. He thought only of future; he never thought of past. Atatürk burned all Ottoman books. He burned our history, our Ottoman literatures."

"Still," Adam said, "he sounds like a great man."

"Great man! Yes, great man. He saved our country. But you see, he was *man*. Not God. Simply man. He was making mistakes." Burak cast his eyes down at the imposing stack of TOEFL study materials.

That afternoon, following his tutoring session, Adam met Oren at the Beşiktaş ferry.

"How'd it go?"

"It was all right."

"Easy?"

"Easy enough, I guess."

They grabbed an inexpensive meal together in a *lokanta,* then headed to Taksim Square to the W. B. Yeats. Jeff's girlfriend, Melodi, approached Adam as he was sitting alone at the bar. He had seen her making her way from table to table: she seemed to know every single person in the pub. Her tight white blouse showed off her heavy round chest, and her gold earrings shimmered as she leaned in close to him.

"You've never danced with me, Adam." She licked her lips and repeated his name—"Adam Dale, Adam Dale"—as if she were tasting him. "You should feel shame, Adam Dale."

He laughed uncomfortably and gripped his cool pint of Guinness. "I never dance."

She clicked her tongue and raised her chin with an air of disbelief. Her eyelids were heavily colored in violet, her lips thickly painted. Adam's heart raced; he felt a pressure building to lean over and kiss her. "Don't mind watching *you* dance, though," he murmured. He thought of Jeff and turned his head away from her gaze.

"I see that." She grabbed his left wrist. Her touch was gentle—just the slightest bite of one of her long nails—but with it he felt a charge run up his arm.

In the morning, back at the apartment, his mouth dry from all the previous evening's Guinness, Adam remembered the $150 Burak had paid him. Down by the pier he treated himself to a new pair of Reebok high-tops, a fancy plaid shirt, and an umbrella for the salty evening rains.

The rest of the week with Burak went less smoothly. On Friday Adam barely survived the three-hour marathon tutoring session, and it ended with the water-polo player missing four straight practice vocabulary questions and hurling a tea glass from the waterside café across the pier into the straits.

Adam was frustrated but took his money and headed to the Yeats on his own.

In the *dolmuş* he realized that this job with Burak hardly qualified as real work. He sensed the ease of the life of an American abroad, the prestige of his citizenship, and though it seemed this prestige suited Jeff and Oren, it felt somehow false to him. He did not entirely understand how these unwritten rules worked—exactly why, for instance, Jeff's refugees were clamoring to get into the United States, why Burak's parents would pay fifty dollars an hour for English lessons. But all that mattered now, he supposed, was the money in his pocket. He decided he would press Jeff's hospitality, and as soon as possible, when he had enough saved, he would find his own place and settle into this city awhile. He'd look for a permanent job, maybe teach at an ESL school—build a life for himself, as Oren and Jeff had done.

At the Yeats, he found Jeff in the back room on the computer, typing an e-mail.

"Can anyone use that?" Adam asked him.

"Just finishing up. Then it's all yours."

He watched Jeff type for a moment, his fingers flying across the keyboard—faster, it seemed, than a person could think. Adam fished into his weathered wallet and found, behind an old ATM card, a scrap of paper with the Lutheran mission's e-mail address.

He'd have to tell his family he was alive. Suddenly it disgraced him to imagine what they would think of his living in a foreign country, as if he were too good for the reservation, as if he were after some kind of white folk's glory. He considered telephoning, but knew he could never bear the call: the familiar voices of his aunt and his sister, angry, worried, asking when he was coming back.

Jeff set him up at the computer and let him use his e-mail account, then showed him the right place to type the address. Under SUBJECT, Adam wrote, *a shout out to the pastor.*

What's up, pastor! he began. He typed with his thumb and index finger joined, searching for the right letters.

> writing you from istanbul. want you to know i'm okay and living the high life. i thought i'd tell you i'm in turkey, staying with a friend. you'd like it here pastor. lots of religious buildings and they pray five times a day. do me a favor. tell my mom i'm fine, that you heard from me. i remember what we talked about before i left and your advice and everything. i've been thinking and i want you understand it ain't my fault what dad does to mom. it ain't my fault half the town deals, or my cousin robbed those houses. i didn't ask for none of that. you come from a different place. you're lucky. once you told me you were sent to do your best and help the tribe. that's fine. you live there, but not really. if you really had to live with all that stuff, see it on a daily basis, sleep in the same

house, you'd want to get out too. you'd be angry too. if i typed faster i'd type more. keep an eye on Mom and Verdena for me.—Adam

He clicked SEND, watching the globe spin in the upper-right-hand corner of the screen, then called Jeff over from the pool table.
"This right?"
The screen blinked. YOUR MESSAGE "a shout out to the pastor" HAS BEEN SENT.
"That's right," Jeff said. "You finished?"

11

JEFF HAD BEEN about to leave his apartment and was slipping on his shoes when he heard the raucous knocking. He opened the door and had no idea what was being said to him, too shocked to see the heavy man appear out of the past, in a synthetic-leather jacket and Addiddass sweatpants, standing in the dim light, offering a red bottle, smiling and nodding at him. Anarbek's hair was graying, his double chin and loose jowls covered in white stubble. The words he was shouting were Russian, a language Jeff had not spoken in years. It took him a long moment, staring, before he comprehended.

"*Zdrastvooitye,* Jeff! Here is the bottle of vodka you like. I need twelve thousand dollars or my life is over."

Jeff stood in the doorway with his shoes on, his keys in his hands. He forced a smile but kept shaking his head, gauging the inevitability of Anarbek's sudden appearance. They embraced clumsily and exchanged a few pleasantries, though Jeff struggled with his halting Russian. Still shocked, he invited Anarbek in, then changed his mind and explained that he was on his way to the European side to meet some friends, and asked if Anarbek wanted to join him.

"We can catch up there," Jeff said.

"And talk business," Anarbek answered.

"Yes, yes, business. Leave your bag. How'd you get here?"

"Flying. In an airplane!"

"Jesus Christ."

In the taxi across the Bosphorus Bridge, Anarbek thanked Jeff for his letter. Determined to avoid the issue of money, Jeff asked after Anarbek's son and for news from the village. Anarbek wanted to know how Jeff's teaching was going.

"I'm not teaching anymore. I thought I wrote you about it. I'm working with—how do you say it?—people who have lost their home. We try to get them sent to America."

"America!"

"Yes, but it's difficult."

"How have these people lost their home?"

"In wars, or politics. Or because of religion."

"Can you send *Mooselmaniye?*"

"It doesn't work like that. I mean, we send a lot of Muslims, but not because they're Muslim. They have other problems."

"Like me?"

"No, Anarbek," Jeff mumbled, "bigger problems than yours."

In the smoky light of the W. B. Yeats they found Adam nursing his Troy, joking with Mehmet, the bartender, about Oren's stiff dancing. Jeff pulled up an extra stool and introduced them.

Anarbek took Adam's hand in his powerful grip. "*Ochyen pri-yatna.*"

"What's that?" Adam asked.

"He doesn't speak much English," Jeff explained. "Says it's nice to meet you."

"How do you say it?"

"*Ochyen priyatna.*"

"Ochen pritna, man."

Anarbek slapped Adam on the shoulders and gave him a wide grin. He leaned over the bar and held four fingers up to Mehmet, and through the pulsing beat of the music called "Wodka!" Then he settled his fleshy elbows against the bar's brass railing. With the rest of the men he looked back and caught in the quivering lights his first glimpse of the dance floor, where Melodi and her friends were winding their hips, their chests pumping. He turned to Jeff, nodded twice, and the wrinkles of his pockmarked cheeks bunched high around his mouth and remained fixed there in a momentous smile.

Adam bent toward Jeff. "He looks a little like my father."

"Who?" Jeff yelled.

"My father."

Jeff glanced up at the Kyrgyz. The resemblance was modest and he had never noticed it before. While Councilman Dale's expressions were nothing but forlorn, there was always a wide-eyed amusement to Anarbek's face, and it lacked the Apache's intensity. "I don't see really see it," Jeff said.

"He does. Tell him."

Jeff translated, and the large man's eyes sparkled and he laughed. Anarbek stood between them, wrapped his heavy arms around both their shoulders, and exclaimed, "My sons!"

With that, Jeff quickly lost track of how many toasts were raised that evening.

In Kyrgyzstan he had always noticed that the more he drank, the more fluent his Russian became. Now, at the Yeats, entire blocks of vocabulary and grammatical rules came rushing back to him. He and Anarbek struggled through a conversation about the current state of Kyzyl Adyr–Kirovka and the bankrupt factory, the dictatorial politics of Central Asia, and more about his job with the refugees. When Jeff brought up Lola and Nazira, Anarbek waved him off. Jeff introduced the Kyrgyz to Melodi and her coworkers, and he stood to greet each one of them, his hand over his heart. "Another old friend," Melodi said to Jeff, laughing. "He's charming!" Finally, late in the evening, Anarbek slid his bar stool closer and asked, "When can you give me the money?"

"Do you understand what you're asking me?"

"For twelve thousand dollars. It will be a loan. I'll pay it all back. In two years. It's for Bolot Ismailov. He's crushing us." Anarbek twisted his hands, as if he were wringing a towel.

Jeff's head spun from the alcohol, from the outrageousness of the request. "Anarbek, if I had that amount of money, I would give it to you. In one minute I would give it to you, and you would never have to pay it back. But—I am serious—I work for a humanitarian organization. Do you know how much my position pays?"

"You used to tell us you made nothing back in Kyrgyzstan." He drew even closer. "I never believed you. How can you be American and make no salary?"

"I was a volunteer! I had no salary at all then!"

"Ha! Working for no money. For two years. Ha! My friend, tell me the truth. Please. This is very important."

Jeff looked him straight in the eye. "Honestly. I make money now. But tell me, how much do you think I make?"

"Twelve thousand dollars."

Jeff laughed and fingered his goatee. "Well, more. Really, I tell you, it's more than that."

"Twenty thousand dollars."

"Close." Jeff nodded. "Okay, you are right, just about twenty thousand dollars."

Anarbek's wild eyebrows slanted. "So what's the difficulty? You cannot share some of that?"

"You are asking for half. What will I have to live on?"

His voice rose in surprise. "Jeff Hartig, you earn twenty thousand dollars! You'll have plenty again next month."

"Next month?"

"Next month! You will have enough money again next month."

"Anarbek! In a *year!* Twenty. Thousand. Dollars. Every. Year. Do you understand? *That's* my salary."

The music had changed—a slow Turkish love song. A few women at the bar sang along in tender, low voices.

"A year?"

"A year!"

"*Neyvozmozhno.*" Impossible.

Jeff swiped his palm slowly down his face, pulling the skin. "It is true. I swear. I am not rich. I have a job, but it does not make me so much money. What do you think Americans are? When I wrote, I was worried you and Nazira didn't have enough to eat. I thought you were desperate. I meant I could send you a few hundred dollars. *That* would be difficult for me. I thought you could buy bread with it. I was not offering to save the village. It was just a small offer, to help you out."

Anarbek's face held the look of a man falling from a great height. "So you make only twenty thousand dollars each year? How do you own a car?"

"I do not have a car."

"What about those apartments?"

"Apartments?"

The Kyrgyz thrust an accusing finger in his chest. "The apartments you used to say cost a thousand dollars each month. That is what you said!"

"One thousand?" He tried to remember. "I was talking about

New York City. But I never *lived* there. Do you even know how far Arizona is from New York?"

"How much can you give me? Can you give me five thousand?"

He calculated for a moment. "I can give you five *hundred*." Through the smoke the disco ball spun lights across the ceiling, like a vision of some distant galaxy. "Even this, I do not know where it will come from."

"Five hundred dollars! It cost me that to fly here!"

"Well, where did you get *that* from?"

"From the factory, Jeff! Nobody is getting their salary this month!" Anarbek grabbed him by the front of his flannel shirt. "Do you know what that will do to the village?" Jeff slipped off the stool and steadied himself with one leg on the floor. Pulled forward, he saw he was far drunker than the Kyrgyz, whose tolerance for alcohol had always been astounding. He regretted now the letter he had sent, in a reflex of guilt, after thinking he had seen Nazira on the Internet. He had led his old friend, a man who had shown him endless generosity, this great distance, only to let him down. He cringed, thinking he was about to be struck.

"Then send me to America, Jeff."

"For what?"

"I'll find work."

"I can't do that."

"You don't want to help us. I was your host-father. My family gave you everything in our home. And now you don't want to help?"

"I want to help, but we don't send people to America from Kyrgyzstan. Your problems aren't serious enough."

To Jeff's surprise, Anarbek let out a great roar of a laugh, kissed him on both cheeks, pushed him back onto his stool so its legs wobbled off the floor, and exclaimed, "My friend! *Tiy bespolezniy!* You are worthless! Just like me!"

Jeff was well aware that nomadic Kyrgyz tradition dictated that guests must never be turned away from a home. Since Adam continued to stay in the spare bedroom, the three of them removed a dusty bookcase from the study, and the large man took over the small room. He slept on an extra twin-size mattress Oren loaned them from the *lise*. The first night, through the wall, Jeff heard Anarbek tossing under the cotton comforter. He heard him wake at four in the morning to forage through the refrigerator and scarf down *suçuk* and two-day-old bread. In the morning the crumbs of the clandestine meal were spread over the kilim in the kitchen. When Jeff went to shower, he found Anarbek in the bathroom, gargling, then hocking into the sink, and he had to wait his turn. In the bathtub fifteen minutes later he discovered the bar of soap enmeshed in a web of curly black hairs, and he did not want to guess whose hairs they were.

Two days after Anarbek arrived, the DHRO sent Jeff on a trip to Syria. The guests were left alone in the apartment, and Anarbek worried how they would get on together. Language was their primary difficulty. With so much overlap between Kyrgyz and Turkish, Anarbek was doing well enough in the city, and though Adam knew only a few phrases, with a pocket dictionary he could make himself understood. Anarbek was suddenly curious about English, and Adam taught him a handful of words: *beautiful woman, hot water, cold water, bread, meat, cold meat, money, blonde, brunette, redhead, vagina, breast, nice butt,* and the numbers from one to twenty (not including eleven and twelve, which Anarbek insisted were irrational). Together they discovered the rich possibilities of communicating with hand gestures, pictures from magazines, and objects around the apartment.

Adam left for his tutoring job that afternoon, and Anarbek spent the day alone in the city. He wandered the Üsküdar streets for what seemed like hours. Startled when vendors cried out from their fruit stalls, he bumped into covered women. Disoriented, he paced down the same alley three different times. Shoe polishers followed him and insulted his scuffed leather loafers. Bearded men chatting on benches outside the mosques quieted down to watch him pass in one direction, back in the other—amused, he thought, by the sight of a lost foreigner. Suddenly self-doubting, he stopped to rest at the water's edge. Maybe he had come for nothing. Should he have listened to Nazira? He ordered a fish sandwich, grilled by a man in a sequined velvet vest, who balanced himself on a rocking boat tied to the concrete pier. Anarbek ate, licking his greasy fingers, then ordered another.

Back in Kyzyl Adyr–Kirovka he had said a hurried goodbye to his wife and daughters. He had explained all about Bolot Ismailov, the years of blackmail, the current threats, how for the good of the village he needed to find Jeff. He had sworn them to secrecy. Lola had hardly been upset by the news of his leaving: after his recent indiscretions, she seemed to want him gone. The real difficulty had been Nazira.

"Think of it," Anarbek had urged her, "as a business trip, for the benefit of us all. I can borrow some of the money Jeff's offered in his letter."

His daughter did not think he should go abroad without planning in advance. He had not written to tell Jeff he would be coming ("It would take too long," he argued), and he had never been to a foreign country. She reminded him that the time Jeff had spent in their village was a distant five years ago. The American had come, he had taught, he had left. "One should not go chasing after the past," she warned. They debated for a week. Anarbek had listened patiently to her concerns, but in his mind he was already gone.

Besides him, there had been only two other passengers on the old Aeroflot plane, but the four Russian stewardesses could not be bothered with them. Halfway through the turbulent flight one of these women tramped through the aisle and spun a Soviet army ration tray of gristly meat in front of him. Anarbek had not eaten it. He was too busy suffering in his seat, which refused to stay upright. He had changed places three times, but behind him the faulty seats all crashed back in the same way, leaving him staring at the ceiling, listening to the high hum of the engine. The only other time he had flown, the summer he had studied in Moscow, the airplane had been full, the flight attendants pleasant. But on this flight, his back aching, his throat dry, he had asked a stewardess for water, and she had told him there was some in the bathroom if he wanted it.

So landing in Istanbul—the city's skyscrapers and beaches gilded in the late morning sun—had seemed like a miracle. He climbed down the steps off the plane, and a yellow shuttle glided across the taxiway to pick up the passengers. It was like a special welcome for only the three of them. The hydraulic doors opened with a rush so quiet, so smooth, he thought he might cry. In the terminal he exchanged money (400,000 lira for every dollar!) and paid for a bus—the strange new bills worked, and he received a handful of heavy change. On the ride along the shore highway he saw, for the first time, the sea. He watched it lapping the coastline: the oil tankers glimmering over the field of blue, the football matches in fenced-in fields along the shore, the blinking neon signs of fish restaurants, and suddenly the staunch turrets of the fortified city walls rising ahead. He remembered his history lessons well enough: centuries ago his Central Asian ancestors had overtaken this city and, fighting their way to the edge of the continents, had carved out an empire. These masses of people around him, jostling for seats, pushing to get off the bus, were his brothers.

That evening, when Adam returned, their friendship was cemented by a love of *kebaps*. The dark American led him across the street from the apartment, and they climbed the shaded hill of chestnut trees to a *lokanta* called Kebapistan. Anarbek could smell the grilling lamb before they entered. In the tiny restaurant they chose one of the four bare tables and sat down amid the rushing and smacking of a small crowd of workers. The waiters and cooks wore white aprons and green-trimmed T-shirts. They danced around, preparing Arabic pizzas and Turkish *pides* flatbread, keeping the wood oven blazing, charring tomatoes and chicken over the coals, chopping onion salads, steaming trays of rice, stirring bowls of yogurt, and trimming thin slices of *döner* from the rotating spit. The choice of *kebaps* was boggling. There was chicken shish or lamb shish, eggplant shish, grilled meatballs, and roasted *döner* meat served in deep sandwiches stuffed with salads, or over rice with sides of spicy bulgur and lemon. There were half-combination *kebaps,* full-combination *kebaps,* and the king of *kebaps* (Anarbek's choice) —the mighty iskender: sliced *döner* over cubed bread drizzled with tomato sauce, a dollop of pureed eggplant on one side, a cool spoonful of yogurt on the other, all topped with a ladleful of melted butter.

The owner had recognized Adam as a regular and greeted them with a partial bow. They stuffed themselves for only a few million lira and washed the *kebaps* down with glasses of chai, served complimentary by a red-faced boy who rushed in and out of the stores along the street, balancing a copper tray of clanking glasses.

After the meal, the two men wiped their mouths and settled back in their seats, toothpicks between their teeth. With his store of thirty English words, Anarbek tried to explain to Adam his reasons for coming to Istanbul, but immediately was at a loss. "Twelve thousand dollar," he finally said. He pointed to his own chest.

Adam laughed. "We all need twelve thousand dollars."

"You help."

He shook his head. "Sorry, man, I don't got that."

"How many dollar yours?"

"Me? I've got nothing. I'm poor. I'm from the rez. You're asking the wrong guy." Adam attempted to explain what a reservation was, and Anarbek understood it was a place, but as hard as he tried to make out its significance, the words sounded like the background noise on a poorly dubbed film.

Anarbek's thoughts were consumed by *biznes*. From morning through late afternoon for the rest of the week he wandered Istanbul, looking for a way to make a quick twelve thousand dollars. With each day that passed he felt a growing dread. But on Friday he sought out Laleli, a district mentioned by his Bishkek airline agent, and was instantly encouraged. The ghetto of hotels and shops catered to businessmen from the former Soviet Union. Signs were written in Turkish and Russian. The restaurants served *pieroshki*, *shashlyk* stands smoked on the streets, and Anarbek felt almost at home. In the morning mustached men stood chatting outside their businesses, one hand thrust in a pocket, the other hand holding a saucer and teacup. After a few hours of exploring, Anarbek grew familiar with the streets. He oriented himself by the colorful signs above the stores: CANABIS JEANS, TUNA TEKSTIL, and FOR YOU COLLECTION FABRIC. He bought aspirin and soap in the *aptekas;* for a snack he bought roasted chestnuts from a vendor outside the Liberty Hotel. The area had an overwhelming hustle and seediness about it, an atmosphere enhanced by rows of naked female mannequins lining the sidewalks, perched in doorways, posing in the window displays. Some wore short black leather skirts, a few wore trim brown leather jackets, but the great majority wore nothing. He was constantly taken aback by the tan, thin, voluptuous plastic bodies. Out of the corner of his eye he kept mistaking them for real people.

He introduced himself to every shopkeeper he saw and forged friendships in Laleli. Most of the businessmen ran import-export shops. They traded in leather, underwear, toiletries, pasta, and tea. In the afternoon he watched them wrapping enormous parcels in hay, duct-taping every square centimeter of the boxes, and rolling them end over end onto the streets, where they would be picked up and shipped east. If they were doing it, he thought, why couldn't he?

He needed to figure out the details of some new business venture like this, free from the critical eyes of his wife, his daughter, and the village. Bolot Ismailov weighed on his mind, the shameless insolence of the younger generation who believed they had ascended to power, and were intent on disgracing him. He scrutinized everything, amazed by the workings of a world he had never imagined. In the bustle of the marketplace, where scrambling merchants tried to outbid each other, he understood that Communism in his homeland was forever dead. He saw the busy bakeries, the restaurants on the clamorous streets full of tireless workers, and he understood, for the first time, that his cheese collective was beyond repair. He eyed the abundant shanks of beef and goat heads hanging in the city butchers, and he knew his factory cows were truly dead. In hotel lobbies he watched the *natashas* with cigarettes—prostitutes in long leather jackets and black fur collars, blowing smoke like dragons from their nostrils—and he understood Baiooz was really gone. Hour after hour, consumed by a mixture of sadness and exhilaration, he found himself awash in a flood of revelations.

He imagined what kind of *ticaret*—import-export business—he could establish. What could he bring back to Kyrgyzstan? What could he sell in Istanbul? What did they need? What had they never seen? He could trade in leather jackets, real warm leather (not the plastic kind he found in Bishkek) that did more than keep the wind out. He could import flavored tobacco to Talas, introduce a new taste for a people accustomed to growing and drying their own meager crops. In the riotous street markets he marveled at heads of lettuce, a food one could crunch on for an entire day and never grow fat. Would the Kyrgyz people buy apple-flavored tea?

He lay awake at night, his eyes wide open, and stared up at the thin cracks in the concrete ceiling. Yes, he was growing old, but he did not feel it yet. As this journey had proven, he had determination and energy enough to give this new life, this world that had sneaked up on him, another go.

And the following evening at Kebapistan, as Anarbek was finishing his monstrous dinner of iskender with Jeff, Melodi, and Adam, inspiration finally struck him. He threw down his fork, clapped his hands over his plate, and yelled, "*Koi!*"

Startled, Adam turned to Melodi and asked, "What'd he say?"

She shrugged. "He says something about sheep."

"This guy's nuts," Adam said to Jeff.

But Anarbek was calculating, and did not even hear them.

* * *

On Sunday he followed Jeff and Adam through the gypsy neighborhood north of the apartment to Fetih Pasha Korsu, a sloping forest overlooking the straits. The hilltop offered views of the intercontinental bridges. They hiked down the winding brick path to a tea garden of low stools and wooden tables. Anarbek stopped to catch his breath. The grassy slopes and cypress trees provided the perfect place for a picnic; and droves of scarved women, their husbands and children in tow, had descended on the park. He was rapt. The forest lay shrouded in a haze of smoke from the grilling meat, and the constant chirping of birds was punctuated by the sounds of children shouting for their mothers, the laughter of men sharing beers, and the arguments of teenagers searching for usable remnants of cigarettes. Jeff led them down to an old exercise trail, a kilometer long, whose metal equipment had rusted and fallen into disrepair. He told them that he came here three times a week to jog the dirt path, up and down the steep curves. His friend Oren was training for the Istanbul Eurasian marathon and occasionally met him here to warm up for his longer runs. Jeff explained to Anarbek how, after school, these woods became a hideout for young Turkish couples, who wandered the jogging trail searching for a secluded place to throw down a newspaper and make out. When he and Oren ran the trails, they never failed to surprise three or four such couples. At first Jeff had been embarrassed and suggested they find a better place to exercise; but Oren enjoyed scaring the young lovers out of the bushes, and argued that this *was* a jogging trail, after all.

Anarbek kept his eyes out for Turkish couples. At the bottom of the trail concrete steps led to a basketball court with two rusted green metal backboards. Adam had arranged to join the bartender of the Yeats there for a basketball game. Mehmet was waiting for them, and he, Adam, and Anarbek challenged a group of teenagers to a game of three-on-three. Anarbek had seen the sport on television but had never fully understood it. Before taking off for his jog, Jeff explained some basic rules, which seemed unnecessarily complicated.

The game began. Adam dribbled effortlessly, without looking at the big orange ball, and passed as often as possible to Mehmet, who threw the ball at the basket and usually missed. Finally Adam passed to Anarbek. He covered the ball in his chest, ran ten steps, forced his way through the defense with his elbows, missed a series of close shots off the backboard, then finally clattered one in and raised his hands in triumph, looking at his teammates. Adam was smiling and clapping, but for some reason shaking his head.

They dominated the young Turks; then they mixed up the teams and the next game was a little closer. Once Adam dribbled in circles around Anarbek, probably just to frustrate him, and the American nearly died laughing when Anarbek shoved him to the ground with both hands and stole the ball.

The teenagers invited them back for a five-on-five next weekend.

12

ANARBEK HAD BEEN GONE too long, and Kyzyl Adyr–Kirovka was barely managing in his absence. The bazaar stalls and village kiosks were taking in little money, there was bickering at the factory over how to evenly distribute the next month's wages, and Anarbek's recent string of girlfriends desperately missed the fruits of his generosity. The people of the village wondered how their lives could get worse.

Pessimism and despair grew so rampant that few cared about the strange rowdy men who were hanging around the bazaar entrance. This group of thugs frightened the Kurdish milkmaids, pursued the young bread sellers into the park, insulted the Koreans and spit in their piles of cabbage salad, and bought bottles of vodka, which they drank squatting in a circle next to Yuri Samonov's table.

The geologist, still in mourning over the death of his son, observed the gang. They would lunch at the *manti* stand, pile dumplings on sheets of newspaper, douse them in vinegar, and stuff them with greasy hands into their greasy faces. By the end of the week, just what they wanted became clear. After lunch, having finished a second bottle of vodka in as many hours, the men were swaying on their haunches when the young girls from the eleventh form appeared. In their starched white blouses and long navy skirts, textbooks pressed close to their chests, the students were prancing through the bazaar on their daily walk home from the Lenin

School. The prettiest of the bunch stopped at a table to buy eggs, but before she could pay the gang had surrounded her. The one with the broad shoulders and thin mustache barked an order at his friends and shoved them out of his way. The group erupted in laughter and dispersed—a few hurried off to taunt the students walking ahead—and their leader had the girl with the eggs all to himself. Even in the dense fog of his drunken mourning, Yuri knew she was Anarbek Tashtanaliev's daughter Baktigul.

He noticed the rough-looking stranger pull Baktigul behind the watch repair kiosk and he thought, if nothing else, he could at least repay his old friend with a warning.

All the next day Yuri worked himself into an alarming drunken stupor, and at four-thirty, drawing down the makeshift wire gate with a crash, he closed his stand. Late dusk was falling. Crows circled overhead and landed on the budding arms of the cherry trees. Yuri stumbled off in the direction of Karl Marx Street. It was approaching dinnertime on this cool summer evening, and even the village children were inside, having their tea. Three ragged pariah dogs followed him as he trudged across the potato field. They arrived on the muddy end of Karl Marx Street, where a pile of burnt trash was still smoking. The animals sensed foreign territory, whined, lowered their tails, turned back, and Yuri found himself alone. On Nazira's porch it took him a full minute to figure out that the bell was missing. He pounded the door with his fist, then realized he had pounded too hard. He should not have come.

Opening her door, Nazira might have expected anyone, but never the geologist, standing as pale and as rigid as a tombstone. He worked his brown fur *shapka* in his hands, and before she could say a word, he apologized for disturbing her. The apology cast such pity in her heart that she invited the Russian into her home. She knew better: Karl Marx Street had eyes. It was not herself she cared about—she had no reputation left to protect—but she did not want Yuri or his wife suffering more than they had in recent months. His coming alone to her house was a sign of great urgency or great drunkenness, and she sensed both.

She seated him upstairs on her softest red felt mat, beside the concrete hot plate she was using to warm the room and bake bread. She could no longer afford to buy bread at the bazaar. Four months ago the government had paid her salary in sacks of flour and a kilogram of butter, and that provided her and Manas with the flat, simple *leposhka* they ate each evening. When her father was home, he would occasionally drop by and slip some kielbasa or mutton into her refrigerator. But, infuriatingly, he had disappeared; and it shamed her now to have a guest—she did not even have a bite of meat to offer him.

Manas slept under two blankets on the floor amid a pile of scattered nature magazines. His fingers were in his mouth—a habit she was trying to break him of—and his hair, normally spiked, was tousled.

She rearranged the magazines. "He likes to look at animals."

"Yes, yes. What child doesn't like animals?" Yuri whispered. "My boy did too."

Nazira did not know what to say.

"How lucky you are," Yuri said, pointing to Manas.

"Lucky? My son has no father. I have no money—I can barely feed him."

"What is important about that? Look at him. What else is important?"

"I am beginning to think I cannot do it alone. I am beginning to think the boy needs a father."

Why was she unburdening herself to this old man? Nazira suggested they drink more chai, and while she scooped the leaves from the carton, she observed Yuri scanning her bare room. She lived like a monk. On the wall hung a lone decoration—a single calendar poster from 1993, six years ago, showing the Statue of Liberty. It had been a present from Jeff.

Yuri eyed an industrial-size pack of yeast on the small table and read the label aloud. "A recipe for Russia's traditional national beverage."

"What was that?"

"You use this yeast for bread?" Yuri asked.

"Of course," she said. "The bread you're eating now."

"Only for bread?"

Nazira tried to mask her smile. "Yuri Samonov! I use that yeast only for bread."

"These last months—my business has been getting worse." He pulled at the frayed cuffs of his pants. "Loyal customers have not been coming. They've found another source."

"I know nothing about it," Nazira said, and turned her head from his fierce gaze.

"My vodka—I keep it up at thirty percent alcohol. Strong! The people like it strong! Then I hear whispers in the bazaar." He lowered his voice. "They've found a cheaper place, they say. A stronger drink."

"Did you come here to accuse me of something?"

"You have been brewing *samogan* and selling it. I know what this yeast is for. And all that sugar I see you buying. Who needs fifteen kilos of sugar a week? A lone mother with a single son? Bootlegging! Nazira Tashtanalieva! Do you know what the police will do when I tell them!"

"You wouldn't. Yuri Samonov, why would you do such a thing? I'm a teacher. I have no salary. I have two mouths to feed. How is a person supposed to survive? I do it because I must. I never tried to compete with you!"

Yuri fingered the paper sack of yeast. "But they tell me your *samogan* is better than my vodka. I have no choice but to eliminate the competition."

"You would not!"

"You have been hurting my business," Yuri said. "A man does what he must."

The threat was too much for her. She stared at the Russian in disbelief, and he stared back, wrinkling his forehead, stone serious. She was almost at the point of tears when Yuri's face broke into a smile, then into full-throated laughter, and then into a roar. It was the first time he had laughed in three months.

"Nazira! Nazira! What would your father think? His daughter brewing alcohol at home. Ha-hah!"

She laughed along with her guest, covering her mouth. "You cannot play with me like that, Yuri. That is not fair."

"Life's not fair, my dear. Life's not fair." He shook his head. "I didn't come here to discuss our common business, though."

"What then did you come to talk about?"

Nazira listened, and what she heard disturbed her more than Yuri's teasing.

"But Baktigul is only seventeen!" she exclaimed.

Yuri further explained his suspicions. She inhaled deeply, trying to calm herself.

"Did you know this happened to me?" Nazira asked. "Is this why you came?"

"This?"

"I was stolen once myself. But I refused to stay in the house." In the years that had passed, she had often looked at her fatherless son, wondering how her life might have played itself out differently. She could trace it all back to that first cause, to a moment's decision: her barefoot flight out of Traktorbek's apartment. What if she had not run away? Had she simply accepted her fate, her family would have been better off.

Yuri searched her eyes. "Nazira, I'm sorry. I did not know."

With a wave she forced away the memories and raised herself off the floor. "*Nyechevo*," she said. It was nothing.

The following day after a cold rain the village poplars glistened in the afternoon sun. Nazira waited at the bazaar. She pretended to be shopping for sugar and a straw broom, but from the corner of her eye, shielded by a silk headscarf, she spotted her sister, chatting among her herd of friends, all gliding calmly across the earthen lot, their schoolbooks piled in their arms.

How had Baktigul grown up so quickly? Recently Nazira had come to realize that, with each passing year, Baktigul had begun to look like a female version of their father. She had Anarbek's round cheeks — vibrantly red, so red they looked stained at times by jam — she had his heavy lips and flat nose. She was slightly shorter than Nazira, but her bosom was already fuller; she wore her hair long (she had refused to have it cut since she was fourteen), and often in a braid.

Baktigul reminded Nazira of her father in other ways as well. Once she took up even the most ridiculous notion, it was impossible to convince her to change her mind. Nazira could remember a period when, as a young girl, her sister had refused to eat anything white. She would not drink milk or swallow radishes or cheese; she refused even yogurt, a delicacy, and the more Nazira pressed, the longer she held out. Lola had to convince Nazira to stop bothering Baktigul about it; eventually she would come around on her own. And that was what happened: one day after school they had caught her eating a vanilla ice cream behind the house. Nazira always remembered the lesson, and it was how she dealt with her sister through her early teens: tell the hardheaded girl the right thing to do and then back away. This summer she had had plenty of practice. Baktigul was studying for her university entrance exams, and Nazira had tried to convince her to pursue acceptance into a technical college, whereby she could earn a steady salary — perhaps in secretarial work or computers. But Baktigul had come across a Russian translation of Colette and had decided she was going to study French. French! As if she would ever be able to earn a living speaking French—she could not even teach it in the village schools. But Baktigul's course was set. She was going to apply to Bishkek International University and study French. Nazira, following Lola's advice, had backed off.

Yet wasting four years studying French was infinitely more desirable than what lay before her now.

Baktigul slowed down by the light-bulb table and cast a shy glance back at a group of squatting men, blinking her almond eyes. Nazira studied the men. From a distance she saw the leader of the group abuse the others. He ordered one to fetch him *manti,* rose and circled them like a sultan, and occasionally kicked them. Even across the bazaar she recognized him. Traktorbek.

Her sister's classmates had walked ahead. Nazira wrung her hands. Traktorbek swaggered up to Baktigul and she looked demurely away, but Nazira knew her well enough to see the flirtation in her manner. The drunken man wrenched Baktigul's arm and began to pull her around the watch repair kiosk. She leaned away from him, as if to struggle, but her feet stepped forward in a reluctant dance. The crowd of bread sellers cleared a path for them; it was a scene they had witnessed before.

Removing her scarf, Nazira charged after them in fright.

Behind the shadows of the kiosk Traktorbek had already taken out a bottle. His arm was snaked around Baktigul's waist and, with her bright teeth and high-pitched voice, she was giggling.

"Aren't you ashamed?" Nazira screamed.

Baktigul looked up and shouted, then jumped back in surprise.

Nazira raised her hand to slap the teenager, but realized she, of all people, had no right. "Get home! Get home before you make our own mother cry in her grave!"

A hot blush colored Baktigul's ears. She hesitated and opened her mouth as if to defend herself, but Nazira glared. Her sister cried out furiously, lifted her books off the ground, and shuffling around the kiosk, disappeared.

Nazira faced Traktorbek. Alone with him, she could feel her courage seeping away. She stepped backward. In the seven years since the abduction, Traktorbek had changed. He had grown larger and wider, his hair was already thinning, above a brown mustache his face seemed older and more cunning, and there was menace in his sneer. He cocked his head to the left with a knowing smile.

"*Eje!*" he said, his mustache curling upward with his grin, "I've been wondering where you were."

"After all these years, you have not moved on." Her voice was cracking.

Traktorbek shrugged. "I have moved on. I've found a better woman than you."

The poplar trees were closing them in, the leaves dripping from the morning rain. Behind her she bumped into the corroded wall of the kiosk. She began edging her way around the metal siding. "Keep your hands off her. If you touch Baktigul!"

His arms snapped up and he grabbed her. With one callused hand he held her around the elbow. "What will you do? Tell me, what will you do? If you weren't such a whore, I would take you again. Only someone else beat me to it." With the other hand he stroked her hair between his fingers. Nazira swatted the hand from her head, but he snatched her opposite elbow, and she stood, caught, in his double grasp.

He stared hard into her; the wolfish sneer violated her all over again. Suddenly, strangely, his expression softened, and his eyes glazed over. He glanced left, then right, let go of her, and stuck his hand deep in his pants, tucking his brown canvas shirt into his gut. He shook his head and lowered his voice. "You ruined me, you know. I've never stopped hearing of it." Nazira grit her teeth and cast her gaze to the ground, listening. He said she had destroyed his life, his plans. He had become the laughingstock of the meat bazaar, had been forced to leave, to support his mother by grilling at a *shashlyk* stand instead of selling whole shanks of beef and mutton. It was no way to live. His family had been permanently disgraced. But the Tashtanalievs would make up for it now.

"What do you want?" she demanded.

"I might want your sister. Maybe Baktigul will be a luckier woman than you."

"My father will never allow it."

"Your father made that mistake once, but he won't this time."

"Leave her alone, Traktorbek. She's a bright girl. She has a future. She doesn't want this."

"That's not what Baktigul tells me."

Nazira could hardly believe this was happening. She turned, gasping, and jogged off into the bazaar, in search of her sister.

Three more days she waited, helpless, for news of her father's return. Baktigul's stupidity infuriated her, and the thought of her absent father angered her further. She needed him to return and put her sister in her place. In the telegraph office she phoned her cousin Cholpon in Bishkek—the last person in the family to have seen her father—and learned that Anarbek had purchased only a one-way ticket. Nazira was sick with worry and could think of nothing else. She asked her sister again and again if she understood what kind of man Traktorbek was, but the mulish teenager answered with quiet nods meant simply to appease her. Baktigul claimed Nazira was merely jealous. "You've spoiled your own life, Nazira. I am not going to let you ruin mine. And how am I to help it if a man falls in love with me?"

Sunday afternoon, in her backyard catching up on chores, Nazira had not yet decided what to do. It was a mild gray day, and she had just finished pounding the house rugs over the fence with a metal spatula. Now, to make a spicy paste, she cut in half the tomatoes she had picked, pushing them through the meat grinder with her red fingers and catching the liquid in a plastic rice basin. All the time she kept an eye on Manas. He was playing in the brown grass, watching ravens poke at the hoed earth of her vegetable garden. Usually observing him at play gave her the greatest reassurance—whatever she lacked, whatever mistakes she had made, she had this boy and he was enough. But now, watching him jog after a bird on his slightly bowed legs, his tanned skin patched with dirt, she was overcome with anxiety. He stopped suddenly and looked up at the sound of determined footsteps coming around the house.

Lola strode into the backyard with Oolan in her arms. Her old friend—long-boned, wide-breasted—had a melancholy look on her face that marred her haughty beauty. She deposited Oolan in the grass next to his four-year-old nephew. The boys whined little greetings, then ignored each other as they scurried around on the damp earth. Avoiding what was truly on their minds, the mothers spoke for a while until Nazira went inside to put water on to boil and carried out a plate of *leposhka* covered with a cloth napkin, followed by bowls of raspberry jam. They ate the bread in silence. Nazira served the chai and Lola dipped two chunks of bread into her steaming cup, carried them over to the garden, and fed the boys the soggy pieces. Finally she squatted in the grass next to Manas and said, "He's been gone almost three weeks. I need him back."

Nazira's heart sank. She gazed at the figures in the grass, and it occurred to her she was responsible for each of them. She had condemned Manas to a life without a father. Oolan was also now left without a father. And Lola, a woman at the peak of her loveliness, had been left without a husband. Nazira had done everything she could to make her family happy, and this disaster was the result.

"I'm sure he will be back soon," she said. "Any day now. What could he be doing in Istanbul, really?"

"You know that's not right. He will not be back. He left with no intention of returning."

She sensed the possibility of truth in Lola's words. Manas began to cry, and Lola lifted him off the ground and supported him on her hip. "Why are you crying? *Tinch*. Hush. Hush, my child." She looked at Nazira. "I can watch him for you."

What was she suggesting? Nazira's mind raced, trying to imagine her father in a foreign land, on a mission to get money from the vanished American. If he had found the money to appease Bolot, he would have been back by now. She looked at her son perched in Lola's strong arms, at his wet nose, his sea-blue eyes, his bristling hair.

Lola said, "You can go and get him. You can bring him back." She bounced the boy in her embrace, and he whined in a screechy voice. "I will watch Manas," Lola said. "You go find your father."

"How can I go? I don't have that kind of money. I can't leave Manas with you for so long. He needs me."

"*I* would go, Nazira, but I've never been away. You have been to the capital, you have been to university. I don't know how to travel like you. We can borrow money from my parents. I've already asked them."

"You haven't."

"Yes. Please find him, Nazira. Remind him that he's left us behind." In an afterthought she added, "His son misses him."

Nazira imagined herself on the bus ride out of Central Asia. A foreign city! And Jeff! What could she possibly say to him? She looked at Lola and murmured, "It's too far. Could you imagine being away from Oolan that long?"

"You won't even be gone a week. I watch Manas nearly every day as it is. He'll hardly know you've left. Please. Do this for me."

Lola set Manas down, sat beside her, and placed her hand on

Nazira's knee. Nazira looked out across the sky, following a single drifting cloud as it approached the brown edges of the mountains. She glanced down at Manas, who was holding his arms out for her to lift him. It seemed she did not have a choice. "I'll go, Lola. I'll bring him back."

That week she moved her son into her old house and packed a sports bag for the journey. She warned Baktigul, in no uncertain terms, to keep away from the bazaar. She said goodbye to all of them at the *otovakzal,* blowing kisses to Manas from the bus window. It took three attempts for the driver to start the bus, but finally, backfiring, it rumbled out of the lot, and Nazira left the village to find the fathers.

13

THE ISTANBUL bus station, a sprawling monstrosity, seemed a hundred times the size of Bishkek's *otovakzal*. Lines of buses stood parked along the three spiraling levels of the concrete building, and dense, incomprehensible timetables littered the windows. Everywhere Nazira stepped the touts circled her and bellowed names of destinations. "Bursa! Buuuursa!" "Adana! Adana! Adaaana!" It was all she could do—hurrying with her heavy black bag—to cross the roads without getting crushed by the speeding buses. They swung around blind corners and unleashed their horns at her.

It had been an exhausting journey so far, and this place offered no rest. She had ridden the village bus twelve hours into Uzbekistan and had not managed a night's sleep since. From Tashkent she found a train to Ashgabat, and then on to Turkmenbashi, where she had to kill an entire day at the dreary port, waiting for the ferry to Baku. Another two days of buses (they were awful; one entire evening a man behind her fondled her arm) had brought her over the Caucasus into Turkey. The delays at the border crossings had been interminable, yet her old Soviet passport and quiet pleas to the officials saw her through. She took a hotel room near Trabzon's police station, but frightened by the sirens, she had been unable to close her eyes. The nights away from Manas were punishing: she felt hobbled, only half able to give herself over to the urgency of this trip. On the final, bucking overnight bus to Istanbul, she drifted in and out of a hazy half-consciousness, which only tired her more; and late morning at last she had exited, delirious, into the riot of Istanbul.

An elderly tout found her a service van to Üsküdar. The journey through traffic and the sprawling environs of the city took her over the Bosphorus Bridge. Through the window she spotted the currents of the straits running, strangely, both north and south. From the waterfront she had no problem finding Jeff's apartment: she simply sought help. She asked everyone she saw, "*Nerede?*" and pointed to the address her father had left her. Women watching from balconies directed her all the way up a street of stairs toward an orange building. She was dizzy with fatigue, and the dread she felt at seeing Jeff again was overshadowed by the thought of actually sitting down and resting.

She knocked twice, and when Jeff finally opened the carved wooden door, he looked jolted. Nazira realized only then that she was unprepared for the confrontation. He had changed. He seemed shorter than she remembered; his hair was thinner and cut to a reasonable length just above his ears. She had imagined she would faint or say something dangerously stupid, but suddenly she found herself confident, completely calm, facing the father of her child.

"*Salamatsizbih,*" she said.

"*Salamachillik,*" Jeff replied, recovering.

A ridiculous scruffy patch of beard clung to his chin. His shoulders were somewhat stooped, and lines of worry had collected at the corners of his eyes. The silence between them lasted an eternal few seconds. She tried to gauge in his expression his level of guilt at abandoning her, but saw none. Neither did she perceive the slightest smile nor sign of joy in his seeing her again. She thought of his concerned inquiries about her in the letter he had sent and, gathering her courage, broke the silence with a smile and the stock phrase "*Ishter kondai,* Jeff?" How are your works?

His eyes flashed in recognition of the ritual, and he answered correctly, in what seemed like a reflex. "*Jakshii.*"

"How is your health?"

"*Jakshii.*"

"Is my father with you?"

Jeff laughed and cleared his throat. "Nazira, why don't you come in," he told her in English, extending an arm, "and see for yourself."

She removed her plastic sandals and stepped shyly into the hall and then the living room. There on the couch, facing the other way, hunched over an opal chessboard, was her father. He was playing against a brown-skinned man—a Kyrgyz, perhaps. Neither looked up, but she could tell from the way her father leaned into the game and stuck out his chest that he was winning. So this is what he had been doing, passing the time at games while the village suffered. She was furious.

"*Shax,*" he announced. Check.

"Anarbek," Jeff called, "guess who's arrived."

"*Bir minoot.*" Anarbek held up his hand, then slammed it down on the corner of the board and let out a great roar of triumph. The young opponent sat staring at the pieces, shaking his head. In mock condolence her father patted him on the shoulder, and only then did he turn. He saw her and his smile vanished. He looked like a man guilty of some horrendous crime.

"Nazira! What are—"

"Ata."

He stood. She could not read the emotions on his face as he stepped toward her. Fear that something had happened at home? Anger at her intrusion into his private life? Amazement that she had suddenly appeared—crossing half a continent to find him in this strange city? Once as a child she had carried an urgent message from her mother to him in the factory sauna, and he had rebuked her for the invasion. She suddenly had the same sense now, that her entrance violated sacred male ground. Her father did not embrace her but simply stood in place, passing uncomfortable glances between the other men.

Jeff spoke very loudly in English. "Nazira, such a surprise. We— we didn't know you were in Istanbul." He repeated this attempt at a joke in Russian for Anarbek, who did not smile. "It's been so— but what are you doing here?"

"I have come for my father."

The brown man on the couch examined her fiercely, and like the others he did not smile in greeting. He was intense and handsome—but lacking, she could see now, any warmth, and his unrelenting gaze made her shiver. He did not seem happy about the distraction from his game. Her arrival, it seemed, had upset them all. She turned to her father, then back to Jeff, unsure whom to confront first, and then she lost all nerve.

After a few minutes of restrained conversation in which Nazira explained her long journey, Jeff took her bag and led her to a room full of books, where a mattress had been set up on the floor.

"Your father's crashing in here," he said.

"Crashing?"

"Staying," Jeff said. "The apartment—well, the apartment's kind of crowded. Will there be enough room for both of you?" He hardly looked at her when he spoke.

"Yes, in my opinion it is enough."

"It's good to see you again, Nazira. I've thought of you lately. I was worried."

"Thank you for worrying, but everything is fine. And I have thought of you too." The words were all wrong. She flushed.

But Jeff was staring at his fingers and had not seen her embarrassment. He shifted on his feet. "Maybe you would like to wash up? I'll get you some towels. We're going to have some dinner up the street in a little bit, and you can come with us . . ." His voice trailed off.

"I am not hungry, thank you. But I would very much like to rest."

"All right. I'll find you something to sleep on."

Anarbek accosted Jeff as he came back into the living room. "Did you invite her? What's she doing here?"

"I have no idea. She's your daughter. You tell me."

Adam couldn't understand them, but he was smiling and clicking his tongue. "What?" Jeff snapped.

"There enough of us for you?" Adam asked. "Better find another place before the next one comes. My aunt might be dropping by soon."

"Keep talking, Adam. See how much longer before I change the locks."

On the ferry to Europe the next morning Anarbek directed Nazira to a scratched wooden bench.

"And how much longer will you vacation in this city?" she asked, sitting down.

"You are all wrong, Nazira. There is no vacation. It's all for a reason, *kizim*," he said. He squeezed himself down beside her. "Jeff would not put up the money he offered."

"I told you, you had no business asking him for that! You think you were doing us a favor, Ata. But do you know what is happening in Kyzyl Adyr–Kirovka since you left?" Nazira described the visit from Yuri, Baktigul's flirtations, then her confrontation with Traktorbek.

"That man is bluffing. He's bluffing." Her father thought for a second. "It's all a game, just to frighten us."

Beneath them the boat engines groaned and the floorboards vibrated. "We must get back as soon as possible," she said. "He's threatened to steal Baktigul. He's going to marry your daughter. Is that clear to you?"

"Quiet now. It is *you* Traktorbek wants, not Baktigul. He's never gotten over it. If I come back with nothing to offer Bolot, it won't make any difference who Baktigul marries. We'll all be ruined. We'll lose what little we have. You see, I'm worried only about our future. How will we live after that?" He explained their options as he understood them: a return home, with nothing to appease Bolot, or another week or so in Istanbul, with the possibility of making lucrative connections.

"Another week will be too late!" she warned, in her urgency switching from Russian to Kyrgyz. "Lola is watching Manas. I can't leave her with the two boys alone so long."

"Nonsense. We must return to the village with a plan. Something to sell." He patted his jacket pocket. "I *have* a plan. You'll see! Lola will understand."

"Your plans! I remember your plans. Erotic films for the cows! An American in the village! This ridiculous trip! Where have your plans gotten us? I can see it. You've been fooled by this city, by all this"—she waved her arms at the skyline—"this foreign *biznes*. Your dreams will ruin us. You were never like this when Ama was alive."

The ferry had pulled out and was picking up speed across the silver waters. Her father's eyebrows clenched, but he ignored the rebuke, reached inside his jacket, then handed her a brochure. "Look at this," he said. The brochure was written in Turkish and English. She began to read it:

ANTIK LEATHER LTD.

We offer low costs and high quality for shearling garments. Antik Leather is one of the oldest and biggest producers in Turkish Leather Industry. Antik Leather has been specialized at processing shearling garments. We have been established in 1982 and now have two factories. One is tannery, and the other is Shearling Ready Made Garment Factory. Our tannery which is shown above photo is been located at Turkey's Leather Processing Center: Yeditepe Leather Industry Region. Today at our two factories, we reached 350 employees, about 9500 sqm closed factory space and US 20.000.000 turning-over yearly. Our production capacities is about 38,000 pieces of ready made garments and 500,000 pieces of processed leather.

Nazira studied the photograph of the tannery at the top of the brochure—a long one-story structure, not unlike the Lenin School, with a red brick roof and no windows. A Turkish flag flapped from a pole beside the front entrance. The grounds were surrounded by green cypresses, and a large sun hung low in the sky above the building. She turned over the brochure.

Shearling is Nature's finest insulator for cold. And it is 100% NATURAL. It will keep you warm and cozy although there is subzero weather. Please do not be shocked by our lowest prices and high quality. Also we have important news for small entrepreneurs . . .

Her father's large, hopeful eyes were fixed on her, awaiting a reaction.

Beneath this paragraph was a picture of a thin woman, with a tight masculine haircut and an overly serious look, modeling a long black leather jacket. One of her hands she pressed to her chin, the other she rested on the shoulder of a man, equally serious, seated beside her. He wore a brown suede jacket, and his hands were folded in his lap. At the bottom of the brochure was the company's address.

Nazira pointed to it. "Is this where you're taking me, then?" she asked, shaking her head.

"No, I'm taking you to their store in the Grand Bazaar, not the actual factory."

She held out the brochure. "And what makes you think you can do business with this Antik Leather company?"

"No, no, you misunderstand, Nazira." He pulled the brochure from her hands. "Antik *produces* the jackets and sells them. But they *get* their skins from another company. In Turkey the business is conducted between family members. This is how it is—how business is run in the world today. You must work with people you trust. This man at Antik buys the leather from his uncle, Hakan." Anarbek reached into his left jacket pocket and removed a second glossy brochure. "It is the uncle who *imports* the sheepskins. Look, he gave me this, but it's only in English. Read it for me."

"I've seen enough."

"Read it!"

She unfolded it.

HAKAN PAZARLAMA LTD.

Importing and Marketing Raw Lamb/Sheep Skins Founded 1992 in Istanbul Yeditepe Organised Leather Industry Zone, and operates now in an area of 12,000 sqm, it includes a refrigerated warehouse of 750 sqm. Which is the first and only one in the sector in Istanbul.

Products: Lamb and Sheep skins for Double Face, Lamb and Sheep skins for Nappa, Sheepskins for shoe manufacturing.

Import from: England, Spain, Australia, Norway, America, South Africa, Switzerland, Sweden, Ukraine.

Objective: Meet the customer's requirements in a professional manner by keeping quality standard high in the sector and providing effective quick service. The company importing raw-skins the most in terms of turnover in Turkey. Hakan Pazarlama having a refrigerated warehouse in the FreeZone provide the best condition for preservation of skin from decomposition and hairslips which are highly important for such an organic material—

Nazira stopped. This technical information was too much for her to process, never mind translate. The ferry had nearly arrived at Eminönü, and as it began its U-turn along the Galata Bridge, preparing to dock, the stone palaces perched on the hills above the port loomed larger.

"Have you met with the uncle, Hakan, then?" she asked, clicking her tongue and returning the beloved documents to her father.

"He has promised to arrange a meeting soon. I will ask again today." He waved the brochures, snapping them in the air. "I have great hope, Nazira. This would be big. Big for our entire village."

"It will take equipment, transportation. Where will you get that?"

"We have our whole factory going unused in the village. Trucks that have not made delivery in years."

"I don't know, Ata."

Anarbek had offered to bring her along on his business rounds, hoping she would share some of his excitement, but she had agreed to come only to convince him to leave Turkey. As they exited the ferry and climbed a pedestrian bridge over the busy shoreline road, he told her how, in his earlier search for a business plan, he had spent time near the Grand Bazaar. He had popped into shops to drink chai with the merchants and followed families to see what they bought, comparing prices and profit margins. Searching for the secret of effective salesmanship, he had even committed to memory the greetings of hawkers ("How can I help you spend your money?"). He wanted her to see this bustling world of commerce—the sparkling jewelers' row, the textured carpets hanging in windows, the handmade purses dangling on lines above the shops. Only then would she understand what had delayed him.

They hurried up the Street of the Market Gate to the bazaar's entrance, an archway outlined in colored marble and inscribed in blue Arabic calligraphy. Inside, the crenelated arches continued; the ceiling vaulted in red and white mosaics over the stores. Her father led Nazira by the arm through the crowds to a quieter section of the market, where jackets hung in dark swaths of brown and black over the cramped shops. He was taking her to meet Faruk, the leather merchant from Antik whom he had befriended. Her father warned her that Faruk had only one arm—his left—so she should try not to stare; and this warning only embittered her more.

"You have a daughter!" the squat, oily-haired man said in rough Russian as they entered his store. "*She's* your daughter?"

"Yes," Anarbek said, "my daughter."

Her father, she saw, had never even *mentioned* his family.

The merchant squinted at her as they shook hands. He had a nervous manner—twitching lips and a bobbing Adam's apple. He sat them down on wooden stools, and a boy brought chai. Faruk handed the glass to Nazira himself, saying, in English, "You are a princess."

"Thank you," Nazira said, blushing.

"And she speaks English, Anarbek! You should take a lesson or two from your daughter. She is smarter than *you!*"

Her father pretended to laugh.

Looking around, she discovered why, of over four thousand shops in the bazaar, Anarbek had chosen this one. On a column in the center of the store hung a poster-size photograph of Hillary Clinton. She seemed to be purchasing a leather jacket. The one-armed merchant, following her gaze, told Nazira how the previous fall Mrs. Clinton had come to the bazaar. Faruk had spotted her and complimented her beautiful hair, and she had bought jackets, from this very store, for Bill, Chelsea, and herself. Nazira wondered if this could be true. But photographs did not lie: there she was in color, shaking Faruk's left hand in an awkward gesture, the famous First Lady with a strikingly white grin, the owner laughing at some joke it looked like he had not understood.

Her father elbowed her and raised his chin. "What a business-man Faruk must be! No? To have sold merchandise to such people!" He turned to the shop owner. "How much did the wife of the president of the United States pay for her jacket?"

"It is between me and the First Lady," Faruk said.

"Of course! Of course!" Anarbek gazed at the man in dreamy admiration.

They discussed details of their potential partnership. From Kyzyl Adyr–Kirovka Anarbek would ship high-quality skins of Kyrgyz sheep to Hakan Pazarlama—the factory owned by Faruk's uncle—which Faruk would then buy for his tannery and use in the production of leather jackets. Nazira could see they were having difficulty communicating and agreeing on general prices, and Anarbek had yet to visit the factory—sixty kilometers outside the city, on the northern shore of the sea.

After discussing business, they chatted awhile, slurping the strong tea. Nazira did not drink hers. She wanted to leave; she wanted only to ask when her father could visit the uncle's factory and get it over with. She knew her father was stalling, enjoying Faruk's company, safe from her questioning. At last the dealer looked at her and said, "I have an idea!" He pronounced the words slowly, the same plastic smile on his face that Nazira had noticed in the photograph. "Why wait for Kyrgyzstan? We can start the dealing now. You can see how well our jackets sell, Nazira. The quality. Quality!" The last word he spoke at her ear, leaning close, with breath that smelled like rotten cabbage.

"Come!" Faruk said, and led them from the store out of the bazaar, across Yeniçeriler Caddesi and into the swirling heart of the Laleli trading quarter. Cars plied the congested streets, people rushed in and out of tiny shops, boxes were taped and hauled off on hand carts, and arguments in ten languages poured from dimly lit alleyways. They followed Faruk to a corner where a tall, blond, heavily made-up woman stood, holding a black leather jacket by a coat hanger. Her painted eyes darted left at the inching traffic on the road, then right at the passing pedestrians. If someone on the street made eye contact, she lifted the jacket and took a suggestive step in his or her direction, a movement that seemed to Nazira some kind of secret signal.

Faruk stopped in front of her, felt the tough leather between his fingers, and said, "*Kak dyela sevodnya,* Sashenka?"

The woman eyed Anarbek and Nazira and swept her curly bangs out of her face. In the histrionic manner of a Russian actress she smiled and pronounced, "Very good today! *Och-yen!*"

"This woman sells jackets for me. There's a large trade here on the street. People look for deals. They know they'll find prices they can't get in the shops, and I give Sashenka a quarter of the profit. If she sells two, three jackets a day, she can make some good money, no? What, fifty or one hundred dollars?"

Nazira pictured that kind of money: fifty dollars a day, three hundred a week, a thousand a month. It was unthinkable. She imagined the new clothes she could buy for Manas and Oolan, a rug for the cold wooden floor in her house, an electric oven now that there was no gas in the village. She could stop brewing *samogan*. But no, they didn't have the time for this.

Faruk stretched his plastic smile. "I give Sashenka a quarter of the profit. I shall give you"—he paused a dramatic second before whispering—"half."

Half? The offer was tempting. What would it hurt to try, two or three days at the most, until her father was ready to leave? She searched Anarbek's face for approval, but he was staring at the tall blond woman's bare knees and nodding, only half listening.

In this way, on just her second afternoon in the city, Nazira found herself employed. The following morning she rolled up the sleeping bag Jeff had given her and ate breakfast with her father and Adam in uncomfortable silence. They had yogurt and last night's bread, and her father made her try, for the first time, a banana. It was soft and sweet, and she had never tasted anything so delicious, but when she told this to Adam, he looked at her as if she were a child. The dark American had little patience. She asked him politely about his family and his work, but he responded only with scornful, curt, one-word answers, and she wondered what she had done to insult him.

Anarbek walked her to the ferry. Alone on the European side, unsure of herself, the traffic swirling around her, she made her way uphill, past the university arch, into the Grand Bazaar and to the leather store, where Faruk greeted her with a kiss on both cheeks, his lips hanging a second too long. He then unfolded a short black leather jacket on a table before her.

"Start at one hundred fifty dollars. Don't take less than eighty," he said in Russian.

She returned to the street where they had met Sashenka. After nine, as the bustle began, Nazira attempted to attract customers: the tourists exiting the hotels, the restaurant owners opening shop, the drivers of boxy Tempra SX's, the Russian *shapka* traders. It made her nervous, standing alone on such a busy street, holding up an expensive leather jacket. She worried someone might just steal it from her and that she would be held responsible. But watching the other saleswomen on the sidewalk eventually calmed her, and she tried to imitate their subtle movements. If eye contact was established with a pedestrian or driver, she took two gentle steps forward, slightly raising the leather coat to signal the potential customer, welcoming him to approach.

Three hours passed without a sale. Nazira daydreamed of Manas sitting on Lola's lap, or petting the neighbor's dog, or chasing sheep in the garden. She missed him with a pain that was almost physical, and as the morning wore on, her daydreams turned into fears. She saw Traktorbek chasing Manas, lifting him roughly, shaking him, tossing him into the air higher and higher and threatening not to catch him.

By late morning Nazira had given up hope of making a sale and was considering dropping this mad game and demanding her father's absolute immediate return home, when a stocky man with a strange Turkish accent surprised her by asking the price of the jacket. She forgot the troubles of home, and with an instinct absorbed from the village bazaar, named a price higher than she had been instructed to: two hundred dollars. The give and take commenced. She bargained carefully, remembering that $80 was the lower limit, and sold the jacket for $120—a huge sum. All the way back to the Grand Bazaar she fingered the bills in her sweater pocket. It was that simple.

Faruk seemed both pleased and surprised when she handed over the money. "Terrific. You are a natural businesswoman," he said. "That jacket was worth only fifty."

He was as good as his word and gave Nazira half the profit on the spot: thirty-five dollars.

She sold two more pieces early that afternoon, an addictive sense of triumph building with each sale. She counted what she had earned again and again. Last year, when teacher salaries had been delayed, the Kyrgyz government had paid her in UNICEF emergency food rations—crumbled bars of inedible dry oats. Now here she was, thick wads of clean U.S. bills rolled in her pocket, almost one hundred dollars in a single day.

Throughout the afternoon she continued to see the mysterious Sashenka, who appeared off and on among the street hawkers of leather coats, fur jackets, and pillbox hats. The woman had a stately air about her, an attitude of experience. She spoke Russian and English and greeted Nazira in both languages, but she bargained with customers in Turkish and in German. While Nazira stood her ground, turning all afternoon on the same sidewalk corner, Sashenka changed sides of the street impatiently, strutting up and down its length, keeping a distance between herself and the other sellers. Strangely, Nazira never saw her make a sale, and she wondered about her own good luck. Was she actually a better dealer? She tried to assuage the unstated rivalry between them with frequent waves and smiles. Late in the afternoon, she had just sold a miniskirt and was passing Sashenka on her way to the shop when the woman stopped her.

"You are getting good at this game," Sashenka said with a forced laugh. "And you are making a lot of money. I have not sold a jacket all week. Why not take me to lunch?"

Nazira said she would love to. In the bright sunlight they ate at a sidewalk café under a red awning that bubbled in the breeze. They chatted for nearly an hour, picking through pieces of chicken shish and roasted eggplant in olive oil. Sashenka's good humor and harsh accents amused Nazira. It turned out she was not Russian, but Romanian. They discussed the underground leather-peddling industry. Sashenka gave her advice: the busiest streets at the best times, the kind of person who will stop to flirt but is not interested in buying, the tricks of knowing if someone is walking away as a bargaining ploy or because you have played too hard. Over chai, Nazira explained how she had come to the city, her attempt to get her father to return to Kyrgyzstan, and his misguided obsession with figuring out a business arrangement between companies in the two nations.

"It seems you may be stuck here for a while," Sashenka said. "I know what that feels like."

"No, I will give my father—and this *biznes*," Nazira gestured to the busy street, "a week at the most."

"Yes," the Romanian said, smiling. "I know what that is like."

A truck crashed by, spewing exhaust behind it.

Emboldened by her success on the streets, Nazira had built up the courage to tell Jeff about Manas. But in the apartment that evening Jeff refused to remain alone in the same room with her. He refused to acknowledge anything had ever happened between them. He never mentioned receiving the letters she had sent, never elaborated on the concern he had expressed in his own letter to her, and when she approached, as quickly as possible he sought the company of Adam or her father, so she could talk no more.

Near midnight, though, she cornered him accidentally. Her father had asked her to fetch him a glass of water before he went to sleep. Passing the living room, she saw Adam sprawled on the couch, reading. He glanced up from his book and quickly looked away. Self-conscious, distracted, she turned into the kitchen and found herself face to face with Jeff. He nearly jumped at her sudden entrance, then laughed uncomfortably. "Nazira, we haven't been alone in many years," he said, and sat down at the round wooden table. He offered her a chair.

She swallowed. "Jeff, I have not forgotten," she said, seating herself.

"I didn't mean you had." His clear voice grew foggy. "I haven't forgotten you either."

She had been caught off guard and tried to figure out how to broach the vital subject at this inopportune time. She bounced back up. "I promised my father to bring water. May I use a glass?"

"You have been here three days. You are no longer my guest, you are family."

"Ah, yes. You are a good host." She managed a smile, opened a cabinet with a shaking hand, and pulled from it two tall glasses. She was about to fill them at the sink, but Jeff came up behind her.

"Don't use the tap. You should drink bottled water. It's safer. Here."

He opened the refrigerator and offered her a plastic liter labeled *Hayat*. Fancy, expensive water, she thought, like something out of a soap opera. Jeff took another glass from the cabinet for himself. She watched him fill them and asked quietly, "I have wondered, Jeff. Why have you not married yet?"

He spilled some of the water on the counter. "Try some of this," he said, offering her a glass. "See how much better it tastes."

She took the glass and pressed the back of one hand against it. "It is too cold. You should not drink such cold water! Your throat will become ill." She met his glance. Jeff returned to the table and sat down slowly. "I'm not sure marriage is in the cards for me, Nazira. I have a girlfriend now, here in Turkey. Her name's Melodi. I'd like to be married one day, but—"

Nazira felt her cheeks coloring. "Yes?"

"I'm not sure *she* does." He sipped his water, smacked his lips, and said in Kyrgyz, "*Eshteke emes.*" It's not important.

"Does she know of us?" Nazira approached the table, slid the chair a bit away from Jeff, and sat down. "Is that why?"

"No, not that." He swallowed. "I think she likes her freedom, her independence. She's not like other women here. She's adventurous. She doesn't want to be married young, with children and everything—a normal, quiet life, you know?"

"Yes, a normal life. Children. And you do not want such things?"

Jeff fidgeted in his seat. "What I'm saying is, if it's not going to work out with me and Melodi, it's time for me to move on again, see more of the world."

"I do not understand you, Jeff. The world is everywhere! You have seen too much of it, I think."

"Listen, someone like me gets bored if I stay in one place too long. I'm not really settled."

"How can you be bored in such a big city? Here you do everything you want. You have money. You take the holidays. Go to films. Eat in restaurants."

"No, it's a different kind of boredom."

"I think you have forgotten Kyzyl Adyr–Kirovka. *There* it is very boring."

Jeff tapped the table nervously with his thumb. "I think I was happy there."

Nazira considered this a moment, then said, "You were happy because you could come and go. We cannot do that."

"What do you mean? You've done that now. Look where you are!" He waved his arm at the window. Across the straits the mosques shone white through the veil of the misty evening.

"But Jeff, do you know what this is costing me?" She wanted to explain how this trip was tearing at her, how it was keeping her from her son, from *their* son. She sought the words she had prepared countless times in her head but found herself for the first time questioning them. Why did he never ask about her life back in Kyrgyzstan? Could he have used her and then left her to suffer the results, like that Eden in *Santa Barbara*? Had he simply played with her? Was he capable of that? Clearly he had never felt anything serious for her. Her body grew stiff, and she thought she was losing all feeling in her chest and her legs. Before she could say anything, Jeff surprised her, reaching across the table and touching her arm.

"I have something to ask you, Nazira. Your father—he mentioned a child once. A son."

She wrenched her arm away, surprised at the strength of her own revulsion. What right did he have, did any man have, to touch her like this?

"Yes," she said fiercely. "I have a son."

"Is he . . . ?" He looked at her in earnest. Five years ago in Kyrgyzstan, Jeff had seemed fresh, innocent, hopeful—there had been a glow of health to this face. Here, in this city, he seemed the very opposite: selfish, dangerously childish. She thought of Traktorbek. *He* at least had wanted her for his wife.

"His name is Manas," she said. She watched Jeff's face drop, and suddenly she lost her courage. "He was an accident. A Russian man I knew from university. He came that year to teach in Talas . . ." She felt the words slip easily off her tongue, the words she had used many times in the past, explaining away Manas's father. She could see relief softening Jeff's eyes. He nearly smiled. She said, "I thought he loved me. But he just came and went. He was— how do you say?—coming and going always."

"A transient."

"Transient? Is this the word?" She shifted in her chair to face away from him.

"Can you handle it? Your son, I mean. Without the father?" His tone had changed; suddenly he was concerned.

Nazira smiled in defiance. "I?" she said, patting her chest. "I can handle it. We Kyrgyz women are used to such things. You have seen our men. They are so lazy. What is the difference, if they stay or not?" She tasted a tiny sip of her father's bottled water—the iciness stung her throat. Jeff Hartig, she thought. It had not been him—it had been his confidence, his foreignness, the possibilities he offered of some other life. "*Durak!*" she said softly in Russian. Fool.

"I know," he said, misunderstanding.

"*Durak. Durak.*"

"I know." He grinned, as if the stilted conversation had cleared the air.

Nazira stood, turned unsteadily, and leaned against the counter. She glanced through the windows at the play of light, the faint hints of stars across the sky. "My father is thirsty," she said, lifting one cold glass from the table.

"Yes, he is," Jeff said, smiling once more. Again that look of confidence, as if they had shared some intimate joke. A pang of hatred pushed at her stomach. Jeff did not know her father. He knew nothing about either one of them.

At the sink, with a splash, she dumped the freezing bottled water from the glass and refilled it with tepid water from the tap—the only kind her father should drink. Jeff remained silent as she strode out of the kitchen. Passing the living room, she saw Adam again, his legs raised rudely on the couch. She had completely forgotten he was there, just the next room over. He did not look up from his book; he refused to acknowledge her creaking footsteps. Americans!

Nazira had never lived in such a strange place with such unfamiliar people, and she did not know how to accomplish the simplest things. Jeff's huge apartment was only superficially clean; she was bothered by the dust on the bookshelves, the strange red sauces that had leaked all over the refrigerator, and the smudged glasses the men had proudly washed. At night she never knew where to sit and spent much of the time alone in the small, stifling hot study, reading Jeff's Lonely Planet travel guides. Each morning she changed her clothes in a mad sprint, afraid her father would come in and swing open the door. Jeff had a laundry machine—a luxury Anarbek showed her how to use—but she felt uneasy about hanging her clothes on the single line on the balcony, among the men's undergarments.

This morning, passing Adam's open room, she saw him doing pushups with his legs raised up on his bed, and she hurried by, afraid he'd catch her looking. The bathroom routine had become a source of torment: she didn't know when was the proper time to use it, and her presence had upset a schedule in which Jeff, then Adam, then Anarbek took turns washing. So for the third morning in a row she waited for her father's healthful clearing of the throat, and when Anarbek finally returned from his toilet, the bathroom was hers. She found that the hot water had run out, that a soaked towel lay in a puddle on the floor. All week now a plastic razor blade had remained on the sink, and though she wanted to throw it out, she imagined it might be Adam's.

At breakfast, Jeff was in a rush to get to work, and he avoided Nazira's eyes. Her father scowled and dismissed any talk of leaving. And Adam made her the most uncomfortable of all, with his long silences.

She found herself more at ease outside the apartment. Her good luck with the leather jackets continued through the week, and her lunches with Sashenka became a daily ritual. It was her only female companionship, and Nazira relished the company. They spoke in Russian about wild subjects, things she never would have discussed with friends in the village—past loves, strange dreams, the habits of men. They chattered as if they had known each other for years, and Nazira felt no danger relaying her secrets: whom would the Romanian tell?

Each day Sashenka drilled her about her progress with her father. Had Nazira convinced him to leave? Had he secured his business connections yet? Nazira would chronicle their previous afternoon's journey around the markets of the Laleli district, into the dark shops of socks, underwear, sweaters, leather, and tobacco. She described her father's intrepid search for someone willing to give him business capital, someone enterprising and kind, interested in helping Turkey's Central Asian ancestors, now that their little country was independent and struggling. From the shop-keepers flowed continuous promises, evasions, and equivocations, but nothing concrete. Only the sheepskin deal with Faruk's uncle, Hakan, looked promising.

Her father, she explained, was tireless; but she could not understand his drive. Capitalism seemed exhausting. She told Sashenka, "If I could just get him home, I'm sure things will work themselves out. We have friends and family back in Kyrgyzstan. How does he expect to get anything done here, so far away, on his own?"

Sashenka assured her that it takes striking out on your own to accomplish something big. There were opportunities in wealthier countries that could not be found in the places *they* had come from. Hadn't Nazira realized this yet? Turkey was developing quickly. One day Kyrgyzstan and Romania would develop too, but the time frame was different. Every country had its own pace, but a human being had only so many years—you had to make your fortune where you could. A person had to survive. Sashenka spoke down to her as if she were a child, yet Nazira argued that she was not as simpleminded and provincial as her new friend thought.

"Let me ask you then, Nazira, who has been buying your leather jackets?"

"Customers on the street. They seem eager enough."

"Friends of his." Sashenka slapped the edge of the table, rattling the empty plates. "Friends of Faruk. That is who is buying your leather jackets. When Faruk has your confidence, you're caught. You'll start depending on him. Pretty soon you'll sell all day for him, and take less of a cut. He'll ask for your passport, and then you'll be working for next to nothing. You'll be desperate, doing him favors. I've been here for three years, Nazira. I too have a family at home, in Romania!"

Nazira felt foolish. "I didn't know."

"You have to be careful."

"No, my father wouldn't let him take advantage of us. We'll leave before any of that can happen."

Sashenka shook her head. "You're such a simple woman! I was once simple too."

They ate their salads, and Nazira tried changing the subject; but about Jeff, Sashenka could offer little solace. "You haven't mentioned it?" she chided. "You are staying with the father of your child, and he says nothing of it to you?"

Nazira explained that she had not had a chance and then, having a chance, had lost her nerve. It was not important really. Manas had been an accident. A *happy* accident, she assured Sashenka. Jeff had not answered her letters, and she had never expected to see him again. "What can I do? Force him back to Central Asia with me?"

"But money!" cried Sashenka. "Support! He's left you with a tremendous burden and he's given you nothing."

Nazira had never thought of her son as a burden. She remembered the way Manas collected his animal magazines, the delight with which he chased the dogs of Karl Marx Street. But now her friend was laughing at her. "You poor girl," she consoled her. "He took advantage of you and just disappeared."

"No. That is not what happened."

Sashenka asked with an ironic smile, "What exactly happened then?"

What *had* happened? She had never attempted to explain it to anyone. "It was just one night," she said. "We were carried away. He was leaving, and there was something so final. We had this friendship. We could talk to each other. He seemed so generous then. And my father—"

"Make the American pay," Sashenka said, listening to her stumble to make sense of it all. "He owes you!"

"Does he?"

Nazira looked into her friend's hard eyes. Sashenka assumed her actress air and drew imaginary lines on the tablecloth. "We women need to protect ourselves. We need rules that every woman must obey, if only to keep our dignity. You are breaking one of those rules, Nazira. You are allowing that man to get the upper hand and get away with it. You have to be stronger."

"I thought I was being the strong one."

"And braver," she said. "You must be braver."

"Wasn't I being brave?"

"Neither. Where is he?" The Romanian stood up in mock seriousness and clenched her fists. "Show me where he is. I'll tear his tiny balls out from under his fat American stomach! I'll make him pay for this."

Nazira raised her hand to her lips. She had never heard expressions like this from a woman's mouth.

Sashenka exploded in laughter and sat down again. With a mischievous smile she said, "I would, you know. No man does that to a friend of mine." She thought for a few seconds. "If your father needs money so badly, get it from the American. Make him pay some every month, for his child."

"No," Nazira said. "I cannot do that."

"Why?"

It occurred to her only then that she did not want Jeff to have a part. She knew now that she had never loved that man, and she didn't have to tell him anything. "Jeff owes me nothing," she said. It was an astonishing thought: her son belonged to her alone.

Sashenka shook her head in frustration. They lingered over the rest of the lunch in an uncomfortable silence. It was only with some effort that Nazira broke the spell to ask for the bill.

14

In the *dolmuş* Melodi leaned against Jeff, pressed her cheek to his, and asked in a whisper where they were going. He had not seen her in over a week. Now, after a Friday night dinner in Beyoğlu, they had not yet decided whose home to return to. Around them the other five passengers sat in silence. The dark Kurdish couple sharing the back seat huddled arm in arm as the driver swerved between lanes, honking his horn in quick blasts. Since Anarbek had come, Jeff had limited his overnights at Melodi's apartment to once a week, as he was uncomfortable leaving his guests alone. He knew he was more conscious of the separation than she was.

He had yet to break the news of Nazira. Now, returning the whisper, he told her that another guest had arrived. She stared incredulously at him.

"And how do you know *him?*" she asked louder, in Turkish.

"It's a woman, Anarbek's daughter. A good friend."

"And she will be living with you like Anarbek? For weeks? For months?"

"I honestly don't know." Melodi's sudden jealously pleased him.

"You cannot ask?"

"Actually, no. I cannot." Trying to calm her, he started to explain the Kyrgyz expectations of hospitality.

"But you are not Kyrgyz, Jeff. You are American!"

"Shhh. I owe them a great deal. When I lived in Central Asia, they were very good to me."

Melodi asked in English, "She is only a friend?"

Jeff felt cramped and leaned forward, his elbows on his knees. The passenger in the front seat swung her head back around, pretending she wasn't watching, and the couple to their right looked steadfastly into their laps, but he knew they too were listening. Through the rearview mirror the driver's eyes darted right and left, searching for gaps in traffic. Jeff held the back of Melodi's soft hand and, intertwining his fingers with hers, squeezed once, then harder—a signal that they would talk about this when the *dolmuş* stopped.

The force of the turning vehicle pushed them against the door as the driver ran a red light and swung through the traffic circle of the Beşiktaş İskele. They waited for the others to climb out, then Melodi slid her way over the shredded vinyl seat, not looking back at Jeff. Outside on the pier, shaded by a mulberry tree, she stood in silence, her arms crossed.

"I need to go back to see if they're all right," Jeff said.

"I think I will not go with you tonight."

"Will you go home?"

She shrugged. "Maybe I will go to the Yeats."

He knew she was asking him to plead. In the past, no doubt, he would have. But he didn't want to introduce her to Nazira—too awkward, and with Nazira in the next room, he would be far too uncomfortable sleeping with Melodi. They had reached a turning point, and he was unprepared.

"You want me to come with you to the Yeats?" he asked. "Or I could take you home first, then go back to my place."

"No," she said. "I'll go alone."

Jeff stared at the wet sidewalk.

"You have changed, Jeff. Since your friends have come, I have always the feeling that you don't want to see me."

"That's not true." His voice was weak. How was she turning this on him? He had asked *her* to marry him.

"Yes, I understand, Jeff. You have an apartment full of guests. You need to go check in on them. Good night then."

"No, it's all right. Maybe they'll be okay."

She stood with her hands on her hips. A young shoeshine boy, his hair matted, his ragged shirt torn at the collar, watched from a few yards off, waiting for them to finish the argument before he approached. Jeff gave him a fierce look, and the boy raised his wooden stool over his shoulder and stepped back to the water's edge.

Melodi asked again, "She is only a friend, this Nazira?"

"Yes. Well, not really." Jeff hesitated. "Actually, Nazira was more than a friend."

Melodi's face—always lively, always bright—grew somber as she gazed at him. She closed her eyes, thinking, then lifted her chin and raised herself to what seemed a new height. "How much more was she than a friend?"

Jeff simply shook his head.

"And now she is living with you? You have invited an old girlfriend of yours to stay with you? It is wrong, Jeff."

"How is it wrong?"

He was growing frustrated. She would not commit, she would not move in with him, but here she was, telling him who could stay in his apartment and for how long.

"Where is she staying?" she asked.

"In the study, with her father. I'm telling you, she won't be here more than a week."

"That is what you said about Adam. You need to tell them all to leave."

"What difference does it make to you?" he asked. "They're friends of mine. They're not living in *your* apartment."

"It used to feel like my apartment, too, Jeff. It was not a hotel. I used to feel welcome there."

"So welcome you could have lived there, and you've chosen not to."

Her head snapped upward as if he had struck her. "Jeff, I think I will go home now. I don't need you to take me. *Iyi geceler.*" She pronounced the words stiffly. This use of the Turkish plural—good nights—had always, in its logic, baffled him. But now it made her goodbye more than final, as if she was wishing him good night for the rest of his life.

"Wait," he said.

She had turned her back on him, revealing the light nape of her neck, his favorite part of her body. In her hoarse voice she whispered, "There is nothing more to say. No, nothing else. I cannot believe you have done this." She swung around again, facing him, and said in Turkish, "Go back to your guests, Jeff. They are important to you. Go back to your friend Nazira."

"I want you to understand. They are not more important than you."

She ran her hand through her hair. "I am beginning to understand. I have given a lot of time for us, Jeff. None of this is easy for me either, with my family and my job. And to come all the way into Taksim from the hospital, to be with you each week. But I do it happily. Why is everything always so difficult for you? You want more and more. You have never accepted all I give. And now it is this."

"Listen, I'm sorry."

"Yes, I am sorry too. We have the Turkish expression: *Akar akar da durulur.*" A stream flows and flows, then settles down.

He smiled weakly, nodding, but she walked off in firm steps to hail a taxi. He was burning to call her back again, to reassure her about Nazira, to admit he had been unwise and had made an egregious mistake. Circumstances divided them, he wanted to tell her—not love. In the twilight the shoeshine boy was still watching, taking in the entire scene. Jeff felt a wave of nausea and was suddenly furious. He wanted to grab the kid by the scruff of his neck and shake him. But he composed himself and strode resolutely to the ferry, to force the waters between him and Melodi once and for all. Sitting alone on the windy top deck he felt part relief and part loss. He looked back at the pier and saw her duck into a taxi; and suddenly he felt only a sharp regret, like a man who has purchased on impulse something he could not afford.

Oren had been thrilled to hear that a woman like those on the Internet was staying with Jeff, and all week long he had been inventing tenuous excuses to invite himself over. He offered to return books Jeff had not, in fact, lent him. He wanted to bring an extra inflatable mattress in case someone needed a place to sleep. He suggested theme nights for dinner: they should all make stir-fry, or he could whip up some real American barbecue for the guests. But Jeff had told him he had enough on his hands at the moment.

Just after Jeff returned home, though, disgusted with himself, Oren showed up. He had the Sunday *New York Times* from the previous weekend with him—he had bought it for twelve dollars at a newsstand in the Hilton Hotel. He bore it into the apartment like a lost treasure, dropping it with a crash onto the living room floor, and then immediately introduced himself to Nazira. Adam made a grab for the sports section. Anarbek perused the bra advertisements. Oren stared at Nazira, who carefully turned glossy pages of the magazine section, afraid to rip them. Adam had discovered pirated copies of his favorite heavy-metal CDs for sale on the streets in Ortaköy, and now he inserted them into Jeff's stereo, and turned up the volume. Judas Priest and Guns N' Roses shook the windows of the living room.

"Can you turn that down?" Jeff asked. He felt like a chaperone.

Into the evening, Adam and Oren sprawled on the woven rugs, their heads propped against antique grain sacks that Jeff had stuffed like pillows. Nazira and her father sat upright on armchairs. Oren entertained them all with a litany of dirty jokes, most of which Nazira did not understand, though she translated for her father, who listened with his mouth open in an expression of genuine puzzlement. Oren showed off his tattoos. He told how he had worked for a summer in northern California as a beekeeper's assistant and then spent an entire hour explaining the mating habits of bees. As a high school student he had studied aikido, and he demonstrated with Adam various holds, throws, and defenses, knocking one of Jeff's inlaid porcelain plates off a stand.

Later in the evening Oren watched the chess game between Anarbek and Adam, offering both of them advice, which, rolling their eyes, neither man followed. From the hallway closet Oren pulled out a backgammon board and challenged Jeff to a match, which he declined. Nazira, conveniently, was the only one left, and she agreed to play him. She sat on the couch, leaning slightly forward, cupping her cheeks as if it helped her strategize, and she gave the slightest blow of air as she moved her pieces. Each time he finished his turn, Oren would lift the dice off the board and hold them out for her to pick from his open palm. Exasperated, Jeff couldn't help but laugh.

He sipped Nescafé and for long minutes observed the scene in his apartment. The percussion of Adam's heavy-metal music was driving nails into his skull, and suddenly Jeff was overcome by a wave of fury, an urge to kick his guests out, boot every last one of them onto the street, let them fend for themselves. But he knew he never would. Near midnight they were still playing their games, Axl Rose was belting out "Welcome to the Jungle," and Jeff served his guests a box of chocolate-covered Turkish delight and wished them all good evening.

The apartment was perfectly quiet early Saturday morning when a steady pounding on the door roused him. The noise interrupted a dream he'd been having in which he was hiking down the Grand Canyon with Melodi. Through the early light streaming from the living room, he blundered down the hallway, furious. Such pounding on a door—this loud, at this hour—he had not heard since Kyrgyzstan, and he dreaded the arrival of some new ghost from his past. The heavy brass bolt stuck as always, and he had barely got it open when Oren crashed in, his eyes wild with excitement.

"We're going on a cruise! Get up!" he yelled. "Get up!" He pushed past Jeff, hurried through the foyer to Adam's room, and rattled the knob. "Everyone rise and shine! Top of the morning, Geronimo! How about a free ride up the Bosphorus?"

Jeff followed him down the hall, trying to quiet him, but he was already smashing the door of the study. "Let's go, you Kyrgyz! *Davai! Davai!*"

"What the hell, Oren?" Jeff whispered.

"School's taking the teachers on a free cruise up the Bosphorus. I decided you're gonna join us. You've all been working too hard."

"You could have asked us last night."

Oren mocked him in an extra-loud whisper. "I forgot. Didn't remember until this morning." He pounded again and yelled, "Let's go, sleeping beauties!"

Jeff pushed his friend from Anarbek's door. "It's seven thirty," he hissed. "Let them sleep."

Adam appeared down the hall in a T-shirt and boxers, his eyes half-closed. Anarbek opened his own door with a lazy frown. "*Shto?*" he asked. He scratched his hairy stomach, stretched his arms, yawned, and hurled a volley of Russian expletives at them.

The hired ferry was docked at the Üsküdar İskele, its top deck crowded with Turkish women who glared out from under wide-brimmed hats and pinched early-morning cigarettes between their fingers. Oren led the group to a row of open whitewashed benches, where they sat down and stared across the waters. To the west the straits shimmered in the morning brightness, the turreted palaces etched in relief against the stark blue sky, but to the north the sky looked threatening.

Nazira pointed to the clouds ahead. "Maybe we should have brought the umbrella?"

Jeff turned to Oren. "If it rains on us, we'll make you regret this the rest of your life."

"Lighten up, Jeff. Have some fun for once."

At exactly eight, earsplitting Turkish pop music clamored from a speaker above the wheelhouse, and the boat pulled away from shore. Oren stood next to Jeff, spread his arms, and jerked his shoulders in imitation of a Black Sea Laz dance. "Get away from me," Jeff said, but smiled despite himself. Nazira seemed smitten with Oren and snapped her fingers, urging him on, while some of the science teachers clapped and shouted his name. Adam leaned both elbows against the railing and laughed. Anarbek descended to the galley in search of breakfast.

The slow boat ride was tedious for Jeff, who had made this trip a dozen times since he had come to Istanbul. He was still reeling from yesterday's scene with Melodi; and staring down at the green depths, lost in thought, he had difficulty showing any enthusiasm when his friends gestured to the sights and asked what they were.

Adam, though, appeared to be completely taken with the boat and the scenery. He swung his head in both directions so he wouldn't miss anything. They sailed northwest against a heavy current, then began the long meandering back and forth across the straits. The captain interrupted the music to point out landmark *yalı*, ornate Ottoman seaside mansions with boathouses built into their lowest levels. People crowded the railings and shot photographs of the Çirağan Palace. The boat docked to pick up another group of teachers near the white mosque of Ortaköy, on the seaside square where Adam said he tutored Burak. Angling back across the water, they passed directly under the Bosphorus Bridge. Jeff gazed up at its expanse with a chill of vertigo, feeling something this large might come tumbling down on them. A man had jumped off these heights and survived. From this perspective, the span seemed too high; surviving a jump like that no longer seemed possible.

The village of Kandili, halfway up the nineteen-mile straits, was famous for its yogurt. When the captain docked, three hawkers carrying plastic milk crates rushed onto the boat, screaming, "YOĞURT! YOĞURT!"

Nazira watched her father buy three cups for himself and shook her head in disbelief. As the boat reached the middle of the straits,

Oren asked her to help him fetch everyone drinks. They descended into the passenger cabin, where they found a bar serving soda, juice, and *rakı*.

"So, you miss Kyrgyzstan?" Oren asked as they waited for service.

"Of course," Nazira said. "It is my motherland. You miss your motherland when you leave it."

Past the bar through the windows she could see a group of wooden fishing caïques bobbing on the waves. An old man leaned over the bow of one boat, pulling seaweed off a tangled net.

Oren said, "We don't use the word *motherland* very often in English."

"Don't you? My English, you can see, is very bad."

"I think it's amazing. Better than people I know in the States."

She threw him a doubtful look. "That is not true."

"It is. I teach English like you, remember?" He moved closer and leaned his tattooed arm against the bar. She puzzled over the paintings on his skin. She found him amusing, but also insincere. He tried too hard to entertain, and he reminded her of a movie star, of a character from one of the Rambo movies. From a speaker above, the driving rhythms of Black Sea music quickened. "So what do you miss about your motherland?"

"I miss my family, of course." Nazira regarded a teacher next to them, gnawing on a piece of sesame-seed bread. "I miss our Kyrgyz foods, my garden, the flowers, the mountains. I miss the horses."

"So you will go back soon?"

"This week, most definitely. I must convince my father he is acting stupid." Nazira shook her head in doubt. "But he never listens to me."

Screams from the upper deck could suddenly be heard against the music. Someone had spotted a pod of dolphins working their way down the straits, opposite the boat. Nazira gasped in astonishment, and they hurried to the windows and watched the gray animals curling through the water, then growing smaller, until they were distant specks, like rocks skimming off the waves.

Back at the bar Oren continued the conversation. "Don't you ever dream of living somewhere else? I mean, when you're in Kyrgyzstan, you're in this tiny village in the mountains. Don't you wonder what it's like in New York? Or Paris? Don't you want to see Australia?"

Nazira was quiet a few moments. Then she said, "I think more about people than places. The people I know are in Kyrgyzstan. My stepmother. My friends. What would they do if I leave them?" She pictured Manas and considered telling Oren about her son. But it had been hard enough to lie to Jeff the other night, and she didn't want to go into that again.

"What if you fell in love with a very handsome foreigner, for example?" He raised his blond eyebrows. "Would you think of living somewhere else?"

She covered her smile and felt the blush spreading on her cheeks. "Where would a woman such as I meet a handsome foreigner?"

"Well, say you did?" He lifted his chest and assumed a regal air.

"I think when I fall in love with a very good man, I will want to be with him wherever he goes. But maybe he would want to be with me too. Maybe he would like my village in Kyrgyzstan."

"Maybe he would."

"But there are too many difficulties in this situation. He would not speak our language."

"He'd learn."

"And he might not like our traditions. We have our guest sing songs at dinner. We eat the eyes of sheeps. Has Jeff never told you?"

"If he loved you, this man, he would learn to sing for you. He'd eat sheep eyes every morning for breakfast."

Nazira laughed. "And you? You do not want to return to your motherland?"

"Motherland!" Oren said, smiling.

"I mean—the United States. You do not want your children grown up in the United States? Or in your home, in California?"

"Maybe, but for me it's more important who I'll have those children with."

"So, Oren, you are searching for a wife."

"Well, yeah." He lowered his voice. "But I'm not really *searching*. I kind of just figure she's out here somewhere and we're going to run into each other."

Oren looked hard into her, a weighted stare. He was suddenly absurd, with his earnest expression, his painted arms and feminine blond hair and shredded cutoff jeans. She glanced out the windows at a ferry floating in the opposite direction.

"You think that's possible?" he asked.

She returned his gaze. "I do not know about those things. I do not know."

"Don't you know? I've been thinking about you. All last night my eyes were riveted." He leaned toward her. "I really like your freckles, and your accent. Your smile too. Why are you shaking your head? I think you're—how can I say it? Exotic. You are exotically beautiful. I'd like to know you better."

Like to know her better? She stared at his pointed chin. It was true, in Kyrgyzstan men could steal women, and the women had almost no choice. But this—this pronouncement of love in a public place, on a cruise, with the Turks drinking cola around them—this was something else entirely. Sashenka had warned her about Western men.

"Would you like to have dinner sometime this week?" he asked. "Just you and me? I know great restaurants in Istanbul."

Nazira rose without answering, taking two glasses of juice.

"Don't go just yet," Oren pleaded.

She had lost her breath. "Yes, it is time to go up."

"You didn't answer my question."

But she hurried up the stairs to the sun deck, where she joined the other men. She gave her father his drink, and Adam shuffled over to make room for her on the bench. It was a relief, sitting next to this one, with no expectation of conversation, and she was perfectly content to gaze out over the railing. After a few minutes, though, Adam surprised her.

"You eat pig?"

"Excuse me?"

"I read that Muslims don't eat pig meat. But I asked your father, and he said sometimes he did. And I asked my student, Burak, and he told me he tried bacon once. He liked it. What about you?"

"I would never eat meat from pigs."

"Why not?"

"Adam, it is not clean."

"Your father doesn't care."

"My father will eat anything."

"Is it because of religion?"

"I never thought of it. We are not very religious, but the Kyrgyz just do not eat pig. They are filthy animals. I cannot even imagine."

"You ever smelled bacon?"

"I don't know what bacon is."

"It smells delicious. I found this Polish butcher in Kadiköy. The only place in the city that sells it. If I fry it up, I bet you anything you'll want to try some."

"That is very kind of you, Adam, but no, thank you."

The morning slid by, the wind rose. Passengers put up the hoods of their jackets, and the sun battled the thick gray clouds. At the narrowest point on the straits the boat passed Rumeli Hisar, the Fortress of Europe, and the air grew cool. Oren stood across the deck, talking to his teacher friends. Anarbek, Jeff, and Adam huddled close to Nazira, and they watched the green shores, lush with oak and pine, approach and recede. The wind bit her ears, and from the loudspeakers she heard a pop song about everything being blue—my house is blue, my car is blue, my girlfriend's blue—and she couldn't understand what it meant.

They glided under the dark expanse of the second bridge, past the Sweet Waters of Asia. Near noon the boat docked at Anadolu Kavaği, the final northern village before the straits opened out to the Black Sea. The sun had not reappeared for an hour, and the sky, still clear to the south, looked dense up ahead. In a garbled voice the captain announced that they would have two hours to climb to the Genoese fortress or eat lunch in the village before sailing back. Nazira's father said he favored lunch first, but Jeff urged him to hike to see the view before the rain came. So she followed the men through the cafés and fish markets, past a simple stone mosque, and they began the climb. The fortress lay three hundred meters above them, perched on the edge of a cliff, a two-kilometer walk along a steep, curving road.

With a squad of teachers, Jeff, Anarbek, and Oren marched quickly ahead. Nazira preferred a more leisurely pace, and to her surprise Adam remained behind, as if to make sure she was okay.

The two of them walked in a steady silence until, at a right turn in the road, her foot slid on the loose gravel. "These paths are slippery," she said.

"No traction," Adam said.

"What does that mean?"

"It means you fall easily. Like that. Careful."

Her flats were not meant for hiking the steep hillside, and halfway up her feet had already begun to hurt. She glanced toward the fortress: the sky ahead was black. "I want to be up there," she said, pointing. "The others are so far in front."

"We'll catch up," Adam said.

And soon enough they did. The men were waiting for them at the top of the hill, on a level stone platform past the dirt parking lot. Her father reached out his hand and helped pull her up and then stood with one arm around her, trying to keep her warm in the wind. "It's perfect," Anarbek whispered in her ear. Before them stretched the Black Sea, an expanse of violent purple water, and over it now, approaching them quickly, loomed a grave black storm, cut by streaks of lightning.

"Rain's coming in just a few minutes," Oren said.

Adam pointed at the storm clouds. "Some view, isn't it?"

"We should see the fortress," Jeff suggested, "and get back down."

Together they hustled along an uneven stone path to the ruins of the medieval fortress, a brown structure of seven rounded towers. In the grass near the entrance, around the fallen slabs of stone, groups of spotted cows were munching tall brown weeds. Anarbek stopped to admire them.

"*Priditye!*" Jeff called.

"Come on," Nazira yelled back at her father. "We don't have time."

She waited for him, but he refused to hurry. After a minute, completely frustrated, she gave up and followed the others. Dinner proposals, offers of pig meat, her father's dallying—she'd had too much of these men. They climbed one by one through a dark hole in the thick walls, emerging into the ruins of the castle, now open to the air. The remains of an outer wall surrounded a wide circle of grass, dotted here and there by sleeping pariah dogs. A few of the teachers sat on the northern stones, laughing, calling, snapping photos of the view, and pointing at the approaching storm. Nazira stepped away from the others, wanting to be alone. She strolled the grounds and noticed carved over the entrance portal an inscription of the cross. At the southern wall she leapt a ditch to reach an earthen walkway. From the steep heights she watched two oil tankers ply their way through the entrance of the straits below, like silver birds crossing a green sky.

Adam appeared from nowhere beside her. She had not heard him coming.

"The others said to find you. They're heading back down. It's about to pour."

"Pour?"

"Rain." The storm had just about reached them. The air was growing darker, more oppressive by the moment, and Nazira felt the first drops on her arm. "I saw a shortcut down there," he said, pointing with his lips—a strange gesture. "We'll cut down through the back of the castle and catch 'em."

She didn't understand why this man, who had rudely ignored her all week, was suddenly so attentive. They turned and jumped over the ditch, then followed the curve in the eastern wall to an opening between the stones. A dirt path led downhill, parallel to the road. The rain began to patter against the dusty earth, and with her poor shoes Nazira could not move quickly on the loose sand. Adam walked close behind her. Once, as she slipped, he grabbed her by the wrist and kept her from falling. His grip and lean arm were unexpectedly strong.

She glanced back up at him. "Thank you, Adam." She was suddenly far more at ease in his presence.

His face was red, his lips tight. "Let's keep going."

A cold wind swept across her ears and the skies opened. The rain cascaded in slanting gusts, the most sudden rain she'd ever felt, and in seconds the two of them were drenched. She clasped the top of her red acrylic jacket. Her hair dripped and she felt the chilling wetness spreading under her light cowl-neck sweater. With each step the heels of her flats slid and twisted down the slick path.

"Take this!" Adam called over the wind.

He had removed his denim jacket and was wearing only a gray T-shirt, now completely stuck to his bony frame. He draped the coat over Nazira's head. She held the front with one hand, and with the other she reached back and felt for his fingers. Squinting, they stumbled down the side of the hill, pulling back vines and branches that blocked the path. The percussive rain fell still harder, and her skirt became splotched with mud. Just when she thought the trail would connect to the road, it curved to the right, the opposite way. Bent over, she plowed forward through the bushes, but with a twist of her arm Adam pulled her off the trail.

He yelled against the storm, "Give it a minute!"

An olive tree with silvery leaves and pungent flowers offered some protection, and they crouched under its lowest limbs. A wave of gratitude swept over her. The rain continued to pour in front of them, but only dripped through the mass of branches above. She pulled the denim jacket to her shoulders, swiped her face, and blinked to clear her eyes. Adam squatted in profile next to her, shivering, breathing heavily. He was still holding on to her left hand.

With her other hand she reached out and brushed back the dripping bangs plastered to his forehead, revealing the scar beneath. His head jerked at her touch.

"In my opinion you are cold," she said. "Do you want your jacket?"

"I'm all right."

He kept hold of her hand, did not turn his head, but instead shuffled his feet slightly closer to her, so their legs were pressed side by side.

"This was not a good shortcut you found," she said, laughing. She hadn't been this close to a man in years, and realized she was enjoying the adventure, Adam's nervousness, the pressure of his legs against her.

"I'm sorry." His melancholy expression had softened.

"Here." She removed the denim jacket and draped it over his shoulders. He leaned back, turned, and glanced at her. She shut her eyes, listening to the rain and thunder, and was reluctant to take a breath. Drops slid off the olive leaves and fell across her face. They crouched in silence for long minutes, her hand folded within his grasp, until finally the rain let up, and he lifted her back to her feet.

15

BURAK EKMEKÇİ was growing frantic—he had less than two weeks to prepare for his TOEFL exam. The morning after the cruise Adam sat with him in the bright sun at the waterfront café, the air unusually fresh after the previous day's rain, but he could hardly concentrate on his student's questions. His thoughts kept wandering to Nazira. He could still feel yesterday's dampness in his skin, the warmth of her body under the olive tree. When they had met up with the others at the port, the two had pretended they'd gotten lost. Jeff bought them both T-shirts at a tourist *bakkal* so they could change out of their wet clothes. Adam had watched Nazira emerge from the restaurant bathroom in her dry shirt, combing through her wet black hair with her fingers. They exchanged a glance but, self-conscious, did not sit next to each other on the ship home and said little for the rest of the day. In the evening, though, playing chess with her father, Adam had felt her eyes from across the room.

"What's wrong?" Burak asked him. "You were not listening to me."

"A woman," Adam said.

"Can I help?"

"Don't know if anyone can help."

He'd thought she was fairly attractive when she first arrived, but each day she'd grown more so. He caught himself going out of his way to catch a glimpse of her in the apartment, and too many times she had seen him staring at her like a fool. He hated to think he'd have to wait until tonight before he could see her again. But at four o'clock he met Mehmet at Fetih Pasha Korsu for basketball, and to his surprise he found everyone at the court: Anarbek in his oversize sweats, Oren and Jeff in their jogging shorts, and Nazira, following them, wearing a bright pink blouse and long flowery skirt, dark sunglasses, and Oren's baseball hat.

Nazira watched them play from the stone steps at the edge of the court, and Adam worried she would disapprove if he scored against her father, so he took it easy. Anarbek's basketball skills had progressed over the previous month. Despite his reluctance to dribble the ball, the big man's natural strength and girth served him well—especially in an inside game, where he pushed the thin Turkish teens out of the way and rebounded for the team.

During the last game, Jeff and Oren returned, sweaty from their jog, and joined Nazira on the stone steps to watch. Afterward, as the players made their way off the court, chatting, Oren suggested crossing the water to the Yeats for a beer.

"You guys go ahead," Adam said. "I'm heading back to the apartment." He glanced at Nazira, and she offered to return with him.

Anarbek and Mehmet were up for the drink, and they tried to convince Adam to come celebrate their victory, but he refused again. Oren seemed slightly put off, but Jeff regarded Adam with a slight smile and convinced the others to leave them alone.

Adam sat down with Nazira on the side of the basketball court, where over the pine trees he could make out the top towers of the Bosphorus Bridge. He concentrated on tracing the mud on the ground with the end of a stick.

"You're a very good basketball man," she said.

"I've been playing a long time. I played in university."

"I always like to play sports. When I was a girl, I used to play football with the boys at school. The teachers were so angry with me. 'That is not a sport for girls,' they said. When I got older, I started watching only."

"In Arizona, the girls play all the time. They're pretty good, really."

"Do they play with you? On your side?"

"Yeah, sometimes. Here, come on, we'll practice."

He led her back to the court and showed her first how to bank in a lay-up, then how to dribble the ball. She pounded it too hard with her flat hands, as if swatting at flies, and once the ball kicked off her foot and she bounded into the woods to chase it. But slowly she caught on.

"That's pretty good," he said. "That's what you've gotta do. Now see if you can take it to the hoop. Shoot a basket." She carried the ball, ran a few steps on the tips of her toes, then heaved it up, and it smashed straight into the rim, just missing her head on the rebound. He retrieved the ball and dribbled with his left hand only, between his legs, then behind his back. She ran in circles around him, laughing, and at last collapsed into a squat.

"You are the winner," she said, out of breath. "Okay, you are the winner. But only for today."

On the walk back to Jeff's apartment, the smell of Nazira's warm skin reminded him of dandelions. She laughed generously at the littlest things: the whistles of street vendors, a grandmother holding a bawling child, a dog howling at the muezzin's call to prayer. He noticed how, embarrassed by her smile, she would cover her mouth with her hand, and he loved how, when she stepped in front of him, her skirt clung to the curve of her hips. These long flowing skirts were so different from the loose black jeans of the Apache girls he had known.

In the apartment he kissed her, for the first time, against the back of the door, and then she pulled him into the living room, across the rugs, still kissing, and they knelt on the couch. He was tentative—he didn't want to make her uncomfortable, but she surprised him. She was more confident, more passionate than he expected. She bit down on his lips, she nibbled his ears, and they worked each other into a dizzy, sweating haze, until Nazira suggested they stop and get some water.

The two pretended nothing had changed when the men returned that night, though Adam sensed that everyone knew. Monday morning, after Jeff left for work, Adam ran down the steps of Kader Caddesi to buy bread and cheese from the waterfront bakery and peaches and bananas from the bazaar. They ate with Nazira's father. She prepared the tea, and Adam showed them how to make grilled cheese sandwiches. He threatened to put bacon on hers.

His weekday schedule with Burak was heavy, four hours each afternoon. But it made no difference; he couldn't have seen her anyway. Nazira continued to sell jackets and accompany Anarbek to his business meetings on the European side. In the evening he met her at Kebapistan for dinner, and afterward, alone, they strolled the misty Üsküdar shoreline, listening to the wailing of the oil tankers. Adam bought her a lemon ice cream at Mado's, and as they walked along Nazira slung her arm through his and offered him tastes of her dessert.

From the pier by the lighthouse Nazira pointed out the Marmara Hotel; its upper floors, the highest point along the straits, gleamed a dim purple in the late afternoon sun.

"A skyscraper," she said to Adam. "I have only seen them in photos, until I came here. What is the highest floor you have been?"

"I went up the Empire State Building in New York once. A hundred floors."

"Is it frightening?"

He pointed to the hotel. "I'll take you up there sometime. You'll see."

She gestured to the dense sprawl of the city, the buildings clambering upon themselves from the edges of the water. "You will live then here in Istanbul, Adam?"

"I gotta find my own place. Maybe you can help me. You'll be here a few weeks, like your dad, isn't it?"

She shook her head. "I can stay only a few more days, Adam. But you must come visit me. I am waiting for you."

Walking back, he imagined a life with her in this city of palaces, in an apartment of their own, or traveling with her to some distant nation whose name he could not pronounce, to her home in the mountains, a place no one on the reservation had ever heard of— true distance.

Nazira found herself humming old Kyrgyz folk songs to pass the morning hours on the street. She could not hide her excitement when she met up with Sashenka for lunch. Describing Adam, her voice had a sudden truer depth. With his dark good looks, his serious nature, his unstated kindness, he was unlike any man she had known. She told the Romanian about watching him play basketball—how she marveled at the grace and assurance of his game, at his magical ability, like something learned in a circus, to hurl the ball from a distance straight through the little hoop. He was modest; he made no effort to impress, he disdained small talk, and she sensed honesty in his straightforward words, his simple phrases, his encouraging exclamations.

Her face that Wednesday was fixed in a half-smile. She listened to Sashenka's own tales—of being ripped off by such and such a customer, of fighting with such and such a company over a telephone bill, of avoiding such and such police officer—with a glowing amusement. And she found her appetite had increased: she ordered extra dishes of eggplant, and after lunch she even shared one of her friend's Turkish cigarettes, coughing the whole time.

"You are in love. I can see," Sashenka said. She swung a finger back and forth. "But stupid girl, you are in love with the wrong man. You should have lost your heart to the father of your child."

Nazira shrugged. "Who can control who you lose your heart to?" She had come to the conclusion that love could not be pursued; it could not be sought in a magazine or demanded in a letter.

"And have you told him about your son?"

"I will. He understands these things. He is very smart."

Sashenka shook her head in amused disbelief. "At least you are not sleeping with him." And then, in an especially loud voice meant to embarrass her, she said, "You have not slept with him yet, have you?"

"I will sleep with him when I please!" Nazira said just as loudly, drawing glances from two Russian businessmen at the next table. The idea had not occurred to her, but suddenly the possibility of being with Adam filled her with pleasure. She was living the brave, modern life of a city woman. And it was only after she spoke the words that she realized they were in direct conflict with her need to return to the village, her impatience with her father.

Sashenka exploded in laughter and treated Nazira to the lunch. She paid with a single ten-million bill and, waiting for change, said, "*Pazhalstah*. One favor."

"Anything."

"Tell me"—she leaned her weight on the table—"how can I find my own American Prince Charming?"

Friday afternoon Adam and Nazira ferried for the first time together to the European side and strolled up and down Istiklal Caddesi, in and out of the bustling music and chocolate and perfume shops. They entered the skyscraper through the metal detector, ascended the escalator, and came across an aquarium so large, the tropical fish seemed to be flying in swarms across the hotel lobby.

"It's a very beautiful lobby," she said. "So many couches!"

He pointed out the registration desk, and Nazira smiled and shrugged and glanced down at the red carpeting. As Adam signed the registration form, he realized with satisfaction that they could have been anyone. He could have passed for Turkish—he was dark enough. He might have been Arab, African, or Jamaican. The desk clerk may have thought Nazira was from China or Thailand. He wrote a false name—Chester Gatewood—on the reception form, paid for the room with two of Burak's hundred-dollar bills, and took the keys. In the elevator Nazira grinned up at him and hugged him close around the waist. Neither had spent this amount of money on anything so frivolous.

In their twenty-second-floor room Nazira ran to the window, and Adam tugged open the curtains for her. Darkness was falling, and through their reflections in the glass the city spread before them in all its grandeur: the minarets, the buttresses, the sea walls. Everything was mirrored in the water of the straits, so it was as if they were seeing two cities—an illusion interrupted only by a cruise ship drifting beneath them. In silence they watched the stars peep out in the sky, wheeling their great arc over the distances.

"I have never seen this," Nazira said softly. "Thank you, Adam."

At the bed he dialed for room service and asked for a bottle of wine. The man on the line suggested he try a red called Yakut.

He cradled the phone on his shoulder. "You like red wine?" he asked Nazira.

She shrugged. "I don't know. Is it tasty?"

"Never had any." Adam spoke back into the phone. "Bring up one of those Yakuts."

While they waited, he spotted a remote control. But when he pointed it at the television and pressed the green button, the air conditioner on the wall behind them beeped three times, then blew a wave of cool air over their heads.

"That feels nice," Nazira said.

She was wearing a black skirt and sitting with her legs crossed over the edge of the bed. She closed her eyes and leaned into the breeze. Adam found another remote control in a drawer and managed to turn on the satellite TV. He kept flipping channels: Hindus praying, a motocross race in Singapore, an Iranian music video, a Spanish aerobics instructor. Light-headed, nervous, they both laughed harder at each channel. He settled on a program showing the film *Scream 2* and stretched out across the bed as Nazira disappeared into the bathroom.

A man in white brought the wine, and Adam paid him with a fifty-dollar bill, giving back the ten dollars change as a tip. The man opened the bottle with a tug, and pushed a cart with glasses into the room.

The air conditioner worked in overdrive, but even using the correct remote control, Adam could not shut it off, and the room was growing frigid. He could hear Nazira behind the door, playing with the hair dryer, turning it on and off, high and low. He suddenly wondered why he was doing this. She would probably be leaving in a few days, and he'd never see her again. The whole thing was unwise, ridiculous, but he felt driven by forces he couldn't stop. She came out wearing her blouse untucked—it fell below her waist and covered half her skirt. She stepped softly to the bed and ran her hand over the sheets. Adam gestured to the wine and poured some for each of them.

"We should make the toast," Nazira said. "It is one of our traditions."

"Go ahead."

She clenched her lips and thought. "To meeting," she said.

"To meeting."

Their glasses touched.

"Not that bad," Adam said. "A fine wine."

"The best I ever tasted."

"Check out this bed." Adam told her. "Check out how soft it is. And feel these pillows. I used to sleep on an old mattress on the floor. I thought it was the most comfortable thing in the world. I'm glad I never tried one of these."

Nazira sprawled on her stomach beside him and crossed her legs above her. He could see the whiteness of the back of her knees. She sipped her wine. "I did not sleep in a bed until I went to the university."

"What'd you sleep on?"

"Adam, we spread rugs on the floor. Every night. Big thick rugs my grandmother made. And many, many pillows."

"Was that comfortable?"

She shrugged. "It was the only thing we knew."

"We'll be spoiled now. No more sleeping on the ground, isn't it?"

"No more sleeping on the ground." They touched their glasses again.

While they drank, Adam told her the story of how he had met Jeff, how Jeff had come to the reservation so convinced he could change things, how he had hired Adam out of high school to work in the teen center, how his cousin Levi had trashed the place and Jeff had left them, but they'd kept in touch.

"Even when he screws up, he means well," Adam said. "He's tried to help me out."

"He means well, yes, but still I get so angry with him."

"Why angry?"

"I like Jeff very much. But he is so alone. Do you know? I cannot talk to him. Sometimes I think he cares only of himself."

Nazira asked more about the reservation. Drawn out, against his will, Adam found himself speaking of his father to her. He said usually he thought he hated the man, but it had to be wrong; you couldn't hate your own father. She sat still and listened silently.

At last they put their glasses aside. He pulled up the sheets, and they both crawled under. Their legs grazed, and they each shifted slightly away, then laughed. He could feel her warmth beneath the covers. The air conditioner, blinking an arctic fifteen degrees Celsius, roared above the bed like an airplane.

"Can you shut the machine off?" Nazira asked.

"I haven't figured out the technology." Adam played with the remote. "I think it's broke."

Nazira sighed. "Back in my village everything is broken. The lights. The door in my house. My television. The school windows. I have a kitchen table with only three legs."

"In Red Cliff," he said, "we've got a junked old refrigerator and swing set in my yard. Every house has dead trucks in front. Housing Authority never fixes any broken pipes. Your water goes out, it's out for weeks."

"We are always losing the water too! I did not think that happened in your country."

"It does, though." He gave up on the remote control and tossed it onto the nightstand.

Nazira was staring up at the back wall, her arms crossed over her chest. "It makes people crazy in my village. Everyone is trying to leave, to Russia, to the capital. My father is afraid to go back."

"What about you?"

"Adam, I told you, I have to go back."

He stroked her shoulder. "You can stay here with me a little longer."

She drew a deep breath. "I never told you one important thing."

"What's that?"

"I have a child, Adam. A son." She looked up and watched his eyes drop. She bent her head and stared forward at the expanse of white sheets.

"A son?" His voice surprised her in its calmness.

She hesitated. "My son has blue eyes. They are so blue. His hair is brown, lighter than our Kyrgyz hair. It looks like this." She pulled up her hair.

"Spiked?"

"Yes. He is so sweet. Adam, he is my life. He was—how to say?—a gift to me." They lay in silence a moment longer. Beside her Adam was scratching his leg with his thumb, and she could smell the saltiness of his skin, at once off-putting and enthralling. She went on, telling him how her son loved horses and could already ride if she helped him up. She was teaching him to read, and he had learned all of his letters, Cyrillic and Kyrgyz. She was even teaching him English words. He could remember the names of many animals in three languages. She paused. "You are disappointed with me?"

"No, it's okay." He touched the back of her neck, unsure what to say to her or whether it was smart to say anything. "It's okay. In Red Cliff the women I know are always having children. How old is he, your son?"

"He is five years old."

"What's his name?"

"His name is Manas."

"I gotta meet him sometime."

Her voice rose. "Would you?"

"Maybe I'll have to come over with you. Meet this kid."

She turned to him and smiled in genuine excitement, not covering her teeth this time. "Maybe you will?"

The horror movie droned on in loud bursts of music. Adam

stretched his feet and curled back his toes. "When I was ten," he said, "my father killed a bobcat. I got the fur. I kept it on my bed, at the end there. Grew up sleeping with a bobcat."

Nazira lay her hand on his chest. "Do you miss your bobcat?"

He looked at her out of the corner of his eye. "I'm too old for it now."

"Am I better than your bobcat?"

Abandoning himself, he slid his arm under her head and pulled her toward him, her eyelashes like feathers against his neck. "You're better than the bobcat," he said. He closed his eyes, more comfortable, he decided, than he had ever been. They nearly fell asleep like that, with the television and air conditioner blasting, their limbs entwined beneath the sheets. When Adam glanced up it was just after eleven. Nazira was stroking the edge of his collarbone and staring into his face. Without a word they undressed each other beneath the covers and made slow, nervous love. The Apaches said everywhere was the center of the world. But Adam felt there, inside Nazira, was more the center than anywhere else. Great powers from great distances had conspired to pull them together. Their bodies arched, and in the middle of her heavy breathing, between her hurried kisses, through her halting gasps, for the first time he knew he had arrived.

They returned to the apartment after two that morning. Nazira expected her father to be furious, but in their bedroom he greeted her with a startling hug. Good news! He had been by the Grand Bazaar that morning, and his long-awaited invitation to the Hakan Pazarlama factory had come. On Monday he would meet with Faruk's uncle and at last finalize the deal to export sheepskin from their village to Istanbul. He wanted her to accompany him to Yeditepe, south of the city, to the Organized Leather Industry Zone, in order to help translate. Bursting with enthusiasm, he spoke without pause for fifteen minutes—he had been holding in this news all day—and he did not even ask where she had been. The roughness of his voice, the sound of Kyrgyz after a magical evening of English, shook her out of her reverie. But the news was good, she told herself. She had feared her father would keep her here for weeks.

In the bedroom, lying on a floor mat, Nazira crossed her arms and listened for Adam's creaking footsteps in the room next door.

Her head spun in a drunken rush, a disorienting amalgam of love and homesickness. From the bed above her, in a state of untrammeled excitement, her father promised, "If this works out, we'll head home next week. We can use your money from the leather sales for the flight. We'll begin preparations for the factory. You see, Nazira? You see? I always told you everything would be okay."

He shut off the lights, and only after the room was dark did he whisper, "And where were you, *kizim,* out so late tonight?" He sounded tired, but there was a teasing note to his voice, a playfulness unlike anything she had heard from him in years.

"I was with Adam."

"Yes, Adam. Adam Dale. I like that one. But he has no money. He's poor."

"Since when has that mattered to you?"

"Yes, you're right." He lay in silence for a second. "So, has there been progress?"

"*Tinch.* Be quiet."

"Perhaps you should ask him to steal you."

"Stop it."

"It is romantic, you know."

She could feel the blood rushing to her cheeks, and in a whisper she huffed, "Ata!"

Her father chuckled softly, and after a few minutes she heard the first of his donkey snores. She listened for Adam again, but the sounds from the next room had ceased. How could she leave him so quickly? She must ask him again to come with her. Smiling into the darkness, she pictured him in Kyzyl Adyr–Kirovka. What would he think of the mountains, the rutted roads, the cheese factory, the statue of Lenin, her house on Karl Marx Street? How would he treat Manas? Soon, she remembered, soon she would hold Manas in her arms, soon Lola would see her husband again, and her father would watch over Baktigul. It was what she wanted, she told herself. It was what she'd come all this way for. She should be happy.

16

ANARBEK AND NAZIRA were to meet Faruk's uncle, Hakan, outside the hotel at two o'clock. Anarbek pulled at his fingers all Monday morning in excitement, on the *dolmuş* to the bus station, on the two-hour bus ride south of the city to Yeditepe, and then in the taxi to the hotel. He had reserved for them an affordable third-floor room at the Kervansaray Otel, on the main street along the pier. After the luxury of the Marmara Hotel, the bare room—two boxy twin beds, stained sheets, faded pictures of sailboats, woolen blankets, and a plywood nightstand with an empty water pitcher—was a disappointment to Nazira. For her father's sake she feigned wonder at the view through the only window, out to the long gray harbor and the dingy shipbuilding yard. This was his moment. She was not here for pleasure, she reminded herself. Whereas two weeks ago she had been skeptical, infuriated at her father's delays, now she hoped with a recharged heart that his meeting would be a success.

They went in search of Faruk's uncle, who, as arranged, was waiting for them outside the hotel doors, sitting against the trunk of his black Fiat Marena. Hakan was a squat white-haired man perhaps a bit older than Anarbek. His legs were crossed, his foot tapped the pavement impatiently, and his fingers worked a set of brown worry beads. He greeted both Anarbek and Nazira with a swift handshake and ushered them into the car. In the back seat Nazira ran her palm along the smooth brown leather upholstery.

Hakan peeled out onto the road, then turned his head and asked if they liked the vehicle, raising his eyebrows and showing his teeth when he smiled. He drove them along the main street of the town, passing slow-moving green army trucks. Soon the metal gates and concrete walls of factory compounds and refineries appeared. Turkish flags flapped at the entrances, and enormous windowless buildings interrupted the view of the sea. At a compound like all the others Hakan suddenly slammed on the brakes; the vehicle squealed and came to a halt in front of a gated driveway. He hopped out, had a word with a uniformed guard, then gestured for them to exit as well. He handed his car keys to the guard and directed them forward, along a sidewalk past the security booth.

Anarbek was astonished by the size of the complex—it was easily five times that of the cheese factory. Small manicured lawns with rows of yellow flowers filled the spaces between two paved roadways. To the right in a parking lot, half full, stood fifteen trucks in an orderly row, their cabs waxed and shining. The main industrial shed was an arching barnlike structure, lying perpendicular to the shoreline, with a wide, flat concrete chimney on which *H. P.* had been painted in giant orange block letters, to be read, it seemed, from land, air, or sea. On the loading dock, protected from the sun and rain by an overhang, lay stacked heaps of sheepskin and calfskin. Hakan led them to his office, on the first floor of a smaller building next to what looked like a garage. He sat them down on red-cushioned chairs, and a woman dressed completely in white, like a nurse, rushed in and served them tea.

Drinking his first scalding sip, Anarbek felt that much of his life had been directed to this moment, to this very interview in the sprawling seaside leather factory. Forces he could not have controlled—the coincidences of time and place, the pressures of the economy, the duties of love and community—had brought him here.

"Kyrgyzstan?" Hakan kept repeating as he seated himself behind his wide, paper-stacked desk. He fingered his chain of prayer beads, which clicked softly as he spoke. "Kyrgyzstan? Our long-lost Central Asian brothers. I was certainly interested in meeting you. Faruk mentioned you have been discussing business. Currently we don't trade with any of the new Central Asian states. But we're certainly interested. Certainly. Your sheepskin, tell me about it."

His hands folded in his lap like a well-behaved schoolboy, Anarbek explained the estimated number of sheep raised each year in the Talas Valley, the extensive summer alpine pastures; yet how, for lack of money, hungry families had to slaughter herds for food instead of putting the wool to better use. With the ready supply of sheep and the low overhead, he could guarantee good prices. When he tripped over certain words in Turkish, Nazira corrected him softly, drawing a wink and an understanding nod from Hakan.

"We take pride, here in our factory, in quality, care, and efficiency. Quality, care, and efficiency. Do you understand me? These are the ideals we expect from all our suppliers. Are quality, care, and efficiency ideals you can uphold?"

Anarbek glanced at Nazira for support, she nodded, and he answered in the affirmative.

Hakan said, "I have some friends in the East, fruit dealers who send out a fleet of trucks to Tashkent each summer. Delivering tomatoes, strawberries. How far is that from you?"

"Not far. A day's drive."

"So it is certainly possible. Come, why don't you have a look around. We can decide if we'd like to pursue this further."

Hakan led them on a tour of the compound, starting in the immense refrigerated warehouse, currently the only one operating in the city—a luxury he could afford because of the sheer size of his company. "I've begun renting a bit of space to some of my competitors here in Yeditepe. A gesture of goodwill, you know. Must support the local industry. Remember, we're competing against the worldwide market." Two buildings served as the tannery. He hustled them through the frenzied activity of 350 workers. Anarbek turned in circles as they walked, taking it all in. Over the screeching and growling of engines, Hakan explained they would have to cure the skins in Kyrgyzstan to prevent rot during shipping. Hakan could send a number of workers to supervise the construction of raceways. He showed them how, when the skins arrived at the factory, they were first soaked in water to soften and remove the salt solution. He directed them to the fleshing stations—screaming machines equipped with rubber rollers and spiraling knives that removed the flesh and tissue. Nazira walked ahead of Anarbek, and he could see her holding a finger under her nose, trying to block out the fetid stench. It was overpowering, but he didn't mind it; he breathed in deeply, and the odor shot through his nostrils like vinegar, the smell of sulfur and ammonia and flesh and blood. They followed workers transferring the skins on mechanized carts to the beam house, where hair was removed by soaking, this time in vats of chemicals. Hakan showed them the milling machines, in which hides were kept in motion for several days. He led them to the bating vat, where the skins were cleaned of lime and softened. From here skins were separated for either the vegetable or chrome tanning processes. In chrome tanning, Hakan explained—for shoes, handbags, wallets, and garments—the hides had to be pickled first in salt and acid.

He hustled them into the second building, in which the final stages of the tanning process were completed. "A well-tanned leather," Hakan said, "can be boiled in water for three minutes without shrinking. Our products exceed even that!" Anarbek looked at Nazira in wonder. Hakan led them down the floor used for chrome tanning, past revolving drums of chemicals where the skins were spun for eight hours, soaking in the chrome, then fixed with additional chemicals. They visited the vegetable tanning floor. In this much slower process, the hides were rotated in solutions of tannic acid for up to four days. "Our leather's like expensive wine," Hakan boasted. "It gets better with age."

"Yes, yes. Wine," Anarbek repeated.

They came to the far end of the factory. Here the skins were wrung out to dry and then split into sheets of set thicknesses, a process handled by a group of men Hakan introduced as his most skilled workers. Anarbek shook a few of their sweaty hands. The chrome-tanned hides were again placed in rotating drums to be dyed, after which they were lubricated with natural fats and chemicals to obtain the final, proper softness. Hakan pointed out the hydraulic presses, printing machines, automatic sprayers, and vacuum dryers used for finishing. Finally, he led them outside and down a ramp to the loading dock. Here the skins were stacked and covered in plastic, ready for distribution.

"This"—Hakan waved his arm, twirling his prayer beads on a single outstretched finger—"this is where your sheep will wind up."

Anarbek had seen nothing like it for twenty years: an entire factory, rumbling with life, its workers hurtling themselves at their tasks with sweat and skill and even, it seemed, satisfaction. To be part of such an enterprise—to supply a share of the skins that wove their way through these machines and emerged to clothe the bodies and warm the feet of the world—it was better than he could have imagined. As they returned to the office, he took Nazira's arm. His heart was pounding. The factory up and running, his employees back to work in Kyzyl Adyr–Kirovka, the trips he would take between Istanbul and Kyrgyzstan. Once the enterprise got off the ground, who was to stop him from assuming, step by step, some of the process of tanning leather—who was to stop him, down the road, from managing his own factory of this kind? All it took was a single step forward. In the office, seated on the cushioned chairs, Nazira was extremely quiet, but he knew her well enough to detect the signs: her slightly upturned lips, the subdued excitement in her eyes. She would not give him the satisfaction of her approval yet, but she did approve, he saw it—she too had gazed at every buzzing machine, every blinking light and button in the factory, at the workers' quickly moving fingers. For once she was not discouraging him.

Hakan offered to treat them to a meal of *köfte* at what he claimed was the region's most famous meatball restaurant. Nazira ate well—unusual for her. Anarbek watched her breaking bread, scattering red pepper over her meat, and sharing the single plate of white-bean salad that Hakan ordered for the table. Hakan even insisted that she drink Coca-Cola, and Anarbek was pleased that she let herself be treated. The terms of the business relationship seemed as settled as they could get for now. Next month Hakan would be sending two workers out to Kyrgyzstan to assess the equipment at the cheese factory, and would supply the required machinery as an advance against payments for the first shipments of sheepskin the following spring.

Then conversation turned away from leather and toward more personal business. Hakan wanted details of their life in the mountains. He said he dreamed one day of fleeing the stressful existence of factory management to a quiet place, where he could ride a horse, do some fishing, read a few books. He was fascinated by accounts of Anarbek's hunting trips and by his explanation of *oolak*, the horseback game of goat stealing whose intricate rules Nazira had to help him explain. They lingered over dinner, the sun began to set, and before it grew too dark, Anarbek said they should be getting back to the Kervansaray Otel and making plans to return to Kyrgyzstan.

Hakan said, "A few old friends of mine will be meeting out at the sports club tonight, to watch the game. Why don't you join us?"

Anarbek turned to Nazira. "Only if it's okay with my daughter." In Kyrgyz she gave him permission to stay out with the men as late as he pleased. But after what had been an exhausting day, she, for one, was going back to the hotel and getting some sleep.

Hakan paid the bill and drove them back along the darkening, unfamiliar streets of Yeditepe to the Kervansaray. Nazira hugged her father good night, her arms tight around his neck, and in the growing exhilaration of the evening he kissed her lightly on the forehead. She shook Hakan's hand, left the car, and disappeared through the tinted doors of the hotel lobby.

Hakan took Anarbek to his sports club, which occupied the bottom two floors of a six-story apartment block. Then they went on to a card house down the street, where they met some of Hakan's friends. Watching the second half of a local football match—the game ended in a frustrating draw—they smoked strong Anatolian cigarettes and drank icy glasses of *rakı* late into the night. Hakan possessed one of the loudest, most infectious laughs the Kyrgyz had ever heard. To one Turk, Anarbek was again introduced as Hakan's "long-lost Central Asian brother"—an expression that delighted him. Camaraderie, strong handshakes, ease of conversation—the sheepskin venture would certainly prove a success. The village factory was as good as saved.

They walked off their drinks along the shore of the Marmara, back toward the sports club. In a daze Anarbek eyed the road of endless lights leading back to the city. It was a clear, warm night. "Too hot to sleep inside, no, Anarbek?" Hakan said. "On evenings like this, there is nothing better than to be out in the air. We should be hunting, or camping!" He gestured across the sea and suddenly stopped. Anarbek saw it too: a huge number of dead fish, turning on the edge of the mild surf, against the cement sea wall. Hakan shrugged it off. "Our waters. The pollution is terrible." He clicked his tongue. "Come!"

They continued on, enjoying the predawn breeze. Anarbek realized he had lost all track of time and thought momentarily of Nazira, alone in their hotel room. He didn't know why she affected him as she did. She was his daughter, not his wife; he wasn't beholden to her, and she had no right to be critical of him. He had suffered and sacrificed for her. The past ten years had not been easy—with the death of Baiooz, the collapse of the factory, the threat of privatization—and he had done his best with what he had. If he had blundered, if he was not always the best husband or father, he could be forgiven. On their return to Kyzyl Adyr–Kirovka Nazira would see him anew—the entire village would, and they would understand the lengths he had gone to secure their welfare.

Hakan and Anarbek returned to the sports club for a late-night meal of baked fish and fried squid. It was the first squid Anarbek had ever eaten, and its rubbery consistency reminded him of boiled tripe. After dinner, the *raki* glasses were filled once more, and while Hakan took on all comers at backgammon, Anarbek wandered the club. In the upstairs room he found the strange billiards table and ran his hand along the soft green felt. He examined the trophies and photographs on the shelves. One wall was covered with newspaper clippings detailing the club's success over the years in football and wrestling tournaments. Another was lined with team photographs, the oldest already yellowed with age. Anarbek found a football team photo from the year of his birth, 1941. He stared into the eyes of the thin, muscular young men. The front row was squatting, wearing cleats and shorts, and the back row stood with their arms crossed over their chests. They looked formidable.

The sports club was nearly empty. Downstairs, Anarbek settled back on a couch next to Hakan, who was playing against the factory's accountant in the final backgammon game of the night. Anarbek picked up Hakan's pocket phone and clicked the power button on with a beep, releasing a green phosphorescence. He shut the phone off with a second beep. On again, off again. The two men looked at him, amused. Backgammon had never been Anarbek's favorite game—he did not trust the roll of the dice, which was why he'd always preferred chess. Still, he followed the moves, sipping what he promised himself would be the last drink of the night, and inhaling the faint licorice scent of *raki* on his breath between each puff of his cigarette.

It was already after three in the morning when Hakan clenched his fists in victory and turned to Anarbek, laughing. "Who's the king here? Eh? Eh?" He patted Anarbek on the shoulders.

"I must get back," Anarbek said. "My daughter, you know."

"Yes, your beautiful young daughter is waiting for you."

They had drunk nothing but alcohol since dinner. Anarbek

asked if he could have some water before he left, and Hakan told him there was water upstairs in the refrigerator in the billiards room. He could help himself.

Stumbling up the steps, then past the pool table, Anarbek realized his clothes smelled strongly of tobacco and his hands were grimy from the cigarettes. Nazira would be annoyed with him. He pulled a liter of drinking water from the refrigerator. The blue label read Hayat. He had just started to unscrew the cap and had not even shut the refrigerator door when the entire building around him began to sway. The floor rocked in a motion that had become familiar to him on the ferries, and he laughed at how drunk he had become. Suddenly the refrigerator rolled to his left, slid against the corner of the wall, and tilted back toward him. He dropped the plastic bottle onto his foot. His eyes shot upward at a groaning noise, and only momentarily did he register the cracking of the ceiling. Allah, Allah! he thought, and his mind flashed down the street to Nazira, across the continent to Baktigul, to Lola, to his son, Oolan. Before he had time to yell, the ceiling rushed at him, the floor dropped beneath, he was floating, and all was black.

17

ADAM AWOKE to the bucking of his bed and fumbled for his shorts on the dresser. He rushed from his room, bumping into Jeff in the blackness of the hallway. "What the hell is this?" Jeff yelled. The floorboards were swaying, as if they were standing on a floating raft.

"I have no idea."

They ran to the living room windows and peered outside. In the coming days Adam would read how the land had purled, rose, and roared around him. For forty-one seconds the quake twisted the steel bridges connecting the continents, toppled outlying neighborhoods, and crumbled entire apartment complexes. A gaseous light exploded from the Marmara. Tidal waves lurched over beaches and drowned shoreside communities. But at that moment he could see only black night through the windows. The electricity was wiped out and, except for the festive sails of a cruise ship below, the sprawling city had fallen into darkness.

The living room rocked, the ceiling moaned, and Adam and Jeff retreated to the kitchen door frame. This was ridiculous, Adam thought as he watched the bookshelves clatter against the cement wall; this was almost funny—like the trampoline ride at the Tribal Fair, and he felt he could have laughed if it wasn't at the same time so frightening. He had seen nothing as terrible as that city around him, emptied of light. Jeff was crouched on his knees, propping himself up on one arm. Adam gripped the door frame. The floor continued to buck, and he thought of his mother and Verdena, at home, informed of his death, an unnecessary death, a wasted life, all his young years of struggling and striving, for nothing, for this, a death in a foreign country.

When the swaying ceased, Jeff found a flashlight in the closet, and they rushed barefoot down the cold cement stairwell, clutching sneakers to their chests, panic in each heavy breath. Adam found himself whispering, "An earthquake. A fucken earthquake." Like them, the people of the neighborhood had fled outside. Some sought refuge in their cars, and many were racing through alleys, searching, he thought, for friends and family. The streets, a riot of confusion, looked like the random exodus after a heavy-metal concert. Police and ambulance sirens sounded, screams erupted from the maze of alleys below them, and only the occasional slash and weave of car headlights cut the complete blackness. He had seen the smoke of forest fires in the ponderosas, heard the raging of flash floods in the reservation canyons, but had never felt the earth shake beneath him. He had never witnessed an upheaval this massive.

They came upon a shadowy crowd huddled around the old Ottoman fountain at the end of the block, a good distance from the taller buildings Adam imagined still might fall. He leaned against one of the rough stone walls, and Jeff joined him, trembling. They stood shoulder to shoulder. Neither spoke. In the first moments of that silence, catching his breath, Adam thought only of Nazira.

When Anarbek regained consciousness, he thought he might be dead. It was so dark, he could have been in a grave. Two things reconnected him to life: the impossible pain he felt with any effort to move and the intense crying of a young child near him. The voice seemed only a meter or two away.

"*Alo?*" he called, his own voice cracking.

"Baba!" The boy sounded weak and hysterical; he must have thought until this moment that he was alone. Baba? The child had mistaken him for his father. Anarbek pictured a young boy—Oolan in his green pajamas, with missing front teeth and close-cropped hair. Painfully he twisted his chest to turn to the voice, but found he could move only his left side. It seemed his right arm was crushed; he had lost all feeling in it, and flailing his free arm, he found that he was pinned at the shoulder by something cold and metallic. The refrigerator: it had saved him.

"I am here," he called in Turkish. "Just wait. Someone will come. Are you okay?" Anarbek gagged on the dust and heard more crying, but he could see nothing. "Are you with anyone else?" He managed to spit out the words, coughing.

"Baba!"

"Please listen. Do you see your mother? Anyone?"

"I don't see her. Baba, it hurts."

He swallowed, his mouth clammy, but there was hardly enough saliva to clear his tongue. He was about to tell the child he was not his father, then changed his mind. "I know," he said, his throat filling again with grains of concrete. The boy must have come from one of the apartments above the sports club. "Hang on. We will be okay. Son, you rest. No crying. Just rest. Someone will help us."

For as long as he could stand it, he called through the wall above him, screaming the single word—"*Yardım!*" "*Yardım!*"—until he fell into a fit of coughing, each spasm a momentary torture. He heard the boy sobbing; Anarbek's screams had frightened him more.

His own fears swelled when he remembered Nazira. He would be okay, he was alive, but what about her? He decided to pray, only with the pounding of his chest his thoughts ran away from him. He thought then of Baiooz, her calming voice of reason. He wished he could speak to her now. He thought of Baktigul and Lola and Manas, and told himself he would rest just a second, and after that, no matter what it took, he would get out and find his daughter. But when he closed his eyes he realized—eyes open or closed—the darkness remained the same.

Jeff's apartment was in the eye of the storm: the city's outskirts were toppled, but the center remained unharmed. The buildings of Üsküdar were built on bedrock, and at dawn the neighborhood police assured Adam and Jeff that it was perfectly safe to return. In the kitchen that morning Adam bent low over the table, absently eating some browning apricots. Jeff had phoned his office and with the help of a Turkish colleague was able to locate the address and telephone number of the Hakan Pazarlama Leather Factory. For an hour Adam watched him dialing, trying to get the connection out of the city, and every time Jeff hung up, Adam grit his teeth. A simple telephone call—the sound of her voice, a single syllable, was all he needed.

Finally Jeff gave up, saying, "The worst is on the outskirts, along the northern shore of the sea. They probably can't get a bus through there."

"But they haven't *called*."

"There are lines down. I couldn't get through—maybe they can't either."

"We don't even know if they have your telephone number," Adam said. "Anarbek never thinks about things like that. You ever tell it to him?"

"I must have given it to one of them." Jeff turned away from him. "They've called here before, haven't they?"

Adam locked his gaze on the table. "I honestly can't remember."

"I'm sure they have the number."

In the afternoon Jeff was at last able to phone the factory and then the hospitals and police stations around Yeditepe. Few calls were answered, and when he got through, nobody offered any help. He said their best chance was to leave the line open and let Anarbek or Nazira find a way to get in touch. Waiting for the telephone to ring, for a key to turn in the front door, they sat helplessly through the afternoon on the living room carpets, reading the papers and watching televised helicopter coverage of the earthquake zone. Nearly once an hour the floors trembled, as if the earth were boiling.

The news was bleak. CNN Turk called it one of the worst earthquakes of the century. Scientists had announced that pressure on unbroken fault lines beneath the city continued at an alarming level. Television astrologers had observed the skies and predicted that a second quake, larger than the first, would hit at any moment.

In the evening Oren came by and invited them to camp with him outside, on the grassy campus of the girls' *lise*.

"It'd be safer," Jeff agreed. "A little peace of mind."

"But what if they call?" Adam asked. "Or come back?"

He refused to leave, and Jeff stayed on with him. Adam paced the apartment, took long cold showers, and opened the refrigerator door without knowing what he wanted. He barely slept that night.

A photograph in *Hürriyet* the next morning showed children bathing in fountains and men barbecuing *kebaps* over small communal grills. Much of the population had spent that second night outdoors in cars, public squares, and parks. Most frightening were the continual aftershocks—already over two hundred of them, more than ten measuring above 5.0. Over and over the city relived the nightmare, and when the earth shook even slightly, from the windows Adam could see that the neighborhood had fled to the streets.

The newspapers reported more than two thousand dead, ten thousand injured, and two hundred thousand homeless, predicting the numbers would rise. Armies of rescue teams—dogs, medical supplies, tents, and body bags—had arrived from every corner of the planet, but it wasn't enough. The government was paralyzed by the scope of the disaster. The military had delayed in acting, and unable to handle the pressure, high-level state and city officials were resigning. Large-scale coordination of rescue efforts was failing. Nobody seemed to be in charge.

"We'll rent a car," Adam said the second evening. "We'll drive and find them."

"No one's renting out cars now. The roads are closed," Jeff said.

"Someone you know can get us out there. Someone at your office."

"I'll ask tomorrow and see if they can help."

The third morning there was still no word. Jeff went to work, and alone, Adam could stand it no more. He felt weightless without Nazira, exhausted. He looked at a map and considered jogging or hitching the forty miles out to Yeditepe to find her. But he wouldn't know where to start, and he didn't have the language to ask anyone there for help.

Jeff returned from his office in the early afternoon and began stuffing his tent, flashlights, clothing, and toilet paper into his backpack. He said he'd had some luck. The DHRO and a dozen other organizations were establishing tent cities. His office was transporting displaced people to the shelters and distributing food, medicine, and water. He had convinced Andrew to send him out to the site, where he would spend the rest of the week helping the relief effort. "It's just past Yeditepe. When I get a break, I'll head into town and try to locate them. They're just stranded out there."

"I'm coming with you," Adam said.

Jeff started to protest but stopped. "There's an extra backpack in the hall closet. I'll get Oren to check in on the apartment."

They packed additional sleeping bags, and the DHRO security

guard drove them in a Land Cruiser toward Gölcük, 175 kilometers southeast, near the epicenter of the quake. The radio announced that the death toll had reached three thousand. The roads were for the most part surprisingly intact, but Adam was otherwise unprepared for the extent of the destruction. Debris from fallen buildings rose fifty feet in the air. Mechanized claws picked like dinosaurs through the rubble. Next to a bulldozer a woman in head scarf and polka-dot skirt sat immobile, her face in her palms. Three men wearing sandals climbed a hill of concrete, pulling at slabs of masonry by hand, and Adam had to suppress the urge to ask the driver to stop so they could help. In Gebze an army regiment in paper facemasks spread disinfectant lime along the street gutters, around piles of green plastic body bags. The ripe smell of death reached inside the Land Cruiser; Jeff had the driver pull over so he could vomit.

In Yeditepe they located the Hakan Pazarlama Leather Factory, and Adam felt a surge of hope: from a distance it looked as if the huge structure had sustained little damage. The entrance gate, however, was closed, the parking lot empty. The driver could find no guards or janitors to give him information. On the main road across from the pier three small hotels still stood. The first two had no record of Anarbek and Nazira; the third had been shut down because of structural damage. Adam began to panic. The driver took them to the station and terminal: buses and ferries were still not running to Istanbul. They circled the ruined town.

In the cafés people sat glumly, shaking their heads and murmuring to themselves. On certain roads the pavement had been thrust upward, and the driver was forced to make a U-turn and retrace their path. Jeff pointed out evidence of the tidal wave—smashed boats and a small marooned ferry. Overturned sailing dinghies bobbed a hundred yards off the coast, jutting like stepping-stones in the water. Jeff said it was time to move on to the tent city. "We don't even know where to look, Adam. We can't keep the driver circling around here forever."

"We're gonna find them."

Jeff was silent. "She's important to you, I know. They're important to me too. But we can't keep this up all afternoon. Other people need this jeep, and I've got to get to my job."

"If you need to go on to Gölcük, then fucken go. I'll get out and look myself."

Jeff shook his head, but he asked the driver to pass one last time up and down the main street. At the very edge of town they paused at a stop sign, and Adam spotted Nazira.

She was sitting alone in the hot evening sun on a stone wall by a statue of a soldier. Her fingers gripped her hair, and she seemed focused only on a fallen apartment building across the street, where a number of men clambered over the hill of debris, shouting and pushing at blocks larger than themselves. One of them was shining a flashlight through the cracks of rubble.

The driver honked his horn, and Jeff and Adam rushed from the jeep. Nazira stood slowly and hugged Jeff first, then Adam longer. "He never came back to the hotel," she whispered, and pointed at the ruins of the building. Adam's stomach dropped. She said, "The people in the factory say he was in the sports club all night. This was the sports club. I am waiting for three days. I think they will find him. They must."

She explained what had happened that night in the hotel. She woke just after three. The bed was shaking from side to side, and at first she thought a truck was passing, until the bed slid far enough it hit the wall, frightening her. She realized the lamp hanging from the ceiling was swinging violently, and a piece of its glass fell onto her back as she rushed to grab her clothes. "The pictures were crashing on the walls," she said. "I ran out of the door, but I did not know the direction to go in the dark." She was propelled by a mass of people fleeing down the hall into the dim lobby. The hotel building, it turned out, had not fallen, though cracks gaped open in its front wall. Some men had climbed back in later that morning and retrieved her bag. She waited for her father and spent the afternoon searching for the sports club. A factory worker verified that he had seen her father in the club late that night, watching a backgammon game, and had given her the address.

"I found the building here, like this."

They stared up at the thirty-foot pile of rubble. The flattened heap of concrete was as large, Adam thought, as the old ruined high school dome. Sticking up among the blocks were broken office chairs and desks, cooking pots, a dusty boot, weathered carpets, and what looked like a crumpled washing machine.

Adam thrust his hands into his pockets, nodded, and said, "Come with us now, Nazira."

"No! I'm not leaving him."

"You can't spend another night here."

"The people"—she indicated a couple of bent women crawling over the fallen concrete—"they have been very kind to me. The rescue workers have been here with dogs. They said they will return."

Adam and Jeff exchanged looks. "It won't do any good to watch the rubble," Jeff said. He helped Adam gently lead her away from the site toward the parked Land Cruiser. "I promise you, tomorrow we'll come back. We'll go to the police and search the hospitals in town. For tonight, just come with us and rest."

In the vehicle Adam slid onto the back seat and took hold of Nazira's hand. He tried to assure her it was true; people could survive for quite a while in a fallen building; he had already seen many such rescues on the news. Jeff said they would notify the Kyrgyz embassy and stay in contact with the police. Her mood darkened, yet she steadfastly refused to admit the possibility Anarbek might be dead, claiming she would *feel* it if it were true. She said her village, her family, couldn't afford to lose him.

The Land Cruiser headed farther east, around the sea, and Adam watched the destruction through the cracked bus window. The area looked more and more like a war zone the farther from the city they traveled. There was little rhyme or reason to the devastation—among intact buildings lay the wreckage of identical structures that had collapsed. Pancakes, the driver called them, using the English word in a way that Adam would have never imagined. Some structures had fallen neatly—Adam could count the number of flattened floors. Others had toppled in a lopsided way, displaying wide cracks. The most stirring sight was the fallen minaret of a mosque. Adam knew little about Islam but loved the majesty of these structures, the sky-slicing rise of the columns above the domes. But this mosque's minaret had collapsed across the roof, its debris scattered over the muddy grass; only its concrete tip remained intact. A few sheep grazed around it.

Adam pictured Anarbek entombed in the rubble; the thought raised a solid, heavy weight in his throat. He tried to compare this grief to that of other deaths he had known—the suicides in Red Cliff, Uncle Sparky's murder—but decided this was different. This man had done no harm; he was hopeful, motivated. To Adam he seemed selfless. He was here only trying to earn a living for his family and village. And Adam felt partly responsible—his friendship had only encouraged Anarbek to stay in Istanbul longer, against what he now knew were the wishes of Nazira.

For another half-hour the Land Cruiser traced the shoreline. The quake had torn down power cables, and a black cloud of burning oil hung over the sea to the southeast. Survivors moved in a daze outside makeshift homes, carrying pails of water. Flimsy roadside tents had been constructed of plastic sheets, shopping bags, and cardboard. Light bulbs were rigged to electric lines, and a single lantern swung above the entrance to one plywood hut.

Opposite the collapsed crane of a steel mill, the driver dropped them off at the DHRO's tent city. Adam saw two thousand tents, most still in packaging. Cardboard lined the muddy paths, and a canvas pavilion erected at the site entrance served as a kitchen. Next to it an army sergeant with a Kalashnikov patrolled a long line of people waiting to use the single public telephone.

Jeff set up his own tent behind the kitchen and told Nazira she could sleep in there. He asked her one last time if she wanted to head back with the driver to Istanbul, but Nazira worried that once she left the earthquake zone, she could not return through the closed roads.

In the open tent Adam convinced her to lie down; and he sat for an hour with her, hand in hand. Her sleeping bag was an old one, stuffed with cotton, worn and soft, and the tent smelled of mildew, like a pawn shop, he thought. Nazira finally began to doze, but it was a restless sleep, and he could see her eyes darting beneath her lids. She was alive, beautiful even in her grief. Her palm was turned up against the outline of her hip, her hands were worn and dry. Every few seconds her thin, limber fingers twitched. Adam left the tent quietly, and in the kitchen pavilion, near Jeff and a dozen Presbyterian church volunteers, he unrolled his own foam mat and sleeping bag—the newer, nylon kind, stuffed with polyester. Over the tent city hung a silence, immense and piercing. Adam tried to sleep, but again and again the ground beneath him seemed to list. It had been doing this for three days, sometimes in a genuine aftershock and sometimes simply in his imagination, but he didn't know which bothered him more.

Jeff and Adam toured the field in the morning. Tents had come from Germany, Japan, and the Czech Republic, and the DHRO had begun to set them up, spread evenly in long lines. The burgeoning temporary city, occupying a plain between the bare green foothills and the sea, seemed to Jeff a cross between a suburban housing tract and a nomadic herding village. "I'm going to have to log in supplies," he told Adam. "You can help out, sorting through those." He pointed to two open truck beds, where volunteers had begun rummaging through boxes and green garbage bags of donated clothes and food, and two nurses were stacking emergency supplies. The nurses brought Melodi to mind, and Jeff battled his ongoing temptation to telephone her. He knew that her European neighborhood, like Üsküdar, had sustained little damage, and he was afraid even a checkup call would open the floodgates between them. He wouldn't show her he was weak, especially at a time like this.

Adam left him, and through the morning Jeff organized priority lists of meals to be prepared and medical requests to be ordered. If he kept busy, he could avoid the thoughts that had plagued him all night—thoughts tracing a straight line between his own actions and Nazira's missing father. He began collecting family names of those living in the camp, to keep track of the numbers arriving and leaving. In the afternoon, with his DHRO colleagues and thirty church volunteers, Jeff helped cook enormous vats of soup and pasta. From plastic bags they distributed loaves of donated bread. The stricken Turks, carrying soiled bowls, lined up in ten rows to wait for food; but before volunteers could dole out the appropriate portions, Jeff had to ask each survivor the terrible question: "How many in your family?"

When things quieted down that evening, he, Adam, and Nazira hitched a ride into Yeditepe to check with the police. On the minibus Jeff asked Nazira if she wanted to send word back to Kyrgyzstan.

"But how can I do that?"

"A letter would take too long?" Adam asked.

"Weeks," Jeff said. "Can you telephone someone in Bishkek and pass the word along?"

"I have a cousin in Bishkek, but what can I say to her?"

"You can tell her you're okay," Jeff said.

"Only me. Only I am okay. How can I say this on the telephone?"

Adam asked, "Have *you* called home, Jeff?"

"I've sent a message," Jeff lied. The possibility his father might be worried had given him a perverse pleasure. Let him imagine the worst for a while.

In Yeditepe they reported Anarbek missing to the police, and the round-shouldered officer at the desk scratched the name and description on a yellowed report form, without a word of consolation or advice. As they left, Jeff said to Nazira, "It's good that we did that. Your father will find out that you are looking for him."

She shook her head. "Jeff, they were no help at all."

At the hospital, beds and blankets had been set up on sidewalks. The building's foundation was cracked, and many of its windows were broken. Jeff learned from a security guard that the hospital staff had moved the injured to a schoolyard and parking lot down the shaded street. The three searched the crowded lot for any sign of Anarbek. Amid the din of traffic and people screaming to get the attention of nurses, the doctors treated patients in the open air. Nazira hurried through the crowds, and trying to keep up, Jeff passed heavily bandaged patients, a young boy with a bloody chest. One doctor, just finished stitching up a wound in an old woman's head, informed Jeff that no major medical procedures could be performed—nobody could reenter the hospital because of the strength of the aftershocks.

Back at the tent city, Jeff called Oren on a borrowed cell phone, but there was no news. Before the volunteers went to sleep, they gathered for a cup of Nescafé at a table in the main cooking tent to listen to the radio. Adam drank only water, and Nazira clasped a teacup with both hands, as if it alone could warm her.

The radio reported that, around the Sea of Marmara, rescue workers from fifteen countries were still hunting through the wreckage for survivors. The estimates of casualties had doubled. Last night it was five thousand; tonight it was ten.

Jeff looked at Nazira. She was staring into her teacup, and he couldn't tell if she was listening.

The news was dominated by stories of faulty construction. Before the quake, through massive corruption, developers had erected illegal neighborhoods. To raise a building required only a single license, easily obtained through bribery. A fatal lack of regulations made the problem worse: once started, apartment buildings had been subjected to no further inspections. Buildings that should have been constructed with elastic features and steel reinforcing rods had instead been built from the cheapest materials, so that contractors could rake in more profits. The most infamous developer erected entire housing communities from concrete mixed with beach sand. His six-story apartments were now a dusty graveyard, and the man had fled the country.

"How could they let him do that?" Adam asked.

Jeff shrugged. "It's corruption. It happens everywhere."

"He's responsible. He's responsible for those deaths."

Nazira quietly left the table and slipped into the darkness, toward her tent.

In the morning Jeff awoke increasingly sick with anxiety; his throat was scratchy from sleeping in the open. The miasma of rotting flesh hung in the air, and his stomach could hold no food. He supervised the extensive preparations for breakfast, which made him more nauseated still. Survivors lined up; they held out their bowls, their faces stern in collective shock. From between the tents, in the murky heat, came shouts of children playing tag.

Adam led a group of teenage boys around the dirt paths, putting up cardboard signs to give each lane a number, so Jeff could locate a family based on its address. As they worked he took it all in: the leaning outhouses, the women boiling water over fires, the makeshift school, the crowded orphanage, the cries of infants, the arguments of families, the electric wires strung overhead, the scrubbing of laundry in tubs, the clothing drying on tent poles, the chopping of wood, the subdued voices crackling from radios, the smell of urine, the leaking water pipes, the splashing of feet in puddles, the squeals of children kicking soccer balls. Three thousand people here, a city twice the size of Red Cliff, but with a collective intensity of suffering Adam could hardly comprehend.

For lunch he helped a crew prepare and serve mutton soup. Nazira quietly cut vegetables, then washed stacks of dishes, and Adam left her to her thoughts. He grew overly conscious of the Turks sitting listlessly near their tents, waiting for something to do. To keep busy, some survivors had volunteered to work in the tent kitchen themselves, and he began to feel superfluous. After lunch he was relieved when Jeff pulled a Frisbee out of his backpack, and the two taught a group of bored children at the orphanage how to throw it.

"What these guys need," Adam joked, "is to learn how to play some real ball."

He located some old coat hangers, rags, and a piece of soggy plywood, and in an hour's work, with the aid of two army cadets, he secured the makeshift backboard to a telephone pole near the orphanage tent. He lined up twenty of the camp's children and in a brief training session, using soccer balls, he taught them the proper way to shoot a basket. He then organized a three-on-three tournament, coaching the orphans, screaming at them in English peppered with pidgin Turkish, which they seemed to find endlessly amusing. "To run. To run!" he ordered. "To throw. To throw. To jump!" The youngest boys and girls imitated his directions, shouting at each other in ungrammatical infinitives.

After dinner two of the children attached themselves to him. Their names were Alp and Doruk, and they were about eleven years old—handsome, dirty, coal-haired boys. They tailed him through the busy kitchen pavilion, hanging off his arms and shoulders. Dark brown dust covered their fingers. Alp, the taller of the two, wore a zippered polo shirt with orange and purple stripes. Doruk had cropped hair, out of which protruded two of the largest ears Adam had ever seen. He wore a white T-shirt with a peeling decal that said 47 Sport. Adam asked if they were brothers. No, they told him, they were best friends. As he understood it, Doruk was living in Alp's family's tent. Alp waved his hands, palms out, and pointed at his friend.

"Doruk father no. Mother no."

Doruk tried to smile, then snatched the soccer ball from Adam's arm and dribbled awkwardly, stumbling once, down to the backboard to attempt a lay-up. Shielding his eyes from the sunlight, Adam watched the kid.

Nazira found him later outside the orphanage, shooting with the boys, and smiled at him. "You have some friends now, I see."

"I guess."

The boys were yelling something at him that he couldn't understand.

"Can you help me out here a minute?" he asked her. "I want to know what happened to Doruk's parents."

Nazira called to Alp and translated for Adam. The night of the earthquake, Alp explained, Doruk's father had woken him up and sent him fleeing from their building. His parents stayed behind to gather his little sister and brothers. Three flights down, safely outside, Doruk turned to wait for his family and saw the entire complex collapse into dust. "Pancake!" Alp said, slapping his palms together. Alp's own family had escaped safely. Now they were trying to track Doruk's surviving relatives but, homeless and jobless themselves, were having no luck.

Adam watched the kid shooting, determined to bank a lay-up. He was haunted by the image of this boy, fleeing the crumbling building, where his family, left behind, had been crushed. Before the sun went down, Adam arranged a half-court shooting contest for the assembled crowd of children and offered the winner a Snickers bar. On his very first attempt, big-eared Doruk heaved the ball overhead. It sailed straight, smashed off the backboard, and sank right in.

To distract herself, Nazira had begun helping young mothers set up a home in the tent city with salvaged bedding, blankets, and carpets. The familiar work was a comfort, and she recognized through it her own need to commiserate with the other female survivors. On her first morning at the tent city she had admired how quickly the volunteers and survivors had set up a huge green tent as the orphanage, and in her free moments, between preparing meals, she would help care for some of the children. The orphanage served double duty as a sort of kindergarten, to keep other children occupied while their parents secured food and clothing. She and some Turkish teachers from Istanbul engaged the kids in playing, storytelling, and drawing, and the crayoned pictures they pinned to the canvas tent wall looked similar, at first glance, to the pictures Manas had always drawn for her. Only on closer inspection did she understand that the blue trees were fallen, green bulldozers pushed at collapsed houses, and purple stick figures played football in a field of tents.

The stocky blond British nurse who supervised the orphanage solicited Nazira's help. She pointed to a carton of diapers and asked Nazira to distribute them to mothers with babies throughout the tent city. Nazira was allowed to give each woman only six diapers apiece, which did not seem enough to her. Unlike the rags she had once used for Manas, these diapers were made of stretchy plastic with a sticky adhesive patch and could not be washed. Around the tent city the mothers were at first grateful, calling out, "Thanks to Allah!" But on realizing how many diapers they were getting, they grew frustrated.

"Only six? That will last me one or two days, at the most!"

One young woman complained that the infant formula she had received for her child had run out. Another middle-aged, pink-faced Kurdish woman approached Nazira, pulled her behind a tent, and in a harsh whisper asked her if she had any Orkids. Nazira thought this must be a different brand of diaper and told her she was all out, but the woman blushed and described what sounded like sanitary pads. She was a simple village woman from southeastern Turkey near Diyarbakır, and she had been living in a shantytown north of Izmit when the earthquake struck. Nazira's heart went out to her, and she said she would check and see if any pads were available.

From the truck of donated medical supplies, the nurse located a light blue carton of something labeled Tampons and handed them over. Nazira said she did not know what they were, but the harried nurse insisted she distribute them. "These'll do the trick," she promised.

"The women are from a village in the south. I don't think they will know either."

The nurse sighed. "Oh, bloody hell! I'll come with you and show them then."

Facing a small crowd of Kurds, with Nazira translating, the nurse peeled the paper from a tampon and explained the cotton wad, the cardboard pieces, the string, and how to use the contraption. She ended with dire warnings about the importance of changing the tampons frequently. When a group of young men approached, the women grew conspiratorially quiet. The eldest Kurd drove the men away.

Through Nazira, a middle-aged woman asked how many tampons could be used at once.

"Oh dear! Only one at a time. Please emphasize this. They must use them one at a time."

A tan, finely wrinkled woman asked if one could urinate while using the tampon. She expressed disbelief when the nurse said yes. One mother asked in a whisper if the tampon would spoil a teenager's virginity. Nazira relayed the question, and the Englishwoman stood still for a second, hips canted to the right, mouth slightly agape. Finally she warned that young ladies might not want to use them if they were worried about this.

On the way back to the orphanage, the nurse thanked Nazira, laughing. "Well, *that* wasn't easy. You make a brilliant translator, though." With the compliment, Nazira felt pride well up in her chest, but she pushed it away. She had no strength to be helping others like this; she had her own problems.

By nine o'clock that evening, after another fruitless trip to Yeditepe, she was worn out. Jeff asked if she wanted to join the volunteers for some tea, but she retired instead to her shadowy tent with a flashlight and spread out her sleeping bag. Suddenly she felt hostile to everyone.

On nights in her old village, managing without water or electricity, she had often dreamt of living in the open like this, in a Kyrgyz yurt in the mountains. But she understood now that it was a humiliation to have to wash in public, to change her clothes in the plastic portable army latrine. She hated the damp sleeping bag and wished she had her old *shirdok*. Late at night like this, when she was no longer busy, all she could think of was her father, and if she did not go mad with despair, it was because she found relief in waiting for Adam. He would come into the tent and stay with her for a while, and then she could make it through the night.

In a few minutes she heard the rustle of nylon, and he crawled in. He sat beside her on the ground, fiddling with his own flashlight as she adjusted her sleeping bag. He told her his frustrations with helping assemble tents for newly arrived families, and his voice was a comfort, though she barely listened to the words. Eventually he fell silent.

She pointed to his scarred forehead. "You never told me, Adam, where did you receive that scar? Basketball?"

"No, my father."

"You were in an argument?"

Adam hesitated. "He pushed me against a wall."

"Why would he do such a thing?"

"It's a long story," he said. "He was angry."

"I don't understand. My father hit me when I was young, if I was naughty, but he did not hit me hard. Nothing like that."

"You? Naughty?"

"I was very naughty as a child, Adam. I listened only to my mother."

"What kind of things did you do?"

"Once I took my father's gun, and Lola and I practiced shooting. Outside the village. At bottles. Bang! Bang! We could have killed each other." She smiled.

"Did he hit you for that?"

"No, my mother hit me for that. My father beat me for once starting a fire in the kitchen. I left the gas tube on too long. When I lit the match everything caught on fire. Even my clothes."

"Anarbek hit you? But it was an accident."

"I was very, very careless, you see. My dress was on fire, and he put it out with a rug. I was crying on the floor. He hit me twice, here, on the face. He was very upset. Then he hugged me. I was only ten. I got many burns."

"That's not the same thing, really." Adam told her then about Levi and the ongoing battle with his father.

"It is terrible. Why did your cousin do such things?"

"I guess he wanted the attention. I think he kind of wanted to be caught." Adam shook his head. "He was just frustrated."

"You helped him then?"

"No, not really. I never thought of it like that."

"You are brave, Adam."

"It wasn't brave. I had to. And a lot of people don't understand."

"I think you were brave."

He was gazing at the top of the tent, and he spoke more of Arizona. In short, choppy sentences, he described the chaparral: the juniper, the blossoming century plants, how the height of the sunflowers in the fall told how much snow you'd get that winter. He tried to explain the putrid smell of a pack of unseen javelina, the rainbow canyons with strips of colored sediment. He described the waterfalls, how the Red Cliff Creek tumbled in three twenty-foot drops before meeting the Salt River. "Summertime my family always used to camp there, next to the second falls. In tents like this. My mom would make spaghetti, and if we caught a fish we'd roll it in corn flour and fry it on the fire. My sister Verdena and me would sometimes share a tent."

"How old is your sister?"

"She's almost twenty now."

"My sister is a little younger then," she said. "I am worried for her."

"Why are you worried?" Adam listened, trying to understand the traditions she explained.

"It's nuts," he said. "If some guy wants you, you don't even have to like him? He can just marry you like that?" Adam snapped his fingers. "If you walk around, any guy can just kidnap you?"

"It is how it is supposed to work."

"If I was your sister, I wouldn't even go outside."

"It is the way we live, Adam."

The outline of a shadow was growing larger on the tent wall. They both fell silent, and Nazira pressed closer to Adam's hip. The large figure halted outside and stood over them, reached for the roof of the tent, and shook it.

Jeff's voice whispered, "I came to see if you guys are okay."

"We are all right," Nazira said.

His shadow knelt down at the front opening. "Do you need anything in there?"

"We're fine," Adam said.

"Here, I brought Nazira some water. And some extra batteries for the flashlight."

She exchanged an embarrassed look with Adam, and he reached outside and took the bottle of water, then the batteries. But Jeff didn't leave. He remained squatting there, in the darkness outside the tent opening, in a strained silence. Nazira suddenly felt they should ask him in, that he wished to join them. But she fought her instincts. It would be too crowded.

"Aren't you hot in here?" Jeff asked at last.

"It is warm," Nazira said, "but we are okay."

More silence. "All right. I'll leave you guys. Good night then."

Jeff stood up. His shadow against the tent grew taller, then shrank, and they listened as the footsteps faded. For a number of minutes Nazira did not speak.

"What are you thinking about?" Adam finally asked.

"My son."

He took her hand and pressed his fingers down into her palm. "Anarbek's wife is watching him, you said."

"I know he is fine, but it doesn't help. Today, every child I see at the orphanage, it gives me pain."

Adam was staring away from her. "I was wondering," he said quietly. "Manas's father. Were you in love with him?"

"No."

"Did he steal you?"

She had to think about it. "No, not in such a way."

"Why didn't you marry him?"

She turned over under her sleeping bag. "Adam, it was not practical."

He faced her, his eyes lowered. "I'm asking too many questions, isn't it?"

"Yes. You are."

He touched her cheek and smiled. "You have two gold teeth. In the back."

"Yes. Three exactly. From when I was young."

"How does that feel? I mean the metal, in your mouth."

"I have never thought of it."

"There are some musicians, in America, who have those too. Rap stars."

"I do not know them."

"It's supposed to be cool. Is it cool for you over there?"

"Cool?"

"Cool. Like, you think you're important 'cause you have gold teeth."

Nazira laughed. "No, Adam, I am not so cool."

"You're pretty cool."

"Stop it. I'm not."

He was quiet, and she held his hand in her fist now and raised it to her face. Outside the murmurs from the kitchen pavilion had subsided. The mournful voice of a muezzin sounded from a distant minaret—the final call to prayer.

"My father is not coming back," she said.

"He's coming back."

"I must not joke myself."

The muezzin's voice grew louder. "Do you pray?" Adam asked over it.

"Yes, I pray for him."

"It's good you do that. I do it too."

"I was always so angry with him. I would tell him he did every-thing wrong. I was not a good daughter."

"It's okay."

"I did not show him the daughter's proper respect. I'll be better if he comes back to me."

"That's right. You will."

"Thank you, Adam."

He stroked her neck with one finger. "I'll get going now."

"Adam. Adam Dale. You have such a strange name."

"It's a normal name. Nazira Tashtanalieva. That's a strange name."

She smiled at him. "I should not love you now. I should think only of him."

"You're right. Just think about him then." After a minute Adam cupped her cheek in his warm palm, then slid his hand to her chin. "I gotta go. Sleep now." He kissed her quickly—his lips dry—and left, ducking through the opening, then zipping it up behind him.

Without Adam there, her exhaustion made her vulnerable to thoughts she preferred to avoid. Over the course of the hot, humid night she plunged into sleep, but her mind stabbed at her and she awoke again. She had been gone from home too long. How could she return and tell Lola that her husband was dead? Was Traktorbek waiting for them, or had he simply been terrorizing the family as a bluff? And Manas must be wondering every minute where his mother was. She felt that she was losing something of her old self, a disembodied part of her, last weekend's youthful convictions that she would one day be happy. It seemed impossible that circumstances would ever again favor her.

In the middle of the night she pulled herself from under her sleeping bag, unzipped the tent opening, and shuffled in her sandals to the bathroom. Even at this hour she had to wait for a free toilet—the tent city had only two portable latrines for nearly three thousand people. She stood in line in the wide open night, her mind cramped with fatigue, and the cool breeze on her face felt powerful enough to knock her over.

In her delirium she had a vision of erasing the past few months of her life, of going backward in time to the moment she had let her father take off for Turkey. Instead of acquiescing, she would absolutely put her foot down and demand he not leave them, demand that he remain with the young wife that Nazira had found for him and the young son he had fathered. She would shame him into staying in Kyrgyzstan, and in doing so, shame him into life again.

Inside the bathroom, her heart leapt when the metal walls around her trembled in an aftershock. She returned, frightened, to her tent, settled down on top of her sleeping bag, and listened to the grating chirrup of insects. She was too hot and restless to attempt sleep; she wanted only to be looking for her father, waiting for the machines that would lift the rubble and pull him free. She tried to think of other things and found herself wondering how those Kurdish women had managed with the tampons, whether or not they had tried them, and if such things actually worked.

In the stifling subterranean heat, Anarbek snapped back to consciousness a second time, to the sound of the child's frightened scream. "Baba! Baba!"

He answered, through the wall of rubble, "I'm here."

"I thought you left."

"I won't leave. Understand? I'm going to try to reach you. What can you see?"

"Nothing. Only dark stone." The voice grew softer. "Baba?"

"Yes?"

"I'm thirsty." The boy said it as if getting a drink from the tap was a simple matter, and Anarbek realized that he was horribly thirsty himself—he couldn't tell whether hours or days had passed. He raised his arm and swatted it around. Above and to his right lay the crumpled steel of the refrigerator. It leaned over a slab of concrete, creating a small open space, allowing him to breathe. A meter behind his head he swiped his free hand and found the plastic Hayat water bottle he had dropped when the building collapsed. It was covered in dust but still unopened, and miraculously, when he shook it, a quarter full. He had just enough strength to unscrew the cap and hold the bottle to his mouth. The liquid renewed him. He tried squeezing out from under the metal toward the child and managed to slide his waist half a meter; then he nearly bellowed at the lightning strike of pain that shot across his back.

Every few minutes he mustered a shout into the void. The choking dust in his mouth, throat, and eyes felt like it would suffocate him at any moment. And he knew he was sweating, losing precious water. He let his bladder loose, then soaked up the wet drops with his shirtsleeve to try to cool himself.

His chest pumping, he was consumed by thoughts of Nazira and the family, imagining how when he was rescued, he would apologize to Lola and his daughters. He would live the chaste, respectful life of a village elder.

Unable to reach the child so close to him, he sometimes spoke to him, insisting that the boy answer. He needed to keep him reassured, raise his spirits.

Straining his thin voice through the rubble, he told the boy his daughters' favorite Nasreddin Hoja jokes. He told him the one about Hoja's shirt being stolen: how, when he took off his pants to lure back the thief, Hoja accidentally fell asleep and awoke naked, with his pants gone too. He told the boy how a neighbor called on Hoja to borrow his donkey. Hoja, however, said he had already lent it out. "But Hoja," the neighbor said, "I can hear your donkey braying in your stables." "Shame on you," Hoja said, "for taking the word of the donkey over my own." He told the boy how

Hoja wished Allah had created horses with wings. That way, Hoja thought, men could fly around the world. But when he got hit with a bird dropping, Hoja decided, in the end, that Allah knows best.

Adam and Nazira hitched a ride to Yeditepe on a packed minibus. The afternoon roads were crowded with ambulances and half-filled trucks. Many gas stations had been destroyed, and each day it seemed to Adam that more cars had been abandoned by the roadside. The smell of scorched flesh from mass burials lingered over the seashore towns—the army burning unidentified bodies to prevent the spread of disease.

They exited the bus a block south of the fallen sports club building. Donated bread, tomatoes, and canned goods were piled high on the street corner, and two women picked listlessly through a heap of secondhand clothing. Opposite them, the hill of concrete and twisted steel was unaltered—most of the people they had previously seen clambering over its heights had given up. Adam could hear a bulldozer and backhoe growling a few hundred yards to the west, beneath the flat orange sky.

A lone construction worker wearing plastic boots climbed down off the wreckage and greeted them. He took off his helmet, and Nazira seemed to recognize him from earlier in the week. "Why do they work on all the other buildings," she asked, "but nobody works here?"

The man shook his head. Until today, he told them, he had heard noises, a voice that sounded like a friend he knew, calling for help. But today he no longer heard anything. "The United Nations is reporting it might be forty thousand," he said. He had heard that twelve thousand bodies had been recovered, and thirty-three thousand were injured. Foreign rescue teams were beginning to give up—in this heat, people trapped without food or water couldn't live more than a week. "But there are always miracles," he said, gesturing to the rubble. "They're still finding people alive."

The construction worker left, and Nazira began to climb up the hill of concrete. "Come, Adam, we will call for him."

"It's dangerous. You don't have good shoes." He tried to pull her back from the crumpled metal.

"He's still alive."

"Of course he is."

"Please let me then." With her skirt tangled at the knees, she stumbled over a bent section of rebar. Adam sighed, and together they scaled the concrete, twenty feet above the ground, calling out Anarbek's name. They circled the remains, balancing on rocking slabs of masonry. Twice Adam imagined he heard movement beneath his feet, but it was only shifting bricks and metal. A few Turkish women came to the edge of the rubble to watch. Nazira called until she was hoarse, and at last Adam had to take her by the hand and lead her down off the pile.

"We'll check with the police. They'll know if anyone's been found," he said.

But in the station the round-shouldered policeman again only jotted down Anarbek's description and the place where he disappeared, writing these notes on yellow report forms and clicking his tongue. He told Nazira that though many collapsed buildings might contain survivors, there was not enough heavy machinery to get to them. "Of course, God is the only one who knows why this happens to us," he said.

They left the station. "God, God, God," Nazira mumbled as they pushed through the heavy wooden doors.

Near the Yeditepe hospital the stench of decay bit Adam's nostrils. The staff and patients had still not reentered the building, but large canvas canopies now covered the schoolyard down the street—a marked improvement over the night before—and a few of the patients, legs dangling uselessly, were pushing themselves around in brand-new wheelchairs. The doctors looked in dire need of sleep, and the conscious wounded stared emptily as Adam passed their cots. A sign had been posted in Turkish and English: ISTANBUL AMERICAN UNIVERSITY, DEPARTMENT OF PSYCHOLOGY, POST-TRAUMATIC COUNSELING. Another sign hung at the gate: FIELD HOSPITAL OPENS AT 9:00. On the far side of the parking lot, the university had set up a pharmacy. Pasted around the schoolyard walls were signs with political slogans advertising the Islamic Virtue Party: LET'S HEAL THE WOUNDS TOGETHER!

Adam was sweating and tired. This searching was useless, he realized. They were about to make a second sweep around the parking lot when he thought he heard a familiar voice calling his name. He turned and saw a sturdy red-haired nurse dressed in white, but he didn't recognize her until she pulled down her facemask.

"Melodi!" She looked weary and unkempt, her dark features

hardened without her makeup. But it was uplifting to find a familiar face here.

"*Merhaba!* I called to you before, but you didn't see me."

Adam pointed to her clothes. "You working out here?"

"For now. They are busing us here every morning from the city. I volunteered. They are very short on health workers." She wiped a drop of perspiration off her face and smiled. "It's good at last to see someone I know!"

"You've met Nazira, Anarbek's daughter?"

At the sound of the name, Melodi seemed to flinch. "No, we haven't yet met."

They shook hands, and Melodi held on to Nazira's, gazing steadily into her eyes.

"How are you?" Nazira asked absently in Turkish. She hardly seemed to register the presence of Melodi.

"You are the first person in days to ask how I am. Nobody says *nasılsınız* anymore. They see you and ask only, 'Did your family survive?' This is our new greeting."

Adam indicated all the rows of beds and IV units, the generators grating away. "It's awful."

"Awful?" Letting go of Nazira's hand, Melodi smiled and shook her head. "Only awful, Adam? It is our *nightmare*. The army has finally begun to help today, but all they do is bury the bodies. They are using an ice-skating rink as a morgue! Allah, Allah! It's not the dead bodies that will spread disease, as everybody thinks, but the unclean water and so few toilets." She clicked her tongue. "And why are you here?"

Her face colored as Adam explained what they knew about Anarbek. She took a long, heavy breath and said, "It is impossible." Nazira turned away from her, but Melodi said, "Nazira, listen, please, give me his surname. I will see what I can find."

Nazira wrote it on a piece of paper, and Melodi disappeared into the nearest tent to check the available lists of names.

"She is Jeff's girlfriend?" Nazira asked.

"Ex-girlfriend. I think she's broken it off."

"She is very kind, and beautiful. Why did she do that to him?"

"I don't know. I never understand anything that happens with Jeff."

Melodi returned after a few minutes, her expression dire. "It's a mess, Adam. Our critical patients are now sent to other hospitals."

There was a great deal of confusion, she explained. Many families could not find their loved ones, and the hospitals had yet to coordinate their efforts to create complete lists of the injured. But all this confusion, she said, should give them some hope that they might track down Anarbek.

Adam asked, "Then where else can we look?"

"Your looking cannot help. He might be anywhere: in Izmit, or Istanbul, or Bursa even. We're getting new patient lists every day. I shall be here all week. Come, check with me tomorrow. I shall leave a message with Jeff's office if I hear anything."

Nazira thanked her.

"Not at all, not at all. May it pass quickly. Please tell Jeff you saw me, and I send my hello."

The encounter renewed Adam's optimism, but on the minibus ride back to the tent city, Nazira appeared more despondent than ever. "I am thinking there will be no more rescues," she said. For the first time she seemed convinced that Anarbek was lost for good. If her father was dead, she would have to go home to the village and inform Lola and the family.

Adam stared out the window. The evening darkness was settling. A farm truck piled high with household belongings rattled past them, and up ahead, where the land began to drop to the sea, he spotted a lone black bull wandering across the road. Halfway through the ride Nazira leaned heavily against his shoulder and said, "My father, he is the only person this could happen to."

He ran a finger up her arm. "Lots of people are lost, Nazira."

"No. It is his punishment. He has no feelings. Since my mother died he does not feel anything. He does not know what he does to hurt others. You see? He does not care how the other people feel. He travels so far and stays away from home, leaving his family to suffer." She pointed out the window. "This is the result."

Across the field of tents Jeff supervised the cleanup after dinner and found Nazira alone at a steel basin, scrubbing a pile of greasy utensils. When he approached, she turned on a hose to refill the basin, as if the loud running of water would keep him from speaking to her. He patted her arm and asked how she was holding up. Nazira lifted a long silver ladle, stained with tomato sauce, and said, "Someone who has lost her father, how do you imagine she should feel?"

"We don't yet know what happened." Jeff took a dirty spatula and spun it in his fingers. He wondered if he should encourage her like this. He never knew the right thing to say. Years ago, in the Peace Corps, he'd once found it so easy to talk to her.

"So much of my life is going wrong," Nazira said, drying the ladle furiously with a cloth. "I feel I am cursed."

"Come on, don't think like that. You've helped so many." His words felt empty to him, inadequate. "I remember how people spoke about you in the village. They depend on you. You're their teacher."

She concentrated on her washing. Her face was showing the effects of long travel, the strain of her grief. Her skin was pale, patchy below her dark eyes, and the flush on her temples looked like paint, pink beneath red.

"Jeff, you don't know," she said. "You never understood."

"What don't I know? I *lived* there, for two years. If anyone can understand what you—what you and your father—have gone through, it's me."

"Yes, you understand so much. Jeff, why then did you never come back to visit? Why did you never answer my letters? Why did you offer money and then refuse us? How could you pretend with us so much?"

He found it hard to believe that, here in the tent city, with the loss of life looming over them—and the possible death of her own father—she was bringing this up now. What was she accusing him of? Was she blaming him?

"We talked about it, Nazira. We have been through all this. I made many mistakes and I've admitted them to you."

She gazed out across the field of tents where children were splattering in the mud, playing king of the hill on piles of sodden bags of lime. "You never understood, Jeff. And you still do not. I think it is too late. I must go back and inform my family." She looked straight at him. "We do not have even his *body* to bury!"

"Nazira, I know you're upset. Look, it's been a long, terrible week." He searched for something more comforting to say. "Why don't we go back to the city tonight? Oren says the roads have opened, and you can come back to Yeditepe every day if you want. We'll get you a change of clothes and a decent night's sleep. Maybe a warm shower."

"A warm shower!" she cried. "I don't need any of that."

She avoided him the rest of the evening, though he caught her glancing at him from across the kitchen tent; and once, whispering to Adam, she nodded in his direction. He decided there was no reason to spend another night in the tent city; he too could return each day as necessary. After the kitchen pavilion was cleaned, with Adam's help Jeff took down his tent and stuffed it into his backpack. He collected their things, and the DHRO security guard drove them all back toward Istanbul. They stopped in Yeditepe to assess the state of the ruined sports club. Nazira stood outside for a few moments, leaning against the vehicle, staring up at what now seemed to Jeff a grave of rubble. At last she asked them to take her back to the apartment. In the jouncing Land Cruiser nobody spoke. For nearly an hour Jeff pretended to sleep, his mind swimming through deeper, more powerful currents, until he felt he would drown under the pressure of so much guilt. He needed simpler rules in life. He needed to be told the right thing to say and do. An old friend was lost, and he didn't know how much of it was his fault, or what might have been prevented. He was guilty of a crime he could not even label. Why hadn't he simply maxed out his credit card and sent the Kyrgyz home, happy, with the money he needed? Instead, against his better judgment, Jeff had let him stay in his apartment, playing at newfound freedoms in a world Anarbek didn't understand. Now the man was lost, both because Jeff had been too generous and because he had not been generous enough. He needed simpler rules.

The highway twisted around the sea, then swept them through the sprawling *gecekondos,* through traffic circles where plastic sheeting tents and houses built of blankets stood on every wet patch of grass, and finally into the city.

Burak's computerized TOEFL exam had been rescheduled for Monday, and Adam resumed their lessons Friday afternoon. Their seaside café was mostly empty; the old backgammon players had not returned to their games.

"Government reporting only seventeen thousand people died," Burak said. "I guarantee to you, it is twice that. At the least." He slid his chair out to sit.

"Seventeen thousand?" Adam asked, sitting opposite. It was more than the population of the whole reservation.

"I am telling you, it is too few!" Burak said. "The government isn't wanting to pay insurance for the deaths. They are lying." He lowered his voice and began tearing off pieces of his paper napkin. "Uff! I have to get out of this shitty country. Everything is shit here; our buildings fall, our government cannot help, our army does nothing."

Adam asked, "You leaving will help?"

"It will help me." Burak patted his muscular chest. "*I* can do nothing. One person can do nothing when a system is shit. A person's only work is to take care of himself. And his family. That is all a person must do."

Adam opened the TOEFL workbook. "Let's finish this stuff." They practiced sentence-completion questions, then reviewed advanced vocabulary words for thirty minutes, and Burak made only one serious mistake—insisting that a praying mantis was a kind of rug.

Adam said he thought Burak was going to pass.

His student beat the side of his head with his fist. "If I don't get too nervous. Tests make me nervous, and I forget everything."

They read over the Turkish papers together and Burak practiced translating text into English. He told Adam that yesterday a survivor had reached the police on a pocket telephone. An Israeli rescue crew had located the man with search dogs, and a group of Turkish firemen pulled him from the wreckage, followed by the bodies of his wife and two daughters. The rescue had made national headlines. The newspapers called the survivor a living testimony to the nation's resilience. Banners on the *Milliyet* and *Star* proclaimed

MAN SAVED BY POCKET PHONE!
A MIRACLE, A POCKET PHONE, AND
A TALE OF STRENGTH!

According to Burak the nation had watched the survivor last evening on NTV news, interviewed in his hospital bed. He was starving, dehydrated, at risk of kidney failure, but he would recover. The photograph in the *Milliyet* showed the man, sheets pulled up to his neck brace, with a weak smile on his lips.

For hours Anarbek had tried to squirm a half-meter closer to the young boy. He seemed near enough—if he could simply free his arm to stretch around the cement block, he might reach the child. But there was no room to maneuver, barely a half-meter of space above. From his new angle, though, Anarbek could make out chinks of light and hints of blue sky, and sometimes he imagined he heard voices calling his name. The light faded and came back—he lost track of how many times. Once in a while he mustered the energy to call out "*Yardım!*" But the effort exhausted him and sent the black pain throbbing in his legs. His tongue was large in his mouth. Each time he called, he sensed his voice was growing fainter. "Don't scream," he finally told himself. "Save your breath." When his thirst grew unbearable, he would take a single sip from the Hayat water bottle, until it was finally empty.

His mind slipped in and out of clarity, but he continued to whisper to the boy. Sometimes it seemed the child had fallen asleep, and Anarbek found himself alone with his whispers. The boy slept for a long time, and eventually Anarbek went under too.

He was flying again, soaring through the air on a jet to America, the aisles filled with boxed goods he was importing from Istanbul to trade in the bazaars of Washington and New York. In his half-asleep thoughts he set up a leather factory in San Francisco and employed Traktorbek's gang. They had joined the ranks of post-Soviet *biznesmenski,* hawking their wares in the global bazaar, competing in the worldwide market. He expanded his business. With Bolot's help he traded in apple tea, in lettuce, in leather jackets, in embroidered towels. He wrote complex business proposals to drum up support for a network of pocket telephones for Kyrgyzstan. One day a cellular technology would connect their mountain villages to the rest of the world. Shepherds could barter on the streets of New York from the pastures of Kyzyl Adyr–Kirovka. He knew someone would see the brilliance of the idea. It was just a matter of time.

He woke from a white distance, unaware where he was or how long he had been gone. He tried to whisper for the boy, but found he had no voice left.

The child made no sound. Anarbek kept up his voiceless whispering, first gibberish, then questions, then prayers to Baiooz, Lola, and Nazira. The boy would not wake. The silent gaps between Anarbek's whispers grew in length, until finally he understood he had slept too long. He had not even said goodbye.

From the living room couch, reading, Jeff heard the turn of the keys, then the quiet whine of the door. He leapt up. In the hallway

Adam was bent over, pulling off his shoes, and Nazira stood behind him, her eyes swollen.

They had ridden back to Yeditepe to check at the hospital again, Adam explained. Melodi had at last found the complete updated lists of patients registered around the Sea of Marmara. Not one contained Anarbek's name. They tried the police station once more, and the officer for the first time took pity and personally escorted them to the site of the fallen apartment complex. The sports club was now a patch of mud. Over the past two days bulldozers had cleared it. The policeman told them that any bodies found had been burned.

Nazira stumbled toward her bedroom, and Adam stayed by her side. The door to the apartment was still open, but Jeff sank against the wall to the hardwood floor. A random, forgotten memory came to mind, a fleeting image of Anarbek at the wheel, driving his crowded Soviet jeep home through the mountains. Halfway through "Ninety-Nine Bottles of Beer on the Wall," Anarbek had changed the words to the chorus, from *beer* to fermented mare's milk. "Ninety-nine bottles of *kumyss* on the wall," he had thundered, reaching back and slapping Nazira's arm, encouraging her to join him.

V

18

IN THE DHRO OFFICE, no one agreed on the best safety measures to follow in the event of another earthquake. Each of Jeff's coworkers had read different reports concerning the best plan of action, but his boss, a traditionalist, insisted the entire staff take shelter under the office furniture. During Jeff's first week back, they drilled this procedure once a day. At random times Andrew yelled, "Earthquake!" and the staff dove under their desks and covered their heads until "All clear!" was shouted. The six-foot-four security guard, however, could not fit under a desk, and during the drills he reluctantly thrust his head under the nearest table, his monumental rear end protruding from it. Laughter spread through the office, first suppressed and guarded, then erupting in a tumult, the first laughter Jeff had heard in two weeks, and as welcome as it was, it seemed a strange, unsettling sound.

Coordination of the DHRO's relief efforts kept Jeff working twelve-hour days. From field reports he knew relief was slowly spreading, and the survivors were slowly being helped. Even if the DHRO could not do all things for all people, even if they could not feed and clothe the masses, they were helping many.

On his second day back from the tent city he suffered through a particularly lousy afternoon. Garbage bags full of donated clothes lay in piles around his desk, the telephone rang incessantly, and at 1:20 another violent aftershock shook the building. The fax machine broke down. His printer was out of ink, and they had no replacement cartridges. He could barely concentrate on his work.

Midafternoon it took him an hour and a half on the phone with a Sultanahmet travel agent to secure two seats for Nazira and Adam on a flight to Bishkek—leaving in two days' time. He had warned his friend against the move (what would Adam even *do* there?), but if it was what he wanted, then Jeff wouldn't stop him. At least, he thought, he would soon have his apartment to himself. Soon he would have his own life again—solitude, the ability to come and go as he wanted, free from their watchful gaze. He could get over Melodi and think about his next move. Maybe he could talk to Andrew about a transfer, perhaps to West Africa. He had always wanted to work in West Africa.

On the phone he paid for the tickets to Bishkek with his credit card—the least he could do. Then he made one final, futile call to the Kyrgyz embassy to see if anyone had located the body.

That evening, still at the office, he realized he had not checked his e-mail since the quake. He found old messages from family and friends, most of whom he'd already been in touch with by phone, but it was his father's six worried messages that especially bothered him. *I'm seeing total destruction on the television,* he had written. *I'm so afraid something's happened to you. Jot me a note, for Christ's sake, and let me know you're all right.*

Jeff wrote a two-word reply: *I'm alive.* Then he reconsidered, deleted it, and wrote in its place: *Dad, I'm sorry I haven't gotten back to you. I've had my hands full. I'm fine.*

One strange address at the bottom of Jeff's inbox caught his eye, and he clicked on the message. He did not have to complete the first sentence before he knew it was not for him.

> Since you left Dad's been on a tear. He fired the principal and all the teachers and closed down the high school. He took down the grandstand at Red Dust Rodeo. Everyone's seen him drunk up at the casino, tossing money into the machines. He's just given up.
>
> Pastor's told me where you are, that you got stuck in the earthquake. Everyone here's just worried is all, and wants to know you're alive. You're all anyone's ever talking about. We've got council election coming in a month. Dad's up for the sixth time, and no one's happy about it. All Red Cliff's wondering who else to run, but there ain't no one. People just

scared of him. Rumor's going round that Adam Dale's coming home, that you'll run. Pastor, Mom, and Marie think the idea's the bomb. You'll win, I guarantee. We're sick of him. Everyone'll vote for a schoolboy college grad like you. Everyone here remembers the SHOT. No one talks about Levi—they think you did the right thing. You just gotta come back is all. People already putting up signs. Mom and Marie breaking out pots for the frybread.

—Verdena

PS: I want my abalone shell back. Don't leave us hanging.

Jeff hoped this letter would be enough, perhaps, to persuade Adam he was making a mistake. He printed it out on his boss's computer, folded it twice, stuck it in his jacket pocket, then left the office. In the kitchen of his apartment an hour later, he handed the printout to Adam. "Some news from home?"

Adam grabbed the paper, and immediately his face flushed. He read only halfway through the message and walked out of the kitchen in a rage. Sprawled on a blue kilim in the living room, he read the rest of it, holding the paper up at the ceiling lamp so the light shone through it.

Jeff joined him after a few minutes. "I got your tickets today, Adam. You know what I think, though." He sank into the couch and wiped his face with his hands. His arms felt like weights; he was exhausted. "You want to make sure she gets back, well, okay, I get it. But staying there?" He shook his head.

Adam scowled, folding the paper. "I did all right here. I'll do all right with her."

"It's not like you can just turn around and change your mind. You don't know what it's like over there, Adam. It's isolated, way up in the mountains. Freezing long winters. No jobs. And the place is falling apart. Half the time there's no electricity." Jeff pointed to the letter. "You've got important things to take care of in Arizona."

Adam slapped the paper. "I don't need to think about all this shit. It's good being away. I forget stuff."

"All right. Just forget about it then."

Adam was growing angrier. "You know what it's *like*, Jeff? I mean the pressure. Watching everything around you die, and there's nothing you can do."

"No, I have no idea. What's that like?" The sarcasm was unintentional. "I *lived* there, Adam."

"And I remember once you told me to get away. 'Gotta get away, Adam. Somewhere with a future.'"

Jeff shook his head. "I was pissed because no one wanted me there. It's different with you. Stop the self-pity already. Look at the goddamn e-mail. They're begging you! You don't go back, who's gonna help?"

"You read this, Jeff? He's tearing the place up. I mean, he's never been able to take care of family; how's he gonna run the town? You forget what was happening? You forget the teen center?"

Jeff was silent a moment. A car alarm sounded from the street below. Adam's eyebrows knotted up, and his voice grew louder than Jeff had ever heard it. "Look, you don't get it. You can take off wherever you want. You're from some happy family down in Phoenix. You don't have nothing weighing on you."

Jeff almost laughed. "Happy! You're so caught up in yourself, Adam, you've never even listened to me. You don't know the first of it. I haven't talked to my dad in years. Happy! Who's ever been happy?"

Adam rolled over on his side and stared at the wall. "You tell me *I* should stop the self-pity. What about *you?*"

A new note had crept into his voice—vindictiveness, and the words stung. Jeff shook his head, saying, "Look, don't suck me into this. I don't ever have to go back there, but you've got to live with this decision. Your family's waiting. At some point you'll want to return. And then what? You're not going to find what you're looking for in Kyrgyzstan. I know. I'm trying to watch out for you here."

"Well, stop it then."

A nasty silence filled the room. Jeff stood to leave, but Adam slammed the heel of his fist on the carpet. "Ah, fuck. I'm telling you Jeff, I don't know what to do. I promised her."

Adam arrived at the shoreside table late the next afternoon and found Burak already waiting for him. It was cloudy, and the wind cut south across the straits under the bridge, churning up pointed green waves. A napkin on the table flapped under the weight of a teacup.

"Well?" Adam asked, approaching.

Burak stood and raised his arms in triumph. "Success! I passed!"

"No shit?"

"I am not shitting." His student was grinning so hard it seemed his neck would burst. "I was very nervous because it was the last chance. I hate taking such exams on the computer. My hands were wet three hours, from the sweating." He gestured wildly as he spoke. "After, at the end of the exam, you can accept or cancel, before they show the score. I am thinking, I did so badly, I must cancel." He pounded his forehead with his palm. "But it is the last chance, so I accepted the result."

"What'd you get?"

He made a thick fist. "Five hundred ninety. I spoke already with the coach of the Queens College of New York."

"Was he happy?"

"He was very proud to me, as my parents are. Adam, because of you I will study in America." Burak grabbed his hand and shook it violently until Adam tore the hand away and sat down.

Burak said, "You don't look glad for me."

"I am. No, I'm real psyched for you, Burak. You earned it. You worked hard."

Across the expanse of water a white fishing boat rocked toward them. He could smell the countless odors of debris lapping against the shoreside jetty. Cypress trees on the opposite shore swayed against the wind. A ferry was plying through the current from Üsküdar to Eminönü, and he wondered if Nazira was on it.

Burak pulled his chair close to Adam, sat down, and reached into his shirt pocket. "Here."

"What's this?"

"My parents say to give you this, as thank you for helping me win the TOEFL." The Turk shoved a roll of green bills into his hand.

Adam said, "Forget it. I didn't do anything. Your English is probably worse 'cause of me." He refused to close his fingers around the money.

With his opposite hand Burak grasped Adam's fingers and in his water-polo grip forced them shut. "You do not refuse a present from the Turks. It is rude."

Adam laughed and nodded once. He gazed past Burak, as far as it was possible to see along the green currents of the straits, all the way to the horizon, where, if he kept his eyes fixed long enough, he thought he could just sense the world turning.

They parted awkwardly, and Adam walked all the way up to

Istiklal Caddesi, listening to the distant wail of the ferry boats, the high-pitched brakes of the street taxis. At the top of the hill he hustled through the sparse evening crowd. Two weeks ago he had come here with Nazira, and the outdoor cafés had been full, the beggars were playing accordions, AC/DC blasted from the open record shops, the trolley car rang its bell at couples on the tracks, and cooks stirred eggplant stews in restaurant windows. He had felt assured of a future with her, of a reality more vibrant than what he had yet known. Now the gray streets were nearly empty. He realized he had somehow deceived himself.

In Taksim Square he smelled French fries coming from a Burger King. He ducked in, ordered a serving, and took them upstairs to the terrace. Red tables lined the roof of the building, but he was the only customer. He slid into a booth. The tabletop was wet with ketchup and soda spills, and he chewed the hot, salty fries, one by one. Across the street gleamed the windowpanes of the French consulate, and on the other side of the square the heights of the Marmara Hotel were lit in purple. The skyscraper blocked his view of the straits, but he knew they were there. The city, once so foreign, was suddenly familiar and cheerless.

He drew Verdena's e-mail out from his pocket and read it again, twice. He turned the facts over in his mind, examining them from every angle. He'd never considered the possibility of replacing his father as councilman: he'd never entertained the slightest interest in politics. Now he realized it was a simple matter of will. The possibility that his family might think he was afraid to run made him furious; then he thought of Nazira, and pushed away the remaining fries.

It was getting late, and he had only tonight to make up his mind. He exited the restaurant, dodged traffic across Taksim Square, and hailed a taxi. He told the driver, an elderly man who managed to steer, smoke, and eat a *döner* sandwich all at once, to take him to Üsküdar. The cab rushed downhill, sped through yellow lights past the Beşiktaş soccer stadium and up the highway to the entrance of the Bosphorus Bridge, where they slowed into a line of stalled traffic. They inched their way across. Adam had never taken a taxi between the continents—he had always used the ferry. From the top of the bridge the monuments of the desecrated city spread in all directions. He contemplated the open heights, the dark waters below, and tried to imagine a nomadic people journeying across straits like this—across the ice, from the farthest tip of Asia, into North America—and making their slow way along the coast and farther down into the deserts, until they had populated the lands, and all great migrations had come to an end.

The traffic sped up; Adam rubbed his dry eyes, and when he uncovered them saw the sign approaching: WELCOME TO ASIA.

Nazira waited by her packed sports bags—all of her father's things, sorted and folded—but Adam did not return to the apartment until after ten that evening. With the door open she could hear him and Jeff speaking quietly down the hall. She made out the words "airport" and "tickets" and grew frightened. A minute later Adam's door shut with a thud. He had not come to see her.

She rose from the bed, left the study, and rapped the hollow wood of his door softly with her knuckles. The floorboards groaned behind the door, but Adam did not answer. After a minute she pounded harder with her palm. "Adam?" she called. "Adam? It is I. Nazira."

He opened the door only halfway. He was wearing a stained white T-shirt and the long pair of black shorts he wore for playing basketball. "I was just changing."

"May I come in?" she asked.

He opened the door wider. "I just, you know, gotta pack up."

"Yes. I too have packed." Nervousness played on his face; thick veins showed in his temples, in the backs of his hands. "What is wrong, Adam?"

"Come in. Come sit."

He tried to lead her over to the bed, but she resisted. "No, please tell me."

He knelt at his duffle bag and pulled out a crumpled piece of white paper from the pocket of his jeans, unfolded it, and handed it to her.

She sat on the bed, reading. With each word a pressure built up in her chest. "Adam!" she said, and leaned back against the bedpost. "I cannot understand it, Adam."

"I promised I'd come with you to Kyrgyzstan, to help with your father's service."

"You will come, no?"

"Nazira, I *want* to come. I want to be with you. But this letter—"

"I do not understand this letter."

"It's from my sister back home. There's this election coming up soon. They want me to run for councilman, something like mayor of the town."

She hesitated, fingering the paper for a moment, then laid it gently on the bed. "It's an honor?"

"Not sure you'd call it an honor." He searched the floor. "It's pretty important."

"You want then to do this?"

He nodded. "I think I gotta." Slowly he reminded her about his father, how the town had no future if he continued to lead, how Adam owed it to his family to return.

"Adam, but our plans? That you promised! You won't come with me?"

"I've got no choice."

She straightened up, ready to leave, to release him from his obligation. When she stood, though, he held her by the arm and directed her back to the edge of the bed, next to him. "I was thinking you could come over to Arizona. Live with me, over there. On the reservation."

"I also want to be with you. But I cannot go to America. I have the duties in my village. The services."

"I mean after. I mean after your father—after the services. In a couple months."

"And I also have Manas."

"You'll bring him. You bring Manas along. He likes horses, you say? We've got tons of horses. I'll teach him to ride fast."

"But—my sister."

"Your sister?"

"And my stepmother, Lola."

"Yeah."

"She has the son, too. Oolan."

"Yeah."

Beside her he had grown stiff. Her head was swimming. Suddenly she saw herself as a ridiculous figure—a foolish romantic, idealizing these hard-hearted men; a pitiable, impoverished woman who, thinking she was capable of higher things, had forgotten her place in the world. "I don't think I can live in America, Adam. I don't like this being far from home. Kyrgyzstan is my—"

"What?"

"My motherland."

"Your motherland?"

"Oren says not to use this word."

He touched her knee. "It's okay, you're right. A motherland. You're right."

"Yes?"

He was silent for too long. Only his thin chest rose and fell. When he spoke, the words were simple and promising, but she could hear in them the deflation of hope. "Maybe a different time, it would work out for us." His deep voice wavered. "We both gotta go back, take care of business, and then we'll see."

"Yes, maybe a different time," she said. She bent her head and tugged down the side of her skirt. This was pain. This was what it felt like to be alone. "I wanted you very much to come," she whispered.

She followed his gaze to his duffle bag, open on the floor, the white, rubber tips of his basketball shoes jutting out. His eyes remained downcast, his voice low.

"Me too."

19

JEFF FOUND THEM a late-afternoon taxi to the airport, and Nazira sat in the front while he, Oren, and Adam crunched into the back. The vehicle lurched. Its brakes squealed. Past the bridge, into Europe, the driver raced onto an open highway, cutting in and out of lanes, and near Melodi's neighborhood Jeff had to lean forward over the stick shift and ask him to slow down.

The city had been in the final stages of modernizing the Atatürk Airport, but the chaos of the earthquake added to the chaos of construction, and now it was impossible to discern what had yet to be built and what, in these last weeks, might have come crashing down. It took the driver nearly thirty minutes to weave through the double-parked buses and stalled cement-mixing trucks. "You're going to be late, Nazira." Jeff worried aloud as they unloaded her bags from the trunk. In Terminal C Adam joined the crowd of people waiting for boarding passes. Jeff pulled Nazira away to a quiet spot near the Air Kazakhstan check-in gate.

"Look, we have this extra ticket. Let me fly with you. It's no problem."

"It is not necessary, Jeff."

"You can't go back alone like this."

"I came here alone. Flying will be much easier. Thank you, Jeff; you are very kind."

He looked away at the earnest embraces of travelers around them: families reuniting, couples stalling before their final goodbye, the funereal hug of two women covered with chadors, who must have suffered a loss. A gray-suited businessman wheeled his father's luggage to the gate. An old Tajik man in a purple skullcap stared at them from a seat a few feet away. Just behind him, a tearful brown child was screaming for her mother in Uzbek. Jeff turned to Nazira again and took her hands awkwardly in his.

"Nazira—I wanted to say—about your son—I can help out."

She looked at him vacantly. "It is okay, Jeff," she said. "We will be fine. It is not your problem." She tugged her hands from his grasp and hurried back to where Oren was guarding her two over-stuffed sports bags. She hates me, Jeff thought. He disgusted her, and she wanted no more of his help. What had he left to offer her, after all? He watched her steps, the lined definition of her calf muscles as she strode away. It seemed impossible, some foggy memory of a distant life, that he had once felt those legs around him. He stood in place, amazed by how little he felt. These weeks had drained him of all emotion.

When he rejoined them, Nazira was complaining that she had never said goodbye to her friend Sashenka. She begged Oren to find her and pass along a message. "You might like her, Oren. She is very pretty. She sells leather jackets on the street in Laleli, near the Antik Hotel. Please tell her I said goodbye. Tell her this: I send an American Prince Charming. Use those words. Do not forget, for me. American Prince Charming."

"Prince Charming." He smiled. "I'll take care of it."

Adam had made no progress in line at the counter, and amid the tumult of the queue gave them an open-armed gesture of exasperation. Squatting by the bags, they waited fifteen minutes more before the loudspeaker announced her Kyrgyz Air flight was twice overbooked. In a panic, Nazira had to elbow her way from Adam to the front of the counter and scream to get her boarding pass. She returned to them, perspiring, crouched on her father's bag, and covered her face in her hands. Adam knelt beside her. Jeff and Oren stood over them, shifting on their feet, watching the crowd. When the flight number was announced at last, they escorted her to the security gate.

She shook Oren's hand first and wished him good luck. "You will find her, Oren. I know it. She is waiting."

"When I do," he joked, "we'll come visit you sometime over there."

She wiped her face with her palm. "You are welcome. If you come, I promise, I shall make you sheep eyes for breakfast."

Out of the corner of her eye Nazira saw Adam, and he was deathly pale. She let go of Oren's hand. "Take care of yourself," he said, and stepped away.

She turned to Jeff. With Central Asian propriety, he shook her hand one final time, fumbling for something to say. "You have enough money for the trip?"

She did not move one finger in his grasp. She wanted to answer him harshly—she wanted to scream, "Jeff, I don't need your money!" This might be her last chance to blame him. She could blame him for everything: her father's death, her illegitimate son, all the false hope. She looked him over one last time, at his baggy blue jeans, his half-buttoned plaid shirt, his scraggly goatee. But he was generous, she reminded herself, and well-intentioned, and she had once dreamt of marrying an American. Her father wasn't the only one who had wanted it. She had foolishly wanted it too, more than anything.

In Kyrgyz she thanked Jeff for his offer. "Thank you also for your hospitality. And Jeff, thank you for the airplane ticket. And for your help—for trying so hard to find my father. I am grateful."

He blushed. "*Eshteke emes*," he said. It was nothing.

She wiped her eyes with the back of her hand and hesitated. Full of dread, she turned to Adam. Neither of them could say what they wanted, she realized, with Oren and Jeff watching, the crowd rushing past them. He made no effort to hug her, or even to kiss her in the Turkish fashion, so they shook hands instead. His palm was wet, but she could not let go. She considered dragging him with her onto the plane. There was the extra ticket, and if she pushed a little harder, if she asked him just one more time, Adam very well might come with her. It took everything she had not to speak, and finally she released his hand. Adam took a step backward, and as she bent for her sports bags, he slipped an envelope into her open purse, next to her boarding pass.

"A little gift," he said. His voice was somber; it pierced her. "Open it on the plane."

Nazira smiled at Oren and Jeff one last time. Then, hunched to her left, dragging the two heavy sports bags, she headed through the gate.

*   *   *

Adam's own flight did not board for two hours. Oren and Jeff offered to keep him company, but they seemed to be talking to him across tremendous distances; he only half-heard their voices. He insisted they leave and let him wait by himself.

Oren tried to comfort him. "Look, I'm sure you'll see her again soon."

"No, it's not going to work out with us." He set his jaw; he didn't want to talk now.

"This will all pass," Jeff said. "Give her some time."

Adam stared hard at his duffle bag. "I'm fine," he snapped. "Just leave me here." He shook Oren's hand, turned to Jeff, and they embraced awkwardly.

Jeff said, "I'm thinking of coming back to the States. Around Thanksgiving. Maybe I'll visit you."

"On the rez?"

Jeff smiled. "If they won't boot me out of town."

"Can't guarantee they won't." Adam stepped back.

"Maybe I'll see you, then."

He could hardly look at Jeff. "Maybe I'll see you."

He didn't bother watching them walk away, but scanned the screen for departure information, found his Lufthansa flight to the States, lifted his duffle, and strode off through the crowd to look for the check-in counter.

Without guests the apartment seemed enormous and empty. Jeff called in sick to work the next day and spent the afternoon slouching alone around the city. He felt he had nothing more to offer this world. His goodwill was exhausted. Thirty, and washed up. For an hour he sat on the jetty by the Kız Kulesi and watched two young boys swim against the current of the polluted straits. Around him Istanbul was still in mourning. The screaming peddlers, the pleading shoeshine boys, the raucous gypsies—none of it had yet returned to life.

It had thrilled him once, when he first arrived here: the sense that this city lay at the center of the world. An ancient earthquake had chiseled out these straits, and the ensuing flood had divided the continents. These roiling currents had swept the cold waters of the Black Sea down to the Aegean and the warm waters of the Mediterranean up to Russia. For over two millennia, from this very point, the city's empires had spread east and west. Its emperors and sultans had ruled from that mighty-walled peninsula. Their gray palaces still loomed over the sea; their domed mosques still peered from the crowns of flowered hills toward Mecca.

But on every hilltop now the concrete had grown outward and over the great peninsula. The vast empire had retreated upon itself. Its peoples left their inherited farms and war-ravaged nations. They fled distant mountain villages and the rusting ports of four different seas. They arrived with oversized bundles, crowded in burnt-out apartment buildings, collected in neighborhoods of shoddy cement structures and crouching cardboard houses. They lit homes with stolen electricity, they heated rooms with toxic coal, they fixed forests of makeshift antennas upon their roofs. And the people kept coming. The city had grown, swallowing suburbs and waterside villages, until entire regions of countryside, once shaded by vineyards and olive groves, were now no more than shantytowns. And no one these days even knew the city's population. Some said seven million, books claimed ten, the news reported twelve, and authorities set it between fifteen and eighteen million—yet still the people came, until there were too many, and it seemed to Jeff the earth itself could not support them.

He left the jetty, and early that evening took a taxi to the W. B. Yeats. Oren was out on a date, Mehmet had not arrived for work, and there was nobody behind the bar, nobody on the dance floor. In the bathroom the owner had hung another Yeats poem, "Sailing to Byzantium," printed in red, above the sink. Jeff made his way to the back room, where he sank into the green easy chair at the computer and checked the *Arizona Republic* Web site. The familiar names of Phoenix neighborhoods—Sun City, Chandler, Apache Junction—soothed him. For the first time in years he missed the heat of the Arizona blacktop in summer, the scent of air heavy with oranges, the saguaro cacti like sentinels on the highway medians. He remembered walking with his mother in a mall parking lot, in southern Phoenix. He couldn't have been more than seventeen. Up ahead he had spotted his father, arm in arm, with another woman. He turned to his mother; she had also seen them. "What should we do?" he asked. Jeff wanted to confront the man, let him know the damage he was causing. They needed to have it out. Instead his mother gripped his arm and said, "Slow down. Just slow down. He doesn't have to know we saw."

The words on the computer screen skated unintelligibly through his mind, until finally he realized the Internet server had failed. It could not find the article he wanted, and with the simple error message a sadness crept over him, a vast emptiness.

He felt a light hand on his shoulder and jumped at the sound of Melodi's raspy voice.

"Why are you here, sitting all alone?"

He turned. She was wearing a tight black silk blouse and jeans, and he noticed the slightest tan line, the outline of a facemask, across her cheeks. She leaned over him to examine the computer screen. "Just waiting for someone," he lied.

"I was so sorry I did not see you in Yeditepe," she said, blinking her glittered purple eyelids. "After the earthquake—you know—I was very, very depressed. I saw Adam and Nazira. Did they tell you?"

He clicked the search button on the keyboard once again. She came around and stood to his right.

"You are angry at me, I know. Please, Jeff, I feel I have only been going to funerals, for days and days and days." She waved her hand, palm out, the old Turkish exaggeration he'd always delighted in.

Let her talk, he thought, she can talk all she wants. It got them nowhere. He scratched his knee.

"I am back at the hospital," she was saying. "We are short of nurses, but I was so tired, I took today off. I came here—I wanted a drink. And you, Jeff?" she asked. "How are you?"

He turned from her again, back to the stalled computer screen, so she would not see his face.

"*Çok üzgünüm,*" she said. "Jeff, I'm so sorry." She began to rub his shoulders from behind. He tensed, but was grateful; he released a long breath. Her strong fingers worked into his shoulders, and he reached up and pressed each of his hands onto hers, remembering the pleasure of holding them, of touching this smooth dark skin. His mother would have adored Melodi. Both of them were stubborn bighearted women who knew how to put him in his place.

She lifted his left hand to her lips and kissed his knuckles. He didn't move. She embraced him from behind, around his neck, pressing her ear against his, whispering comforting thoughts in Turkish, thoughts he could barely understand. "*Geçmiş olsun,*" she said at last. May it all pass quickly.

On the screen the error message appeared: the Web site could not be found.

It was very sad, he thought, what had happened between them.

The smallest things that divided. All the ways people managed not to save one another. He did not want to move, not one inch. He wanted only to surrender to this life. He thought it would do him good to stay here awhile, just like this, in her grasp, cheek to cheek. There were worse places to be. He felt a wetness on his neck, Melodi's own tears running down under his T-shirt, sliding cold along his chest.

"Come here," he said, turning to face her. He pulled her around the easy chair, then solidly onto his lap.

In the overbooked plane Nazira had to steal a seat from a Kyrgyz man who had foolishly chanced the restroom. Her luggage blocked the aisle—neither sports bag would fit in the overhead compartment. She argued with a stewardess who demanded she move them, until the woman finally huffed and gave in. Nazira settled into the lumpy seat. The Russian businessman to her left would not share the armrest, and above her the reading light did not work. She felt as if she was already home.

She closed her eyes during takeoff. The unfamiliar turbulence of the flight—Nazira's first—made it hard for her to breathe. Nothing held the airplane up; the deserts and mountains of Asia swam kilometers below her feet. She passed the first hours remembering her duties to her father. She would have to get the relatives in Cholpon Bai to assemble the yurt, the women would sing the *koshoks* for three days. She could barely remember the words: "When our father was with us, we could touch the sky. Now we have been separated from him, now we are left alone . . . May your daughters live a long life, may your sons always be happy, they are my gift that you left me, they are the ones on whom I can rely . . ."

The men would enter the yurt, singing, "Dear father, I will never see you again." Lola would help her bake the *borsok*. Nazira would need to ask the men to slaughter a horse. For three days the village guests would come; the women would cry and sing and wet their faces. This is what they must do, even without the body to wash and bury. On the morning of the third day the village mullah would recite the *janaza*—their final farewell.

If Adam had come, what would he have thought? He could have helped slaughter the horse. He might have learned how to assemble a yurt. Would he have wailed, like the other men, during the *janaza?*

His gift! She pushed her seat upright, removed the envelope from her purse, reached inside it, and slid out a thick bundle wrapped in manila paper. It took her a moment to decipher Adam's rough handwriting: *N—This will help awhile. Use it for your son.—A.*

She unwrapped the paper and found, secured with a rubber band, a stack of crisp one-hundred-dollar bills. The pile was heavy in her hand, like a brick. She lowered it into the folds of her skirt, between her legs, and checked that the Russian to her left was still asleep. One by one she counted the bills. Ten thousand American dollars.

Her heart skipped, and she fumbled with the green money, trying to get the edges of the bills lined up evenly again. At last she hid it away in her purse. It was too much—she couldn't keep such money on her body. Sweat dripped down her arms, and suddenly she worried that with this money she would never make it back to her village alive. She clutched her purse to her stomach for the rest of the trip.

The plane landed in Bishkek at dawn, and she climbed down the stairs onto the steady ground. The airport hosts were dressed in traditional Kyrgyz costume—red felt vests and fur-lined hats—and they offered the passengers warm pieces of bread before herding them onto a rusted airport bus. A faded poster on the bus still advertised the thousandth anniversary of the *Epic of Manas*. Another proclaimed MENCHEEKTESHTEEROO. The shuttle bus backfired and sputtered but managed the two-minute drive to the terminal without breaking down.

It was a long taxi ride to Bishkek's *otovakzal*. There, she loaded her luggage in the lower compartment of a bus leaving for Talas. Halfway through the eight-hour trip they pulled into the rest stop in Kazakhstan. The maggot-filled outhouse reeked worse than she remembered, but Nazira did not mind much. She had expected it, even with a strange anticipation. At the Kyzyl Adyr–Kirovka bus stop a benzene seller offered her a lift to the village. She said nothing to him of her father or of where she had been for nearly a month. They piled her things into his truck and drove along Fifty Years of October Street, past the new mosque (still under delayed construction) to the cheese factory, where she would store the luggage. Later she would drag it home to Karl Marx Street.

The door to the factory office was locked. Nazira pressed her face against the dark window, blocking the late afternoon sunlight. "*Alo?*" she called and patted the glass pane. Somebody should have been working. She stood on her toes and looked in again. Her father's office was barren; there were no books on the shelves, no papers on the desks, no calendars on the walls. Abandoning the window, she dragged the oversize bags to the stables. The sliding door lay open, but she found the building ghostly empty: not a single cow remained, not even the smell of cow. She pushed the bags against the aluminum wall and in a panic hurried along the muddy street that led to her father's home.

Crashing through the gate into the courtyard, she found, sitting on the tea bed—not Lola and the children, as she had expected—but Baktigul. A beige silk *platok* was tied around her sister's head, and behind her a powerful figure drew forward. Traktorbek. He was lounging on the cushion like a sultan, poised to pull red chunks of dripping *shashlyk* off a skewer with his teeth.

Not one of them moved. From the kitchen window Lola spotted Nazira and shrieked in surprise. She called inside to the children, and through the door a small figure shot out of the darkness and into the dusty courtyard.

Suddenly Traktorbek, Lola, and Baktigul were all speaking at once, but Nazira heard nothing. She was aware only of her child running toward her, screaming, "Ama, Ama!" Over the last few years she could never be sure if time in this village marched forward or backward, but it no longer mattered: with her father's death, it seemed all time had stopped. Manas clutched her legs and held them. Ten thousand dollars—Adam's gift to her—would be enough to raise him, to keep his body clothed, his stomach fed, as he grew. She bent and embraced him, kissed both of his ruddy cheeks, lifted him and squeezed him tight to her chest. "Uff! You've gotten so big!" she said, and gave her son one long kiss above his wet nose, between his blue American eyes.

She lowered him to the ground and looked up. Baktigul was beaming triumphantly. Traktorbek had risen, and was addressing her politely. "*Eje,*" he had called her. Big sister. "*Kosh Kelingiz!*" He was welcoming her into her own home, the home in which she had grown up, given birth. Nazira froze; she didn't know which direction to turn. This squat, shiftless hooligan, who sold meat in the bazaar, who had dreamed of opening a gas station in the capital, had upset the balance of the family. But now she had no choice.

Now the balance must be regained; now, more than anything, they would need a man. Steeling herself, she stepped forward to offer her hand.

"Thank you, brother," she said, grimacing. "How is your health?"

"*Jakshii.*"

"How are your works?"

"*Jakshii.*"

"And how is your family?"

"*Jakshii.*" Traktorbek smiled, offered her an infuriating half-bow. "And our father?" he asked. "Has he come back with you?"

Nazira steadied herself, then turned to bear Lola the unbearable news.

From the plane window Adam could see through the clear air of Arizona. He would not allow himself to think of Nazira or Anarbek, and to take his mind off of them, he had just finished for the second time an old *Newsweek* article describing Bill Clinton's visit to a South Dakota reservation—the first president to set foot on Indian land since 1936. In his speech the president promised that rez town immediate access to the Internet.

He forced Nazira's face from his mind, conjuring up instead the city he had left last night, remembering the statues and photographs of Atatürk. Father Turk, the people had called him. Adam pressed his forehead to the window. The Red Mountains, small as goose bumps, swept past below. The plane approached Phoenix and he spotted Sun Devil Stadium, and then the Arizona State campus. The plane canted, circling the downtown towers, over Bank One Ballpark, and then over the capitol.

The family met him at the gate. His mother was twisting her thin gray hair, and Aunt Marie Anne stood with her fists on her hips, a prescient authority in her cold expression. Adam dropped the duffle bag.

"Mom."

Lorena came close, reached up to his face, and touched his forehead. Her fingers drew lines over his nose and over the arcs of his ears as she took him in. He accepted the affection without moving his head; he felt almost impenetrable, and the rage was gone. When he spoke, he directed the words straight into her eyes. "Came back to see you."

She grasped both his hands and offered him her defeated smile. "You gained weight."

"It was those *kebaps*," he said.

In the parking lot the seats of Jeff's old Toyota pickup scalded his legs as he slid in. Marie Anne drove them out of Phoenix, and halfway home they stopped at McDonald's and switched places. Adam drove the last two hours to the reservation. The high desert spread before them through the burning late-summer haze. Saguaro and cholla dotted the dry cliffs. He drove through the mining towns of Globe and Miami, beyond the Wal-Mart, and higher up, toward the Salt River Canyon—the swift expanse of cliffs, the dazzling light—and higher still, into the piñon pines. He rolled down the window, and warm, clean air lapped against his face. He could practically smell home—the manzanita berries, the wild horses— and in those smells he knew the steady peace of sacrifices rightly made.

"Tell me what's been going on," he asked his aunt.

Marie Anne uncrossed her arms and seemed to think about it, as if she had to travel far back into her memory. Adam wound the truck through the canyon. When they reached the top, his aunt cleared her throat and looked straight ahead. In pure Apache, the sound of the syllables a benediction, she told him the news: who had won that year's Fourth of July rodeo, who had taken off to Tucson and gotten into all kinds of trouble, who had been fired from the sawmill.

His mother pushed him playfully in the side of the head with her palm. "Istanbul, heh? What were you thinking? Six *months* I am praying nothing happened to you." She gripped his elbow. "Now look there," she said. "You're almost back." She pointed across Adam's chest, over the steering wheel, to the hill in the distance, the mesa rising behind Lonely Mountain.

He slowed the pickup at the Turnoff. A spray-painted sign stood next to Uncle Sparky's memorial:

Don't Screw Up Vote A. Dale.

"What's this? I didn't tell you I was running."

Marie Anne said to his mother, "Go ahead."

His mother nodded, speaking almost in a yell. "Your father's thinking he might not run for council again. Says he's tired of fighting for this town. Says no one's appreciating him."

"Afraid he'd lose, isn't it?"

"You'll run?"

He shook his head, smiling. "Didn't say I'd run."

Let them beg if they wanted him, let the whole town beg. He stepped hard on the gas and made a right at the Turnoff, following the only paved road. Each time he had left Red Cliff, he returned to find that the town seemed smaller, as if the outside world had grown. Now he had been halfway around the earth, as far as a man could go. Crossing over the pass, he could see it in the distance, the strip of the white deflated school dome, the corrugated iron roofs blinking in the sun, a town so small it seemed like nothing, like he could palm it in his hand.

ACKNOWLEDGMENTS

My deepest gratitude to

My agent, Dorian Karchmar, an inspired reader and a tireless coach, and my editor, Heidi Pitlor, for her creative vision and utter dedication. They are true *chong kishi,* and a first-time novelist could not have been more privileged.

To my father, Ron Rosenberg, for the words of wisdom that kick-started this book; my mother, Marilyn Crain, for a decade of long-distance phone calls; as well as Teri Rosenberg, Howie Crain, Linda and Jerry Marsh, Dan and Sharyn Rosenberg, Lori and Darren Ruschman, Todd and Barbara Marsh, Steve Hamm, Allison Hamm, Jessica Crain, and Melissa Crain.

Bol'shoe spasibo to Alan and Mimi Drew, Joe and Alycia Campbell, Todd Schleicher, Mayram Tulebaeva, my fellow K1–K3 Peace Corps volunteers, the Iowa Writers' Workshop, Lori Glazer, Larry Cooper, and the staff at Houghton Mifflin, as well as the entire Howell crew.

And to my students in Turkey, Arizona, and Kyrgyzstan, for providing me with understanding, inspiration, and hope.

I would also like to acknowledge a debt to Keith Basso's *Wisdom Sits in Places* (University of New Mexico Press, 1996) and Ustun Reinart's article "Of Diapers and Tampons: Women and the Earthquake" (*Women's International Net Newsletter,* Issue 95A, October 1999).